Summer Crossing

SUMMER CROSSING

A Novel by

STEVE TESICH

Random House
New York

All rights reserved under International and Pan-American
Copyright Conventions. Published in the United States
by Random House, Inc., New York, and simultaneously
in Canada by Random House of Canada Limited,
Toronto.

Grateful acknowledgment is made to the following for
permission to reprint previously published material:
  Walt Disney Music Company: Excerpt from the lyrics
to "ZORRO." Words by Norman Foster. Music by
George Bruns. © 1957 Walt Disney Music Company.
Excerpt from the lyrics to "ENCYCLOPEDIA" Words
and music by Jimmie Dodd. © 1955 Walt Disney Music
Company. Reprinted by permission of the publisher.
  Intersong Music: Excerpt from the lyrics to "There
Goes My Baby" by Lover Patterson, George Treadwell
and Benjamin Nelson. Copyright © 1959 by Hill & Range
Songs, Inc., and Jot Music, Inc. All rights administered
by Unichappell Music, Inc. (Rightsong Music,
Publisher). International Copyright Secured. ALL
RIGHTS RESERVED. Used by permission.

Library of Congress Cataloging in Publication Data
Tesich, Steve.
Summer crossing.
I. Title.
PS3570.E8S8   813'.54   82-40125
ISBN 0-394-52759-3   AACR2

Manufactured in the United States of America
Typography and binding design by J.K. Lambert
98765432
First Edition

To Sam, Julia and Marya
with love and gratitude

*Man has places in his heart which do not
yet exist, and into them enters suffering,
in order that they may have existence.*

—LEON BLOY

Summer Crossing

Chapter 1

His name was Presley Bivens. He was from Anderson, Indiana, he weighed 167 pounds and he was smiling at me. He had been here twice before, won both times, and was back again to try to make it three in a row. He wasn't at all what I had expected from a legend.

The Civic Center was filled to capacity, the spectators were screaming, the cheerleaders were cheering, but he didn't seem to hear a thing. He seemed friendly, relaxed, not like an opponent at all. And he kept smiling. The referee warned him for stalling a couple of times, but he really wasn't stalling. He just wasn't in a hurry. He seemed to know what the outcome of the match would be. That he was going to win. That he had won already. As far as he was concerned, he was back in Anderson, Indiana, standing on his living-room rug and looking back on all this, remembering how he beat me.

There was only a little over two minutes to go in the match and I was ahead six to four, and yet I was the one who was nervous. He just kept smiling. He had little round pig eyes that got rounder when he smiled. There was nothing about him to suggest the greatest wrestler in Indiana history. His chest was flat, covered with a fuzz of blond hair, his arms were soft, his legs underdeveloped, his skin pale. All he had was that neck of his, a massive, frightening neck; dinosaurs had necks like that. His small, round head sat on top of that prehistoric neck like a Crenshaw melon on top of a fire hydrant. He kept talking to me. When I scored my first takedown he told me in his southern Indiana twang, in his high-pitched nasal voice:

"Nice move, kid. Reel puhrtee."

He kept calling me "kid." He was my age and he kept calling me "kid." He was behind with a little less than two minutes to go, and he was relaxed. I was winning and he was smiling. No, he wasn't what I had expected at all.

The crowd was for me. Some called out my name. C'mon, Price. You got him. You got him now. Others called out the name of my high school. C'mon, Roosevelt. He's all yours. You got him. Coach French was down on his knees at the edge of the mat screaming instructions.

"Stay away from him! Don't fall for it! Don't let him do it!"

In a state of few legends and most of them basketball, Bivens was a wrestling legend. He was two-time state champion at 165, he was undefeated in three years and all his victories were by pins. I had heard about him long before I met him. Anybody who had ever gone against him said the same thing. They all thought they had him, they were always ahead on points, he was always on the brink of defeat and then something happened. Everybody knew about that trick of his. Coach French had first warned me about it weeks before the state finals. When the two of us drove down to Indianapolis in his car, that was all he talked about.

"You know what he does, so don't fall for it. All he's got is that neck bridge. That's all he's got. So don't fall for it. Go for points. You hear me?"

The last two-minute period began. I was down. The ref blew the whistle and I escaped. Two more points. I was now ahead eight to four.

"Nice sit-out, kid," Bivens twanged. "Reel slick."

He came toward me. We tied up and strayed off the mat. The ref made us break and walk back to center circle. The ref winked at me on the way back. He wanted me to win. Everybody wanted me to win. A small group had come down from Anderson. They had talked to me before the match; even his hometown people wanted me to win. Everyone wanted the legend to fall.

Bivens and I looked at each other from the perimeter of the circle. He checked the clock. Less than a minute and a half to go. He came toward me. We tied up again. He suddenly dropped and went for my ankle, and without thinking I stuck my forearm across his face, faked left and went right and had another takedown. Two more points. The score was now ten to four. Coach French jumped to his feet. In his twenty-five years of coaching he had never had a state champion. I was going to be his first.

Bivens was flat on his stomach. I was on top of him. He struggled to his knees. My right arm tightened around his waist. He tried a reverse but I saw it coming and caught him in midmove. I stuck my right arm between his legs and lifted up. My left arm slipped around his neck. He was on his back now. I was on top, going for a pin.

"Let him go. Don't do it!" Coach French screamed, waving a towel. I could hear him clearly. And then I realized that the crowd was still. They were all on their feet but they were perfectly still. Coach French continued to scream, but I shook my head at him. I was going for a pin. I felt Bivens' body surrendering beneath me. One of his shoulder blades was already on the mat. The other was inching closer. I shifted my weight toward that shoulder and felt it dropping. The ref sprawled out on his stomach and watched, waiting for the shoulder to touch the mat.

And then suddenly Bivens bridged on his neck. The move was so quick and powerful that I had no time to react. My whole body rose, and as it did Bivens twisted his, catching me off balance. Our positions reversed instantly. He was on top going for a pin. I was on the bottom.

I can still win, I thought. I'm ahead on points. Even a near fall would only give him three more. I can still win. I kept calculating as I desperately tried to keep my shoulders off the mat. They were so close I could feel the heat of the sweaty mat rising up to meet me.

"Forty-five seconds," the ref called out. He wasn't supposed to tell us how much time was left, but even he wanted me to win.

Bivens was still in no hurry. He had his head on my chest and he seemed to be taking a nap. I couldn't understand what force kept me down. I could not feel him trying. I was all effort; he was none. He lifted his head, resting his chin on my chest, and looked at me. Our faces were inches apart. He smiled at me. Don't torture yourself, he seemed to be telling me as I struggled to keep my shoulders off the mat. Why are you struggling so hard? Defeat is not such a bad thing. It really isn't. It won't hurt. He suddenly seemed very familiar, painfully familiar. I knew those eyes. That smile. And I felt embarrassed and ashamed for having tried to beat him.

I looked away and exhaled and as I did all resistance went out of me. I eased back into defeat as if into my proper place. The referee slapped the mat with his hand to signal the end of the match.

Coach French's old Mercury smelled of spilled coffee and pipe tobacco. On the way down we had made a deal. If I won, I'd get to drive back. I had really been looking forward to driving the car. Coach French sucked on his pipe, shook his head and pushed the speedometer past seventy. He seemed to be hoping for an accident, something to make an already rotten day a truly disastrous one. He stared into the dusk as if looking for it. The radio was on. The Drifters were singing.

"There goes my baby
Moving on . . . down the line . . ."

Coach French turned the radio off.

"Damn you, Price! You had him! I tell you, you had him! Oh, damn!"

He still couldn't believe it. He turned the radio back on. He kept doing this. When he had something to say he would turn it off, let out some of his frustration and then turn it back on again. Music and recrimination at seventy miles an hour on Highway 41. I fingered my second-place medal, trying to think positively. Second place wasn't that bad. Second in the whole state of Indiana.

We sped through dusk and into the night.

Coach French turned off the radio.

"Dammit, Price. You gave up."

It was as simple as that. I had given up. But it surprised me that he had noticed. When you give up you always think that it's a very private moment deep in your soul where nobody can see. Coach French saw.

"Whatcha have to go and give up for?"

"I don't know, Coach."

"I wish you hadn't done it. I sure as hell wish you hadn't done it."

I shrugged.

"You had him. You know that?"

"Yeah, I . . . I thought I had him."

"You did! You did have him. You had him. And then you know what you did?"

"Yeah, I know, Coach."

"You gave up."

"I know I did."

"I wish you hadn't done it."

"I didn't know I was going to, Coach. I just . . . I don't know."

"You could've been driving the car now, right?"

"Yeah."

He turned the radio back on. Coach French talked like he coached. His wrestling philosophy was based on learning a few moves really well and using them. His conversation was an out-growth of his wrestling philosophy. Twenty-five years coaching and never a state champion. I looked at him. I wondered how many times he had made this trip, full of hope one way, full of despair and disappointment the other. There would be no next year. He was retiring.

We stopped at a gas-station restaurant to eat. Both of us ordered a cheeseburger and a milkshake. It seemed impossible to be heart-broken while slurping milkshake through a straw, but Coach French was working on it.

"You see this place?" He gestured with his pipe. It was a dreary place. Everybody was overweight and pale and wore clothes that didn't fit right. They were all eating something that didn't taste as good as they thought it would. Using a lot of napkins, probably because they were free. "Looks like a rotten place, doesn't it?"

"Sure does." I smiled.

"But you know what? This rotten place would look like the best place in the world if you'd won the state championship."

I put my cheeseburger back on the plate. I was sure that in his many years of coaching he had stopped in this same spot before and used that very line on other losers. I was now a part of that tradition. Winners have their traditions, losers have theirs. He paid and we left.

"You want to drive?" Coach French offered.

"That's all right, Coach."

He started speeding again. In the distance we could see the eternal flames of the oil refineries, one higher and brighter than the rest belonging to the Sunrise Oil Company. East Chicago, Indiana. Home.

I thought about my dad. For the last year or so I had not been able to get through a day without thinking about him. I carried him inside me like an extra organ I did not need but had to care for.

I flinched as Coach French turned the radio off.

"Tell me, Price, I really want to know. What made you do it?"

"What's that, Coach?"

"Give up like that."

"I don't know," I said. My dad's image would not go away.

"You didn't have to get pinned."

"I know."

"You had him."

"Yeah, I know."

"All you had to do was hold on for thirty seconds. That's all, right?"

"Right, Coach."

"And then I saw you. I saw it happening. I saw you giving up. Why did you do it, son?"

"I . . ."

Out of nowhere I started sobbing. Coach French, the softie that he was, looked thunderstruck.

"Hey, don't. C'mon, don't. You shouldn't listen to me. I'm a stupid old man who's been coaching too long. What do I know? I know nothing. Don't . . ."

I couldn't stop. Had I known I was going to start crying, I could have figured out a way to stop. It was a shock to both of us. He left the radio on for the rest of the way.

"You can let me off here," I said as we passed Aberdeen Lane.

"I'll take you home."

"Here's fine, Coach. Really." I didn't want to go home right away.

"It just wasn't meant to be, that's all," he said as I got out of the car. He tried to smile. "There's always next year."

And then he remembered that he was retiring and that I was graduating and that there would be no next year. He blinked slowly, as if pulling down the shades on hopes for the future.

"Goodnight, Coach."

"Goodnight, Danny."

He drove away slowly toward his retirement. His left rear light was out.

The first thing I always noticed on Aberdeen Lane were the trees. I had seen pictures of towns in Vermont and New Hampshire with tall, beautiful trees on every street. In East Chicago we only had Aberdeen Lane. Either the trees wouldn't grow in the rest of the city, or nobody bothered to plant them, or when they planted them and they grew, they just didn't grow as tall, as wide, as beautiful.

Even now, in mid-March, in the middle of the night, the trees seemed fine, just fine, although they had no leaves on them and wouldn't have any for some time. The light from the streetlamps, the light from the houses, TV lights from second-story windows shone through the bare branches as I walked slowly, scraping my soles on the sidewalk.

I didn't know anybody who lived on "A" Lane. We all knew that they were better off than the rest of the people in East Chicago, richer and, judging by the lights in the windows, stayed up longer at night. The houses were all brick, most of them two-storied; the lawns were large, the grass on them greener than on other lawns, and several had underground water sprinklers. Just about every other car parked in the street was a new station wagon.

The last time I had spent any time on Aberdeen Lane was in October. I needed twenty leaves for a leaf collection for my botany class. I spent a quiet afternoon picking up leaves off the ground— silver maple, sugar maple, Dutch elm, pin oak, mulberry. The day branded itself on my memory: the peace I felt, the sense of progress I was making, the scent of autumn and the sight of the falling leaves on a windy day.

So I got off here on purpose to see, before I went home, if the peace I had known that day would still be here to ease the shame and the pain of my defeat.

I tried to think positively. Second wasn't bad. Second in the whole state of Indiana. Not bad at all. I imagined a lineup of all the wrestlers from the state in my weight category. It was a long line that stretched around the block, and in that long line I was second best. There would be no pressures on me. Nothing special was expected from you when you were second. Everyone would respect how close I had come without wondering how far I would go. My two friends, Larry Misiora and Billy Freund, both of them wrestlers who hadn't even made it out of the regionals, would not feel a gulf of superiority between us. There were many points in my favor.

I wondered if only losers bothered having positive thoughts. In the back of my head the image of my father fluttered. I could think about other things and still think about him. He was one of those transparent images that could be superimposed over what I saw and thought to make me see the world through his eyes.

I stopped in the middle of the block. The green house that was for sale in October was still for sale. I leaned on the trunk of the silver maple and tried once again to recapture the October peace I had felt.

A car appeared at the end of the block, turned right and came down the one-way street the wrong way. I moved behind the tree to escape the glare of the headlights. The car stopped on the other side of the tree; the headlights stayed on for a few seconds and then went dead. A man stepped out of the car and stretched. He stood right under the streetlamp, looking like an actor about to speak on the stage. He didn't seem as old as his silver-gray hair, nor as young as he dressed. Fifty, maybe. He looked across at the green house, examined some keys and then walked across the lawn toward the door. After much jiggling he got the door unlocked.

"It works," he shouted.

"Too bad," I heard a girl's voice call from the car. "I was hoping we'd have to break down the door."

It was too late for me to come out from behind the tree. They would think I had been spying on them. So I pulled back even more to make sure they didn't see me.

The man went inside the house. Several lights came on, including a floodlight that lit up the lawn.

The car door opened and a girl came out, turquoise earrings shimmering in the night. She lit a cigarette and threw the burning match away. Dark hair, olive skin, high cheekbones.

"Rachel," the man called from the house.

"That's my name," she muttered to herself.

"Rachel!" The man appeared in the doorway. "You coming?"

"That's what I'm doing. I'm coming. Here I come." She seemed in a bad mood. When she walked her hips did not move.

The man moved away from the doorway as she came in. She walked past him without stopping. He stood looking after her for a second or so and then he, too, disappeared.

Rachel, I thought. I had never seen a Rachel before. I was quite conscious of words and I knew when I used them for the first time. I was seventeen, it was the summer of 1960 and I was sitting on Mrs. Dewey's porch when I used the word "irrational" for the first time in my life.

I left. When I reached the corner of Aberdeen Lane and Northcote, I looked back. Rachel and the gray-haired man were walking toward the car. I watched them unloading it, carrying suitcases and boxes into the house, and then I headed home. Behind me, down by the library, a train clattered through the night. The locomotive whistle blew. I could tell by the sound that it was the New York Central heading east.

Irrational. I had only used it once. The rule was you had to use the word three times before it became yours.

My dad was sitting at the kitchen table when I came in. He had pulled down the overhead lamp close to the table, and the small bulb was the only light in the house. My mother put in 150-watt bulbs. He took them out and put in 60-watt bulbs. If one drew a line anywhere in the world, the two of them would automatically stand on opposite sides. He was doing the Chicago *Sun-Times* crossword puzzle.

"Hi, Dad." I always had to be the first to speak.

"Yes, hi."

"Mom at work?" I knew she was.

"Yes, night shift. All month."

I opened the fridge but I wasn't hungry. Had I won, I would have eaten something.

"That's why we have to defrost the fridge so often. You stand there with the door open."

I shut the door.

"I lost."

"Lost what?" he said and turned his head. He looked young in the dim light. A little man whose thick, luxurious hair didn't have a single gray strand in it. He could have been a schoolboy doing homework. People said we looked alike. I had my father's face and my mother's body. They were still fighting it out for my soul.

"The match. I lost the match. I got second."

He smiled his sad smile and nodded his head. It was his smile that I had seen on the face of my opponent. I didn't know what struggle my dad and I were engaged in, but I knew I was home and that he had won, and without knowing the specifics of our combat I once again felt ashamed for having tried to defeat him. I showed him my loser's medal as a token of reconciliation.

"Life's like that, you know. People lose. You'll get over it. Don't let your mother make you feel bad about losing. She will, you know, if you let her."

I thought about taking a shower. Had I won, I would have taken a long, hot shower and replayed the match.

"I'm going to bed."

"Yes, me too. Pretty soon," he said without looking up.

"Goodnight, Dad."

"Yes, goodnight."

Chapter 2

We all just sat there. The giggles and the whispered wisecracks had died down a long time ago. We were waiting for the bell to ring so we could leave the classroom, and although it was clear that the class was over, that Mr. Geddes, our English teacher, was going mad in front of our eyes, we all just sat in our seats and waited for the bell to ring. Nobody moved. Hands lay still on desktops or in laps, postures were frozen and the only sound other than the ravings of Mr. Geddes was that of my friend Billy Freund, hiccupping once every few seconds in the seat behind me.

Mr. Geddes' voice rose and fell, his mouth opened wide and then shut, his eyes bulged and then withdrew into their sockets.

"Blue flame." He raised his right index finger high above his head for emphasis. "Blue . . ."

He chortled, showing us his tongue and teeth.

"I will now use it in a sentence. Here goes." He chortled again. "I have been burnt by the blue flame."

He nodded his head and growled like a dog. "Yes, I have . . . g-r-r-r." He loosened his tie. Then he looked at it. Then he looked at us. Then he screamed.

"My God, it's a blue tie. Navy-blue." He loosened it some more until the loop came out to his chin and then he stuck the tie into his mouth and winced like a horse taking the bit. He clamped his teeth around it and continued speaking.

"G-r-r-r, blue suits. Blue stockings. Do you know, g-r-r-r, what bluestockings are?"

He waited. Needless to say, nobody raised a hand. An eyebrow, maybe, but that was all.

"Blazers! From blue flame we move on to, g-r-r-r, blue blazers. I will now use it in a sentence. Here goes: Billy bought a blue blazer."

Behind me, Billy Freund hiccupped. Larry Misiora looked at me. Even mean Larry, a madman of a different kind, sat still, and for once in his life he seemed afraid.

Mr. Geddes' face was covered with sweat; wrinkles I had never seen before scarred it, expressions I had never seen before replaced each other in rapid succession. He seemed angry when he smiled. He seemed happy when he cried. Everything was reversed. It had been such a bland, ordinary face for so long that I found it impossible to connect Mr. Geddes, our old English teacher, with this raving, terrifying creature that sat at his desk. His face never stopped. It kept going through an agony of expressions. In our biology class we once saw a film on childbirth. The mother's face went through a lifetime of changes in the film. Mr. Geddes seemed to be in the process of delivery.

"G-r-r-r," he growled, gagging on his blue tie.

We had thought at first that it was all a joke. It began as a classroom discussion of metaphors in poetry. Mr. Geddes had brought up a popular song to demonstrate that popular songs used some of the same images as poetry. He digressed for a while to remind us that if it had the word "like" in it, it was a simile; if it didn't, it was a metaphor. He asked for examples of popular songs built around metaphors. Somebody mentioned "Blue Moon."

I hadn't been paying attention. I had my own metaphors and my own problems. Although it had been almost a month since my loss in the state finals, and the sharp pain of defeat was gone, a lingering pain remained, a sense that there would be no second chance, a realization that my career as an athlete was over. I kept avoiding Coach French. We had known each other for four years, but now we seemed to have only that one night in common. He tried not to hurt me but he couldn't help himself. Had I won, he kept telling me, I could have got one of the few wrestling scholarships to Indiana University or Purdue. Bivens got one to Indiana. I guess it just wasn't meant to be, he kept telling me. Even when he didn't say it, it was in his eyes. That expression became a greeting between us. Hi, how are you. I guess it wasn't meant to be. I guess not. The further I got from my defeat, the more I seemed to have lost. My friends Billy Freund and Larry Misiora downplayed Bivens' victory and stressed how close I had come, and although this was my own line of reasoning, I suspected them of being secretly glad I had lost. The wrestling season was over. We didn't have another sport. We felt our finely tuned bodies losing their edge. We were slowly slipping into the arena reserved for has-beens. This irritated and depressed all three of us and made mean Larry Misiora all that much meaner and angrier. We were used to being tired at the end of the school day, and the absence of that wonderful exhaustion after a hard workout left us full of excess energy and with no outlet for it. We talked about setting up a gym in Freund's garage, we talked about running every day, we talked about wrestling in AAU meets, but we knew it was just talk. School was ending and we didn't know what to do with our lives except cling to each other. And we clung to each other half for support and half, I felt, to make sure nobody got away on his own.

At home, my mother and father alternated between periods of total silence and open hostility to each other. When they talked, they tried to inflict pain. When they were silent, they seemed to be devising new weapons. On rare occasions they were civil, but since all three of us knew that it wouldn't last, even those times were not free of anxiety.

So I had not been paying attention to Mr. Geddes during the early part of the class. I was concentrating on my own problems, the fog of problems that was gradually enveloping my life. By the time I heard the giggles and the whispers, Mr. Geddes was on his way. By the time Freund punched me on the shoulder and whispered in my ear, "I think Mr. Geddes is falling out of his tree today," everyone else in the classroom had grown quiet. We all watched as he went mad.

"Picasso had his blue period." Mr. Geddes at this time still seemed capable of going either way. At first it was the suspense that made us pay attention. "Have you heard of Picasso's blue period? Have you heard of Gainsborough's 'Blue Boy'?" He waited for a reply. "Have you? How about *The Blue Hotel*, by Stephen Crane? How about *Blue Juniata*, by Malcolm Cowley? How about *Blue Voyage*, by Conrad Aiken?" He waited for a reply. "Well, how about them? Or is 'Blue Moon' all you know? Is that all you know? 'Blue Moon'?"

"BLUE," he wrote on the blackboard. A couple of kids made moves to leave while his back was turned but sat down immediately when he faced the class.

"I will now use it in a sentence. Here goes: I am blue. Not like Paul Bunyan's ox, or the noses of the upper classes, or the blood of Bostonians, no, not like that at all, but blue in my own way. Yes. I am blue in my own way. That is a sentence. I will now diagram it for you. Here goes."

He picked up the chalk again and began diagramming the sentence on the blackboard. The chalk broke in half, but he didn't seem to notice. He was confounded. He kept trying to draw straight lines but they came out wavy and zigzagged: a signature of a madman. And that's when he seemed to realize what had happened to him. He let out a shriek, threw the chalk in the air and the suspense was over. From then on it was just the horror.

The tie was still in his mouth, but he was now tightening the knot, gagging himself, trying to silence himself. The tie pushed back the corners of his mouth, thrusting into view his back teeth and his trapped, swollen tongue. The tongue moved, trying to shape sounds.

"U-u-u-u-u?" He could no longer say "blue." He pointed at the word BLUE on the blackboard and then at himself. "U-u-u-u-u!"

The bell rang and we flew out of the classroom. Once in the corridor we stayed together. We all wanted to say something but nobody spoke. We were afraid of words. They didn't seem safe anymore. Kids from other classes, other classrooms, poured out into the corridor and down the stairway. They were all talking and laughing. We felt like some doomed voyagers who had been trapped on an island, and we ran toward the jabber and the noise of our classmates as if they were a rescue party.

School was canceled for the day. We were told to go home, but most of us remained. We hung around outside, the way we did during fire drills. From silent spectators the kids in my class turned into star witnesses describing in giddy detail all they had seen and heard. A lot of them, like Johnny Wasco, had never had an audience before and would never have one again. They talked and they couldn't believe that their schoolmates were listening.

An ambulance with a flasher and a siren sped past the front of the school, cut through the parking lot and disappeared around the back. "U-u-u-u," the siren whined. We didn't see Mr. Geddes taken away. It was as if the sound of the siren came and the sound took him away. "U-u-u-u."

The three of us walked home slowly; Billy Freund, Larry Misiora and I. As usual, we took Baring Avenue; Freund was on the right, near the curb, Misiora on the left, I in the middle.

"Poor Mr. Geddes." Freud shook his head. His name was Freund, but a substitute teacher a couple of years ago had called him Freud and that was all it took. "Poor guy. That was terrible. Terri-ble. Hmmm."

"Nice school we got, huh?" Misiora flashed his mean grin. "Great place, isn't it? Fine teachers, too. I mean, Jesus Horrendous Christ, we've been going to class taught by a crazy human being."

"He wasn't always crazy." I felt obliged to defend Mr. Geddes. He had, after all, praised some of my compositions. It now grated on me that in all my years of going to school, the only teacher who ever praised me personally went insane. Poor Mr. Geddes. From then on, whenever anyone mentioned his name, it would always be Poor Mr. Geddes.

"I wonder what made him go like that?" Freud, the heavyweight on our wrestling team, had a voice like a foghorn. He spoke the way he walked. First one foot then the other. First one word then the other. He pushed his father's fedora hat back on his head. "Maybe it was a woman?"

"He didn't have no woman." Misiora spat on the street.

"That could do it too." Freud shook his big head, but he shook it slowly. "Maybe we'll go crazy too. We got no girls. I thought when I was a sophomore that by the time I was a senior I'd have a girl. So here I am, ready to graduate, and I don't have one. I don't know how you get 'em."

We walked silently for half a block. Our teacher had gone mad in front of our eyes, but personal problems were personal problems. None of us had a girl. None of us knew how to get one. We knew we were missing out on something. I certainly did. Once again I thought of my dad. He was a man who had perfected the look of someone who was missing out on something. Was it love, I wondered. I didn't know enough about it to know.

Misiora, who pronounced his name "Missurah," as in "wide Missurah," took the slingshot out of his pocket and began shooting at the stop sign ahead. He was a dead shot. Freud looked and blinked each time the rock hit the steel sign. An old woman stepped out on her porch and seemed ready to give Misiora hell, but one quick glance at him made her change her mind. There was a look in Larry's wild blue eyes that said he just loved trouble. Even the black guys in school didn't pick fights with him. He was a better wrestler than I, but he didn't win often because he didn't try to beat his opponents. He tried to hurt them. He didn't care what the score was. His haircut said it all. It wasn't really a crew cut and it wasn't a flat-top and it wasn't a DA. Blond bristles stuck out in all directions and here and there the bare cement-colored scalp showed through. He cut it himself. And he did it on purpose to look ugly and mean. Any guy that could do that to his own head was capable of anything.

He spat in the direction of the old woman, and she retreated back into her house, as if summoned by good sense.

"I tell you." Misiora grinned, looking around the street, like some cynical estate-appraiser at a bankruptcy. "Home town." His eyes seemed to peer inside the houses we passed, at the lives inside the houses, at the slipcovers, the tablecloths, the closets full of cheap clothes, the gaudy shower curtains, the lawn chairs waiting for summer, the people waiting for holidays, the interiors of people and places, and his grin seemed to condemn all of it and all of them to worthlessness. "One of these days . . . boy . . . I tell you . . ."

He reloaded his slingshot again, letting the sentence trail off. He had developed a habit from Mrs. Dewey of leaving his sentences unfinished. From years of wrestling, trying to lose weight to make weight, spitting for hours at a time to shed an ounce, he had developed the habit of spitting as he walked. He walked down Baring Avenue, holding his loaded slingshot, the rubber straps pulled halfway back, looking for a target. My mind went back to Mr. Geddes' class: the use of imagery in poems. The loaded slingshot pulled halfway back seemed like a perfect image for Misiora.

A train rattled in the distance, its whistle blowing. It was a freight train. I could tell by now. It was heading toward Chicago.

Misiora fired his slingshot and hit another stop sign. Freud blinked. Misiora reloaded it again. His pockets were full of rocks.

"I saw this article in a magazine. In *Field & Stream.*" Freud waited for Misiora or me to cut him off, and when we didn't he continued walking and talking at the same pace, lumbering along like a big brown bear with a fedora hat.

"And in this article, they said how there's all these jobs in Alaska and Montana and places like that. What you do is work for the Department of Game and Fish."

Misiora snorted.

"Yeah, they got this department." Freud took in the snort and continued. "Department of Game and Fish. And they need people to have these jobs. For example, you keep track of herds of elk and write down how many elk you see and where. Or you count how many trout you saw in a stream. They give you a cabin to live in. They had a picture of this cabin. Man, it was a nice cabin. Had a fireplace." He smiled, seeing it all. "We could buy boots and those sheepskin jackets. You know. I still have the article at home. You can send for stuff. You fill this thing out and they send you stuff, applications and stuff. It'd be nice, you know, for the three of us."

Misiora looked at me. Whose turn was it, his eyes asked me, to tell Freud he was full of shit?

"Freud," he said, "you know what?"

"What?"

"You're full of it."

"You got any better jobs in mind?"

"No."

"Then why am I full of it?"

"Because you are. Some people are and some aren't. You're one of those who is. Counting trout in a stream!" Misiora shook his head.

"We gotta have a job when we get out of school, don't we? I mean, don't we?" Freud asked.

We knew we did. After eighteen years of living, years and years of dreaming and daydreaming, reading books, writing essays, walking home together countless times, yearning for that first kiss from that first girl, laughing at jokes we had since forgotten, after countless nights on Mrs. Dewey's porch and countless workouts in the gym, it all boiled down to a job. We had jobs last summer as stockboys in the National Supermarket. We had jobs the summer before that, too. We always had jobs: washing cars, cutting grass, wrapping Christmas presents in large department stores in Hammond. But that was different. This was our last year of school. Our last summer was coming up. It changed everything. We didn't really want to work during our last summer. We didn't know what we wanted to do, but we didn't—at least Larry and I didn't—want to have jobs. I was afraid of getting a job without having the start of school in the fall to end it. All three of us felt, I think, that the next jobs we found would be the jobs we would have for the rest of our lives. It made us anxious and indecisive. For the moment, at least, we didn't need money. We had our meager savings. We didn't have girls or cars and so even the little we had was more than we needed. We used to go to movies, but the approach of summer made us somehow too impatient to sit through movies, so we just stopped going. We waited for something to happen to us. Something happened to all those others who graduated from our school. Something would happen to us, too.

"I hate April," Misiora said, flatly. "Everyone hates March, but I hate April. You know why? It's just like March."

There were few trees on Baring Avenue and they stood far apart from each other, like old friends who had gone their own ways. None of them had leaves yet. The buds were appearing, however; small hints that change was in the air. I wished that lives of human beings, my life, could go through the same cycle as the lives of trees. In one year, you get through it all and then begin all over again. It seemed better than waiting and wondering and worrying what, if any, fruit your life would bear. I sometimes felt trees rustling inside of me. At times my own sexuality overwhelmed me, made me dizzy with yearning for something I had never had, for love, perhaps, and then suddenly a tidal wave of loneliness would come over me, as if at eighteen I had already lived my life and I were an old man who was trying to remember, and couldn't, the loves and days of his youth. It alternated like that. Everything was behind me or everything was still ahead of me. But it all seemed to boil down to a job.

A Sunrise Oil Company truck backfired as it went past us. It startled Misiora and he instantly took it as a personal insult.

"You mother!" He pulled back the slingshot and fired a large rock at the back of the tank. "Like I said." He flashed his dagger grin. "This is what's the matter with this country."

Freud raised his eyebrows slowly. Misiora's non sequiturs still perplexed him. "Like I said," Misiora said quite often about things we weren't talking about at all. Maybe he was thinking about them.

"You know," Misiora went on, "you're walking down the street thinking your own hateful thoughts and some jerkoff jackass rumbles along and disturbs you. It's not nice." He looked after the truck. "One of these days . . ."

"I guess you're lucky," Freud said, lowering his eyebrows ponderously, like some lonely old lady lowering her Venetian blinds at the end of the day.

"Oh yeah, tell me why, O Freud?"

"Well, your dad works for Sunrise. I bet he can get you in. If nothing else works out, you always have that."

"Ah." Misiora raised his arms in the air. "That's why. You know what, Freud? You're right. My worries are over. I'll follow in my dad's footsteps."

"You can't kid me," Freud snorted. "I can tell when you're being sarcastic. Man, I don't have to use sarcastic in no sentence. All I got to do is hang around you."

"You don't have to, Freud. No law that says you have to hang around me."

We walked on silently. I could tell that Freud was sorry he'd said anything. There was nothing he hated more than to hear how we didn't have to hang around together. In his mind we had to. In his mind the truest definition of friendship was that you went down with the crew.

We walked on, silently. We crossed the railroad tracks and, as so often happens with friends who have spent a lot of time together, all three of us looked left at the same time and then right at the same time, our feet in step like some three-man army on parade.

We sat down on the cement slab outside the public library and looked at the traffic on Chicago Avenue.

"Nice place we live in," Misiora said. "Our two biggest streets are named after other cities. That should tell you something." He was alluding to Chicago Avenue and Indianapolis Boulevard.

I let the remark go. The air was getting misty and smoggy and the traffic lights on Indianapolis Boulevard glinted in the distance like harbor lights. You could smell the steel mills and the refineries. The odor prickled the inside of my nose and made me feel I was going to sneeze. On certain days you could watch the soot fall like black snow.

"Hey, look." Freud pointed. "There goes a '56 T-bird."

We looked. There it went.

"Sure wish I had a car," he sighed. For some reason he took off his fedora, placed it in his lap and ran his fingers slowly across the edges. Kids in school made fun of his hat. It didn't stop him from wearing it. It was his father's hat. He loved his father very much, and his death had made Freud cling to us all the more. He could go a day, two at the most, without some show of affection from Misiora and me, and if he didn't get it, he'd start rubbing against us, leaning on us, like some lonely St. Bernard. If he'd had a tail, he'd have wagged it.

"We going to Mrs. Dewey's or what?" he asked.

Misiora blinked. I shrugged. Neither of us answered. Freud

leaned on me. From profile, he looked handsome. He had a nice straight nose, deep-set black eyes and a childish pout. You could see his long black lashes going up and going down when he blinked. His metabolism was just slightly faster than evolution. He moved slowly; he walked slowly; he thought, ate and wrestled slowly; and when he leaned on you, as he did on me, he even leaned slowly— fifteen, twenty pounds at a time until his full weight rested on you and he sighed to a stop.

"See these shoes?" He moved his big foot slowly. "They're my dad's." He kept his voice down, not wanting to rattle the cage in which Misiora lived.

"They're nice," I said.

"Yeah. My mother was going to throw all his clothes away. That bitch. But I put them all in the garage. Everything almost fits me." He rubbed his shoulder against my back like a bear rubbing against a tree. "What a bitch she is. I still can't get over her selling his car like that." Lady Macbeth plotting murder in the night was in Freud's mind far more worthy of sympathy than his mother for selling his dad's 1960 Buick. "Didn't even tell me. Just sold it. Like it was nothing or something."

Stragglers from our school walked past us. They waved. We waved. Misiora didn't wave. He didn't shoot rocks at them either, so they probably took it as a friendly greeting and kept right on going.

Fat Patty Campbell began singing "Blue Moon," and the girls in her group laughed. I could tell they were talking about Mr. Geddes. One of them put her scarf in her mouth in a merciless imitation of the poor man. I did not consider myself overly sensitive or caring, but I did want Misiora at that moment to deliver a couple of painful rocks on their fat asses.

"Stupid cows," I muttered.

"I like cows," Freud said, smiling. "Milk cows especially. My dad took me to this farm in Crown Point once and I saw some. They walk like they're all running for president, real important, their big ole jugs swinging like bells. You ever see a milk cow drink water?" He shut his eyes and exhaled a sound of delight. You ever hear Caruso sing, he could have been asking. "They put their mouths in a stream and you'd swear they're doing nothing . . . they don't make no ripple or nothing in the water . . . it's like nothing's going on, but they're drinking, all right. Oh yeah!"

Misiora nudged me.

"Look who's coming."

He turned. I turned. Freud unleaned himself in stages off me.

Beautiful Diane Sinclair was walking up the street alone. Her black hair bounced as she walked. Her eyes looked past us; her lips parted in a smile of somebody listening to herself being introduced to an adoring crowd; she smiled past us; and then the outline of her breasts, and then her perfume, and then the few loose strands of hair dancing on the back of her neck, it all went past us like a galleon loaded with treasures and perfumes bound for other ports.

Misiora jumped off the cement slab and walked after her. We followed. A small adjustment in her posture told us she knew we were right behind her.

No matter how many times we saw Diane, her beauty depressed us. We stared at the outlines of her undergarments, we smelled the perfume trailing after her and we got more and more depressed. We were convicts being led to a firing squad by the warden's daughter. When you realized, as all three of us did, that no matter how long we lived, no matter what we did, we would never kiss, never, never kiss Diane Sinclair and that somebody else would, it made the rest of our lives seem like a long quest for second best.

We crossed Chicago Avenue and followed her past the parked cars and scattered shopping carts outside National Supermarket, edging closer to her, dropping back and then edging closer again. She turned the corner and the three-man army turned with her.

She adjusted her posture again, twitching her left shoulder as if flicking flies off her body.

"Diane!" Misiora called out. Freud and I were startled. You didn't talk to Diane. We had seen Misiora do many startling things, but this one took us completely by surprise.

"Die-an!" Misiora split the word in two and flung the angry syllables at her. "For God's sakes, Diane, time's running short. Here we are, ready to graduate and go our own wonderful ways, and it occurred to me that you've never spoken to us."

As Freud and I edged back, Misiora edged forward toward her.

"I understand, of course. We're all so very busy, but still the fact remains, Diane, that we've been in the same school, sat in the same classrooms, for over four years. Five, almost. And not a word! I tell you . . . I mean, I tell you, Diane."

She turned her head slightly. We could see the tip of her nose, the corners of her smile.

"Maybe you don't think we like you," Misiora went on. "Well, nothing could be further from the truth. You want to know something? We think you're beautiful. We dream about you, Diane. And if you stopped and turned around and talked to us, do you know what would happen? You would make us happy for the rest of the day. There, I've given you the facts."

He actually seemed to think she was going to stop and talk to us. He actually seemed to be thinking that. She continued walking, sailing, a galleon oblivious to the chatter of the seagulls in her wake. Misiora's face hardened. Tendons bulged out on his neck. He hated her at that moment. He hated the impossible.

"Diane, my dear, I have only one more thing to say to you. If your pussy is as tight as your heart, you must be one helluva fuck."

"I guess you'll never know," she replied, without changing her stride or her posture.

"Yeah, it looks bad for me. But I'll tell you another thing since we're suddenly on talking terms. I'd just as soon cut off my prick as give it to you."

"Maybe if you cut it off I'll take it."

She turned the corner again, but Larry didn't follow. She went into her house without so much as a look back at us.

"I tried," Larry grinned, "but I guess it just wasn't meant to be."

He looked at me. I had used Coach French's line as an excuse for my defeat and now Larry used it just to hurt me, to remind me that he wasn't the only one who had lost. Freud didn't get the connection and took it at face value.

"Yeah, when things weren't meant to be, they weren't meant to be."

We started walking again.

"So?" Freud asked, expecting us to know what was on his mind.

"So what?" Misiora said.

"We going to Mrs. Dewey's or what?"

"No." Misiora spat. I almost hit him. His spitting was suddenly getting on my nerves. He put his slingshot away and left, making it clear he wanted to be by himself. Freud sadly watched him go.

"You want to come over to my garage? I put a radio in there."

"I don't think so," I said.

"I can't live with my mother no more. I'm moving the stuff from my room to the garage. I sure miss my dad." He shrugged, his big shoulders going up and then coming down like a slow elevator.

Streetlamps were coming on. It was getting dark. I felt my mind drifting away.

Freud put his arm around me as if trying to hold me in place.

"What's with him?" he asked.

"With whom?"

"Misiora."

"I don't know. He's just . . ." I was beginning to leave my sentences unfinished too.

"He's going to do something."

"What do you mean, 'something'?" I was getting impatient.

"You know. Something. I can just feel it. He's going to do something terrible," Freud whispered.

We split up. I waved. Freud waved. Half a block later, I forced myself to turn around, and just because Freud expected it, I waved one more time. He waved back. His father's hat made him look like some huge lonely detective, ponderously seeking clues through the night about what to do with himself.

Chapter 3

The kerosene lamp flickered in the darkness, making shadows on the walls. It was only four in the afternoon, but it seemed like midnight. Heavy rain was falling. Thunder rattled the windowpanes; lightning flashed every few seconds, creating images like X-rays of the world outside.

"Bad storm." My mother crossed herself in her Byzantine manner, and then she made some signs to protect us from it.

She was a very superstitious woman. Whenever it thundered she would turn off all the lights in the house and light up the kerosene lamp that she had brought over from Jugoslavia, from Montenegro. The Devil made it thunder. The Devil made lightning bolts. The Devil hated electricity and bright lights. A kerosene lamp was harder to see. She was always making bargains with God and trying to trick the Devil. She had left Montenegro over twenty years ago, but she had kept all her old ways.

I always relaxed in a storm, and the worse the storm the better I felt. I loved snows that paralyzed the city, floods that made movement impossible, roads washed away, city cut off: nothing to be done. The roads to the future seemed cut off too, in a bad storm, so I didn't have to worry about it. There was nothing I could do. How pleasant that felt.

"Bad storm, yes, but I have seen much worse. Sure. Two days and two nights, once, I remember. It made thunder and lightning for two days and two nights."

Over twenty years in America and she still talked like a foreigner. Her vocabulary had stopped growing years ago. It was as if she had decided that's that, that's all the words I need, thank you.

We sat at the kitchen table. Her back was to the windows. I was on the opposite side; the kerosene lamp was in the middle, flickering, making shadows on the walls. We drank Turkish coffee from turquoise enameled demitasse cups with gold handles. I didn't like Turkish coffee, but I drank it to keep her company. I drank it because she thought I liked it. I really liked the storm. Here I am, I thought. Cut off. If the storm keeps up I'll never have to get a job. It was like war. Sometimes, in moments of personal crisis, I hoped for wars to break out and make whatever decisions I had to make unnecessary.

"Here, want to smoke?" She offered me a cigarette. She knew I didn't smoke, but she loved to offer.

"No."

"Sure, I forgot. You don't smoke."

She lifted the cover off the lamp and lit her cigarette on the burning wick. She held it between her thumb and index finger, and when she inhaled, her slanted, slightly Oriental eyes narrowed. She stared at the wick as if it were illuminating some other world, some other time, that she remembered. She didn't look like my mother now. She was simply a woman thinking her own thoughts. I thought mine.

How was it, I wondered, that my father had picked her to be his wife? Surely he could tell—one look at her was enough to tell—that this foreign woman with Oriental features was not the woman for him. She was taller, stronger, handsomer. Why, then? Unless he wanted to have a live-in reminder of his inadequacies. Even more astonishing was that she had accepted him. She talked about the men in her family; they were all tall and dark, ferocious warriors all of them, heroes all of them.

She smoked her cigarette, her gold tooth flashing through the smoke. A permanent sneer lay on her lips, the semisensual sneer of a superior being. If she had doubts, it was about the rest of the world, not about herself. My father and I did it the other way around.

She looked up at me and I looked away. At times I thought she could read my mind.

A lightning bolt hit not far away.

"Mmmm." She nodded. "That was good one." She crossed herself again and lowered the wick. The Devil was getting close.

"I guess Dad's waiting out the storm."

"Yes, if he is smart."

She turned her demitasse cup over on a paper napkin. The coffee grounds would fall down the sides of the cup, making strange patterns. She would then read and interpret the patterns. She was a fortuneteller like her mother. I didn't believe in that stuff, but I did listen. Sometimes I would let her read mine. Never when my father was around. He hated all that savage mumbo jumbo. I declined this time, too. It was a wonderful storm. I didn't want to be reminded of my future or of what lay ahead.

She waited for the grounds to dry and had another cigarette. Once again she offered me one.

"I still don't smoke."

"You don't smoke cigarettes. You don't drink whiskey. You don't dance." The litany of my sins. "You don't chase women. You don't gamble."

"C'mon, Mom, I wouldn't know where to go even if I wanted to gamble."

"Sure, sure, I bet you do all these things when I am not around."

I always stopped short of convincing her that I wasn't a rake. It felt pleasant to have her consider me one, she wanted me to be one: her son, the smoking, drinking, gambling, womanizing rake. That was the son she wanted.

She reached out across the table and placed her hand on my biceps.

"Mmmm, what is this? Big muscle. Are you strong?"

"Yes."

"Real strong, like bull."

"Yes."

"And girls, they like your muscles, hmmm?" She smiled.

"I don't know." I shrugged in a way that could be interpreted as a modest "yes."

"I know." She held the cigarette in her teeth. "I know what girls like. She's not very skinny, is she?"

"Who?"

"This girl of yours."

"No," I lied, and having no girl, I tried at least to imagine one so I could keep the conversation going.

"And what does she do, this girl who is not too skinny, this girl of yours. Does she make sounds you like to hear, hmmm? Does she move her hips? Does she make you happy?"

"Yes," I lied. I was getting hypnotized by the flame and the sound of her voice. I imagined girls from my school moaning in my arms,

Diane Sinclair moaning in my arms, Mrs. Dewey moaning in my arms. I wanted to hear more.

"And you, you make her happy, too?"

"Oh, yes, I do."

Her face beamed. That was the kind of son she wanted. Not one like my father, but like her. She leaned back in her chair. Her face changed.

"Sometimes in the spring we would take flocks of sheep to new pastures. Big mountains we have in Montenegro. So big. Many flocks of sheep on different sides of mountain. And mountains make echoes. You hear sheepbells ringing. You think they are very close, so close, but they are not. They are far away. And you hear boy shepherds playing flutes, playing love songs, and you think they are very close, but they too are far away. And you wonder who that boy shepherd is who is playing flute so lovely. You wonder all day . . . you sing the song he plays and you imagine how he looks. And then at night you make fire to keep away wolves. Big wolves in Montenegro. So-o big. You lie down by fire, you go to sleep and then like in dream you hear noise. You hear sheepbell ring. Ah, something is coming. But you are so sleepy, you do not awake. And then you hear footsteps very close and you open eyes and you see one of those faraway boy shepherds who make lovely music . . . and he is standing by the fire, and he is taking off jacket and putting it down on ground next to you. Then he lies down next to you and his hands brush away your blanket, and his hands pull up your skirt and then you make love. Not conversation. Just love. Then he go away. In the morning, you wake up and you do not know for sure if maybe boy was just dream. But then when you stand up, you feel here, in the bottom of your stomach, you feel, ahh, it was not dream. Then you smile and you put two fingers in your mouth and make loud whistle and all the sheeps jump up and all their bells ring and you feel so very happy to be girl who is living."

She leaned forward in the chair. The story was over. She looked like my mother again. I liked hearing her tell stories about the old country. Her face changed as she talked about it, became younger, girlish. It made me feel good to know that it was possible to look back on your life, at the happy moments in it and not be saddened that they were gone. I wondered what moments I would have to look back on. The day I collected leaves on Aberdeen Lane. Yes. That wrestling practice in my junior year when I just could not get tired, and after three hours in the wrestling room and an hour lifting weights I went and ran up and down the bleachers and I still wasn't tired. I felt eternal. I would and could go on forever. Maybe I would remember this afternoon too: thunderstorm outside, midnight at four P.M., my mother talking, kerosene lamp burning and shadows on the walls.

She picked up her coffee cup and scrutinized its interior, one eye half shut like some Oriental trader appraising suspicious jewels. She looked at the cup. I looked at her.

"Mmmm." She nodded. "Yes, that I knew already."

She turned the cup slowly in her hand and then she stopped suddenly. Her mouth opened. Her face paled. She arched her back as if a spider had run down her spine. She had seen something in the cup. She crossed herself twice and spat over her shoulder. Her hand was trembling.

"What's the matter? You see something bad or what?"

"No-thing. Big fooey. I see nothing. Too dark, I can't see." She was a good storyteller, but a terrible liar.

She got up and carried the cup, like some diseased object, to the sink and washed it out under the tap. She let the water run. Running water had a soothing effect on her. Whenever she and my dad fought, she'd go to the sink, turn on the tap full blast and just stand there listening to it until she felt better.

I didn't really believe in her fortunetelling, but I was glad it wasn't my cup that had frightened her. I wondered what she had seen.

She shut off the tap and smiled as she turned around.

"I am getting old. It is true. Not so good at telling fortunes. When I was young, I was so-o good. Now? No more. Maybe I need glasses. Your girl, the one who is not too skinny, she wear glasses?"

"No, no glasses, Mom."

"That's good. She is not Catholic, is she?"

"No, she's not." I didn't even feel like I was lying anymore. Since I didn't have a girl, she couldn't possibly wear glasses or be Catholic. My father was Catholic.

"That is good. Only two kinds of peoples I don't have good times with. Catholic peoples. And German peoples." She paused, suddenly suspicious. "She is not German, is she?"

"No, Mom. She's certainly not German."

"Ah, good. You are smart boy. God in heaven, he has big heart.

He loves all peoples. He loves Catholics and Germans too. That is why I don't have to love them." She had a truly astonishing relationship with God. "And she is very beautiful, yes?"

"Oh, yes. Very."

She beamed and clapped her hands.

"So, what is her name?"

"Rachel." The name slipped out of my brain and fell out of my mouth like a dislodged brick. It caught even me by surprise.

"Ray-chel?"

"Yes, Rachel," I said.

Chapter 4

I sat in my English lit class writing the name "Rachel" in my notebook. I wrote it straight and I wrote it embroidered. I didn't know why I was writing it. Maybe if I wrote it enough times I would find out. I turned the page and continued writing it on a clean sheet of paper. Rachel.

Miss Mashar, a young substitute teacher who had replaced Mr. Geddes for the remainder of the term, stood in front of the class and talked about *The Scarlet Letter*, by Nathaniel Hawthorne.

"In its own way, *The Scarlet Letter* is a love story," she was saying. She loved that opening phrase. A few minutes earlier she had said that "In her own way, Hester was the precursor of modern heroines in literature." I had run across that word "precursor" before, but I knew that I had never used it. It seemed like a nice word to try. I started writing it down in my notebook, but by the time I got to the letter "r" I changed my mind and wrote "Rachel."

Every time somebody raised his hand to ask Miss Mashar a question, she seemed delighted to be addressed as "Miss." It had been a long, hard struggle, but she had finally made it and here she was, a Miss. Miss Mashar. She was very young and she just couldn't get over the thrill of it all. She never sat down, however. It was as if that desk and that chair, his desk and his chair, were responsible for Mr. Geddes' insanity and were still infected with it. When she touched the back of the chair with her hands, she quickly pulled them away.

The bell rang.

"Who's Rachel?" Freud asked me as we headed for our locker.

"Nobody, why?"

"You were writing her name in your notebook. I'm so used to cheating, I peek over your shoulder even when there's no test. Ha!" he laughed. Although he was painfully slow in everything else he did, Freud was a quick laugher. A "ha!" and that was that. Like a gunshot.

I clicked up the handle on my locker, "Ra-" I let it drop, "chel."

Misiora joined us just as Diane Sinclair went by. He stared at her as at an old enemy, but she didn't seem to notice. Freud passed out chewing gum and we all took a stick. Misiora, of course, threw the wrapper on the floor.

We always took the long way out of the school so we could go past the gym and the wrestling room. We just couldn't get used to the fact that it was all over. The smell of stale sweat and wintergreen coming from the room was like ballroom music to a wheelchair-bound old man who knew he would never dance again. As we crossed the gym, we ran into Mr. Lukach, the football coach. He had a whistle around his neck. He always did. Freud slunk back when he saw him.

"Hello, boys." He winked at us. Coach Lukach was one of those men who are constantly trying to improve their image. Right now, he seemed about three weeks into a correspondence course in how to develop a twinkle in your eye.

"Hi, Coach." We all nodded.

He almost slapped us on the back, but then he remembered that we weren't football players and he didn't. He only slapped football players on the back.

"Big day coming, eh? Gonna graduate soon." He winked again.

Freud leaned on the wall of the gym, looking down at his feet. Coach Lukach took a small step toward him and then he took a step back, as if to get a better overall look at Freud.

"Well, Billy?"

Freud shrugged, wincing as if in pain.

"Can't say I didn't try, can you? Can't say that."

"No, Coach. I can't say that."

Coach Lukach had lusted for three years after Freud's big body. He wanted that body on his offensive line. He tried everything. He even slapped him on the back and squeezed his neck, but Freud would not go out for football unless we did, and Larry and I didn't want to.

"You would've made a great tackle. I don't make mistakes. I know you would've. Maybe even all-state. And you know what, Billy? Had you listened to me, right now you'd have yourself a football scholarship to Indiana or Purdue or even Notre Dame. But no, you wouldn't listen, would you, Billy?"

"I guess not, Coach."

"So now what're you gonna do?"

Freud scratched his head. He seemed to be thinking very hard, trying to answer the question.

"Well . . . maybe the three of us here . . . I don't know."

"You'll regret it, Billy. You'll regret it for the rest of your life." The coach winked and left, playing with some loose change in his pocket.

"Thanks, Coach," Freud said. Then he looked at us, shrugging apologetically for being so damned submissive. "I don't know. I have a hard time, you know, talking back to men whose first name is Mr. or Coach. My dad taught me to have respect for grown-ups."

We left the gym.

"I don't think I would've made no all-state tackle." Freud put his arm around Misiora, trying to tell him and me that he had no regrets. Without being conscious of it, he was also reminding us that he had sacrificed football for friendship and now as graduation approached he expected us to keep that in mind. At least that was how it seemed to me.

"Lukach is full of shit," Misiora said. Freud nodded, as if hearing a revelation.

Misiora looked at his watch. "Let's go visit Mrs. Dewey."

Freud and I looked at our watches too. Her husband wouldn't be home for a couple of hours, so we had some time. We headed up Indianapolis Boulevard in our usual formation: Larry on the left, I in the middle, Freud on the right.

"I don't think I would've made no all-state tackle. Do you?" Freud asked me.

"I don't know."

"I don't think I would've."

He had a hard time walking in a straight line. He either kept bumping into me or straying off into the postage-stamp-sized lawns that fronted the boulevard. The approach of graduation was making him anxious. He was getting drunk on anxiety, stumbling around as if intoxicated.

"Nah, no way in hell could I make all-state," he kept mumbling

in that foghorn voice of his. "That Lukach." He leaned over to look
at Misiora. "Boy, you're right there, Larry. He's full of shit, that's
what he is. You know."

"Yeah, I know. I know." Misiora was getting tired of the subject.

"Telling me a thing like that," Freud went on. "I'm not going to
regret it for the rest of my life. I'm just not going to." His voice
lacked conviction. He looked at me and Larry for support.

"Hey." Larry smiled. "C'mon, Big Freud." He put his arm
around him. "You can't let a guy like that get you down. Can you?"

"I guess I can." Freud shrugged.

"Well, don't." Misiora tightened his grip on Freud's shoulder.
"You've got something, Billy, that's more precious than any scholarship."

"Yeah, what's that?"

Misiora grinned. "Us. You've got us. Right, Daniel?"

"Right," I said.

I was puzzled by Misiora's shift in attitude. He really seemed to
be trying to get Freud out of his depression.

"You know what I'm going to do, Billy?"

"No, what?"

"I'm going to paint you a gloomy picture," Misiora said. Freud
smiled. Misiora used to do that a lot. Whenever Freud or I got upset
by something, he'd paint us a gloomy picture—a picture so gloomy,
in fact, that by comparison our unhappiness seemed trivial. I smiled
too. We loved to hear his gloomy pictures.

"All right." Misiora took a deep breath and, keeping his arm
around Freud's shoulder, began. "Here's how it is. You went out for
football. You got the job as starting tackle. Not only that but you
made all-state just like that asshole said. And not only that but you
got a full scholarship to Purdue. So off you go to Purdue next fall.
A hero!"

"And what about you guys?" Freud asked.

"Never mind us. Daniel and I, we're out of your life. You're at
Purdue. We're here."

"Yeah, but won't you come and visit?"

"Hey, this is my story. All right. Anyway," Misiora went on
again after a short pause. I could tell by his eyes that he had just the
right gloom for Freud. "There's this big game. Purdue against
Michigan. You make this great tackle but you get hit on the head.
And do you know what happens?"

"I get killed," Freud said.

"No, nothing that easy. You get knocked out. Out cold. And then hours later when you come to, do you know what happens?"

"No." Freud could smell the gloomy part coming up.

"You don't remember a thing, that's what. Not a thing." Larry made a zero with his fingers and showed it to Freud. "You don't remember what team you play on. What dorm you live in. Your name? You don't remember your name. Daniel and I, we come and visit you in the hospital. You don't remember us. Don't remember ever knowing us. Zero, that's what you remember." He showed him the zero again. "Hey, you remember that Halloween five years ago when all three of us dressed up as Robin Hoods and your dad took pictures of us?"

"Sure, I do." Freud smiled.

"No, you don't. Not anymore. You've got amnesia, Freud. You've got tackle-induced amnesia. You don't remember beans. Not us. Not your dad. Not your dad's Buick. Nothing. Zero."

"Christ." Freud clutched his head.

"There you go." Misiora lowered his voice, a storyteller coming to the moral of the fable. "Now, aren't you glad you didn't go out for football?"

"Sure am, Larry." Freud nodded. He was really too smart to be cheered up by the story, but what cheered him up was the fact that mean Larry would actually drop his meanness for a while and concentrate on him.

We crossed the intersection of 147th Street and Indianapolis Boulevard against the light. A driver honked his horn at us.

"Here." Misiora flung him a finger. "Sit on this." He seemed relieved at finding an opportunity so quickly to show us that he was back to his old mean self again.

A factory whistle blew at Blow-Knox Steel. My dad worked there, and although I knew he was at home, the whistle made me look toward the foundry and I saw it, I saw the street and the boulevard and the chimneys and smokestacks and the flames of the oil refineries through his eyes. His image stayed with me for a few blocks and then left, receded to return again.

Mrs. Dewey was sitting on her porch when we came up her street. Either she always sat there when the weather was nice, or she knew when we were coming and sat there to wait for us. She crossed her legs and smiled. "Hi, guys. Hello."

We replied with short, abbreviated waves, reeking of self-conscious nonchalance.

"Hi, Larry. Hi, Danny. Hello, Billy." She made her voice go deep for Freud's benefit and he smiled like a dog whose itch had been scratched. "Haven't seen you guys for a while. Whatcha been doin'?"

"A little of this," Misiora said, "and a little of that. Little, in short."

He always softened around her. His body, his head, his face, his thoughts seemed to be constructed out of corners and edges that relaxed only when he saw Mrs. Dewey. His mean blue eyes almost lost some of their meanness in her presence.

"Gonna graduate soon, eh? Diploma time." She smiled and started humming "Pomp and Circumstance."

We sat down in our usual place on the porch steps, at her feet, slouching into our spots, moaning from habit as if we had just come from wrestling practice, forgetting temporarily that our last season was over.

"Yes." Larry turned toward her. "Once we get that diploma, a whole new world will open up to us."

"It just might, Larry." She paid no attention to his cynical tone. "Why else would everybody be going to school? I'll tell you one thing. I sure regret dropping out like I did. Less than one year to go, tsk, and I had to go and drop out. I sure regret it now. Let me tell you . . ."

"You think you'll regret it for the rest of your life?" Freud asked.

"Well, I don't know about that, Billy. At this rate, I'll have so many things to regret, I don't know if I'll be able to squeeze that one in."

She chuckled. She was the only person I knew who truly chuckled. When she did, two deep dimples formed, making her look fragile and vulnerable, as if they were cracks that could make her break.

"Whatcha gonna do," she sighed. "I wanted to get married, so I got married. I didn't even get a honeymoon out of the deal. Bimbo promised me a honeymoon." Bimbo was her husband. "But then this job came up, and, well . . . tsk . . ."

She left the sentence unfinished. She seemed destined to go through life without ever completing anything. Something was always getting left out of her life: a year from school, a honeymoon from a marriage; even the wall-to-wall carpeting in her living room wasn't really wall-to-wall because Bimbo balked at the cost.

A car roared down the street, slowed down as it went past her house and then roared away again, horn blowing, several hands waving out of the open windows. She waved back. We recognized the guys in the car. They were juniors from our school. Next year at this time, they would probably be sitting here, talking with her. Our replacements. She'd had a group of seniors when we met her, and now she had us. Next year it would be them. She was in her late twenties, but she loved to sit and talk with high-school boys. She loved to hear about school gossip, about dances and proms and homecoming games. It was as if she were trying to complete that year of school on her porch. We felt at ease with her. She was the only grown-up we knew who wasn't really an adult, and sitting around and listening to her gave us a comforting feeling that life after school maybe wasn't all that impossible. There was something else, too. She had about her an aura of homey sex, of sex not in the bedroom with the lights turned off but on the couch with the TV turned on. We *knew* she made love. It wasn't just some rumor. We knew she did, and her experience where we were totally ignorant, her knowledge of this mystery, made us want to be with her. She didn't mind that we peeked up her dress and down her blouse; on the contrary, she made those sights available to us in a very easy, giving way. Our inhibition kept us from pursuing the matter to its natural conclusion. Our hopes were that something would happen. It was our last summer with her. Something was bound to happen.

"You guys got any plans for the summer?"

The three of us looked at each other, checking in with one another, wondering if one of us had some secret plan that didn't include the other two. I saw nothing in Freud's eyes except doglike devotion, but Larry seemed to have something in his that he didn't want to share.

"Yeah, I plan to get a tan," Larry said.

"Ha!" Freud laughed.

"Boy . . ." Mrs. Dewey fiddled with a button on her blouse. "I used to love making summer plans. Nothing I liked more. I tell you . . . maybe we could all four of us take a drive to Wisconsin Dells. Ever been there?"

Three heads shook, no.

"That'd be a nice trip. Bimbo has to go and visit his cruddy parents in cruddy Iowa somewhere and while he's there, we could all go to Wisconsin Dells. It's not far. We could either take a day trip or stay overnight or something. They have these boats, you know, that go through the Dells."

"What's a Dell?" Freud asked. We all looked at him. He was instantly sorry he asked.

"You mean like in Wisconsin Dells?" Mrs. Dewey asked.

"Yeah. I mean, I know what Wisconsin is, but . . ."

"You don't know what a Dell is?" Misiora cut him off.

"No, I don't."

"What're you, stupid or something?"

"I guess I must be." Freud accepted the verdict calmly.

"Everyone knows what a Dell is."

"You mean you never heard of Wisconsin Dells?" Mrs. Dewey sounded just like a schoolgirl.

"I heard of it. I heard of it." Freud clutched his head. "I just don't know what a Dell is, that's all. I'm all for going there, though. Sounds great to me."

Mrs. Dewey chuckled and ran her fingers through his hair. Kindness was never wasted on Freud. He beamed. One fact was very clear to me: none of us knew what a Dell was.

Mrs. Dewey went on to elaborate her plans. We would get up real early, get a full tank of gas—no, we would get a full tank of gas the night before, then get up early and drive for a couple of hours and then stop for breakfast at some restaurant. She even knew what we would have for breakfast. Pancakes and sausages. And then we would drive on to the Dells and, depending on how much fun we were having, we'd either stay over or come back. If we stayed over, we'd find a motel somewhere. She dropped that word "motel" like a hand grenade. "Motel" to us was one of those words so loaded with implications and possibilities that it could have been one of the lands in Disneyland: Motel-Land. She talked. We listened. Cars drove by. Cars parked. People were coming home from work. The empty spots in front of the houses were getting filled with cars. Through the windows of the houses I could see TV sets coming on.

"What's that?" Misiora interrupted her just as Mrs. Dewey was launching into the menu for the dinner we'd have in Wisconsin.

"What's what?" she asked.

"That." Larry pointed to a bruise on her arm, a bluish-yellow mark cut in half by the sleeve of her blouse.

"Oh, that!" She ran her fingers across it. "I bruise real easy. Bimbo pushed me and I fell back against the door. It's nothing."

"What'd he push you for?"

"Oh." She made a face. "I don't know. I think I was crying or something and he can't bear to see me cry. Gets real mad. 'Whatcha cryin' for?' " She tried to imitate his voice. " 'I'll give yah something to cry about.' So he pushed me."

"What, he beats you!" Misiora's eyes narrowed.

"No, he doesn't 'beat' me. Not 'beat' beat. You know. He biffs me around. That's all. Just biffs. Never with a fist, although he keeps threatening. He knows I'm afraid of getting hit with a fist. I never should've told him I was. Now that he knows, he keeps threatening me. He says if he ever catches me crying again, he'll let me have it with a fist."

Misiora stood up—jumped up, actually.

"You tell him, Lavonne. You tell him if he ever lays a finger on you again, I'll put his ass in a slingshot and bounce it down the street like a marble. You tell him that for me."

"Well, now, Larry." She put her hand on his shoulder and lowered him onto the steps again. "I'm not going to tell him that. That would just mean trouble for all of us."

"I'll tell him," Misiora said through clenched teeth.

"No, you won't."

"He'd do it," Freud said.

"I know he'd do it. But I don't want him to. Things are bad enough as it is. No sense making them worse."

"If I hear that he hit you, if I hear that, Lavonne, I'm not kidding around now, if I hear that I'll break his fingers off and stick them up his ass one by one."

Mrs. Dewey chuckled. The image made her laugh.

"Oh, he won't hit me. All I gotta do is stop crying. That's all. So I'll stop. Silly to cry. I don't even know why I do."

"I cried when my dad died," Freud said, "but that was different. I knew why I was doing it."

Mrs. Dewey sighed and began talking about her dad. She used to sing when she was a young girl and he just loved to hear her sing.

"He'd come home tired from work, sit on the couch and open a beer and I'd sing him a nice song. And you know what he told me once . . . He said, 'Honey, as far as I'm concerned, this is as nice as life gets.' That's what he said. He even paid for me to take music lessons from this Russian woman. A violin, yet. She said a violin was like a duke . . . no . . . no . . . aristocrat." Her eyes lit up. "Yes, she said a violin was the aristocrat of musical instruments. Nobody in my family had any musical ability except for me so they all wondered like crazy where in the world I got it from. Where could she get it from?" She chuckled. "If I'd kept up my lessons . . . but . . . ah, well . . ."

I stood up. I had to go. I liked Mrs. Dewey. I liked Larry and Freud, but I felt dishonest sitting there. I wasn't really listening. I was a participant, but not a wholehearted one. Part of my heart was somewhere else.

"I gotta go home."

Mrs. Dewey looked at me and then at Larry. She wanted Misiora to stay. Freud didn't know what to do, go with me or stay with them. To see him sitting there, pondering this decision, you would have thought he was at the crucial crossroads of his life.

He stayed.

"Bye."

"See yah."

"Bye, Danny." Mrs. Dewey waved. "I bet you're not going home. I bet you gotta girl somewhere."

"Ha!" I heard Freud's laugh.

The conversation, I knew, would now turn to girls and love and Mrs. Dewey's tales of high-school love affairs. There's nothing like love, she said repeatedly, nothing like it. I tell you . . .

I walked away yearning for happiness or tragedy all my own. Something all my own.

My dad was sitting at the kitchen table when I walked in, his elbows on the tabletop, his head in his hands. He was doing his *Sun-Times* crossword puzzle and my entrance did nothing to spoil his concentration.

"Hi, Dad."

"Yes, hello."

I took an apple out of the fridge and bit into it.

"Must you!" he snapped.

I paused in midbite.

"You sound like a horse when you eat like that. Chomp-chomp-chomp. Maybe your mother likes it that way, maybe that's how they do it in her country, but I don't like it. Take a knife, cut yourself a nice slice like a civilized human being and eat it quietly. All right?"

"Sure, Dad."

I took a knife out of the drawer and cut myself a small slice. Although he wasn't looking at me, I slouched over. I always did that when he was around. It made him feel bad that my mother and I were so tall and he was so short. My mother wouldn't dream of slouching.

"What's an eight-letter word for sea mammal?"

"Ah-h." I started thinking aloud just to show him I was on the job.

"Never mind. I got it!"

He started writing. If you sent in the correct solution to the crossword puzzle, you won five hundred dollars. He really wanted to win. He had been trying for over a year. He also played this thing called TOTO, having to do with the German soccer league. If you guessed the scores for the upcoming week, you could win a fortune. He was involved in other things, too. All kinds of things, which he kept in a steel box in a corner, padlocked for privacy.

I slouched into the living room and sat down on the couch. He turned his head, looked at me and then went back to his crossword puzzle.

"Mom at work?" I asked.

"Yes."

"You working tonight?"

"What else?"

I had left Mrs. Dewey's porch to be here with him. I felt obliged, no matter what the circumstances, to spend some time with him. It never turned out the way I wanted it to, but I kept doing it.

The fridge kicked on and its shaking and the buzzing filled the silence. I chomped on the apple, the fridge drowning out my noise.

My dad leafed through a dictionary, looking for a word. His right hand kept returning to a spot on his neck, his fingertips touching the spot gently. It was a bump of some kind.

He wrote something down again.

He hadn't always been like this, solitary and aloof. A few years ago something had happened and he had changed. I had no idea what caused it, but the change was drastic. He and my mother began fighting or not speaking to each other and the atmosphere in our house became cold and warlike.

His hand left the bump on his neck and wandered into his hair. He had beautiful, wavy hair, so thick he could hardly comb it, and when he did, he always looked at the comb with delight, observing that not a single hair had fallen out. It was his pride and joy and it dominated his appearance like a headdress of eagle feathers.

"What's an eleven-letter word for serpent's tooth?"

"What kind of tooth?"

"Serpent's. Serpent's. Eleven letters."

"Ahh, I don't know."

"You don't, eh? What do you know?"

"A few things, I guess."

"Like what?"

"I don't know." I shrugged.

"You going to flunk out of school?"

"I don't think so. I'm graduating next month."

"And then what'll you do?"

"I don't know."

The fridge kicked off. It got real quiet again. I wished I had something to tell him, some incredible news. At times, I would have liked to come inside all cut up and bleeding just to see if it would snap him out of his mood.

"Dad."

"Yes, what?" he replied without turning around.

"How's work?"

I knew it was a dumb question as soon as I asked it.

"Miserable, that's how. Those animals I have to work with . . . beer and women, that's all they know. Beer and women. Most of them are foreigners. More and more of them. They talk in their own language and sing these songs and laugh like hyenas. Your mother would probably find them attractive."

He flipped through a dictionary, counting letters, thinking. The clock inside my body ticked off two minutes, a wrestling period. The apple had made me thirsty, but I didn't want to walk past him to the kitchen to get a drink.

"Daniel," he said suddenly and turned his head and all that hair toward me.

"Yes, Dad."

"I named you that."

"Yes, I know."

"Your mother wanted to give you one of those foreign names, but I wouldn't have it. Do you know why I named you Daniel?"

"No."

"You mean I never told you?"

"No, I don't think you did, Dad."

"You sure I never told you?"

"Yes."

"Why don't I tell you now. You see, I named you Daniel because . . ."

He smiled. And since he rarely smiled these days, it creased his face in a strange, disconcerting manner. His scalp moved; the tips of his ears rose and hid in his hair. He stopped blinking.

I looked at him and waited for the explanation of my name. I had the knife in one hand and the apple in the other.

Then a frightening thing occurred. He opened his mouth as if to speak. A second passed. And then another. He said nothing. His smile began going away, wrinkle by wrinkle, and his unblinking eyes and open mouth left him looking aghast. He shook his head, as if trying to deny something, and his eyes, having totally forgotten about me, found me again. He seemed startled by my presence. I felt like an unwitting peeping tom who had peeked through the keyhole of his brain. He stared at me suspiciously, wondering how much I had seen.

He stood up and came toward me. I dropped the apple from my hand and held on to the knife.

"Do you know what?" he almost whispered, coming toward me, stopping a few steps away.

"What, Dad?"

"Something," he said, "something's going to happen. Mark my words."

He smiled. I smiled. I relaxed a little. I realized he was imitating my mother, making fun of her fortunetelling.

"Isn't that how she does it?"

"Yeah." I nodded. "Just like that."

"You're going on a trip," he continued, trying to imitate her accent. "Yes, a long, long trip."

"That's her, all right."

He tried to laugh. I tried to laugh. He was doing it for my benefit. I was doing it for his. Behind his game, I sensed something else operating—a coverup. He wanted me to forget what I had seen, and although I didn't know what it was, his desire to cover it up gave it importance.

He laughed again. I laughed again. Satisfied that he had erased something from my mind, he walked back to the kitchen. His stockinged feet were covered by the cuffs of his long, gray pleated slacks and he walked noiselessly across the carpet, then the linoleum, back into his chair.

"Six-letter name," he asked me minutes later, "wife of Jacob?"

"Rachel." The name tumbled out of my brain again.

He reexamined the puzzle and wrote it down.

"I think that's it."

I was in bed when I heard him leaving for work. I was still awake when my mother came home from her job. I shut my eyes and pretended to be asleep when she opened the door to my room. She stood there for a while, looking at me, and then left.

Chapter 5

My father stayed in bed all day Saturday. He came out of the bedroom a few times to go to the bathroom, wearing blue pajamas and brown slippers and holding a comb in his hand. He combed his hair in the bathroom and then, slippers slapping on the linoleum, he shuffled back into the bedroom, leaving the door open. He looked pale and even smaller than usual, the way people do when they're sick.

"It is flu," my mother said. "It comes and then it goes away."

The bump on his neck had grown redder and larger. It looked like a boil.

"He is small, weak man." My mother, aware of the open door, lowered her voice. "He works very, very hard. It is good he stays in bed and rests."

She took his food to him. He loved cabbage soup, so she made him cabbage soup. She even went out and bought him the Chicago Sun-Times. When he wanted a sharpened pencil, she took a kitchen knife and sharpened it the way a peasant whittles a stick, yellow chips flying, half the pencil gone, but it got sharpened. She stayed for a few minutes in the bedroom and I could hear them talking. Their voices were soft and lovely to hear. My mother and father talking gently to each other. It felt like home. His voice didn't carry like hers, so I couldn't hear what he was saying.

"You are not to worry," she said. "You just lie in bed like Turkish pasha and I bring you what you need. Everything will be fine. Everybody gets sick."

He said something I didn't understand. I heard her laugh.

"Yes, it is true. Even I get sick. Sure. And when I get sick, you be good to me and when you are sick, I am good to you. No, no . . . why do you cry? You can tell me."

Whenever my dad got sick, things got nice around the house. My mother submitted to his whims; she forgot past grudges and hostilities and took care of him in a touching, motherly way, free of even a trace of resentment. Things were never as nice, as free and easy between them as when he was sick.

Freud came by on Sunday.

"Allo, Fraud," my mother greeted him.

"Ha!" He laughed as he always did when she mispronounced his already mispronounced name.

"Shhh." She put her finger to her lips.

He and I went outside.

"My dad's sick. Flu or something."

"He'll be okay. People who get sick a lot do okay. My dad was never sick and then . . ." He sighed and then remembered why he had come. His face lit up. "Listen, this is Bimbo's weekend to be volunteer fireman and Mrs. Dewey said we could all go for a drive in her car. Not to the Dells or anything, but a drive . . . you know . . . get a hamburger or something. Misiora's with her now and I came to get you."

"I have to go to church with my mother," I lied.

"Oh." He nodded, disappointed. "I'll tell them. Church is important. I never go, but I know it's important. I'll see you Monday, huh?" He ran off. A little dog shot out of the yard down the block and ran after him. "C'mon, pup!" Freud bellowed.

My mother came out a little later. She was dressed for church, and she looked beautiful.

"Your father is sleeping. He will be all right."

"Sure, I know."

"You have not come to church with me in long time."

"I guess not."

I used to go, but my father, a non-practicing Catholic, objected to my going to my mother's heathen Byzantine services.

"Maybe you will come with me now."

"I can't," I said. "The guys are picking me up. We're going for a drive."

"Oh, yes, I know what kind drive you are going on. Yes, I do."

She smiled, winking at me. Had my mother's worst fears about me only been true, I would have lived an incredible life.

"I will pray for you, son," she said as she walked away. She turned the corner. The bus stop was three blocks away. My father didn't believe in cars, TV sets, radios, record players . . . modern garbage, he called them.

I felt a little guilty. Having lied to my friends and my mother, I began lying to myself, pretending that I had no idea what I was going to do next. I knew, but even as I headed toward Aberdeen Lane, I tried to pretend that I wasn't going there. In my mind I saw myself walking right past it, not even pausing to look. But when I got to the corner of Northcote Avenue and Aberdeen Lane, I stopped. I had lied my way to here, and now the truth was that I had no idea what I wanted. To catch a glimpse of her, maybe. To hear her name again. Rachel.

Slowly, as if looking for a reason, I started down the lane. Church bells rang.

I was going to walk past her house, but when I saw that her car wasn't there, I was both disappointed and relieved. I stopped and leaned on a sugar maple tree. The house looked the same. There were no signs that anyone had moved in. Same curtains. Same window shades. I allowed myself to wonder if perhaps I had imagined it all: the girl, the earrings, the man with the silver-gray hair calling her name—Rachel.

"Hey, you!" I heard her call. I pushed off the tree as if it were a hot stove. I recognized her voice, but I couldn't see her. I turned to leave.

"Hey, you. I said, you!"

And then I saw her. She was in the second-story window, pointing her finger at me.

"Stay right there!" she cried, in a voice used to obedience. I stayed.

The front door opened and shut and then the screen door on the porch opened and she ran out, slamming it shut behind her. She was barefoot, wearing faded blue jeans and a flannel man's shirt much too big for her. One sleeve was rolled up past her elbow, and the other had come undone.

"You stayed!" She smiled. Her green eyes were swollen, as if she had been crying.

"Well, you said . . ." I pointed to the window where she had been.

"Why were you looking at my house like that?"

"Like what?"

"Like you were doing. Like this." And she leaned on the maple tree to show me. It hurt to see the accuracy of her imitation of me. When you're eighteen and living in East Chicago, there's nothing to cling to except the notion that you're inimitable.

"I don't know. I was just looking."

"You were thinking," she said slowly.

"I wasn't thinking," I lied. "What was I thinking about?"

"You live here?" she asked.

Later I would get used to it, but for the moment her skipping from one subject to another unsettled me.

"No, not on this street. I live near the park." I pointed.

"Is there a park here?"

"There are two parks. Well, actually, there are three. There's Kosciusko Park. I live near there. Then there's . . ."

She cut me off again.

"You any good at screwing things in?"

"I guess so. I don't know. I guess I am."

"Let's find out." She took me by the elbow and led me to the side of the house. "You better be good."

"I didn't say I was good. I said . . . I didn't know."

She dragged me forward, her black hair bouncing, turquoise earrings dangling. From extreme profile, her face had the smooth, flowing shape of a Grecian urn I had seen in a book at the public library.

"Here it is." She stopped and pointed to a water spigot on the side of the house. A rolled-up hose with a sprinkler lay beneath it. "I wanted to water the lawn, but the hose won't screw in. The silly thing just kept going around and around."

I picked up the hose and looked at the attachment. I examined it while she waited impatiently. I wanted to look at her, but I didn't. She leaned on the house, standing on one leg.

"So?"

"I'm looking."

I wiped some dirt from the interior with my finger and pressed down on the loose washer.

"Don't tell me that's what it was." She made a face. "If you tell me that's what it was, I'm going to be real upset. I am."

I aligned the attachment with the outlet and turned it slowly. The threads slipped into the grooves like hands into mittens. As soon as she saw that it was going to work, she grabbed me by the back of my shirt and pulled me away.

"I want to do it. I want to do it."

She rubbed her hands and turned the copper fitting slowly, savoring the movement like a safecracker. She bit her lips. She flashed her eyes at me. She seemed delighted that it was working. When she finished the job, she pulled back and looked at it.

"What do you think?" she asked.

"Looks good to me."

"Now we turn on the water. No. No. Take the sprinkler into the yard first."

She couldn't wait. It was one of those sprinklers that move back and forth. I dragged it to the middle of the lawn, expecting her to turn the water on in my face, but she didn't.

"A little more to the left."

I hated direct orders, but for some reason it was fun to obey her. I moved it a little to the left.

"That's it. Perfect. Now come here. Quickly . . ."

I ran back.

"*Now* we turn on the water. You want to do it?" She considered being generous and changed her mind instantly. "No, I want to do it. Here goes."

She turned the handle. The hose shuddered. A second later, the sprinkler began fussing as if startled out of a deep sleep, and then it sputtered, and sputtered again, and then long jets of water shot out into the air.

She clapped her hands.

"Look at that. We did it!"

She hugged me on the spot. She hugged me the way little kids hug kittens: quick and rough and then on to other things. She ran out onto the lawn. I followed.

"We're a great team, you and me," she said. "We are." She smiled. The corners of her eyes wrinkled. She squinted when she smiled, as if she were staring into the sun.

The sprinkler moved, arcing from the house toward the street, the water hitting the branches and the young spring leaves of the sugar maple tree.

The water and her smile relaxed me. My stiff shoulders loosened.

"What's your name?" she asked.

"Daniel Price."

"No middle name?"

"Well, yeah." I shrugged.

"What is it?"

"Oh, it's . . ."

"C'mon. C'mon. Tell me." She shook me by the shoulder.

"You won't laugh?"

"I never laugh. Not if it's important that I don't. Is it important?"

"I'd rather you didn't laugh."

"I won't. Really. Will not laugh."

"Boone," I said.

"Daniel Boone!" She opened her mouth. Then she got quite serious. "You know what? I'm going to have to take back what I said. I'm going to laugh. Daniel Boone." She started laughing. "Daniel Boone Price."

"It was my father's idea. I don't know why he . . ."

"Do people call you Boone?" She laughed. "Hey, Mrs. Price . . . can Daniel Boone come out and play?"

Some people can laugh and make you forget that they're doing it at your expense, make you feel good just seeing them laugh. That's how it was with her.

"I'm sorry." She stopped. "I hope I didn't hurt your feelings."

"No, you didn't."

She almost seemed disappointed.

"Well, now that I know your name, I'll tell you mine."

"Let me guess," I said.

"How silly. What do you mean, guess? You'll never guess it." Her face changed as the game appealed to her. "Oh, go ahead, I don't care."

She drained all emotion out of her face and looked at me.

"Go ahead," she said.

"I'm waiting."

"Waiting for what?"

"For a sign," I said. I loved the position I was in.

"A sign! You really are silly. You are!"

"Your name," I intoned like my mother when she read fortunes in her Turkish coffee cup, "your name is"—I looked at her and was suddenly overcome by how beautiful she was—"Rachel."

She flinched.

"I told you you'd never guess it. My name is not Rachel, so there."

I flinched this time.

"It's not?"

"It certainly isn't. And what if it is? Big deal. All right, all right, so you got it. How did you know?" she asked, trying to appear disinterested.

"Oh, it's just one of those things I can tell sometimes."

"What else can you tell?"

"That's all. For now," I added quickly.

She tilted her head and took what can only be described as a long, hard look at me. It was as if she were making a reappraisal, and so open was her stare, so concentrated, that I felt the very outlines of my body, the boundaries of my shoulders, the size and shape of my eyes, nose, mouth, my every feature, as if by looking at me she were describing me out loud to herself at the same time.

"Do you believe in destiny?" she asked.

That was one of those words. I had read it repeatedly, and I had heard it spoken, but I had never used it myself.

"Destiny." I used it for the first time. "Yeah. I believe in destiny."

"So do I. Maybe it was destiny?"

"What?"

"That we met. That you knew my name."

I couldn't tell if she was joking or not.

"Maybe so."

"I have no middle name. My last name's Temerson."

She offered her hand. We shook.

At the beginning of every wrestling match I shook hands with my opponents, and after four years of shaking hands, I was able to tell certain things about them the instant our hands met. I could tell the weaklings who squeezed real hard trying to impress me with strength they didn't have from those who feigned a weak grip just so they could shock me with their strength when the match began. I could tell who wanted to win and who wanted to lose and who didn't really care one way or the other. When Presley Bivens shook my hand before the championship match, I felt like a job applicant shaking hands with the director of personnel. All I could tell about Rachel's hand was that she was letting me hold it and although her face was that of a beautiful girl, her hand was that of a woman far more mature than I. She let me hold it and then she took it away, smiling that squinty-eyed smile of hers. It was strange. Her face was so open, her smile so direct that it was like looking at an open book, but a book written in a language I did not understand.

A car pulled up—a blue Packard with New York license plates. Both of us turned. It was the man with the silver hair. Rachel's face changed instantly when she saw him. The puffiness under her eyes, the telltale signs that she had been crying, which had vanished while we were alone, now returned suddenly, by sheer force of her will, and she greeted the man with them. He got out of the car with a large old camera in his hands. He slung the straps over his shoulder and, making a detour to avoid the water from the sprinkler, came toward us, looking down at his feet, up at us, down at his feet.

My long experience with my mother and father told me right away that the two of them had had an argument and were now both looking to see who would make the first sign of reconciliation. He seemed older than I had remembered him from that night, or maybe it was just that it was daylight now and Rachel was so young and I was so young and we were standing in front of a tree in bloom.

He smiled at me, then past me at Rachel. I recognized it as his sign of reconciliation. She responded to it. I felt like one of those screens through which people in prison movies talked.

"Didn't I tell you you'd make some friends here?" he said to Rachel, stopping a few feet away from me.

"His name's Daniel." Her lips puckered playfully as if she were getting ready to say "Boone," her eyes flashed at me and then she moved on. "Daniel Price."

"Hello, young man." He kind of bowed at the waist and I kind of bowed back at him.

"He's my father," Rachel said, and I kind of bowed again.

"Do you live around here?"

Before I could say anything, Rachel cut in.

"He lives over by Kosciusko Park. There's three parks here, you know."

"Well, they sure hide them well," her father said. He had a soft voice and gentle eyes. His face, however, was a series of strong, straight lines: a straight nose, straight mouth, many wrinkles in his forehead and two deep diagonal ones running down his cheeks that were perfectly straight, as if drawn with a ruler.

"They sure have a lot of industrial plants here, don't they?" he asked me.

"Oh, yes. A lot. That's all we have."

"There's a name for this area, isn't there? They call it something."

"The Region," I replied quickly.

"That's right." He smiled. "The Region. Yes."

I felt like he knew the answers but was asking me to be nice.

"The Region." Rachel walked between us. "That's a silly name. The Region! What kind of region?"

"It's just the Region," I said.

"Actually, it's da Region, isn't it?" Her father looked past Rachel at me.

"Yeah, that's how we say it here, all right. Da Region."

He smiled. I smiled. Rachel didn't smile. She seemed irritated that we knew something she didn't.

"I'm going inside," she said.

"Would you like to come in for a cup of coffee or something?" Her father gestured toward the house.

I did, but a quick flash from Rachel's eyes told me to decline.

"No, I, ah, I have to go to church with my mother."

"Ah, that's right. It's Sunday," he said. "Well, we hope to see you again, young man."

"Thank you. I hope . . ." I tried to talk like he did and almost got lost. "I hope to see you again, too."

"Bye." Rachel waved and left.

"Bye," I said.

"See you soon, young man." Her father followed her.

I walked away. The screen door slammed shut once and then it shut again, although not as loudly. When I turned around, both of them were gone.

The word "Rachel" had brought me to Aberdeen Lane, and I was leaving with a new word in mind. Destiny.

Yes, it all seemed to fit. Even my loss in the championship match had a purpose. Had I not lost, I would not have gone back to Aberdeen Lane and I would not have seen Rachel that night. Why else did I just happen to be there when she arrived? Destiny. Why else was there a thunderstorm that kept me inside with my mother, why else did she ask me about my love life at that very moment, and why else did her name, Rachel, just happen to fall out of my brain where I didn't even know it was lodged? Destiny.

"Destiny." I said the word out loud. It had a wonderful sound. Destiny. Like the name of a rolling river that would sweep me away and turn jobs and plans and careers and worries about life into silly things that stayed behind on the banks of the river as the water carried me on.

It wasn't up to me anymore. Nothing was up to me. It was all out of my hands. Destiny.

"Rachel." I said her name out loud. "Ray"—the first syllable spread my lips into a smile—"chel." The second moved them forward as if in a kiss. Rachel.

Chapter 6

Having a destiny was like having a secret identity, a secret mission. I could sit in my geometry class proving the theorem that parallel lines can never meet and it would suddenly hit me that nobody in the classroom knew who I really was. Freud didn't know. Misiora didn't know. My teacher didn't know. My parents didn't know. It made me feel wonderful, almost giddy at times. I could enjoy all the things that bored me before because I knew they were temporary, because I knew that the real me, the secret me, the me with the destiny, was meant for something else. It was a source of perpetual joy and anticipation, my destiny, like the feeling I used to have when I was a little kid weeks before Christmas, the feeling that every day, no matter how long and tedious, was wonderful because it was bringing me that much closer to the real goal itself: Christmas Day.

Not only did I have a destiny, but I had an address for her: she lived on Aberdeen Lane and her name was Rachel.

I started going there regularly after school. When Freud and Misiora wanted to know why I couldn't go with them to visit Mrs. Dewey, I told them it was because my father was sick and I had to stay at home with him. It was true that my father was ill. Although he kept going to work, insisting that he was all right, it was obvious that he was not. The boil on his neck was getting bigger. It was infected, but he refused to see a doctor. I noticed his fatigue, his ashen face and the ever stranger glow in his eyes, but I was not really concerned. I was almost glad that he was sick because it gave me an easy excuse for Freud and Misiora about why I couldn't go with them. I had a vague feeling that other people had their lives too, a vague feeling that I was hurting my friends, lying to them, a vague feeling that I was ignoring something tragic in my father's life, but it didn't matter; only my feelings for Rachel were not vague, only they mattered.

"Hello, young man." Her father usually greeted me at the door and then he called her. "Rachel, your young man's here."

I loved being called "young man," loved being called her young man, loved seeing her appear, always acting surprised to see me.

"Daniel! What a shock."

"Hi, Rachel."

I used every opportunity I could to say her name. I loved saying it. I even loved when she mocked me for it.

"Hi, Daniel," she'd say, imitating my voice. "How's school?"

I'd usually make up something to say. I'd embroider the truth a bit to amuse her, and if she laughed I felt victorious. I spent a lot of time thinking up and storing up stories to tell her, and in the process I felt my heart opening up. There I found things that I only wanted to say to her, that I only wanted to share with Rachel.

"How's school?" she asked me one day.

"It'll be over soon."

"And then what?"

"I don't know."

"You don't? Are you sure?"

Her father wasn't at home. We sat by the fireplace and she looked at me in a way that seemed to imply that she had something in mind, some answer that I hardly dared consider. Her green eyes glowed.

It took a while, but the same thing always happened. Her eyes, when I first arrived, seemed dull and lifeless, cold, almost, despite her smile, and then as we talked, as I thought my thoughts and stumbled for words, they would begin to glow, gradually but perceptibly, until they shone and sparkled like sunlit marbles in a pool. And always when they reached a certain intensity that made my head spin, she would stand up and turn the lights out, so to speak, and I would go home thrilled once again that I had caused such a radiance in her and mystified by its abrupt conclusion.

Her father was a professional photographer. He spent a lot of his time building a darkroom in the basement. The house had belonged to his aunt. When she died and the real estate agent could not sell it, he had decided to move in.

"We all need a change sometimes," he told me. "Rachel and I had been back East all our lives and this seemed like a good opportunity to see another part of the country."

"Yes." I nodded. We all need a change. Yes.

He always seemed glad to see me when I came, and yet he always left for the basement after a few minutes. I certainly didn't mind being left alone with Rachel; it was just that I noticed his polite evasion of me. Everything he did was polite, with a slight smile and quick bow, but our eyes seldom met.

Rachel called him by his first name, David. When I seemed surprised by this informality, she just shrugged.

"I don't like the words 'Father' and 'Dad.' I don't. I especially don't like 'Dad.' " She made a face. "It sounds terrible. Dad. He's got a name, doesn't he? He calls me Rachel. He doesn't go around calling me 'Daughter.' That's why we have names, right?"

"I guess so," I said.

"What do you mean, 'you guess'? There's nothing to guess about. I just told you how things are. You're always saying 'I guess this . . . I guess that.' "

"It's just something I picked up."

"If you can pick it up, you can drop it, so drop it." She put her hand on my shoulder. "Okay?"

"Sure."

It would never have occurred to me to call my own father by his first name, and for that very reason she seemed all the more original and fascinating. She didn't just do things and say things, she had a reason for doing them, a theory.

She never answered questions directly, not even the simplest ones, and since I was eager to know all about her, this evasion both irritated and intrigued me and made me ask questions all the more.

We were sitting on her porch one day. Her father was hammering away in the basement working on his darkroom.

"They're not going to make Packards anymore," I said, pointing to his car.

"That's why I like it. It's the last of the line. A ruin in the making. I love ruins. Don't you?"

I wanted to love them because she did.

"Yes," I told her. Then after a short pause I asked her, "You're from New York, right?"

"I never said that."

"No, it's just that the license plate on the car—"

"That doesn't mean anything." She cut me off.

"Usually—" I began, but she cut me off again.

"Usually!" She raised an eyebrow as if appalled that I would use such a word. Then she smiled. "Yes, you're right."

"You are from New York?"

"No, the car's from New York."

"Where are you from?"

"Correct me if I'm wrong, Daniel Boone, but if I did tell you it wouldn't really make any difference, would it? What if I told you I was from Massachusetts? Or from Connecticut? What would you really know that you don't know now? The fact is I'm not from here, from da Region, and you are."

"How do you know I'm from here?" I tried to make myself mysterious, too.

"Because of the kind of questions you ask. Where I come from, people don't ask questions like that."

She never talked about her family, and so a few days later I asked her, "Is your mother alive?"

"I certainly hope so," she said.

We were walking slowly down the boulevard. The shops that hadn't closed already were closing as we walked past them.

"So where is she?" I asked.

"My mother?"

"Yes."

"You mean where is she right now? Right at this instant?"

"No, you know—"

"Right now," she interrupted. "Let me see. If I know my mother, right now she's going through the newspapers for the second time looking for things she might have missed."

"Why doesn't she live with you?"

"Why do you want to know?"

I shrugged. "I don't know. Everybody I know has a mother. So, I guess . . ."

She interrupted me. "You're guessing again." She shook her index finger at me and picked up the pace slightly. "Well, I have a mother too. I have a mother and a father and they're both . . ." She paused suddenly. Her intonation changed when she resumed. "They're both alive and well."

I understood. They were divorced. I didn't know anybody else whose parents were divorced. Nobody ever got divorced in East Chicago. Rachel, a daughter of divorced parents. It added a dimension to her. A girl from a broken home. Divorcee's daughter.

"Do you miss her?"

"What do you think?" She looked right at me.

"You probably do," I said.

"You're probably right."

She almost kissed me as we parted for the night in front of her house. My heart beat madly at the mere possibility of a kiss.

"Goodnight, Daniel."

"Goodnight, Rachel."

I was in love. I felt like the first person who had ever really fallen in love. The very first. I felt like an explorer who had discovered a strange, beautiful country, and I wanted to tell everyone about it. About her. About me. What it felt like. How I went to bed thinking about her, woke up thinking about her, went through the day thinking about her. I wanted to say it out loud in front of witnesses. I am in love with Rachel. But there was nobody I could tell. My father was sick. My friends would have felt betrayed, had I told them. I wanted to tell my mother, but having lied to her about Rachel already, it would have seemed silly to bring up the truth now. The person I really wanted to tell was Rachel herself, but I felt afraid. Something told me I had to go slowly, or as slowly as I could. It was difficult, because I wanted to say it, to hear myself say it, after years of waiting and being certain that I would go through life without ever saying it, to finally say it: I love you.

We were washing her father's car one day. She was wearing cut-off shorts and her favorite flannel shirt with rolled-up sleeves. It was still spring and there was little sun, but she seemed to get a tan instantly. Her legs were brown, even in back of her knees. Her hair hung loose, her earrings dangled. I sponged. She rinsed. She just loved rinsing the suds off, aiming the hose and squinting as if she were using a machine gun. I stared at her and did my job. She ignored me and did hers. Every now and then, she would stick her index finger under the hem of her shorts and pull them down in a very businesslike manner. Words were tumbling out of my head into my mouth. I felt incapable of containing myself anymore. I was going to blurt it all out.

"What's the matter with you today?" she asked, her finger on the trigger of the hose.

"Nothing."

"You're real quiet."

"Yes."

"Are you thinking, or what?"

"Yes."

"Stand back."

I stood back. She pressed the trigger. One second she seemed like a serious young woman, the next like a little kid playing with water. I was going crazy.

"Looks real nice." She examined the car. Then, very casually, as if asking for the time of day, she said, "What're you thinking about?"

"I don't know," I replied.

"You don't! I always know what I'm thinking about. You shouldn't have thoughts just flying through your head like bats through a barn. You should know what they are. I bet you know."

"Yes, I do."

"So-o?"

"I was thinking about you."

"I thought as much." She smiled, and pulled down her shorts. "And what about me?"

"Well, I guess . . ."

"Now you're not going to start guessing again, 'cause if you do . . ." she threatened, and aimed the hose at me.

I stammered, hoping she'd pull the damn trigger and put me out of my misery. I couldn't say it, not what I wanted to say.

"You're beautiful," I finally said.

She wrinkled her face. She seemed irritated.

"You are," I went on. "You're very . . ."

She dropped the hose on the ground and covered up her ears.

"I don't want to hear that. I don't," she said, looking away. "I don't know what to say when people tell me that. What am I supposed to say: Thank you."

"No. You don't have to . . ."

"Well then, what? I don't know what to say when I hear that. I hate it when I don't know what to say. You won't say it again, will you?"

"No."

She walked slowly toward me. I had no idea what she would say. Not a clue. I never did.

"I can't wait," she said softly, stopping next to me. "I just can't wait to be old. An older woman. Forty or so. You know . . . with all those nice wrinkles they have. I just love the wrinkles you get when you get old. I do."

She pushed up on her cheeks with her hands, wrinkling her face. I wrinkled mine. She laughed.

"Now, just stay like that and I'll be crazy about you," she said. She looked at me with such tenderness that I felt safe in telling her everything that was in my heart. But just as I opened my mouth to tell her I loved her, she cut the moment off.

"So, how was school today?"

I went home swearing that I would stay away from her the next day, but a promise that ran contrary to my desire made the day longer than I had ever expected, and by the time dusk fell my resolve collapsed and I was back on Aberdeen Lane, knocking on her porch door.

Nobody answered. Their car was parked in the usual place, and from inside the house I could hear the radio playing. The Ames Brothers were singing "Blue Moon."

I knocked again.

"Rachel," I shouted through the screen, "Mr. Temerson!"

Just as I was ready to give up and go home, her father appeared. "Oh, it's you. Come in, young man, come in." He waved me inside. I followed him. He was wearing an Oriental bathrobe that came to his knees. His calf muscles bulged like grapefruits. I didn't expect him to have any muscles at all. That was my department.

"Have a seat."

I sat down in an old easy chair by the fireplace. I waited for him to call Rachel. He shut off the radio, took a half-finished drink from the end table and sat down himself.

"Would you like a drink, young man?" He bowed his head. "I'm having gin without tonic."

"No, thank you."

"I have no tonic. There simply is no tonic in the house." He lifted the glass and paused, amused in some strange way by his last remark. Then he took a drink. He was either drunk or on the road to it. His eyes were bloodshot. "What would you like? What can I get you?"

"Oh, nothing. I'm fine . . . Thank you, Mr. Temerson."

"David, please." He still didn't look directly at me. "Rachel calls me David. You call me David."

He crossed his legs and I couldn't help noticing his calf muscles again.

I waited for him to call Rachel. He sipped his drink, slowly running a finger over his lips after each sip.

"Rachel's not here," he said.

I stood up, ready to leave.

"No, no, there's no need. You can stay, can't you?"

I sat down.

"You don't have to stay, but you are certainly welcome. My house is yours. My daughter is very fond of you, you know."

"Yes, well, I don't know," I mumbled.

"She's an interesting girl, isn't she?"

"Rachel? Yes, she's . . . real nice."

"Nice?" He smiled. He looked amused again. "Sorry, I guess I just never thought of her in quite that way, but you're probably right. She probably is real nice."

He had another sip. He ran his finger over his lips.

"Do you have a girl right now?" he asked.

"You mean like a girlfriend?"

"Yes, I suppose that's what I mean. Like a girlfriend."

"No, I don't."

"Have you ever had one?"

"You mean like a girlfriend?"

"Yes."

"No."

He had another sip.

"Do you like girls?"

I tried to figure out what he meant. "You mean, like in general?"

"Yes, do you like them like in general?"

"I guess so. I don't know. Yeah, I guess so."

He smiled. "Rachel says you 'guess' a lot."

"Well, I guess . . ." I stopped. My face flushed.

"Oh, you needn't worry. We do talk about you some, but we don't talk about you all the time. She doesn't tell me everything."

He reached down and picked up a camera. I hadn't noticed it there. He took off the lens cap. It dropped to the floor and he hardly took notice of it.

"Have you ever made love to a girl?"

My first impulse was to lie. My second impulse was to consider it a very strange question. My third impulse was to have a drink.

"No, I never have."

"But you want to, I imagine."

I couldn't understand why I was enjoying this turn that the conversation had taken.

"Yes, sure."

"Not 'I guess.' "

"No."

"You think about it a lot?"

"Yes."

"Wondering what it will be like, right?"

"Yes."

"Seems too good to be true, doesn't it?" He smiled sadly. "Too wonderful to ever happen. You're positive it'll never happen to you."

That was exactly how I felt about it.

"Sometimes," I said. "Most of the time, actually."

"Yes." He played with his camera. "I remember. It was a long time ago, but I do remember. It's so easy to forget what it was like, what it is like to be young. I make a point of trying to keep it fresh in my mind, but it doesn't really work."

He advanced the film, cocking the shutter.

"The problem with love is this," he said, but not necessarily to me. "It's both a sickness and a cure and you never know which one you're getting."

He suddenly lifted the camera and looked at me through the viewfinder. "You're a very attractive young man. In some parts of the country you would be considered handsome. I don't know if that's the case in this particular part of the country." He seemed to enjoy looking at me through the camera. It made it easy. Once again, eye contact was avoided.

He pressed the shutter. I smiled. He advanced the film and aimed the camera again.

"You've had pictures taken of you before, haven't you?"

"Just for the yearbook . . . wrestling team, things like that."

He took three pictures in a row. I had no idea what my face was doing. After each click, I realized that I should have been smiling and remembered that I wasn't, or was pretty sure I wasn't. It was hard to think with a camera pointed at me, and yet I was thinking. It was just that I didn't know what I was thinking about.

"Now think of Rachel," he said, and hid behind the camera.

I didn't want to think about her but my mind obeyed him. He pressed the shutter once, twice, several times, click, click, click, and I wondered if he was taking pictures of me or of what I saw in my head. My mind was like a slide projector. Each click from his camera, each advance of his film caused a new image to pop into my head and before I could remember what it was, a new one replaced it. Click! Click! Click! I saw Rachel, I saw my mother, my father. I saw him, Mr. Temerson, in my head and in front of me, click, click, click, but I could not hold the images long enough to see what they were like; a pair of eyes, a gesture, a heartbreaking smile, brief glimpses was all I saw, as if I were running through a gallery at breakneck speed.

"That's it. We're out of film, young man." He put the camera in his lap. "Out of tonic. Out of film."

I stood up.

"Going?"

"Yes."

I glanced at the camera. I was leaving, but some part of me was staying behind to be developed in his darkroom in the basement.

"I'll tell Rachel you came. She went out for a walk. If you'd care to wait for her . . ."

"No, I have to go home. My father's not feeling well."

"I am sorry to hear that. It's nothing serious, I hope."

"No, I don't think so."

He didn't walk me to the door.

It was dark when I went out. The streetlamps were on. I was only wearing a T-shirt and it was damp with sweat. I had no idea that I had been sweating that much. A light breeze was blowing, and it made me feel hungry and cold. It was only then, walking away from the house, shivering, that I could reflect on my visit with Mr. Temerson. It seemed like a dream to me, a trance. The reality of the darkness, the hunger in my stomach, the cool breeze in my face brought me back to a more familiar world and made the one I had left even stranger. To keep the chill away, I started running and as soon as I started, it hit me: I knew where Rachel was. I just knew. It was destiny again. Destiny was calling me, telling me where she was, pulling me toward her.

I took a right on Northcote Avenue and from there it was a straight shot, five blocks away, to Kosciusko Park. She was there. I just knew it. As I ran, I formed my plan. If she was there, then

I would tell her that I loved her. I ran through the night like a man with a mission, with a message for Rachel. I allowed myself the pleasure of a game. Each TV light I saw in the windows of the houses was a sniper. I was running through enemy territory. Would I get there in time? Dogs were barking as I zigged and zagged, dodging bullets from the TV sets. I considered getting wounded, but there was no time.

As soon as I got to the park, I saw her. The park was deserted except for one solitary figure moving slowly through the trees. The park lights were on and I could see her long shadow even when she disappeared behind the trees.

"*Rachel!*" I shouted. The shadow moved. She appeared. I ran toward her.

I half expected her to run toward me, but she didn't. It didn't matter. She was here and I knew she'd be here. It was destiny after all. It was.

"*Rachel!*" I called her name again, leaping across the grass, waving my arms as if we had been separated for centuries and were about to have a reunion.

"You're all worked up, aren't you?" she said when I stopped in front of her, panting, sweaty, thrilled.

"I knew you'd be here," I told her, "I just knew it."

She didn't seem that glad to see me, or maybe it was that she just wasn't as thrilled about it as I was.

"You're all sweaty. What've you been doing?"

"I ran from your house."

"You were there?" she asked, as if waiting for an explanation, a full report.

"Yeah, your dad and I sat around . . ."

"Was he drinking?"

"A little, I think."

I was getting sidetracked. I wanted to get to the message.

"What did he say?" she asked.

"About what?"

"About anything. What did the two of you talk about?"

"Love," I said.

"No, you didn't."

"Yes, we did."

"I bet."

"How much?" I stuck out my hand. I wanted to hold hers. I really wanted to hold it.

She looked at my hand and then she looked at me and then she smiled. If she wasn't reading my mind, she was certainly flipping through the pages.

"Rachel," I said, my hand beginning to tremble, "I—"

She interrupted me. "I really like the way you say my name. I like the way it sounds when you say it."

This made me very happy, so I decided to please her. "Rachel," I said.

She wrinkled her face. "No, not like that. You're trying now. I like it the way you normally say it."

"Rachel." I tried again.

"That sounds terrible. You've lost it completely now. You have." She started walking away.

"Rachel." I was getting desperate.

"It's getting worse and worse. You better stop." She started to run. "Look, I gotta go home. See you tomorrow." She waved.

I felt crushed. I started running after her. "Rachel! Rachel! Ra-chel! Ra-chel!" I called.

She started laughing. She laughed as if somebody were tickling her, merrily, nervously, wanting to stop but unable to do so. She leaned on a tree. I stood in front of her, waiting for some verdict.

"God, you're silly. You are, you know. You should see your face. So terribly sad and worried. Like this." She made a face and laughed some more. "That's how you are. Silly. Sil-ly."

"Rachel," I said.

"Ahh, that's better."

"I love you." It came out in one piece and not one word at a time the way I thought it would. I felt drained, as if I had nothing left to say. Ever.

Her eyes widened and she looked directly at me and in her eyes I could see not the fact, but the temptation of loving me. She was playing it out in her mind. What would it be like to love this boy?

Once again I waited for the verdict.

"Stop looking like that." She brushed her hand against my cheek.

I stopped. Or tried to stop. I didn't know what I was doing.

"And does it feel wonderful to love me?" she asked.

"Yes."

"I think I'll need more details than that. And does it, hmm . . ." She sucked in her lower lip, pondering the next question. "And does it feel like anything you've ever felt before?"

"No. Never."

"Good. I think you're on your way. And does it, ahh, do you feel it in your stomach? Like you had swallowed a cherry pit and it's getting hotter and hotter and bigger and bigger and it hurts and feels good at the same time."

"Yes."

She clapped her hands.

"I think you really are in love. Congratulations!"

She embraced me and kissed me twice on each cheek, as they do in the foreign legion movies when they give you a medal. Only they weren't quick kisses. Her lips lingered on my face; her parted lips nibbled gently on my cheeks and I could hear the sound, the popping bubble-bursting sound of her wet lips pulling back from my skin. A shudder ran through my body. My eyes shut.

When I opened them again, she was brushing her hair back, thinking.

"What happens next?" I asked.

She smiled. "That's just what I was going to ask. Do you know what it means when two people ask the same question?"

"No."

"It means that neither of them knows the answer, that's what. Something will happen. Our story has begun. Now I have to go home. I do. No, I don't want you to walk me. You stay here until I'm gone. Don't say anything else and don't call my name. You might spoil it all. All right?"

I nodded.

She left. I was hoping she would turn around and wave, but she didn't. She walked across the grass, through the tree trunks, across the street and down the block and then she was gone.

Our story has begun, I thought. The fact that she had said it, not I, made it even more official.

Chapter 7

Freud was wearing his father's shoes. They were these massive wing-tipped cordovans with drilled-out designs on the toes and the heel. The sole extended a good quarter of an inch all around like a little shelf. They were too big and too wide and when Freud plopped his feet down, the shoes plopped first and Freud tried to keep up with them. He wasn't walking in them, he was following them. It changed the way he moved, but he was proud of them.

"My mother was going to give them to Goodwill. Boy, that woman's so sentimental, it makes me want to puke. Goodwill! My dad's shoes. They're like new."

"They sure are big," Misiora said.

"Yeah." Freud grinned, taking this as a compliment. "My dad was a real big guy."

"That must account for the shoes." Misiora kept it up.

"Yeah, he had real big feet, too."

"You could water-ski in those, Freud."

"Yeah, I could," Freud grinned, happy and proud. He was wearing his father's hat and his father's shoes and he thought he looked great.

We were walking to school down Magoun Avenue.

"Assembly today," Freud said.

"Yeah." Misiora spat. "I hope we don't have that same speaker we had last year. That guy . . . I tell you . . ."

He looked at me. It had been a couple of blocks since I had said anything. My mind wasn't on Magoun. It was on Aberdeen Lane. I had spoken the words: I love you. That made me feel different, committed. It was as if I had enlisted. I felt aloof and slightly superior, like a man wearing a uniform.

Freud, by sheer coincidence, let drop his latest plan.

"You know, I picked up this brochure. It's from the Army."

"You mean like the Army in Army and Navy?" Misiora asked.

"Yeah, like that. Only it's from the Army. And they have this thing now. It's called the Buddy Plan. It's for guys who're buddies. And if these guys want to sign up, well, they sign up for the Buddy Plan and then, the Army guys, they say they'll make sure that we stay together. Sleep in the same barracks and march around in the same unit or whatever it's called. Like if the three of us wanted to do that, well . . . you know . . ."

We walked some more. Nobody said anything.

"Anyway," Freud said, after a while, "it's called the Buddy Plan."

"What's the name of that plan again?" Misiora asked.

Freud laughed: "Ha!" It sounded hollow and disappointed, but he was grateful for the opportunity.

Other kids walked past us. We were really dawdling. Old men and old women stood in their windows watching us go by, making sure we didn't throw any candy wrappers or gum wrappers on their lawns. They cursed us when we did, and seemed disappointed when we didn't.

Fat Patty Campbell waddled past us with two fat girlfriends. For most of the year, fat girls and skinny girls, pretty girls and ugly girls would walk to school together. But as summer approached, they all seemed to group with their own kind. The truce was over. Bathing-suit season was approaching.

"Hi, Billy," Patty said. Her girlfriends tittered.

Freud looked stunned. Who, me?

"Say hi to the lady." Misiora hit him on the back of the head.

"Hi, Patty," Freud said. Then he shrugged at us, one shoulder at a time.

"Hey, Pattycakes." Misiora hurried after her. "Patty, I've got something for you."

Patty turned around to see Misiora aiming his taut slingshot in her face.

"Why didn't you say hi to me?" Misiora said in his mean voice and let the empty pouch go.

Patty winced and then, realizing she was unhurt, shook with anger.

"Why don't you grow up, Larry. Why don't you just go home and grow up!"

"Why don't you sit on my face and I'll guess your weight, Pattycakes."

"If that's what you like, you better ask Mrs. Dewey to do it for you." She shook her red face at him.

"What did you say?" Misiora clenched his fists.

"You know what I said. Everybody knows . . ."

Freud and I grabbed Larry before he could do anything.

"Hey, c'mon, Larry. Take it easy."

"She's just stupid," Freud thundered in his ear.

"This goddam town. Jesus Horrendous Christ, I hate this town. If you so much as spit, the gossip will have you barfing in the streets. You scratch your ass and they'll say you crapped in your pants. I tell you . . ."

Then he calmed down.

"You can let go of me now, Freud."

"Okay," Freud said, "I will."

We checked to see that Patty was far enough away and then let him go. Both of us took a step back as we did. Larry grinned.

"I don't know what got into me. It's not like me to lose my temper."

We headed for school again.

"Yeah, I know what you mean," Freud said, half a block later, alluding to God knows what. Walking or talking, you always had to wait for Freud's other shoe to drop.

"Everybody gossips," he explained. "My mother, she gossips too. Yeah. She tells me stuff about this Italian foreman at the factory. About the chief of police. About the mayor's son. About your dad . . ."

"What about my dad?" Misiora grimaced.

"Oh, not your dad. Daniel's dad."

"What about Daniel's dad?" Misiora asked.

"He's my dad," I said. "You mind if I ask the question?"

"You don't seem to be here today, Danny boy, so I just thought I'd take your part."

"What about my dad?" I asked Freud.

His mother worked as a secretary in the same steel mill as my father. When husbands die, the mills try to employ the widows.

"She just gossips, you know." Freud seemed sorry he had brought it up.

"Yeah, but what does she say?"

"Oh, stuff. You know. She says how the workers are talking about your dad being sick and all."

"I told you he was sick."

"Yeah, I know. She says they say how he's acting . . . sick . . . you know. That's all."

I could tell that wasn't all, but I didn't want to know the rest.

"Did I ever tell you what I think of this town?" Misiora asked, as we went into the school.

We filed into the auditorium. Misiora pushed a couple of freshmen aside who were crowding him. They fell back and bumped into a couple of juniors who also pushed them. The freshmen laughed. They liked the attention. Freud got separated from us as we looked for seats.

"Look." Misiora nudged me.

I turned and saw Patty Campbell maneuvering Freud into sitting next to her. He looked at us with desperation in his eyes: a comrade getting caught behind the enemy lines. He still had his hat on, and as he sat down, Patty told him to take it off. He did.

Misiora whispered in my ear, "I think Patty's realizing she's not going to get anyone better, so she's going after Freud. Ain't true love touching?"

We sat down. Mr. Wallace, our principal, introduced the speaker, who, he said, needed no introduction. The speaker came out. Most everybody, except Misiora, applauded.

The speaker was a little old man, but full of energy. He practically ran to the podium, waving, rubbing his hands, smiling.

"Oh, shit," Misiora groaned, "I bet he's an optimist."

I had told Rachel that I loved her, but she hadn't said that she loved me. That was what I was thinking about. She didn't say she did. But she didn't say she didn't. I was new at love, and I think my first major discovery about it occurred in the auditorium on that day. It wasn't enough to love somebody. You wanted her to love you, too.

"So." The little old man raised his hands over his head. "This is East Chicago Roosevelt. The Rough Riders!"

Applause and cheers. Misiora slumped in his seat.

"What a wonderful time to be young." The speaker shook his

head with delight. "I tell you, you're a lucky bunch, you are, to be young at a time like this. And what's more, our country's lucky to have you. You are future leaders; the future scientists, the future artists, architects, builders . . ."

The list of occupations continued.

"He's worse than optimistic," Misiora groaned. "The sonova-bitch thinks he's inspirational."

"Your future is waiting for you, and what a future it is. Limitless! That's what it is! Limitless!"

He spread out his arms to show us just how limitless it was. He went on. There are doors to the future, he said, and some of the doors have combination locks on them. Our education was the combination. Other doors have keys. Our ambition was the key. There were also other doors that had to be knocked down, broken by our resolve. He got all excited as he waved his fists, knocking holes in these doors. And there were still more doors. The last doors weren't that easy. Before we could get through them, we had to find them first.

"And find them you will!" he shouted at us. "How? Ingenuity! Curiosity! Do you know what you are? You are pioneers, you are conquistadors, explorers!" He stood on tiptoe at each word, bouncing up and down, calling us, in the end, lucky rascals.

"You lucky rascals, you!"

Then he went on to tell us about great men who had made their fortunes with nothing more than a thin dime in their pockets and a dream in their hearts. He tapped his pocket when he mentioned the dime and thumped on his chest when he mentioned the dream. Ben Franklin. Edison. Ford. Carnegie.

"Do you know where these men are today? Do you? Look around!"

Heads turned in the auditorium.

"They're probably sitting next to you. Yes. They are your school friends. They are you!"

I looked at Misiora. Misiora looked at me. "I'd like to strangle him," he said.

"The future is out there." The speaker pointed toward the back of the auditorium. "Go get it! And when you do, when you get there, keep going! Ever onward! Thank you and God bless you!"

He ran off the stage.

Patty clung to Freud the rest of the day, and she convinced him to walk her home when school was over. He wanted us to get him out of it, but Larry gave him his blessing instead: "Oh, go ahead, walk her home." Freud left with her, his hands on his stomach, like a handcuffed prisoner of war being led away. She gave him her books and he took them. Her fat girlfriends, abandoned for the moment, walked behind.

Misiora looked at me. He had sent Freud away on purpose. He had something on his mind that he wanted to tell me, but he didn't seem to know how to start. I had something on my mind, too. We walked silently, thinking our thoughts.

Misiora's house was right across the street from the Sunrise Oil Company. The refinery operated twenty-four hours a day, seven days a week. Men were always walking up and down the steel ladders, on the catwalks around the huge tanks. Enormous men, walking through the guarded gate on their way to work, suddenly shrank to insignificance in comparison to the monumental structures around them. A mile-long chain-link fence surrounded the refinery. Somebody was always wrecking the fence. Somebody was always fixing it. The flame always burned on top of a steel chimney, flickering high in the air like a flag.

Larry and I sat on his front porch. The porch faced the refinery. We were eating some horrible peanut-butter cookies his mother had made. She was warm and friendly, just like his dad, but a mercilessly bad cook.

"Do you think you're smart?" Misiora asked me, spitting out half a cookie.

The question took me by surprise. We had been sitting there silently for about half an hour, and this was what he finally had to say.

"Who said I was smart?" I defended myself.

"Nobody said. I'm asking you. Do you think you're smart? Real smart."

"I don't know. I don't think so. I'm eating your mother's cookies. I can't be all that smart, can I?"

He didn't laugh.

"Then how the hell are you going to find one of those fucking doors to your fucking future if you're not smart?"

The little old man had really upset him.

"Forget about that guy," I said.

"You forget about him! Jesus Horrendous Christ, you forget about him!"

The front door opened and his mother stepped out, carrying a tray of cookies, wearing a red apron with a yellow parakeet on it.

"I was just wondering if you boys would like . . ."

"No more goddamn cookies, Mom. All right!" Larry threw the two he had in his hand at her. She flushed, and backed into the house silently.

Larry jumped up.

"Damn!" He pointed to his house as if that gesture were making everything clear. "Godlousydamn! She thinks, do you know what she thinks, what my goddamn parents think . . ." He shook his head, pulling on his hair. "They think it's a big deal to get a high-school diploma. They do. Goddamn big deal! They never got past grade school, neither of them, so they have all these moron-type notions now about the great strides I have made. I'm going to be the first in the family to graduate from high school. Now, that's something! Isn't it? Dream come true." He kicked the porch railing. "My smart son, my daddy calls me! Our smart boy, my mother calls me. Shit! They're so stupid. They're so stupid, stupid, stupid." He kicked the railing repeatedly, his face turning red, the tendons in his neck bulging.

"I come home and they just beam when they see me. They just fucking beam. Here he is: Mr. Brains. That's me, in case you didn't know it. Mr. Brains!"

He calmed down a little, but looked at the door as if daring his mother to come out.

"You know what they're like. You've seen them. Marshmallows. Everything is 'lovely and nice.' So lovely and so nice. You look out of our house and you look right at that fucking refinery and you smell that shit they call air and they think it's 'lovely and nice' because my dad can walk to work and not only that, he can walk home for lunch. How lucky can one man be? That's his big deal. He walks home for lunch. He walks home beaming and my mother stands by the window, beaming back at him. 'Here he comes.' How lucky can they be! He walks home for lunch and their son is Mr. Brains!"

His voice was getting louder. I was afraid his mother could hear, but then maybe she knew, maybe she knew when she heard Larry's voice getting louder to walk back, back toward the alley, out of hearing range. She seemed like that kind of woman.

"I knew they were stupid," Misiora went on. "When I was eight years old I knew they were stupid, and since then all I've wanted to do was make sure I didn't grow up to be lovely and nice and stupid like them. Well"—he nodded his head slowly—"it would appear that my own dream has come true. I have made it. I'm a success. I can honestly say that I'm not nearly as stupid as my parents. That only leaves one question: So what?"

He unbuckled his belt and started pulling on it absentmindedly, tightening it around his waist, loosening it, tightening it.

"That goddamn school. I hate that school! All it did was teach me to feel bad. My education's made me smart enough to realize that I'm not going anywhere." He turned his head away from me, and then he let it drop on his chest. "You see, I thought, your brain . . . I thought . . ." His body began to shake. "I thought it was like the rest of your body . . . you know . . . if you work out, it gets bigger and better . . . but it won't . . . it just won't . . . it just won't budge." He slapped his head. "It's like there's a box around it and I can't get out of the box. And if you can't get out of the box, they shouldn't tease you with doors. Man, if you can't get out of the box, how the hell're you going to get through the door? I should've stayed ignorant and happy like my parents. Only it's too late for that. I'm too smart for that now. I tell you . . ."

He fell silent. I didn't think he wanted me to say anything, so I didn't.

Smoke hissed out of the refinery, rising, disappearing into clouds. Men walked through the yard, surrounded by a fence, like termites through termite mounds made of steel.

The huge, flag-like flame flickered and waved above it all.

"You see that?" Larry pointed to the security gate. "You see that gate? That's my door."

He turned his head toward me. His eyes, a little cloudy now, were beginning to burn again. As I looked at him, I was reminded of the conversation I'd had with Freud:

"He's going to do something."

"What do you mean, 'something'?"

"You know. Something. I can just feel it. He's going to do something terrible."

It was all there, in his eyes.

Chapter 8

"**D**oes your father like me?"

"No," Rachel said, "he hates you." Then she laughed and started walking faster. "Of course he likes you."

It was night. We were walking south on Whiteoak Avenue. Rachel had felt cold and I had given her my high-school jacket to wear. She seemed to enjoy wearing it, and looked around the dark avenue as if wishing to find a mirror to see how she looked in it.

"What does he say about me?" I asked.

"I'm the one who says things about you, he's not."

"And what do you say about me?"

"Oh." She clutched the jacket around her. It wasn't that cold. She just liked clutching it, I think. "All kinds of things."

"What kinds of things?"

"All kinds of things. Who can remember all of them?"

"Can you remember one?"

"Yes," she said, "as a matter of fact, I can."

She said nothing more. She knew I was waiting to hear. We walked in silence. Whiteoak Avenue had no streetlamps, and we could hardly see each other. Every now and then a car would go by, and when the headlights hit our faces we would look at each other. Her eyes shone with delight and mischief as she waited for my strength to wear off.

"So." I finally gave in. "So what is it? What's the one thing you remember?"

"Well, since you asked"—she took my arm—"I told him that you're in love with me."

"And what did he say?"

"He said . . . let me see . . ." She pretended to be thinking. "Ah, yes. He said: 'That certainly was quick.' "

"Is that all he said?"

"I think so."

"Did he ask you how you felt?"

"He never asks me how I feel. He knows how I feel. I make it very easy to tell how I feel."

"I can't tell how you feel."

"You just haven't known me as long as he has."

We walked some more. I was enjoying the walk. I just wanted to enjoy it more. I wanted to know if she loved me.

"I love you," I said.

"Still?" She laughed. "After all this time?"

"I do, you know."

"I know. You told me. And I even told my father."

"And did he ask you if you loved me?"

"He doesn't ask me questions like that. He knows if I do or don't."

"And do you?"

"He knows. I know. You're the only one who doesn't know."

"So why don't you tell me?"

"Can't you tell without being told in words?"

"No, all I can do is guess, and you said I shouldn't guess so much."

"You shouldn't. Stop guessing."

Headlights from an approaching car hit her face. I looked at her, but she turned away. Before she did, I saw something in her face that I had not seen there before: pain. I had seen similar looks in my mother's face, in my father's eyes, but never in somebody so young. I had always thought that such painful expressions were reserved for the parents of the world, for grown-ups. It startled me a little to see it in her.

"Rachel," I said.

"That's it. That's how I like it when you say my name. Just like that, Daniel Boone. I could tell you loved me the first time you said my name. I remember it. I do. It was our Destiny Day. Our D-Day. Remember?"

"Sure."

"And you guessed my name."

"Yes," I said. I was beginning to think I had guessed it, beginning to forget how I came to hear it, beginning to play tricks with circumstance. As we walked, I found it difficult to remember what it was I had been planning to do with my life until I met her. It was all vague. I knew I was still somebody's son, somebody's friend, but that too was vague, and once again the only things that weren't vague were Rachel and my feelings for her. We weren't just walking, we were going somewhere. A part of me was happier than I'd ever been. I almost didn't want to know if she loved me. That answer lay ahead and lent an air of purpose to every step I took. It was a goal to be reached.

We took Walsh Avenue back toward Aberdeen Lane, walking arm in arm. Whenever she caught herself walking in step with me, she changed stride.

"How come you never call me on the phone?" she asked. "You don't, you know."

"I don't have a phone. My father doesn't believe in phones. He thinks they're luxuries we don't need."

"That's interesting. I like people with weird ideas like that. What else doesn't he believe in?"

"Cars. We don't have a car. We don't have a television."

"Hi-fi?"

"No hi-fi. We have a radio my mother won in a lottery, but we can't listen to it when he's around. It makes him upset."

"What an interesting man!"

I had never thought of my father in this way. It made me happy that she found him interesting, although she had not met him. "Yes, and your father is interesting, too," I said.

"He's a good man and he loves me very much." She took her arm away. "I'm all he has, and he knows that someday I'll have to leave him. A time comes when we have to leave."

"Yes, I know," I said, wondering if she had used "we" to mean she and I or just we in general. I didn't press for a clarification.

"It's sad, isn't it. You love somebody and he loves you and yet you know that you'll have to leave."

Her house was completely dark except for a reddish glow coming from a basement window, a strange, steady glow as if an unflickering flame were burning down there.

"What's that?"

"Safety light," she said. "It's David. He's in his darkroom doing dark things," she added with a touch of mock mystery.

"He took pictures of me."

"Yes, I know. Can I keep the jacket?"

"Sure."

"It's about time you started giving me presents. I like presents."

"What would you like?"

"Surprise me." She flung her arms around my neck. "I bet you want me to kiss you," she said, smiling. The red glow of the basement light was right behind her and I could not help wondering what it was her father was developing down there.

"Yes, I do," I said.

"All right, Daniel Boone. Here it comes. A kiss!"

She drew me toward her. Her parted lips parted mine. Her tongue touched mine briefly as if tasting me, as if she had been wondering what I tasted like, and when she pulled back, I saw once again not the fact of love, but the temptation in her eyes to love me.

"Thanks for the jacket," she said and went inside. She didn't turn around. She went straight inside.

It only hit me when I started walking away that I really had nowhere to go. My father was at work. My mother was at work. The house was empty. Misiora and Freud were at a drive-in movie with Mrs. Dewey. So I stopped and leaned on a tree, an elm, and, looking at Rachel's house, I thought about her.

The red light went off in the basement. A lamp came on in the living room, and then I caught a brief glimpse of David as he pulled the curtains shut. He was wearing a white sleeveless T-shirt and smoking a cigarette.

I stayed there for at least an hour thinking of her, enjoying the night, the silence and my thoughts.

Chapter 9

H*ey, La-rry!"* Freud cupped his hands around his mouth and called.

Misiora was late for school. Freud and I had been waiting for about ten minutes. Across the street the morning shift was about to begin at Sunrise Oil. The men from the midnight shift were coming out through the gate.

"I wonder what's keeping him?" Freud checked his watch again.

"I don't know."

He began winding the watch. It was his father's Bulova. He had spent almost ten dollars getting it to work again.

I watched the weary men coming out through the gate and I thought of Rachel. Her kiss was still on my lips, a real kiss, a lover's kiss, and I wondered if any of the men I saw were in love like me. No, I decided. Not a one. I felt quietly happy, profoundly intelligent and emotionally generous. A kiss can do that. I took pity on all those men. Poor guys. Look at them. Trudging home with their empty lunchboxes, bent over, exhausted, joyless. Rachel's kiss made me want to rush up to them and proclaim that it was easy to be happy. Life was wonderful. I felt wise beyond my years.

Freud saw me looking at them and misread my thoughts.

"All those guys," he said. "I bet when they were our age they were worried too. And now look at them. They all got jobs."

I put my arm around him in a friendly but slightly condescending manner. I was so full of love for Rachel that it created an excess and I let it spill over his big shoulder.

"Did you write your poem?" he asked.

"What poem?"

"You know. Your poem. For Miss Mashar's class."

"Oh!" I suddenly remembered. "No, I didn't."

"You didn't!" Freud was shocked.

Several days ago Miss Mashar had read us some poetry by John Donne, and then she decided that it would be fun if we all wrote a poem to celebrate our last week of school. She believed that "in our own ways" we were all poets. Everybody had laughed.

"I guess I just forgot all about it," I said cheerfully. Freud wrinkled his forehead, wondering why I was smiling. Forgot about it, I thought. I'm so in love with Rachel that I forgot all about my class assignment. My forgetfulness thrilled me.

Misiora came out of his house tucking his shirt into his trousers.

"We're going to be late." Freud flashed his father's Bulova again.

"In that case, there's no hurry," Misiora said. "The tragedy has already occurred."

We walked to school slowly, aiming for the second class.

"We had a conference," Misiora told us. "That's the word my dad used: conference. Do you know what the conference was about?"

"No," Freud said.

"My graduation present. They wanted to know what I wanted for my graduation present."

"You got nice folks." Freud smiled sadly.

"Oh yeah, they're real nice. Nice and lovely. And you know what, Freud?"

"What?"

"I'm the apple of their eye."

My second class was a study period, and since I had nothing to study, I thought about Rachel, life and the world. In my state of love-induced euphoria I dreamed up outlets for my newly discovered generosity toward those less happy than I. Daydreaming there with my head on the desk, I loved everybody and wanted to do something to make their lives happier. Misiora, Freud, Mrs. Dewey, my mother, my father, I loved them all more than ever. I finally settled on my dad. I imagined myself bursting into our house. There he was, sitting at the kitchen table. Dad—I rushed to him—I've decided. You're going to be happy from now on and I'm not taking "no" for an answer. We're going out, you and I, we're going for a walk. That's right. Just the two of us. I saw him smiling, trying to resist but finally giving in. I saw my mother coming home from work, finding the two of us talking, wondering what had happened. I saw the three of us: a small happy family. I saw it all.

The bell rang.

I continued daydreaming on my way to Miss Mashar's class.

"Very nice," Miss Mashar commented after each poem. Didn't I tell you, her smile seemed to say, that in your own ways, you are all poets.

Most of the poems began with the lines "Roses are red, violets are blue . . ." The concluding couplets were not very funny, but I felt generous and laughed along with the rest of my classmates. Only Misiora didn't laugh.

"Billy," Miss Mashar called, "did you write a poem?"

"Yes." Freud stood up. He took a folded sheet of paper out of his pocket. He licked his lips as he unfolded it.

" 'My Dad,' " he announced. His voice changed as he read the poem, as if somebody were strangling him.

> "My dad drove a car
> And smoked a cigar
> And when he died
> I cried."

Then he sat down, his chin shaking.

"Very nice," Miss Mashar said. "Very, very nice, Billy."

It was all he could do to keep from crying.

Johnny Wasco was next. He read a poem about how he got his finger cut off in wood shop. Everyone laughed at the last line: "I didn't see the saw but the saw sawed me."

There were three more "Roses are red"s in a row, and then it was Misiora's turn. I expected him to say he didn't have a poem, so I was startled when he stood up to recite.

"It doesn't have a name," he said. He seemed very calm, his arms hanging down, slightly bent at the elbows like a gunslinger's. "It's just something."

"Poems don't necessarily have to have names," Miss Mashar said.

"Thank God." Misiora grinned and, leaning back on his heels, began to recite. He was the only one who didn't read his poem. He had no paper in his hands. He stared right at Miss Mashar as he recited:

"I bet, I just bet
that some man is an island."

The first line startled me out of my lazy, daydreaming mood.

"And I bet that the sun
on some days is not shining
anywhere contrary to the somewhere-
the-sun-is-always-shining
school of thought."

The kids in the class began making faces and looking at each
other.

"And I'll betcha anything
that although we all gotta die
some no-good bastard
some real sonovabitch
will sneak through
and live forever and
not pay one cent of tax."

He grinned. "End of poem," he said, and sat down.

Miss Mashar had to quiet the class. The words "bastard" and
"sonovabitch" had got them all excited. They all wanted to say them
out loud. Miss Mashar, as a way of elevating the level of discussion,
began talking about meter and rhyme and how not all poems had
to rhyme. Larry's poem, she said, belonged to the free-verse category.

Nobody in the classroom, not Miss Mashar, not even Larry himself, seemed to think much of what he had recited. A pang of envy
clarified my own opinion of it. How could Misiora write something
like that?

"Daniel," Miss Mashar called, "did you write a poem?"

"No." I shook my head. "I forgot."

She seemed relieved.

For the rest of the school day I debated with myself whether I
should tell him that he had written a wonderful poem. But some
nameless feeling was creeping into my mood of generosity and
goodwill. I said nothing.

Mrs. Dewey was waiting for us outside the school in her car. The motor was running, radio blaring. She honked the horn when she saw the three of us coming out. "How's about a Dairy Queen, guys?" She leaned out of the window. "My treat."

Larry got into the front with her and Freud jumped into the back, leaving the door open for me.

"I have to go home," I said, shutting the door.

"Sure, sure." Mrs. Dewey winked at me and drove off.

It was a little unsettling to know somebody for over ten years and then to discover you didn't really know him at all. How could Misiora write a poem like that?

I walked home slowly. "I bet, I just bet that some man is an island." The first line of his poem kept going through my head. I didn't like the envy I felt. I wanted to feel the way I had felt this morning: happy, generous, eager to embrace those less fortunate than myself. I had a sudden, almost ravenous hunger to do something nice for somebody. I remembered the daydream I'd had in the study hall about my father, and I headed home determined to make it come true.

He wasn't home. It was almost five o'clock. He was late. I sat down and waited for him.

The time went by. I peeked out of the window. A light rain was beginning to fall. It was almost six o'clock now. He was very late. I decided to go out and look for him. It was the rain, I think, that did it. The thought of looking for my father through the rain seemed to me an indisputable act of a generous, wonderful son.

I took the route he took when he went to work: up 149th Street to Indianapolis Boulevard, down the boulevard to Pierson and then a right at Pierson straight to the factory.

The half-hearted rain continued to fall. A taxicab went by, windshield wipers moving. You could go for months without seeing a cab in East Chicago.

I imagined running into my dad. I saw him at the end of the block and I ran toward him. Dad, where were you? I was so worried. He smiled, pleased by my concern. Look at you, he said, it's raining and you don't have a jacket. It's nothing, I shrugged, I was so worried I forgot about it. Instead of going home, we went to a bar for a drink. Everyone knew him there. They greeted him as soon as we walked inside. This is my son, Daniel, he introduced me. They had all heard about me. So you're Daniel. Your father's told us so much about you. The waitress winked at me. My dad treated everyone to drinks and then he raised his glass and made a toast. To my son.

I went inside several bars near the factory, but he wasn't in any of them. I looked up and down Pierson. I looked up and down Railroad Avenue. I saw a black man trying to get his car started, but I couldn't see my dad anywhere.

Maybe, I thought, maybe he went home with one of his friends from work. I knew he didn't have any friends at the factory, but now I wanted him to have them. I sensed that my morning daydream was collapsing in the drizzle, that I lacked the spirit to make my father happy on my own. The desire to see him happy was still there.

I walked up and down different streets near the factory. Strange men were coming out of narrow houses in small groups. Their work day was over. They had showered and shaved and changed clothes and were now going out somewhere. They talked in strange languages. One of them sounded like my mother's language.

And then I saw him. I spotted him at a distance. He stood on the corner of Perry and Railroad Avenue. The loud-talking foreigners walked past him and he looked after them. I couldn't tell if he was lonely for their company or scornful of the noise they made. I was too far away to read the emotion in his eyes. He looked so small. All the men who walked past him were bigger than he.

I thought of going up to him, but I was curious to see what he would do, where he would go. He didn't see me. Sneaking around parked cars, through the rain, I edged closer to him.

He stood erect under a tree. The tree trunk was inches from his back, but he would not lean on it. His collar was buttoned, his tie was tied. Every now and then he reached up and tenderly touched the boil on his neck. The collar was cutting into it. It hurt him, but he would not unbutton it. He looked down Perry Street toward Indianapolis Boulevard. Drops of water dripped off the branches and fell on his shoulders. He just stood there, looking down Perry Street, thinking.

What, I wondered, is he thinking about? If I came out of my hiding place and asked him, would he tell me?

He touched his boil one more time and began walking. I followed him down Perry Street, ducking behind parked cars to make sure he didn't see me.

Several little black kids, all holding hands, all barefoot, stomped past him, slapping their feet on the wet sidewalk. They parted their hands to let him through and then joined them again. He hardly saw them.

He stopped on the corner of Indianapolis and Perry. He just stopped and stood there, looking at a house with a green door. That's what it is, I thought, it's the house of his secret love. He looked around. I ducked behind a car. Yes, that's what it is. He was making sure nobody saw him.

He just stood there, looking at the house, making no move to go inside.

The curtains on the windows of the house were drawn. Lights were on. The silhouette of a woman appeared and disappeared.

He stood there for at least half an hour, and then reluctantly he crossed the street. He looked back over his shoulder at the house on the corner. Then he turned and continued walking.

I followed him up Indianapolis Boulevard. He walked slowly, aimlessly. That wasn't what I wanted to see. I wanted to see him happy. Maybe there was something about me, about my mother, about the house we lived in, that made him perpetually gloomy. Maybe, I reasoned, he had some idea in his head that ran counter to showing happiness in front of his family. Maybe he saved his happy moments and showed them when we weren't around. I followed him through the rain, hoping for a glimpse.

C'mon, Dad, I urged him. Do it. Just once. Let me see you happy.

We passed several restaurants, a few bars, and at each place I hoped to see a couple of men walking out, seeing my dad, waving to him, he smiling and waving back and then all of them going inside again for a drink or two and me standing outside, looking through a window, seeing my dad happy, smiling, a different man. But the closer we got to home, the clearer it became that no such event would take place.

My heart was sinking. I had imagined such wonderful moments for him. I had imagined myself causing them to happen. It still wasn't too late, I kept telling myself. I could still run up to him, embrace him and try. But his despair seemed contagious and my grip on my own happiness not as secure as it had seemed this morning. One look from his eyes, I feared, just one look and I might lose it completely.

Not far from home, I couldn't take it anymore. It seemed pointless to follow him. I stopped and watched him drift away down the boulevard. Then I took a right and headed toward Rachel's house.

It had been a long day and I had no love left to spare.

"What have you been doing?" Rachel asked me. "You're all wet."

"So are you."

She was wearing her father's Oriental bathrobe. I remembered Mr. Temerson's round calf muscles as I followed her to the living room. Rachel's hair was wet and she was combing it.

"I just took a bath," she said lazily. She sat down on a pillow on the floor and continued combing her hair, the comb pulling her head back, revealing the long line of her neck. She smelled of shampoo and bath oil. The tips of her bare toes were still red from the hot water. She seemed soft, languid, boneless. Her eyes regarded her own body as much as they did me.

"So, where were you?" she said slowly.

"Oh, I just felt like walking through the rain."

She smiled as if she weren't listening. Her toes wiggled slowly. She stretched herself, the hem of the bathrobe rising over her knees.

"Where's your dad?"

"Upstairs." She pointed with her comb. "Reading."

I reached over and put my hand on her foot. Her skin was warm and even the bony ridges seemed rubbery and malleable.

"We read poems today in my English class." I wanted to keep my hand on her flesh, but I felt I had to talk if I wanted to keep it there. "We were all supposed to write a poem and then read it in front of everybody."

"Did you write one?"

"Yes," I said, my hand gliding across her loose calf muscle.

"So let's hear it."

"I can't remember it. Just the first line. That's all I remember."

"Let's have the first line, then."

"I bet, I just bet that some man is an island."

She held the comb in her hand, waiting to hear more.

"That's all I remember," I said.

"You're lying," she said, pulling her feet away. I let my hand rest on the carpet as if I didn't even notice. She yawned, smiling. "I should go to bed."

I stood up. I saw her breasts as she rose. She looked at me and then, squinting as if an idea had come into her head, she began combing my hair. She leaned back to inspect her work. The floor creaked under her feet.

"No," she said, "I don't like it." She messed up my hair with her hands. The loose sleeves of the bathrobe fell down over her elbows. My arms went around her waist. I kissed her. Her lips parted slowly, lazily.

"I'm so sleepy," she whispered.

She saw me to the door and I could hardly hear it shut behind me.

I planned to tell Misiora about his poem the next day, but somehow the time was never right. Nor could I find the right moment to bring it up the day after that. And then other matters took over.

Chapter 10

We had another assembly, only this one was just for the graduating seniors, the class of '61. Representatives from "business and industry" in the region came to counsel us on the job opportunities in their firms. A guy from Blow-Knox Steel, where my dad worked, came; a guy from Inland Steel, a guy from U.S. Steel, a guy from Jones and Laughlin Steel, U.S.S. Lead Refining, Calumet Iron and Supply, M and T Chemical, Cities Service Oil, and a guy from Sunrise Oil—all kinds of guys dressed in suits and ties, smiling at us, answering questions, handing out brochures, recruiting. These guys didn't talk about "doors" or dreams or ingenuity. They talked jobs. They talked about how much you got paid an hour. How many weeks of vacation you got and how soon. Medical benefits. Security. Pension upon retirement.

"Do you have a buddy plan?" Freud asked the guy from Inland Steel. "You know, like in the Army."

"Not exactly, not on paper," the guy replied, "but I'm sure we can work something out. We're big at Inland, but we're flexible."

Freud took every brochure that anyone offered and walked around the auditorium from representative to representative, like a kid at a carnival. Patty Campbell followed him around with brochures of her own. He seemed bewildered by her pursuit, an innocent man chased by a bounty hunter.

The highlight of the assembly was the unveiling of a new corporate logo for the Sunrise Oil Company. This was done, according to the representative from Sunrise, as a special gesture in honor of the graduating class of '61. All the other representatives seemed a little irritated by the announcement, but they gathered around just as we did for the unveiling.

The guy removed a felt covering from a canvas, and a lot of people smiled instantly. The new symbol was a sunrise, but a cartoon sunrise. The sunrise had little arms and little legs and a huge happy smile like it was real glad to see us. "THE SUN ALWAYS SHINES" read their motto underneath the figure. A couple of our teachers began applauding, and the rest of us joined in. Even Misiora applauded. He seemed relaxed, but a little distant, as if we had never had that conversation on his porch. The taste of his mother's cookies came back to me as he applauded.

The rest of the school day was spent waiting for the day to end. Exams were over; those who were going to graduate would graduate, those who wouldn't knew they wouldn't. The teachers had nothing to do but banter. They couldn't even tell us what we were going to be covering next year because there would be no next year.

I thought about Rachel. A time comes when we have to leave. She did say we. We. She and I.

Just before the last class ended—health and safety, of all things— I heard a siren. It stopped in front of the school and everybody rushed to the windows. Firemen were jumping off the truck and running inside the school. The siren continued. "U-u-u-u." Everybody in the classroom, including the teacher, remembered Mr. Geddes. "Blue-blue-blue," the siren seemed to be wailing. Mr. Wallace, our principal, came into the room just as we were all getting ready to rush out. He told us to take our seats. Everything was under control. It was just a false alarm.

"I like that Sunrise character. He's kind of cute," Misiora said, as we were leaving school.

"Yeah," Freud said, "he is. Real happy."

"The sun always shines." Misiora grinned.

Patty Campbell was waiting on the corner for Freud. He saw her and pulled his father's hat down over his eyes, directing his father's shoes away from her. That's when I saw my mother walking down Magoun Avenue. Freud saw her too.

"Hey, there's your mother," he said.

She waved to me and smiled the way only people from other countries do: openly, broadly, too broadly. Then she stopped on the corner and waited for me to come to her.

As I left the group, Misiora left too, leaving Freud alone, with a ream of brochures in his hand. Patty Campbell and I passed each other at the intersection, she on her way to Freud, I on my way to my mother.

"See you tonight," Freud shouted after me. "Don't be late!"

We had no plans to meet tonight, but he was trying to short-circuit any plans Patty might have for him and give himself an out. I couldn't help coming to his aid. "Nine o'clock, right?" I shouted back.

"Yeah, that's right. Nine!" Freud looked a picture of gratitude.

"What is at nine o'clock?" my mother wanted to know.

To explain the whole situation seemed too complicated.

"Oh, a bunch of us are going out."

"To have a good time, eh?"

"I guess."

Kids from the school walked past us. Most of them waved or said something. I did likewise. My mother looked on. She seemed happy that I had so many friends.

"Is something the matter?" I asked her.

"Nothing. I wanted to see you. That is all."

Her words said one thing, but she made sure to convey the opposite meaning with her eyes. We started walking. She looked at the houses, at the lawns.

"I always wanted to have house of my own. In America I was sure I would have house of my own. Always landlords. All my life landlords."

She lit a cigarette and smoked it, holding it with her thumb and index finger. I was surprised she didn't offer me one. When she inhaled, the wrinkles on her already wrinkled face were accentuated. I thought of Rachel. There's a face, I thought, that Rachel would like. Nice wrinkles. She exhaled through her nose.

"When he was young man your father was funny," she said without any introduction. "So-o funny." She smiled, her gold tooth shining. "Like a boy. He was not boy, but he was like a boy. It is too bad you did not see him like that. But I saw him and I remember."

She flicked the cigarette with her teeth, knocking the ash off. I could never understand how she did that.

"I was not very long in America, maybe six months, when this little man, he starts follow me around. He was like boy. Like a boy who will grow up. Only he was a man. And he starts follow me around. He starts wait for me when I come out from work. He starts speak to me. Only I don't understand English so good. I don't know what he says to me and he speaks plenty. Once he wait for me when I come out from work and he give me flowers. Yes, he give me flowers. That I understand." She laughed, smoke blowing out of her nose. "I think to myself, this is nice man. And he look at me so-o funny. He look at me all the time like I am something special. Like I am something he very much needs. Yes, it is true. Like that he was looking at me. All the time."

Details of their courtship were something neither of them talked about. I didn't know why she was talking about it now.

"I never meet man like that in Montenegro. Men there tall. Don't say much. This man short and he say plenty. And he have nice hair. Such nice hair. Long with waves. I like him." She looked at me. "I like your father. When I meet him, I like him, and now we fight and make arguments, but in my heart . . . I like him."

She waited for me to say something.

"I know," I said. "I know you like him."

"Good. I am glad you know that."

She lit another cigarette. This was unusual. Two cigarettes in a row were usually reserved for laundry day and storms.

"Sometimes it happens . . . people think they will have some kind of life. They are sure they will have some kind of life and then it becomes that they get different kind of life . . . and they don't want make acceptance . . . it is no good to fight . . . how you say in English . . ." She waved her hand through the air, hoping to catch the word.

"Destiny," I said.

"Yes. Destny." She made the word sound foreign. She left the "i" out of it and made it shorter, harder. Not like a river at all, but like a rock. I didn't like the way she pronounced it.

The railroad-crossing gate started going down as we neared Chicago Avenue, and we hurried across the tracks. I walked. She ran ahead of me. Although she could see clearly that the train was at least a quarter of a mile away, she was and would always remain a true foreigner who believed American trains were capable of erratic shifts in speed and could suddenly move up to supersonic levels and run over you.

We walked silently as the train racheled behind us. Ra-chel-ra-chel-ra-chel.

Once we were far enough away, on the other side of Chicago Avenue, she began again.

"It is now hard time for your father. He is not so good in his health and he thinks . . . he thinks too much . . . his poor head is always full of sad thinkings. We must be nice to him. Even when it is very hard, we must be nice. He tells me you are never home when he is home."

I felt stung by this. Why had I thought that he didn't notice, that he wouldn't notice such a thing?

I shrugged. "I used to stay home, but . . ." I shrugged again.

"What does that mean?" My mother mirrored my shrug. "When you do this . . . what does that mean?"

"I don't know. I guess it means that I don't know. I don't know what to say to him. I don't know what he wants me to say to him. It's hard to just be there not knowing what to do."

"So it is hard. To regret is much harder . . . to regret because you did not do right thing. It is terrible thing, to regret. There is not much time. Do what is right."

"What do you mean, there is not much time?"

She hesitated. "Soon you finish school," she said. "Who know where you go then . . . when you see your father again."

"I wasn't planning to go anywhere." I felt a little irritated. My most cherished, secret ambition, to leave . . . and she was treating it like a walk to the store.

"So many things I was not planning to do and I did all of them and some of them twice." She put the cigarette out and looked at her wristwatch, a man's watch. "I have to hurry to catch train."

She embraced me and then pushed me back, making it clear she wanted to walk to the train station alone.

"I will see you tonight. If you are asleep, I will see you in morning. Do what you want. I have told you to do what is right, but you are old enough to make decision."

Old enough to take on an extra load of guilt. She walked away. The South Shore Line train station was a mile away. From there it was a forty-five-minute ride to Chicago and then another fifteen-minute walk to the building where she worked as a cleaning woman. And then the same thing again to get back home. She didn't have to work, but she wanted a house of her own and my dad didn't make enough.

Already I was dreading spending an evening with him. I wanted to be with Rachel, and his need for me, if in fact it was a need, struck me as a nuisance, an emotional detour I hadn't planned for.

The light was on in the kitchen when I got home. It wasn't like my mother to leave a light on in the house unless something important was on her mind. The fridge began to rumble. I sat down at the kitchen table to wait. The faucet was dripping. I just looked at it. I was sitting in my father's chair, and my elbows were on the tabletop just like his usually were, my head resting in my palms like some despairing figure perched atop a cathedral from the Middle Ages. Was this what it was like to be my father? Work day all done, fridge rumbling, faucet dripping, hours before bedtime. I tried to put on his life the way Freud put on his father's clothes, and although I was only guessing at his wardrobe, it weighed me down with despair and brought to mind the way my mother had pronounced the word "destiny." Destny. A rock.

I jumped out of the chair as if it were diseased. I went to the fridge and drank some milk.

What am I afraid of, I wondered. My father is coming home, that's all. And yet it felt like I was in an arena waiting for my wrestling opponent to show up.

I was ready to run to Rachel's house when I caught sight of my dad's steel box. It was in the corner as usual. The padlock was in its place, but it hung open.

I knelt down, took the lock off and waited a few seconds. The steel box was my dad's darkroom where he left things to develop. I lifted open the lid.

The Sunday edition of the Chicago *Sun-Times* crossword puzzle lay on top. It was half finished. I looked at some of the words: concertina, felucca, Rachmaninoff, caftan. There were a couple of other words that didn't look like words at all. I put it aside. Duplicates of other weeks' entries in the crossword-puzzle contest, none of which he had won, were there too. I glanced through them as if they were family pictures and put them aside. I knew I would find nothing new, but I kept on rummaging. It was something I started doing a few years ago, going through his things whenever he forgot and left the lock open. It began as a hunt for clues to the change I sensed in him: the aloofness, the despair and the growing malice, the need to hurt me, my mother, the world. I kept hoping, as I was hoping now, to stumble upon his diary where I would find out all about him, where it would all be explained: why he was like he was, what he thought about me, how he wanted me to behave toward him, how he really loved me and my mother despite the way he behaved. But he didn't keep a diary, or if he did, he kept it somewhere else.

I found his ragged crossword dictionary and put it aside. Half a dozen sharpened pencils with a rubber band around them. A couple of movie magazine pictures of Anna Magnani that he thought looked like my mother. His expired passport. We had all been going to visit Jugoslavia with my mother as our personal guide, but then things changed, he changed, life changed. On the bottom of the box were passports of another kind. Passports to a better life. Scraps of paper torn from newspapers and magazines and matchbooks. Enrollment forms to be filled out. Start a business in the privacy of your own home. Mason Shoes: Sell our exclusive line of shoes. Invisible Weaving, with a picture of a cigarette burn in the upholstery and then another picture where it was like new. Just three orders a day and you could be making . . . Boxes to be checked off. "You bet I want to make from 150 to 200 dollars a month in my spare time. Send me the free introductory kit." There was a scrap of paper to start a rubber-stamp business, another one for a home study course in refrigeration, franchise offers, coupons for self-improvement, learn ballroom dancing at home, tune your own car and eliminate unnecessary bills, develop your body and add inches to your arms and chest, and still more business offers: sell lightbulbs that last forever. You bet I want to be financially secure.

I put back everything inside the box and shut the lid. The front door opened as I was slipping the padlock through the hinge. I recognized my dad's footsteps shuffling along the corridor. I pressed the lock shut and stood up. Then I quickly went to the table and sat down. The second door opened and my dad walked in.

God, he looked exhausted. He didn't even see me.

"Hi, Dad."

He was too tired even to be startled. The lunch-bag trembled in his hand, the brown paper rustling.

"Yes, yes. Hi. You're home?"

"Yeah, I thought I'd . . ." I didn't know what to say.

His head hung low, leaning to the left to keep the boil from rubbing against his shirt collar. Although he worked as a laborer in a steel mill, he always went to work with his collar buttoned, wearing a tie and a jacket.

"I didn't expect to find you here," he said. He put his lunch-bag in the fridge. Half a sandwich was probably left over, uneaten. He checked the sink for dirty dishes and then shuffled into the bathroom. When he came out again a few minutes later, he had combed his hair, opened his collar and loosened his tie. He had been looking at his boil. I tried not to look at it, but could not help myself. The way he carried his head thrust it into view as if he were determined that I not miss it. It looked like a cherry tomato. I couldn't understand why it didn't burst after all this time.

He opened the fridge again and looked around.

"What's this!" he cried out. "What is this?"

He held a milk carton in his hand, shaking it.

"It's empty. There is no milk inside." He shook it again for my benefit. "Why is it in the refrigerator if there is no milk inside? If it's empty, it's garbage and should be in the garbage can, not the refrigerator."

"I guess I forgot to throw it away," I said.

"You drank all the milk and then you put the empty carton back into the refrigerator, is that what happened?"

"Yes, I think so."

He shook his head angrily. The movement hurt his boil. He grimaced, showing his teeth.

"It's not much to ask for, is it, that after you drain the last drop of milk from the carton, you throw the carton away? Is that too much to ask for?"

"No, Dad."

"Well, then, why didn't you do it?"

"I forgot."

"You forgot! You forget all the time! What would happen if everybody decided to be like you? What if everybody forgot to do what they were supposed to do?"

I said nothing.

"What would happen, I said?" He repeated the question, still holding the milk carton in his hand.

"I don't know, Dad."

"Chaos, that's what. Chaos! We all have to do little things every day. That's how order is maintained. Little things have to be done."

He kept gesturing with the milk carton. I was worried that he was going to put it back in the fridge, rediscover it and then launch into another tirade.

"You and your mother, maybe you think you're too big, too grand, too, too whatever to do little things. Is that what you think? You think little things should be done by little people, is that how the thinking goes around this house?"

"No, Dad."

"*Father!*" he screamed. "I don't like that word 'Dad,' I am your father."

"Yes, Father."

I just knew that he was going to put the milk carton back in the fridge and I didn't know what to do about it. I had the strange sensation that my thoughts were making him do it, that my anxiety over it was going to make him commit the very act I was trying to avoid.

And then he did it. He put it back inside and slammed the door shut. I looked away. When I looked up, he stood there, realizing what he had done, blinking slowly, trying to figure a way to wriggle out of the blunder.

I wanted to disappear, vanish. I wanted to make it easy for him, to pretend I didn't see any of it, but his eyes drew mine to them.

"Do you know"—his voice was now soft, whispery, like leaves being raked—"do you know what's happening to me?"

"No, Father."

A strand of his lovely hair fell down over his face. He brushed it back, slowly, lovingly, as if his hair were all he had left of value. He walked to the table. He grabbed the back of the chair for support and then eased himself into the seat.

"Do you think about me," he asked, "when I'm not here, when I'm working at the factory, do you think about me?"

"Yes, Father." I was so glad I didn't have to lie. I did think about him. "I do."

"It's hard work. Hot and dirty in summer. Cold and dirty in winter. And sometimes when I'm working, I wonder if anybody's thinking about me."

"I am."

He hadn't washed up well at the factory. There were dirt stains on his hands, his face, his neck.

"We had overtime today, but they sent me home. Because of this." He pointed to his boil. "The workers complained. They said it made them uncomfortable. So the foreman sent me home. He said I have to see a doctor."

"It probably is a good idea. Sometimes doctors can fix everything up."

He tried to smile. "And other times they can't, is that how it is? Other times they can't."

"Usually they can," I said, trying to keep my voice easy and conversational. He wasn't listening.

"I argued with them. With the workers. With the foreman. I argued with all of them. Your mother loves it when I work overtime . . . her kind of man works overtime all the time. Yes. So I wanted to surprise her with a bigger check, but they told me I had to go home. So I screamed at them. I screamed and screamed at them . . . and then I got so weak. I had to hold on to the machine to keep from falling. I felt like falling. But I didn't. Not in front of them! This one . . . this one foreigner there . . . he said: The little man is going to fall. I heard him say it. And I wouldn't. *The little man,* I said, *is not falling. The little man is holding on.*"

He got all upset. He was back at the plant in the thick of the argument. He held on to the edge of the table, his head shaking, his body trembling, his knuckles turning white.

After a while he calmed down.

"I wish you and your mother had been there to see me. She likes strong men. And I held on. I was strong."

The memory of his triumph relaxed him. His fingers loosened their grip on the table.

"Daniel Boone," he said, trying to smile. "Daniel Boone Price. I gave you that name."

"Yes, I know."

"Your mother wanted one of those foreign names: Marko or Milan or Miroslav, but I wouldn't have it. I'm American. My son's American. He's going to have an American name."

He was getting excited again. His heart beat faster. I could see the echo of his heartbeat under the boil on his neck. The whole red, swollen infection throbbed.

He saw me looking at it. "Does it make you uncomfortable, too? Like the men at work. Does it?"

"No," I lied, "but it's probably a good idea to see a doctor."

"And what do you think the doctor will say?"

"I don't know."

"And does your mother know?" he asked.

"No."

"She doesn't! The great fortuneteller doesn't know." He seemed pleased. "And here I thought she knew everything. I know some things she doesn't know." His head dropped. Strands of hair fell over his forehead. He brushed them back and looked up.

"Smiles on a summer night," he said, as if divulging a mystery.

"It's a movie, isn't it?" I asked, after I couldn't tolerate his questioning stare and the silence.

"A movie. Is that what you think it is? And who was in that movie?"

"I don't know. Maybe it's not a movie. I just thought I heard it."

"I saw it," he said softly. His exhausted eyes were fixed on me, trying to tell me things. I didn't know what we were talking about, what his eyes were telling me, why there was so much pain in them.

"What do you suppose is inside of here?" He pointed to his boil, scrutinizing my face for any sign of disgust.

"I don't know."

"Do you want to know? I'll tell you. It's a secret. But I'll tell you. Do you want to know?"

I nodded.

"All right. Then I'll tell you. But it's a secret. Can you keep a secret?"

"Yes."

"There's mean blood in here." He pointed to the boil again. "Dead things. Old dreams that died. We all have them. Our heads are full of them. Mine is. Full of them. There was a time when my head felt like a birdcage . . . clean and neat . . . and there was a nightingale inside . . . and it used to sing in a clean, sweet voice . . . the song of my life."

He began crying.

"Father . . . please . . . don't."

I didn't understand why he was crying, but his sorrow was filling the room, riding me into the ground like an opponent I didn't know how to fight.

"The poor little bird," he whimpered, "not an eagle who can soar . . . not a hawk who can fight in the skies . . . but just a little thing." He cupped his hands to show me how little. "A little nightingale . . . and it had a little song . . . and it used to sing . . . until the world broke its little heart . . . oh, the pity of it all . . . the poor little thing . . . killed by a smile."

What smile? I wondered.

He sat across from me, lost in thought, silent, his face wet with tears, but not crying anymore.

I stood up. He blinked and noticed me.

"I'll go buy some more milk," I said. I had to get out of there. He just blinked at me.

I tried to walk past him, but he grabbed my wrist. I shuddered. His hand was cold. So cold.

"Don't ever hope," he said. "Promise me you'll never hope."

"I won't, Father."

"You promise?"

"I promise."

"Never?"

"Never," I swore.

"It can kill you," he said.

"I'll be right back. I'll just go out and get some milk."

He held on to my wrist. He seemed to be hanging from it, trying to pull me down into his lap. I pulled back. I was getting as cold as the hand that was holding me. I didn't know how to extricate myself without hurting his feelings. I kept waiting for him to get tired, for his grip to loosen, but he just held on. The little man held on.

Then he laughed.

"Your mother tells me you have a girl." He was sitting. I was standing. To look at me, he had to tilt his head back, and when he did, his Adam's apple looked like another boil about to burst.

"I know her name," he said and laughed again. "Do you know how your mother pronounces it? Wretchel. Is that her name: Wretchel? Is that it?"

"Rachel," I said, as if conjuring up a comrade, calling for help.

"I think I like Wretchel better. Yes, I do like Wretchel better."

"Her name's Rachel."

"Wretchel? Is that what her name is, Wretchel?"

I tried pulling my arm away again, but he held on. His grip tightened around my wrist.

"You didn't think your old father was strong, did you? You thought you were much stronger than me, didn't you?"

He pulled me down suddenly and kissed my cheek. His breath was sour, sickly.

"There," he said, "I let you go."

I went to my room to get some money for the milk. When I came out, he was kneeling in the corner by his steel box, tugging on the padlock.

"Now why did I do that?" He ran his fingers through his hair. "I was sure I left it unlocked. I lost my key. What am I going to do now?"

For a split second, I felt like explaining, taking the blame, but I didn't want to get involved in another go-around.

"I don't know what to do now," he said, as I rushed out of the house. He seemed to be praying.

Chapter 11

We graduated the next Tuesday, and for various reasons none of our parents came to the ceremony. Misiora simply didn't want his parents to come. Freud had had a fight with his mother and she refused to show up unless he apologized.

"Ha!" Freud said. "Fat chance."

The day before the graduation, my dad collapsed at work and had to be taken to the infirmary. He came home that night, his boil lanced, his neck bandaged, humiliated by his collapse. As he was coming in, I was going out, wearing my cap and gown. Rachel wanted to see me in my graduation outfit and my thoughts were all with her. I ran toward her house, my gown flapping, my mind scheming to use the occasion to get another kiss from her. I even saw how I would open my robe and close it around both of us as we embraced.

On graduation day, my mother, my father and I left the house together. They were all dressed up. We split up after a couple of blocks. I hooked up with Misiora and Freud, and they caught a bus to Indiana Harbor. My dad had an appointment at St. John's Hospital. I hadn't got my kiss from Rachel the night before and that was what was on my mind. I was replaying our scene the way I used to replay my wrestling matches, trying to figure out where things went wrong and why. She just didn't feel like kissing, she said. I should have let it go, but I didn't. I tried to talk her into it; I tried to make deals. I opened my robe and tried to convince her to embrace me so that I could wrap the robe around us the way I had planned. She wouldn't. "It's not a debate," she said. "You can't convince somebody to feel like kissing when she doesn't. I have other things on my mind. That's all. That really is all."

She smiled. I pouted. We parted. All I could think about was the kiss I didn't get, wondering what it was she could've possibly had on her mind that was so important.

Even as I watched my mother and father get on the bus and the bus pull away, even though I knew I should be thinking about him, that I should be worried about him, I wasn't. The tragedy of the kiss that slipped away seemed greater to me than anything else at that moment.

Misiora carried his cap and gown; Freud and I wore ours.

"Guess what Larry got for a graduation present?" Freud asked.

"I don't know," I said.

"Guess." Freud seemed all excited.

"I don't want to guess."

"Tell him, Larry." Freud nudged Misiora.

"No," Misiora sighed, "I'm too thrilled for words. You tell him."

"A car." Freud jumped at the chance. "His dad got him a '59 Chevy. Isn't that something? Huh?"

"I guess you might say"—Misiora played with the tassel on his cap—"that my happiness is no longer in doubt. I am all set. I tell you . . ."

"If I had a car"—Freud licked his lips—"I'd be driving it now. Go ahead." He nudged me. "Ask him why he's not driving it."

"I don't want to ask him," I said.

"Since you asked," Misiora said, smiling, "I'll tell you. It's because it's a graduation present and I haven't graduated yet. I can only handle one thrill at a time. The thought that I'm going to be a genuine high-school grad, I mean, the mere thought of it makes me blind with delight, and if I were driving a car I just might hit somebody with it. I just might. The thrill of it all . . . and all."

Freud sometimes missed everything. You'd be pulling his leg and he'd be thinking you're shaking his hand.

"Yeah," he said, "I guess that makes sense."

Trouble began as soon as we got to the school.

"Shit." Misiora spat. "What're they doing here? I told them not to come."

His parents sat in their car, all dressed up, watching us walk toward them, smiling nervously, obviously hoping that Larry had changed his mind and would let them attend the ceremony after all.

"I'll be right back." Misiora spat again and walked toward them. Freud and I stopped.

"I wish I smoked cigarettes," Freud said as we stood there, trying not to look or listen to Larry screaming away at his mother and father. "I mean, this is one of those times when lighting a cigarette might be just the thing to do."

Misiora walked away from the car. The car started up. His parents waved to us as they drove past.

"Good luck, boys," Mr. Misiora shouted.

"Congratulations." Mrs. Misiora smiled.

I wondered if they would drive home right away and take off all those nice clothes they had put on or if they would keep them on for the rest of the day.

"I can't believe this is it," Freud said as we ambled inside the school. "I mean, this is it. When we look back on this day we'll know that this was it."

Mrs. Dewey watched us march into the auditorium as the under-graduate members of the orchestra played "Pomp and Circum-stance." She was all dressed up in pink and white and she waved to us with her gloves. Some people can't stay away from weddings; others favor funerals; Mrs. Dewey liked graduations. She sat there among all those mothers and fathers, and either the sight of us or the sound of the mournful music moved her to tears. She was probably crying in part over that semester she never completed and never would complete.

We heard speeches. We were called up in alphabetical order to receive our diplomas. We heard some more speeches. And then it was all over.

"Well, that was that," Freud said, as we walked out of the school with our robes unbuttoned. He looked through the dummy diploma we had all been given, the rolled-up piece of paper with a ribbon around it, and pressing it to his eye as if it were a telescope, he thundered in his foghorn voice: "Hey, you know what? The world does look better when you're a high-school grad. Here, take a look!" And he laughed, "Ha!" After a second pause, he laughed again, "Ha!"

Nobody seemed to want to go home. The kids in robes, the parents in their best clothes, the teachers—everybody just stood around, mingling, as if we were all going to be called back inside.

Mrs. Dewey hugged each of us, biting her lips, shaking her head, crying, talking in incomplete sentences.

"God, just think . . . It seems like only . . . I don't know . . . Look at you, guys . . . graduates . . . It seems like only yesterday you were . . . and now here you are . . ."

And she hugged us all over again, kissing us on our cheeks, pushing us back to take a good look at us, crying and then kissing us again.

"You won't forget about me now . . . now that you're big shots and all . . . will you . . . if you do . . . I tell you, if you do . . ."

Patty Campbell watched from a distance, waiting her turn.

It all felt to me like some final farewell at a train station. Passing motorists slowed down to take a look at us. Old people stood in their yards across the street and looked on. Was this, I wondered, was this one of those days I would remember forever? I looked around, hoping to find something that would leave a lasting impression on my brain.

"Boy, I bet there's nothing like graduating, is there?" Mrs. Dewey began fiddling with the pearl buttons on her white blouse. "I just know there's nothing like it. Maybe I'll take some adult education courses and get my diploma. Maybe I will." She chuckled.

I saw her husband's car pull up behind hers, but I didn't say anything. Mr. Dewey, the infamous Bimbo of the beerbelly, got out and headed right for her. He had foul mood written all over him. By the time Freud and Misiora saw him, he was right behind her.

"C'mon, Lavonne, let's go home, huh," he said. He spoke without looking at her, without looking at us. He spoke to the sidewalk. His voice and his posture were those of a man who was trying to be reasonable, but determined to remind one and all that he had a foul temper he was keeping under control.

"It's graduation day, Bimbo." Mrs. Dewey wiped her tears with her gloves. She carried the gloves as a decoration. She never put them on. I was sure she thought they made her look classy.

"Don't call me Bimbo, huh, Lavonne." Bimbo kept right on staring at a spot on the sidewalk. "And don't cry. You know I hate it when you cry. You know that. So why do you do it?"

"It's just . . . I don't know . . . it seems like yesterday, that's all . . . God, caps and gowns everywhere . . ."

And she started bawling. Just as nobody chuckled like Mrs. Dewey, nobody bawled quite the way she did.

"C'mon, Lavonne, don't do that." He took her by the elbow. "C'mon. You got no business being here, anyway. What're you hanging around here for? It looks ridiculous. C'mon. Let's go home. Stop crying, already. I'm tired and I don't want no fight, Lavonne. I really don't want no fight, but if you keep this up . . ."

"I won't. I haven't cried in a long time, have I?"

He started pulling her away. It was hard to tell if she was resisting or not. Misiora looked on, twitching, waiting for some signal from her to do something that never came.

Bimbo led Lavonne into her car and then he got into his car. She drove away. He followed. They both put on their turn signals at the same time as they took a left on Magoun Avenue and drove away.

"I bet she gets it today," Freud said.

"She better not," Misiora said. He tore the tassel off his cap and threw it away.

Patty Campbell, her fat mother on one side, her fat father on the other side, walked through the milling crowd toward us—toward Freud, actually.

He saw them.

"C'mon, let's get out of here."

He hurried across the street. Misiora and I followed. We didn't look back to see the impression our hasty departure made.

"I don't know," Freud muttered when we joined him. "Patty thinks we have so much in common. I don't think she understands. She's fat. Her folks are fat. She probably thinks I'm fat, too. What she doesn't realize is that I'm not fat. I'm big. They're all big and fat. I'm just big. Besides, even if I was fat, there's no law that says I have to hang around with a fat girl, is there? There's no such law."

"They got their eye on you, Freud," Misiora said.

"I know they got their eye on me. Fat chance they got of getting me."

He paused. It struck him suddenly that he might have said something funny. He considered it for several seconds and came to the conclusion that yes, indeed, he had said something funny.

"Ha!" he laughed. "Fat chance!"

A Sunrise Oil Company truck rumbled past us. Their new corporate symbol was freshly painted on the sides and the back of the truck: a yellow, smiling sun, its little cartoon arms waving. Misiora waved back, imitating the smile.

"It's so cute. It really is cute," he said.

Chapter 12

I t was a little after five when I got home. My mother and father were not back from the hospital yet. I walked around the house in my graduation robe, trying not to get depressed. There had been nothing remarkable about the day, nothing to separate it forever from the rest of my days, and yet it was supposed to be a big day in my life. School was over. The door to the past was closed. I saw no doors to the future opening up.

I started humming "Pomp and Circumstance" and marching around the house. I really didn't want to get depressed. For once it felt as if the decision was up to me. I could go either way.

I went in my room and dug up my old leaf collection. It was in a red binder, one leaf per page. I turned the pages, slowly looking at the leaves. I brought the binder close and smelled them. The color was faded and even the smell was faded; a faint trace of autumn was there, however. I tried to inhale the atmosphere of the day when I had picked them: the quiet, leisurely day when I had nothing in my head but the prospect of another leaf to find. It had been such a wonderful day. I remembered the fact but not the essential details, not the texture, not the one or two magic details that would allow me to experience it again. I was trying too hard. The day was gone. There was nothing I could do about it. For some reason I found that hard to accept.

It had all started last night when Rachel refused to take part in the scene I wanted to play. I flipped the pages of leaves—some were cracking off in places—thinking about her, wondering how and why she could refuse me a kiss when she had kissed me before. It was that kiss, that missing kiss, that had followed me around all day, a constant reminder that everything was not all right. Up until last night, I was sure of nothing but my feelings for her, her feelings for me. Now everything seemed vague.

I put the leaf collection away and began walking around the house again, humming. I tried to see her side of things. A guy shows up and before she can say anything, before she can even invite him into the house, he flings open his graduation robe and tells her to jump in so he can wrap the robe around her and kiss her. Pretty damn unreasonable. Crazy. That's what it was. In my mind, I exaggerated what I did to make it seem even more unreasonable. The more unreasonable my actions were, the more reasonable her refusal. And that's all I wanted. I wanted her refusal to make sense. To be something I had caused to happen by acting foolishly. That way, if I acted differently in the future, the little breach that had formed between us could be repaired. I could not bear to feel estranged from her. I hadn't even realized to what extent my plans revolved around her until her refusal to kiss me suddenly took the future away.

I walked around the house, humming, replaying our scene, adding specifics that had never occurred just to stack the deck in favor of her refusal. By now, I was not only opening my robe, I was a would-be rapist. I was reaching out for her in a slimy, sex-maniac manner, my eyes bulging, my mouth foaming with lust. Of course she refused. A girl like that would refuse. I was glad she refused. I was delighted.

I walked around the house faster and faster. I was getting real excited. I circled the kitchen table, humming, and skipped through the living room. My mind was churning, creating possibilities I had never considered before. It was my mind and my thoughts and yet they felt new, different.

I laughed out loud at something my mind thought up, as if it were a suggestion made by a second party.

Yes, I liked that. That's what I would do. I would do it again, wearing my graduation robe again, only I would do it differently.

I ran out of the house, slamming doors behind me.

The sun was close to setting and all the industrial particles in the air were glittering and glowing red. It was still officially daylight. There were no cars with headlights on yet, and I instantly launched into a destiny game as I ran. If I got to Rachel's house before the sun set, before I saw a single headlight, then everything would work out fine. I was making a deal with destiny. I was testing it. I felt brave, heroic—a Greek hero, working against the clock and the Fates all in one.

I ran as I used to run: all out. I hardly bothered to look at the traffic as I ran across streets. Brakes screeched, horns blew, voices yelled at me, but I was running at full speed and paid no attention.

I had to grab hold of the Aberdeen Lane street sign and swing myself in the direction of Rachel's house, I was running so fast. I made it with seconds to spare. The sun was setting. I stopped to catch my breath and in the distance saw a set of headlights heading west. I had made it.

Triumphant, sweaty and full of hope, I knocked on Rachel's door. By now I was feeling lucky. Instantly I rolled my destiny dice again. If Rachel opens the door, I win. If her father opens it, I lose.

The porch light came on. The door opened. Rachel appeared.

"Oh, no," I said, beating her to the punch, "it's not you again, is it?"

She seemed a little startled, and then she caught on to what I was doing. She smiled. "And what do you think you're doing?" she said.

"Oh, Rachel, Rachel." I launched into my brand-new self-mockery act. "I want a kiss. I want a kiss. Can I have a kiss, can I please, oh, please, oh, please, can I? Huh, Rachel, can I?"

She laughed, leaning on the door, looking at me, her chin tucked in the bend of her elbow, her back arched. "What're you, drunk or something?"

"A kiss." I stuck out my hand like a panhandler. "Spare a kiss, Miss? How about a peck? A little peck."

"No, never," she laughed.

"Does that mean yes?"

"Never, never."

"Does that mean there is hope?" I wrung my hands and then pulled my hair in despair, wobbling around in front of her, crying mock tears and then wiping them with the long sleeves of my robe.

"You're disgusting," she laughed, and ran inside.

She left the door open and I heard my name mentioned twice, once by her and once by her father. She came out, twirling car keys in her hand.

"I didn't know you could drive," I said, as she started her father's car and pulled out.

"Even though you're a high-school graduate, there's still a lot of things you don't know."

I calmed down as she drove. She turned on the radio. We heard an excerpt from President Kennedy's news conference, and then after the news, as we drove up Indianapolis Boulevard through Whiting, music came on and we listened to the music. She didn't say anything. I didn't say anything. It felt fine. Every now and then she turned to look at me. It felt real fine.

"I saw you," she said, as she took the ramp to the Chicago Skyway.

"Saw me where?"

"Today. Outside your school. After the graduation."

"No, you didn't."

"Did so. Who were those two guys you were with? The big one and the blond one."

"They're my friends."

"Thank God you have friends. I was worried for a while that I was it."

"Why didn't you say something?"

"I didn't feel like talking, I felt like spying on you. I took a picture of the three of you with David's camera."

Whenever she turned her head, her turquoise earrings swung, catching the light of passing cars. I remembered the first night I had seen her.

"Are you staring at me?" she said, keeping her eyes on the road.

"Yes, I am."

"And what're you thinking?"

"You really want to know?"

"Yes, unless it's filthy and nasty and dirty and slimy."

"It's not."

"Then I want to know," she said.

"It feels like we're married . . . driving around like this."

"How would you know what it feels like to be married?"

"I don't. But I hope it's like this."

"What, me at the wheel, is that it?"

"Maybe so. You seem to like it at the wheel."

"I do."

She stayed on the Chicago Skyway until it turned into the Dan Ryan Expressway and then headed back.

"For somebody new here, you sure seem to know your way around," I said.

"Maps. I'm good at maps."

On our way back, just before we got off the Skyway, a big sign greeted us: LAST EXIT BEFORE THE INDIANA TOLLROAD.

"Do you know any place where we can park," she said, "where it's quiet?"

"Whiting Beach."

I told her how to get there. We drove past refineries and steel mills and across countless railroad tracks and finally came to Whiting Park and Lake Michigan.

"People swim here?" she asked.

"Most do. Some drown."

She shut off the engine and rolled down the window. She listened. We could hear the waves sloshing against the shore. She lit a cigarette.

"Were those two guys your best friends?"

"Yes. The blond one's Larry Misiora. The big one's Billy Freund. Everybody calls him Freud."

"Really?"

"Yes . . ."

"I had some wonderful friends myself. I did. Girlfriends. There was Valerie and Julie and Nancy. And they really liked me. I can tell when people like me. And they did. You know what we did once?"

"What?"

She turned around, lifted her legs and stretched them out across my lap.

"It was a couple of days before Christmas. It hadn't snowed at all yet. I was lying in bed and it just hit me suddenly: It's going to snow. I knew it was going to snow. I just knew. So I called Valerie and Nancy and told them to meet me in front of my house. To show you the kind of friends I had: They both came. It's going to snow, I told them, and I want to see the very first snowflake of the year. We bundled up in our jackets and waited. My mother woke up. I told her what we were doing and she made us some hot chocolate and went back to sleep. We drank our hot chocolate and waited. I hate waiting. I hate waiting for red lights, for people, for things I want, but I just loved waiting that night. The three of us huddled together, Valerie cracking jokes, doing imitations of guys—she's real good at doing guys, especially the way guys dance, you know, real cool and all. And Nancy laughing at anything we said. Oh, it was so silly and nice. And then the air got real still. It had been windy, but it suddenly stopped and I knew this was it. I looked around. We all did. And I saw it first. There it was! I saw my snowflake. And we ran toward it, laughing and making noise and I held out my hand like this. It landed in my palm and melted. It started snowing hard after a while. Both of them stayed over that night. We all slept in my bed, our arms and legs all jumbled up. It was so silly and so very nice."

She put out her cigarette slowly, still thinking, probably, of that night when the snowflake fell. She brushed her hair back with her hand, the gesture that of an older woman, the face it revealed in full that of a young girl, homesick for her friends. Her feet lay on my lap. My hand reached inside the loose-fitting legs of her jeans and stroked her ankle.

"I sure miss them," she said. "I miss having girlfriends."

"Maybe you'll meet some girls here you like."

"I don't want new ones. I want my old girlfriends. They're the ones who loved me. Till I got pretty. Shit." She stomped her feet in irritation, kicking me in the stomach. "I wasn't very good-looking when I was young and then I don't know what happened. I felt it happening, but I couldn't make it stop. Valerie's and Nancy's boyfriends started looking at me funny. They got much louder. They started calling me on the phone. They . . ." She waved her hand in disgust. "You boys are really horrible. You are, you know. You spoil everything. You just come along and spoil everything."

"I think for once I'm innocent," I said.

"Yeah? You wouldn't give a damn about me if I weren't pretty."

"Sure, but what about you? If I weren't so handsome and so gorgeous . . ."

She laughed. She seemed grateful for the opportunity to laugh. She poked me playfully with her foot, appraising me with her eyes.

"You're funny," she said. "Tonight you're funny."

I covered up my ears. "I hate compliments."

"Now, that's not funny!"

"I'll show you something funny. We've known each other long enough and I think it's high time you saw it."

"What is it?"

"Excuse me while I get it out . . ." I opened up my robe and pretended to unzip my trousers.

"What're you doing?" she screamed.

"I'm going to show you my tassel!" Before she could say anything, I whipped out the tassel from my graduation cap and wiggled it in front of her eyes. "Isn't it pretty?"

She pulled it out of my hand, laughing, wiggling it in the air herself and then covering her eyes and laughing some more.

"We better go home," I said with a straight face, "before you get any ideas."

"You're truly silly," she said. "You do know that, I hope." She put her feet back on the floor and started the car. "Don't tell me," she said. "I want to see if I can get home from here by myself."

She backed out and drove slowly through the winding streets of Whiting, pausing at intersections, narrowing her eyes, getting her bearings. When she got back onto Indianapolis Boulevard, she smiled and nodded her head. "There. I did it."

It was such a childish gesture that for once I felt older.

"Pretty good, huh?" she said, not content until she got credit.

"Sure was. You've got a great sense of direction."

She seemed satisfied now, and with both hands on the wheel, she drove back.

As soon as she parked the car in front of her house, I sensed that something was going to happen. I had sensed it during the whole drive back. We didn't talk. The radio was off. We just sat there thinking and I felt my thoughts leaving my head and going into hers.

"What *are* you thinking about?" she asked me.

"You," I said.

"You love me, is that what you're thinking about?"

"Yes."

I thought of scents I had never smelled, sounds I had never heard —not words, sounds. I thought of my fingers slipping under her clothes. She seemed to know all my thoughts. They went from my head into hers and came back at me through her eyes.

"And how long will you love me?" she asked.

"Forever."

She reached out and guided my head so that it rested on her shoulder. Our ears were touching.

"You can't see my face now," she said.

"No."

"And I can't see yours either." Her lips touched my neck as she spoke. "But I'm imagining what you look like at this moment. Are you imagining me?"

"Yes."

I thought of straps slipping off her shoulders. I thought of her hands touching me.

"Do you realize that we'll never know if what we're imagining is true? For all you know"—her tongue touched my neck as she spoke; she seemed to be writing with it across my flesh—"for all you know, Daniel Boone, I could be looking very bored right now. For all I know, you're pouting behind my back. Are you?"

Her tongue skipped across my neck like a pen across paper.

"No." I squirmed.

My heart was going crazy. My neck felt so sensitive I thought I would scream. My spine tingled and ached. My hands reached inside her flannel shirt. She moved her head back, brushing her hair against my face, grazing my cheek with a turquoise earring.

"You're not pouting," she said, and then she kissed me. Each time she had kissed me before, there was a feeling of a stopwatch timing her, a sense that she would pull away at any second. This time I could not hear the clock ticking. She kissed the corners of my mouth, she nibbled on my lips, her tongue touching mine, pulling back and touching it again as if she were still writing messages with it. My hands moved up her waist slowly, over the bumps of her ribs, into the hollows and up again until they reached her breasts. I felt the tiny goosebumps around her nipples and this made my whole body break out in goosebumps.

All this was new to me. I had never touched a girl's breast before, never been kissed like this, never felt the heat of my own desire setting another person aflame.

She pulled away suddenly. Her eyelids trembled, her eyes glowed. I had caused this to happen, I thought. Her parted lips moved as if she were ready to smile or speak, as if she herself didn't know what she was going to do.

How her eyes glowed. And I had put the fire there. Me. New, it was all new to me.

"I have to go inside. I do." There was almost a trace of regret in her voice, but she didn't wait around long enough to allow me to exploit it. She left instantly. She rushed out of the car and ran across the lawn as if the fire in her eyes were something she had to get inside the house before it went out. I was left sitting in her car with my tassel in my hand. I felt triumphant. I twirled my tassel and got out. My first step on the ground told me I was back in tune with destiny.

For the first time that day I felt as if I had actually graduated. The erection in my trousers was my diploma. It preceded me like a bowsprit as I sailed toward home, a hero. I had made Rachel laugh. I had caused her heart to beat faster and made her eyes glow. I had touched her breasts!

I took off my gown and slung it over my shoulder, conscious of the dashing image that I made. I was conscious of everything: every step I took, every car that passed, every house number. I felt I could remember it all if I wanted to. I knew I would remember this night forever. I had a night to remember. As I looked at the lawns and the houses, I allowed myself to feel pity for all those poor people living inside of them, all those "others," of whom I was no longer a part, who had no such night to remember and possibly never would. My brain felt raw, as if a thin layer of skin had been removed from it, as if a dustcover had been removed from it, and it could now send out thoughts and receive impressions from the whole world.

I was sorry about only one thing. I wished that Rachel had worn lipstick so that I could have lipstick marks all over my face. I wanted to walk into the house covered with them.

A porch light suddenly came on in the house in front of me. The door opened and a woman appeared in a housecoat, holding a small puppy in her arms. She dropped the pup on the porch and shook her finger at him.

"You should be ashamed of yourself," the woman scolded him, "doing a thing like that on the rug. Bad boy! Bad!"

The bad pup cringed, tucking his tail between his legs. The woman shut the door and turned off the lights. Instantly the pup changed. He shook himself all over, popped his tail out and looked around, ready for a night on the town.

I whistled at him. He followed me to the corner and then headed across the street in a different direction.

I didn't hesitate as I normally did before going inside my house. I didn't slow down at all. For once, I felt ready even to take on the chronic gloom and despair that my father carried with him. It would not envelop me tonight. This was my night.

My mother was sitting at the kitchen table when I walked in. She was still wearing her best clothes, the clothes she had worn to the hospital. She was smoking. The fridge was rumbling.

"God, am I hungry," I said loudly. "Is Dad asleep?"

"No."

"What, he went to work?" I said, opening the fridge.

"The doctors at the hospital said for him to have to stay there. It is bad news. It is cancer."

Chapter 13

Neither my mother nor I slept that night. She kept making coffee and smoking cigarettes, washing out her cup, her pan and her ashtray in the sink and then making some more coffee. I could tell that she had no intention of going to bed. There was an all-night vigil look to her. Perhaps in Jugoslavia, where she was born, this is what they did when a member of the family fell ill. There was a feeling she projected of somebody doing the right thing. A little after two in the morning she lit her old kerosene lamp and turned off the electric lights. Maybe this too was part of some old-world ritual. In the flickering lamplight, her face looked tired but calm, serene almost, like that of a soldier doing his duty. There was nothing she could do for my father except this: stay up and think about him.

I sat with her at the kitchen table and lied. My eyes lied. My face lied. The very posture I had assumed, slumped over, my head resting in my hands, my elbows on the table, was a lie. If she projected serenity, then I projected concern for my father, and my concern was a lie. My whole body was lying. I kept my hands on my head to cover up the thoughts inside, half afraid that when she looked up, she could see right through my skull and see those unspeakable thoughts for herself.

I felt cheated, irritated, annoyed by the timing of my father's illness. Just when the horizon of my own life seemed to be expanding, my confidence growing and my sense of myself crystallizing, he had to get sick and pull me back, force me, at least outwardly, to think about him, to consider him, and abandon myself.

"Do not be so worried." My mother completely misunderstood the cause of my agitation. "Maybe God will be good and make him get better. Such things happen."

I felt monstrous. I held on to my thoughts and guilt clung to every one of them. How could I be so callous? My own father was in the hospital with cancer. My own father. Hospital. Cancer. I tried imagining what it must be like to be in his position, what it must be like to be this little man, my father, whose life had been spent, from what I had seen of it, in a forlorn state of gloom and unhappiness and whose life might now be ending. The least he could expect would be to have his own son, his only son, feel for him at such a time. I tried, but something rebellious and selfish would not let me. I wanted to concentrate on my own happiness and not his tragedy.

I wanted to dissociate myself from his life, from the possibility of having such a life; from the blood in my veins, partially his blood, which could make me have a life like that.

Why now, I kept thinking. Why on this night of all nights? It was as if he had waited, or so I accused him, for just this night to give in to cancer. I had entered the house ready to fight him, to preserve my hopes, and he, even in absence, had won again. I imagined him lying in his hospital bed, savoring his victory.

The later it got, the more nightmarish my thoughts became. My inner struggles left me totally exhausted. Several times my mother suggested that I go to bed, but I felt obliged to refuse and keep up the sham of a concerned son. I could not go to bed if she didn't go to bed. I was so tired and confused and guilt-ridden that I no longer knew what I was trying to prove by staying up. Maybe I was hoping to become so exhausted that even my guilty conscience would collapse and I could have some peace by default.

To keep my mind occupied, I began counting the number of times the fridge kicked on and off in an hour. My mother smoked and drank coffee, talking about my dad, about his cancer and how she had suspected for a long time that something was terribly wrong with him.

"Maybe you did not notice, but he was different once. Then he changed. He was laughing in the old days, he was very much happier man and then he made big change. I did not know why, but I could tell. Now I know why. Yes. It was cancer. All this time. It was doing things to him, but we did not know. Doctors in the hospital, they tell me cancer sometimes takes many years. It goes through body very slow sometimes and it makes person act strange. Yes, that is what it was with your father. Cancer. I am sure."

She went on and on, blaming the cancer for their arguments, for the strange way my dad behaved, for all those years in which his dark, gloomy moods ruled our house and made unhappiness the permanent atmosphere of our family. She seemed to find relief in her explanation, gratitude almost that it was cancer and not something else.

"Yes, it was cancer. All this time. But we did not know," she kept saying, fixing me with her stare to make sure the point was driven home.

The fridge, I found out, kicked on and off nine times an hour.

The kerosene lamp went out by itself shortly before sunrise. Despite her vigil, my mother's face looked lovely and strong. I doubted mine did.

Our landlord, Mr. Kula, who lived in the house next door, came in around seven o'clock. My mother had apparently left his telephone number with the hospital in case of emergency, and he came to tell us that they had called. He seemed annoyed that she hadn't told him ahead of time about the arrangement.

"It's all right—an emergency is an emergency—it's just that I like to be informed, that's all."

My mother left to talk to the people from the hospital. Mr. Kula lingered a few minutes.

"Is it your father?"

"Yes."

"I didn't know. They just said they wanted to talk to Mrs. Price. Do they know what's wrong?"

"They think he has cancer."

He sighed and shook his head. "I hope he has insurance. He's probably covered at the plant."

"I don't know."

"You better find out. Cancer can be quick, but it can also be slow. Hospitals are expensive. My wife had an appendix and that's nothing and yet it cost. But cancer . . ." He shook his head.

My mother came back just as he was leaving. "We have to go to hospital," she said.

For some reason, Mr. Kula just stayed there, leaning on the doorframe, listening, blinking.

"They talk funny English at hospital. You will come with me to tell me."

"Sure, Mom."

"Thank you for telephone." My mother tried to smile at Mr. Kula.

"Oh, think nothing of it. In times like these . . ." He shook his head, but wouldn't leave.

"How will you get there?" he asked. "I know you don't have a car."

"We will take bus," my mother said.

"If I didn't have to go to work, I'd take you." He started out. "Buses don't run regular this time of day. I don't suppose you can afford a taxi?"

"We will take bus."

"I'll call Larry, Mom. He's got a car. He can take us." I waited a second or so for Mr. Kula to offer to let me use his telephone, but since he didn't, I ran out with some loose change to the pay phone on the corner. When I came back, Mr. Kula was still there. It angered me the way he was looking at our house, us, the house of a man, the family of a man, who has cancer.

"Where does he have the cancer?" he asked.

"Thank you for the telephone," my mother said sharply, not trying to smile this time.

He took the hint and left.

Misiora showed up in no time at all and like a good friend said nothing. He just shrugged when my mother thanked him and muttered something about "Anytime, Mrs. Price."

"I am glad my son has such good friends," she said, and started crying.

I sat up front with Misiora. My mother sat in the middle of the back seat by herself. Larry drove slowly, carefully, as if she were asleep and he were afraid to wake her up.

I seemed to be crossing different emotional state lines with every block. One block I would think about my dad, the next I would think about Rachel; one block I would be overcome with pity for him, the next I would feel the same old irritation at the timing of his illness and wonder when I would see Rachel again and when I did, if we would resume where we had left off. I was too tired and too disoriented to feel guilt anymore. My eyes hurt. I shut them and slumped down in the seat, my knees on the dashboard. Although I didn't want to, I remembered the drive with Coach French after my defeat in the state finals.

Misiora stayed in the car in the parking lot outside the hospital.

My mother and I went inside. I held the door open for her. She was surprised by the gesture and smiled nervously. I did too. The strange place was making us feel like strangers.

She couldn't remember the name of the person she had talked with on the telephone, and I had to speak to several people, who made us sit down and wait while they "looked into the matter." Finally a nurse told us where to go and we went there.

I couldn't see any patients. It was all doctors and nurses and day janitors. One of the janitors was Brad Davidson, the greatest all-around athlete our high school had ever produced. He had graduated two years ago when I was only a sophomore. I looked away, embarrassed, as he walked past us, pushing a broom.

I found Dr. Hurst's office and we went inside. I held the door open for my mother again.

Dr. Hurst was very young, but his large forehead and wire-rimmed glasses gave him an imposing appearance. He shook hands with both of us, and then all three of us, as if on command, sat down at the same time.

"I know it won't help much to say this." He leaned toward us as he spoke, looking mainly at my mother. "But cancer, unfortunately, is not that uncommon in this area. The heavy concentration of industry is wonderful for employment, but it seems to be causing an epidemic of cancer, all kinds of cancers. The only reason I say this is to remove any sense of being cursed, singled out. Many families of our cancer patients tend to feel this way, and they shouldn't. You shouldn't." He looked at me and I instantly nodded my head, agreeing.

"The second thing to keep in mind is that cancer is not contagious. You can't get it from somebody who has it. This is not an opinion. It's a medical fact. It is bad enough for our patients to be stricken with this disease without being treated and shunned as potential carriers."

He looked at me again and I nodded.

"Mr. Price"—he paused—"has cancer in his spinal cord. There are various treatments that are available. None of them are guaranteed to produce results, and unfortunately none of them are available in this hospital. It seems that our area has magnificent facilities for producing cancer and none for treating it. I would suggest that you transfer Mr. Price to one of the Chicago hospitals where they are better equipped to do what they can for him."

"We only want very best," my mother said.

"Yes, I know you do. I have made some preliminary arrangements for transfer and if they meet with your approval, Mr. Price can be moved today."

"Yes, good," my mother said. "Thank you. I give approval." She looked at me to check whether she had phrased her acceptance correctly. "I work in Chicago. I can visit him every day," she added.

"I'm sure he will appreciate that," Dr. Hurst said and stood up. My mother and I responded immediately by standing up ourselves.

"Mrs. Price," Dr. Hurst said, "may I talk with you in private for a second?"

She didn't seem to know what this meant.

"You can wait for us outside." He motioned to the door and walked me to it. "We won't be long."

I stepped out. He shut the door. I waited for about ten minutes, not moving from the spot. I kept looking around, afraid that my dad might appear. Although I knew he was probably in bed, I still kept looking around for him.

My mother came out.

"We will now go visit your father. I know where he is," she said.

"What did he say?" I asked her.

"Dr. Hurts"—she mispronounced his name—"he wanted to tell me certain things."

"I know. What kind of things?"

"Nothing very much." She lied badly. "He is nice man."

She led and I followed. We climbed the stairway to the second floor, and then walked down the corridor, looking at room numbers. Before I knew what I was doing, I started playing my destiny game. If my father's room number is even—I rolled the dice—then Rachel and I will make love. If it's not, we won't. I looked down at the floor and followed my mother.

She stopped. I almost smiled when I looked up. Number 218. We went inside. Now that I was successful, I was sorry I hadn't played for higher stakes.

The windows in the room were open and the draft from the door caused the window shades to billow out. A man, not my father, sat up as we came in and then lay back again, disappointed.

My father was awake, his back propped with pillows, reading a newspaper. He lay the papers on his lap as we came toward him.

He looked no different from the last time I had seen him, but since I knew he had cancer, I saw it in him.

"Hi, Dad." I spoke first.

"Yes, hello. Hello." He looked at my mother. "Did you bring my comb?"

"Sure I bring it. You say bring it, I bring it. Sure." She took his comb out of her purse and gave it to him. We stood by the bed while he combed his hair. He examined the comb when he was finished, for loose hairs, and finding none, he seemed content. My mother told him how a friend of mine had driven us here and how I had been so worried about him that I didn't sleep all night.

"I slept fine," he said. "They gave me pills and I slept. I didn't like the dreams I had, but I slept."

His lanced boil looked much better. For a split second, I forgot that he wasn't in the hospital because of his boil. Then I remembered and once again saw the cancer in him.

My mother asked him about the food they served in the hospital. He told her. She asked him if he wanted her to bring him something special. He said he didn't. Then she told him about Dr. Hurst's recommendation, only she mispronounced his name again. He corrected her.

"It's Hurst. Hurst. Not Hurts."

"Eh, I am foreign woman. What do I know." She let him have his criticism. "But he says that in Chicago they have things to make you all fine."

"They do!" he said with exaggerated joy. "In Chicago yet! All this time and I didn't know. They have things in Chicago to make me all fine!" He stared at her with ugly, probing sarcasm. Even Misiora's sarcasm seemed like mild stuff compared to his.

"Yes," my mother went on, "they have good hospitals there, to make you better."

"So you think I should try to live, is that it?"

"Sure, you live. My God, how you talk. You live long time."

She was having a hard time talking. A sad, defeated smile appeared on my father's face as he watched her struggle to keep from crying. What did it all matter, his smile seemed to say, what was all this fuss about something called life.

"I was just checking," he said. "I didn't want to do anything before checking with my family."

"I will be back," my mother said and took me by the arm. I didn't know what she was doing. She led me out of the room into the corridor.

"You go home with your friend. Dr. Hurts, he tell me they will take your father in ambulance. I will go with him and then I will go to work. But you, you go home."

"No, I want to come with you," I lied.

"You want to come and I don't want you should come. I give orders, not you." She put her hand on my shoulder. Her voice got softer. "You look very tired. It is enough your father is sick. I don't need to have to worry about you also. Now you kiss your father goodbye and you go home and sleep."

We went back inside.

"I should get sick more often." He tried to make a joke as I kissed him on the cheek. He embraced me and held me in his arms. The newspaper fell to the floor.

"I'll come and visit you, Dad."

"Yes, yes. You love me, is that how it is?"

"That's right, Dad."

"And I love you," he said. "You're all the sons I have."

My mother looked on, crying.

"Bye, Father."

"Yes, yes, goodbye."

I opened the door. The window shades billowed out. I took one last look at my parents and left.

Brad Davidson was standing outside the hospital when I came out. He was smoking a cigarette. He looked at me without recognizing a former schoolmate and kept on smoking. He had put on weight since his glory days.

I found Misiora leaning on his car. I told him about my dad, what the plans were. He seemed to be paying attention, but his eyes kept straying toward the entrance of the hospital where Brad Davidson stood smoking a cigarette. Finally I had nothing left to say. I saw an ambulance pulling up and wondered if that was the very ambulance in which my dad would be transported to Chicago.

"He was all-state in everything." Misiora kept looking at Davidson. "Football, basketball, track. He had more scholarship offers than Terre Haute's got whores. Damn." He shook his head. "He shouldn't have come back. It must hurt like crazy to go away a hero and then come back like that. Let everybody see that nothing worked out. I bet he thinks about it all the time, don't you?"

"I don't know."

"I bet he does. He looks like he's thinking about it now."

It always surprised me the way Misiora could be affected by somebody else's troubles. He just didn't seem the type. If he could have, he would have gone up to Davidson and painted him a far gloomier picture than the one he was living in now just to cheer him up. I felt badly for Davidson myself but my concern was not as deep as Misiora's.

"Seems like anybody who tries to leave East Chicago comes back. There must be a way, I bet."

I bet, I just bet . . . I remembered the opening of his poem.

Brad finished his cigarette, looked at his watch and walked back inside the hospital.

"You wanna go home?" Misiora asked.

"Yeah."

On the way back, he drove past the Sunrise Oil Company. Painters were painting the huge storage tanks with the happy sun character.

"My dad thinks I'll make foreman in no time at all. What with my education, you know."

"You getting a job with Sunrise?"

"It's a tough choice." He spat out of the window. "It's either that or become another Andrew Carnegie, but I'm leaning toward a job with Sunrise. The sun always shines, you know."

"What's Freud going to do?"

"Something wonderful, I'm sure. And you?"

All I could think of was that I was destined to make love to Rachel.

"I don't know," I said.

"We're all going to do something wonderful," Misiora said. "After all, we are the Rough Riders, aren't we?"

He started singing the school song.

"We are the riders
Mighty, mighty riders
Everywhere we go-o
People want to know-o
Who-o we a-are
So-o we tell them
We are the riders . . ."

He sang, tapping with his hands on the steering wheel. Although I was exhausted, I was beginning to feel better, freer. My dad was being taken to Chicago. Cancer was being transported across state lines. His misery, his hopeless smile, that atmosphere of perpetual defeat would no longer inhabit my home. I could bring Rachel there. It was my home now.

"Mighty, mighty riders," Misiora sang on.

Ahead of us, the railroad barriers started going down, lights flashing, bell ringing.

"C'mon, Larry, let's make it," I said. If we make it across and don't have to stop for the train—I played my destiny game—then everything will be wonderful. I had no idea what "everything" stood for. I had no time to be specific. Just everything.

Misiora swung into the wrong lane and then he zigged and zagged around the barriers and bumped across the tracks. The locomotive whistle blew but we were safely across. Once again I had gambled and won. All the signs looked good.

Chapter 14

A week after my father went to the hospital, a man came from the telephone company and installed a phone. It was my mother's idea. She wanted the hospital in Chicago to be able to reach us in case of emergency. She also showed up one day with a TV set under her arm, carrying it as casually and lightly as if it were a pillow. Her reasons for getting the TV set were much more complicated and convoluted. First of all, my dad had a TV in the hospital and he seemed, according to her at least, to be getting used to it. When he got out, he might want to have a TV in his home. Second, I was at home all alone and should have something to help me pass the time. And then there were important things happening on the national and international scene and we should keep up with world events.

She carried the set into the living room and plugged it in. She sat down crosslegged in front of it and turned a knob. A picture came on. She clapped her hands. "It works!"

She really was like some savage. She looked at me, beaming, as if it had required some special voodoo of hers, some special touch, to make the set come on. She tried all the channels. All of them worked. She snorted, delighted with herself. I could see her thinking: This is easy, no big deal.

She found President Kennedy on one of the channels and she paused. He was having a news conference. Maybe this was one of the national scenes we were supposed to keep up with.

"There is a man," my mother said, touching the screen with her finger. "Irish John Kennedy." Her eyes beamed, looking at him. "I saw him on television where I work. Three times I saw him. He is a man who fits his trousers. Oh, yes. Your father, he is Irish. John Kennedy is Irish. It is strange country, this Ireland."

When the news conference was over she looked for Kennedy on the other channels, as if he had gone somewhere else for a while, and when she couldn't find him, she turned the TV off.

I saw very little of her. She was either working or visiting my dad at the hospital or riding the train to and from Chicago. She slept no more than five, six hours a night and yet she looked wonderful, more beautiful than ever. She moved more quickly, she laughed louder— my dad didn't like her to laugh loudly, but since he wasn't here, her laughter rattled the dishes. She was a woman who liked to do her duty and do it well. Her duty now was to visit my father daily, on Saturdays and Sundays too, and she did it gladly. She told me how he looked, if he had had a good day or a bad day, how touched he was by her visits, how the other patients and nurses and doctors were commenting on what a good wife she was and what a rare thing it was, devotion like hers, these days. There was a glow about her of somebody who was doing her job. Both of her jobs were in Chicago: her job as a cleaning woman, her job as a wife, and when she came home, she beamed in the afterglow of jobs well done.

Even before the addition of the telephone and the TV set, the house felt different without my father there. His absence made the walls look brighter, the interior more cheerful. I no longer had to watch my step. I did not have to worry or wonder how I could sneak my enthusiasm for life into the house without him seeing it, staring at it, smiling that hopeless smile at it. Only now did I realize how much he had controlled my thoughts. I was not quite ready to blame him for my defeat in the state championship, but I was coming closer and closer.

Despite my promise, I did not visit him at the hospital. I could not concentrate on two people at the same time, and I wanted to concentrate on Rachel. I wanted to make love to her, and either I created an atmosphere of urgency about it or I truly felt it, for it seemed to me that a clock was ticking and we were fighting the clock. If we didn't do it soon, anything could happen. The one thing I feared the most was my father recovering before we had made love. His return home, I was sure, would doom the whole relationship. I don't know why I felt this. After all, our affair—I began thinking of it as an affair—had begun while he was still home. Maybe it was destiny again. At a crucial moment in our affair, destiny had stepped in and removed him, clearing the way for us to consummate our affair. I didn't really like the word "consummate" but I used it in my thoughts because it sounded so officially mature and final. Throughout history and literature, at least from what I had read, men and women had fornicated away but only a chosen few had consummated a love affair, and Rachel and I were among those chosen few. The act itself was a total mystery to me. Having never made love to a girl, certainly having never consummated a thing in my life before, I didn't really know how to daydream about it. Out of this total ignorance, I fashioned appropriately ignorant conclusions. Making love to Rachel would make her mine. It would remove all doubts, settle all anxieties about our future; the door would open, I would enter and from then on, both of us would be in another world. It would consummate everything.

I went to her house on the very evening after my father was taken to Chicago.

"God, you look all weird," she said at the door. "Is anything wrong?"

"No, nothing's wrong."

"Well, stand still, then. Why are you twitching around like that?"

I was afraid to stand still. I felt I had consummation written all over me and I didn't want her to read it.

"Can we go somewhere?" I said. "Let's go to my place."

"We're having dinner. You hungry?"

"No."

"Well, you have a choice. You can either go away or you can come in and watch us eat."

I came in and watched them eat. Her father looked at his plate.

"It's wonderful moussaka." He offered at least three times, "You sure you don't want some?"

"No, thank you. No."

"Good thing, too," Rachel said. "The way he's twitching around, it'd be all over his lap, if not the floor. Calm down, will you. You're giving me a stomachache."

"Looks to me"—her father smiled sadly—"like the young man's in love."

His smile reminded me of my father's smile.

Rachel looked up at him, but he kept his eyes on his plate. She wouldn't give up, however. She just kept staring at him. It got very silent and very still at the table. I felt excluded, as if I weren't there at all. Finally, he could no longer resist. His eyes lifted. They looked at each other across the table, her eyes transmitting, his receiving, and then it was all over. Rachel cleared the dishes, the clatter of plates making everyone feel better.

"I still haven't developed those shots I took of you," he said. "I've fallen a little behind."

He saw that I was looking at Rachel walking away toward the kitchen and waited patiently for my attention to focus on him. I almost apologized when I realized what I was doing, but he just waved his hand and smiled that smile again.

"You see," he went on, "I tend to shoot a lot of film and let it pile up so that I myself don't know what I've shot after a while. And then I start developing, hoping for a pleasant surprise. Some people leave money on purpose in their winter clothes and then, come early December or late November, when the weather gets cold, they take the clothes out, put their hands in their pockets and get a pleasant surprise. Well, I do the same thing with my unexposed rolls of film. Do you ever do that, Daniel?"

That was the first time he called me by name.

"I don't have a camera," I said.

"No, no, I mean, leaving money . . ."

"No, I don't."

"I guess it's not something young people do. It's more of an older man's trait."

Rachel came back. He stood up.

"I guess I better go see what surprise I can find in my darkroom." He paused. "I won't forget about your pictures, Daniel."

Rachel took her time wiping off the table, giving more attention to the few crumbs and stains than to me. We seemed to be having an argument with each other in our heads. I was thinking away at her and she was thinking right back at me. I had expected her to embrace me and kiss me as soon as her father was gone. She knew I expected this and didn't do it.

"You can't just come in here like you did," she finally said, "and expect to have things your way."

Although the tone of her voice hurt me, it pleased me that she knew what I was thinking; that it wasn't just a feeling, but that, in fact, our minds could talk to each other without our saying a word. Surely that kind of closeness was reserved for the chosen few.

"I gotta go," I said.

"Go ahead."

When I saw that she wasn't going to walk me to the door, I panicked. I knew the kind of night I would have if I left without some reconciliation between us, and I didn't want to have that kind of night. I couldn't push her. She was too strong. Standing there with her back turned to me, wiping the damn table with a wet sponge, she looked like the strongest person I had ever seen. I couldn't bluff her. I was too weak and she knew me too well. She just wiped the table, her neck stiff, her feet set, her hips rigid, her torso twisting at the waist so that a quarter-inch of flesh showed under her shirt whenever she leaned over. The sight of that flesh tightening and then filling out as she swung back and forth across the table made me taste, once again, what it would be like to make love to her. I could taste the peace I would feel. I envisioned her surrender, my victory, our consummation.

She turned her head and flung a cold stare at me.

"I thought you said you were going."

A conniver began conniving inside of me.

"I'm afraid to go home," I said.

Her eyes narrowed. She scrutinized my reply as if the words I had spoken were hanging there in midair.

"Afraid of what?"

"Never mind. Look, I'm sorry. I never should've come. It's just that I didn't know what else to do so I came here to see you."

I waited for that split second when I saw her neck softening, her shoulders turning toward me and then I started out.

"Goodbye," I said.

"What's the matter with you tonight?" She caught up with me at the door.

"It's my father," I said. I was glad she didn't turn on the lights. It was easier to lie in the darkness. "They found out he has cancer. They took him away this afternoon to a hospital in Chicago and I . . . I don't know . . . I'm just all . . . I don't know . . ."

"So why didn't you tell me right away?" She sounded both angry and conciliatory.

"It didn't seem right to burden you with it."

"You're not just silly. You're stupid. That's what you are, stupid." She embraced me. "No wonder you've been acting weird. I thought you were . . . I don't know what I thought."

Her cheek pressed against mine. I circled her waist with my arms. Her body softened, conforming to the contours of my body. I could feel her breathing on my neck, feel her lashes blinking against my ear. And then, overcome by yearning for her and the conniving tricks I had to employ to get her in my arms, I started sobbing. It caught both of us by surprise.

"Shh, shh." She rocked me gently in her arms. "Don't."

"I . . . I . . ." I couldn't speak because I couldn't tell her what I wanted to tell her. I loved her and I wanted to make love to her. It was that simple, but it was somehow too late for simplicity. I could smell the disaster if I told her everything now, if I confessed.

"Shh, don't. These things happen. They do." She kissed my eyes. "Don't."

"I'm afraid to be home by myself." I couldn't stop conniving. "My mother works and . . ."

"I'll come. I can't tonight. I can't. David is all depressed about his work and . . . I just can't."

"But you will come. Some other time?"

"Of course I'll come. What do you think?"

"I love you, Rachel." I had to say it. I had to say something that was truthful.

"I know you do. I really do know." She paused. "And I love you, too."

I didn't know if I had forced that sentence out of her, tricked it out of her, bullied it out of her or not. I didn't care. I heard it. She loved me.

"Now you be strong," she said and took me by the shoulders. "Will you?"

"Yes."

"Good."

"It was destiny, wasn't it, Rachel?"

"What?"

"That we met and all."

"Of course it was. What do you think?"

Freud stopped by the next day to inquire about my dad. He had talked to Misiora, and Misiora had told him about the cancer.

"Boy, I sure hope he pulls through, I sure do." He kept standing, refusing to sit down, as if it would have been disrespectful under the circumstances. I told him my mother had ordered a telephone.

"I can call you then, huh?" He smiled. "It'll make it easy to stay in touch. I love getting telephone calls. Even when they're for my bitch of a mother, I still like to hear them ring."

His father's wardrobe seemed to be invading his body. Every time I saw him, he had something else of his father's on. This time it was a vest. He kept sticking his fingers in the vest pockets and pulling them out.

"I got a job," he said after a while. "Strictly temporary. I'm going to work for the park. Cut grass and turn on the sprinklers and pick up and stuff. I'd like to have some spending money and I don't want to ask my mother for it. It's strictly temporary, though. If you and Misiora want to do something together, you know, the three of us, just say the word. I know you got more important things to think about, what with your dad and all, but . . . I just didn't want you thinking I was deserting the gang."

He took his father's hat off and looked at the maker's label. Then he put it back on.

"How's Patty?" I asked him.

"I don't think she likes summer. You know, girls wearing shorts and swimming suits. I think she's waiting for the summer to be over. She's not bad, though. I'll grant you she's fat. She says it's not her fault. Heredity, you know. Boy, she's got one fat heredity. But she's not an awful person. Really, she's not."

In his own lumbering way, he made it clear that he didn't want to be teased about her anymore. He made a U-turn in the kitchen with his father's shoes and left.

"See you, huh?"

My mother brought back detailed reports from the hospital: how my dad looked, what he ate, what he said. She woke me up one evening so that she could tell me about her visit.

"Do you know what he said?" She sat on the edge of my bed with tears in her eyes. "He told me this: All my life, I had only one dream and that was to be a husband and a father. It didn't matter what else happened to my life. A husband and a father." She wiped her eyes. "That is what he said. Those were his words."

He was beginning his radium treatment and although the treatment was producing some painful side effects, my mother looked on the bright side.

"They have radium in this hospital, they have famous Jewish doctors, they have everything. I have talked to the nurses and families of other patients who come for visits. None of them come and visit every day like I do, but when they come, I talk to them and they tell me this is best hospital. When Mayor Daley gets sick, they tell me, he goes only to this hospital. All the big shots go there. Yes, they have everything."

I kept waiting for her to ask me why I didn't visit him at the hospital, but she didn't. She never mentioned it. She seemed content to be the one who was doing the visiting, the reporting, the crying. I couldn't tell if she was trying to spare me or if she wanted all the emotions for herself.

I saw Rachel every day. We went for walks. We went shopping for groceries at Kroger's. We put new spark plugs in her car and she called her father out so that he could hear the difference in the sound of the engine. She let me drive the car and we drove around town, talking in a strange new way about all kinds of things. I saw Freud in his uniform, cutting grass in the park. I told Rachel about him and although I didn't intend to, I found myself sounding patronizing, as if Freud and his life were some speck that I could hardly see from the mountain peak of my own destiny. On our way to Miller Beach in Gary, we had a flat tire and Rachel insisted that she change it herself. She wouldn't let me do anything except loosen the nuts, and as soon as she saw that they were loose enough, she took over the job. Everything we did, every look we exchanged, even when we were talking about things that had nothing to do with us, was filled with the anticipation of our imminent lovemaking. It was just there between us, like music, and the inevitability of that lovemaking made the waiting for it a source of constant joy. I didn't push her. I didn't hint. I didn't have to. I could tell it was coming. Like Christmas, around the twentieth of December, when you could just feel it coming closer and closer and you almost wanted to prolong the waiting.

We talked about everything except ourselves. When I saw Misiora roar past us in his car, with Mrs. Dewey in the front seat, I told Rachel about them and once again that patronizing tone got into my voice.

"Poor woman," I called Mrs. Dewey and then went on to paint a complete picture of her incomplete life.

Rachel told me about her girlfriends: Nancy, Julie and Valerie. "Julie got pregnant. She knew she couldn't have the baby so she had an abortion. She was all happy at first because it had come off so easily, and then it hit her that the baby wasn't there anymore and she started crying, and crying and crying. She just couldn't stop. We spent the night with her, and Valerie and Nancy were so nice to her. They were so nice. God, those two girls! They hugged her and cried with her and all four of us were like sisters who loved each other."

I told her about my dad. She told me about hers. He was working on a portfolio in the hopes of having an exhibition. His work, according to her, had been quite popular back East a few years ago, and then something happened. Either his work changed or the public's taste changed. He was now, in Rachel's words, "trying desperately not to be desperate."

"He's going through a crisis," she said and I mentally made a note that "crisis" was one of those words I had never used. "He's getting old and he doesn't want me to stay with him if I feel I'm missing out on something. He wants me to have my youth."

"Sounds like a nice man," I said.

"He is. He really is."

"He's not that old," I said, full of patronizing generosity.

"I know. But he just feels like something's coming to an end. Some phase of his life. It's sad."

When the telephone was installed, I called Rachel right away.

"I never talked to you on the phone," she said.

"I know. How do I sound?"

"Strange."

"Here, you want my number?" I gave her the number and then, after a few idle remarks about how it was getting hot even at night, we hung up.

Later that evening, the telephone rang. It startled me. I had never heard the phone ring in my house before.

"Hello?"

It was my mother.

"Where are you?" I asked her.

"I am here. At the hospital with your father."

There was a pause and then he came on.

"Hello, Daniel."

It seemed like years since I had heard his voice, and although he was far away, across state lines, it brought back that old atmosphere of hopeless despair. I half expected him to materialize in front of me.

"Hello, Father. How are you?"

"I'm still alive, Daniel." He made it sound like a warning.

Chapter 15

Three days later it happened.

As soon as I woke up I knew that this was the day Rachel and I would make love.

I lay in bed remembering, replaying our scenes from the night before. I remembered everything.

We had gone riding in her father's car. I had her drive past the factory where my father worked and then I asked her to park right across from the house with the green door where I had seen him stop that night in the rain.

"Why are we stopping here?" she asked me.

"I don't know," I said. And I didn't. Maybe I just wanted to retrace his steps from that night and be happy in the very places where he had seemed so forlorn.

I leaned over and kissed her.

I lay in bed remembering how easily I had done it. It had even surprised her.

"You're getting pretty sure of yourself." She leaned back.

"No, it's just that I love you so much, that's all."

"You sure do go on about love a lot," she said.

"Makes me feel good to say it."

"It won't always be like that, Daniel."

"Yes it will. Always."

"It can be a real sickness." She nodded her head, smiling. "And it can be a cure, and a time will come when you won't know which is which."

My eyes lit up.

"Who told you that?" I asked.

"I read it somewhere," she said.

"No, you didn't. I know where you got it from."

"Where?"

"From your father," I said slowly, not trying to disguise my triumph.

She took it all in, my words, my elation, all of it.

"And how do you know," she said, "that he didn't get it from me instead?"

I didn't expect that reply. Instantly our positions were reversed. Sensing my confusion, she went right after me.

"Real smart guy, aren't you. A high-school graduate and he thinks he knows everything. So tell me, smart guy, how do you know he didn't get it from me?"

"I don't."

"You don't is right." She poked me several times with her finger. "You don't feel so smart now, do you?" She kept poking me in the chest, in the same spot, not so much for emphasis as to hurt me. Then, realizing that I wasn't going to fight back, that she had won, she pulled back and softened.

"I don't like to be accused of being influenced by anyone. I say what I say. I do what I do." She smiled. "You see, love's not always fun, is it, Boone?"

She started the car, and as soon as she started driving she left our argument behind.

"You ever get up in the middle of the night?" she asked me as she took a right on Indianapolis Boulevard.

"Sure. Sometimes."

"It's become a habit with me. I get up and go to the sink in the bathroom for a drink of water. And then, while I'm drinking"—she paused, reliving the moment—"I turn on the light. I look in the mirror, but my eyes, used to darkness, can't focus at the start. Then they begin to adjust. And gradually I see myself appearing in the mirror, clearer and clearer, until finally there I am. Oh," she sighed, "I love that. Watching myself appear, emerge as if from a fog. I wish my whole life could be like that. I wish that every day things would become clearer and clearer and that I could be aware of it all and keep track and remember every moment of my life as it came into focus."

I envied her ability to formulate so precisely a wish that had been fluttering vaguely through my own mind.

She stopped the car in front of her house. She made no move to get out. We sat there silently for a few minutes.

"Maybe I'll surprise you tomorrow," she finally said.

"How?"

"Wait and see."

I lay in bed remembering the look in her eyes as she spoke those words. Wait and see. I contemplated just staying in bed and waiting for her to come.

There was a knock on my door.

"Are you awake, Daniel?"

I shut my eyes. I didn't want to be disturbed. I wanted to think about Rachel.

My mother came in, stood in the doorway for a few seconds watching me and then shut the door quietly and left. A little later, I heard her dialing the telephone. I listened. I heard her put down the receiver without saying a word.

When I got up, she was sitting in the kitchen, drinking Turkish coffee and smoking. She looked tired. The work, the visits to the hospital, the lack of sleep, were catching up with her.

"I called your father on the telephone," she said, "but he did not answer."

"Maybe he's asleep. It's still kind of early, Mom."

She considered my reply half-heartedly. I sat down and had some coffee. She waited till I'd had a few sips.

"It is not going good," she said. "I did not want to worry you, but I have to, Daniel. The cancer, it is spreading. The doctors tell me it is spreading into his head."

"The brain?"

She winced, waving her hands as if wanting to wave away the word. She preferred thinking of it as the head.

"You can't ever tell," I began babbling. "They really don't understand how cancer works. Sometimes it just stops by itself. So, maybe . . ."

"Oh, Daniel, Daniel, I know you are more educated than I am, but I have seen your father. Last night. Last night he was talking to me and he was not talking right. He was asking me to make smile for him. It was so very strange. He wanted I should smile. So I try to do what he wanted. No, no, he says, not like that. Smile for me. I want you to smile for me like that. I did not know what to do. I kept making tries, but he got very angry at me and he called me very terrible names. Yes. It is in his head now. The cancer. It is in his head, God help us." She crossed herself, looking up at God.

Smiles on a summer night, I remembered my dad saying.

She couldn't get over it. "I did not know what he wanted. Smile like that? Like what should I smile? I did not know. I kept making tries to smile. It was so painful. Then he began to scream at me and call me terrible names and the nurse came in and gave him a shot. I started to cry and he once more wanted me to smile. His doctor, he is very best doctor, he told me that this is how it will be. His head is not his own. It was cancer screaming at me and calling me names. It was cancer, Daniel, not your father."

Her hand shook as she sipped her coffee. And once again she asked me, as if I were accusing her:

"How could I smile? I could not."

"Of course you couldn't, Mom," I said. "Don't be upset."

"It is too late for that. Too late for don't be. I am upset and we must prepare to be more upset. We must prepare, son, for terrible things."

She left for Chicago around noon. Her job didn't begin till four, but she wanted to visit my father before work.

I cleaned up the house. I vacuumed the carpet. I washed the dishes. I could almost hear the hum of my own activity.

The cancer was spreading. Yes. But it was spreading far away, in another state. The worse my father's condition seemed, the more I felt compelled to dissociate myself from it. The more certain his death seemed, the less I wanted to be related to a man facing that destiny.

I was somebody else entirely. My life was just beginning. My mind had no cancer in it. My mind was just waking up. My mind had images of Rachel in it. My mind had images of us in it. My mind snapped shut and would not allow my father inside.

I watched TV all afternoon, fine-tuning the images on the screen, thinking of nothing for hours at a time. I was in training once again, only instead of training my body, I was training and disciplining my mind. Every now and then, just to test myself, I would allow a brief image of my dad into my head and then I would get rid of it, push it away like a plateful of food that was bad for me.

When dusk fell, I began waiting for Rachel in earnest. The house was full of ghosts of my father and mother, their loveless glances, their arguments, their silent stares. I needed Rachel to come. Our lovemaking would cleanse the house of ghosts from the past; it would chase them away the way the sign of the cross made demons flee.

There was a knock on the door. I jumped. I turned the TV off and then I turned it on again and left it on. I opened the door.

"Rachel?" I tried to seem surprised.

She stood in the hallway, half in shadow, half in light, the dividing line cutting her smile in two. She knew I had been waiting for her, so she stood there looking at me, smiling, knowing I wouldn't mind waiting some more. Aware of the effect, she moved her face completely into the shadow and then completely into the light, smiling, her turquoise earrings dangling.

"Guess what?" she said.

"What?"

"I brought your pictures." She showed me a manila envelope and walked inside. "It's not a bad place," she said, looking around.

"I never said it was a bad place."

"No, it's just that you never talked about it." She stopped in front of the TV set. "I don't suppose there's anything on with Katharine Hepburn in it?" she said.

"I don't know."

"Probably not."

She was wearing perfume. The house will smell of Rachel all night, I thought.

"You mind if we shut the TV off?" she asked.

"No, I'll . . ."

She beat me to it.

"I like shutting things off," she said.

It got very silent without the TV.

"Here." She waved the manila envelope around. "You want to see your pictures?"

I took the envelope. She sat down on the couch. I stood in front of her and pretended to be looking at the pictures. She brushed her hair back.

"I've never seen you like that," she said.

"Like what?"

"Like you are in those pictures."

I tried looking at the pictures again, but her perfume and her dangling earrings and her eyes were in the way.

"So terribly sad."

"What?"

"You," she said, "in the pictures. You look so sad. And much older. It's strange."

She looked around the living room.

"No family pictures?"

"Oh, we have some, but we keep them in a drawer."

"Can I see them?"

I went to my parents' room and rummaged through the drawers till I found our album. When I came out, she had her shoes off, her legs crossed, wiggling her toes. I sat down next to her and opened the album.

"That your dad?"

"Yes."

"You sure look a lot like him."

"Not really."

"That your mom?"

"Yes."

"Too bad you don't look like her. She looks great. God, look at those wrinkles. She's got even better wrinkles than Hepburn. She's so dark. How come you're not dark?"

"I don't know."

"She Greek?"

"No, Montenegran. That's in Jugoslavia."

"I know where that is. I know that whole area. I'm from Greece."

"No, you're not."

"My soul's from Greece. In my other life, I lived in Greece. I did. I can just feel it."

She waited for me to disagree with her so that she could say something.

"Your profile," I said, "reminded me once of a Grecian urn."

"Oh, very nice. I look like a pot."

"Not a pot. An urn. That's like a vase."

"God," she moaned, "you think I don't know what an urn is."

She seemed eager to quibble over anything. I hadn't expected this. She looked at the pictures in the album. "You really do look like your dad, you know." She wiggled her toes, waiting for me to disagree. I decided to go the other way.

"Yes, I know."

"You're just agreeing with me to agree. I hate that. I really do hate that."

"Maybe I better turn the TV on," I said.

She laughed. When she did, I became aware of her perfume again.

"You ever been to Greece?" She readjusted her legs. Her knee landed on my thigh.

"I've never been out of Indiana, except to Illinois, which is the same thing."

"We almost went to Greece instead of coming here to the Region. Almost. You know, sometimes I feel like one of those women." She paused. "You know, one of those women in a Greek tragedy. Gods push me one way, but I don't want to go the way they're pushing me. I want to go the other way. That's how I feel. Like the gods are going to get angry with me pretty soon. You like Katharine Hepburn?"

The sudden change of topic made me almost want to scream.

"Sure," I said.

"What do you mean, 'sure'?"

"I mean I like her."

"Why did you say 'sure'?"

"Everybody likes Katharine Hepburn."

"Oh yeah?" she said. "Then how come I know a whole bunch of people who don't?"

"You don't know a whole bunch of people who don't." The hell with it, I thought, if she wanted to quibble, we'd quibble. "You're just being . . ." I couldn't think of the right word. "Why are you being like this?"

"Like what?"

"You know how you're being . . . You're being . . ."

"I like your shirt," she said.

"Stop changing the topic! Will you for once stop doing that!"

"Why, don't you think it's a nice shirt?"

"What is the matter with you? Huh? Tell me, will you please tell me, what is the matter with you?"

"Don't scream at me. I hate that."

"I hate it too. I don't want to scream at you. I just want . . . Rachel . . . I've been waiting for you all day. All day. I love you. You love me. It's so simple and we're . . ."

"It's not as simple as you make it seem." She leaned her head back, making her long neck look even longer.

"Sure it's simple. I love you. You love me. That's simple."

"I've said it once and I'll say it again: It's not as simple as you make it seem."

"What's complicated about it? Tell me!"

She seemed to be thinking. I waited.

"You know what?" she said.

"What?"

"I really do like that shirt you're wearing."

She looked at me challengingly, ready for anything; ready for us to split up and never see each other again. It was all there in those damn green eyes of hers. I couldn't even imagine what it was like to have strength and resolution like that.

"Do you know why I came here?" she said. When I didn't reply, she poked me with her finger. "Do you? Hmm? If you don't know . . ." She smiled, and when she smiled I became aware of her perfume. It was like a trick she had. She smiled: I smelled the perfume. "If you don't know, all you have to do is say 'No,' and I'll tell you. Do you want me to tell you? Do you?"

I nodded.

"Oh, good. He's alive. The reason I came here, D.D. . . ." She paused. "That stands for Dear Daniel. If I ever write you a letter I'll just start with D.D. and you'll know what it means. The reason I came here is because David developed your pictures and you looked so sad, so terribly sad in those pictures. I'm a real sucker for sorrow. So I came to cheer you up. I didn't see any sorrow in your face when I came in."

"That's because I was glad to see you."

"Go ahead," she said, placing her hand on my shoulder.

"Go ahead what?"

"Show me."

"I don't understand."

"Show me how sad you can be."

"Rachel . . ."

"Show me. I want to see. Like in the pictures. C'mon, don't pout. Move on to sorrow, Daniel. Let me see it."

"Rachel, I don't know how to . . ."

"Think, Daniel. Think of sorrow and let your thoughts appear." She touched my cheek and then her hand came to rest on my neck. Her eyes were wide open, focused on me, unblinking. "Think of sorrow, Daniel. Think of losing something or someone you love. Think of hopes going up in flames, dreams in ruins."

She was not an easy person to deny, not when her hand was on my neck, not when her own face seemed to be reflecting the words she was using. I must have reacted to something I saw in her. As contrived as the situation was, something moved me.

"Rachel," I said. I wanted to tell her that we shouldn't do this. She seemed near tears and I wanted to comfort her. I wanted to remind her that we were so very young and that our whole life was ahead of us, the two of us, the chosen two, but I didn't have a chance to say anything. She winced as if in pain and pulled me toward her, her fingers digging into my neck.

The album fell to the floor.

She kissed me and kept on kissing me, so that I found it difficult to respond, to jump in and do my part. Her lips moved all over my face, my eyes, my neck, as if she were looking for a particular spot to settle on; she moaned as she moved, as she looked, as she kissed me and kept on kissing me, kept looking for that magic spot, oh, where is it, where is it, she seemed to be moaning. Her lips overlapped mine, then they moved, as if to speak, and, closing for a split second, opened again, opening mine, and her tongue touched mine, and it was not like kissing, it was like two animals touching, like two hostile dogs testing each other's scents, intentions, baring their teeth, snorting, growling softly, ready to bite.

She was struggling, or seemed to be, with herself, and her struggle spilled over into a struggle between us. It was like a wrestling match and I once again became aware of the clock ticking, only I didn't know how much time I had left, how many more minutes I had; all I knew was that seconds were going by and that any second she might change her mind. I felt this in her whole body, I felt it in her kisses, which were taking my breath away, and I hurried, before time expired. I fumbled with her clothes. I fumbled with my clothes. Zippers unzipped, buttons unbuttoned or fell to the floor. I wanted to look, but there was no time to look at the parts of her body I had never seen. I couldn't tell if she was helping me or fighting me. The distinction got lost in the rush toward consummation. I couldn't even think. There was no time for thinking. I would think about it all afterwards. I would replay the scene in my own time and enjoy the moment in retrospect.

She lay beneath me, but her body kept moving, her head kept moving so that I could not see her face clearly. I wanted to see it. I wanted to see her eyes looking at me as I went into her, but she would not stop moving her head from side to side and her eyes flashed past me like searchlights looking for somebody or something else. I thought I heard her say something, but I could not make out what it was. A word? A name? A sound? I felt her hand on mine and then both of our hands touched and guided me toward her. I felt the damp, hairy softness parting, I caught her scent, and then as she bent her legs and her knees pressed against my ribs, I entered where I'd never been before. The blood drained from my head and I felt dizzy, wet and warm.

"Rachel," I said, wanting to hear her name, to remind myself where I was, with whom I was. I could not hold my head up. It was as if a defective gyroscope were twirling inside my brain. I let my head fall onto her breast and then I moved my cheek along her flesh until it came to rest next to hers. I wanted desperately to see her eyes, to see the expression on her face, to see what she was thinking and, more than anything else, to see, to really see the confirmation of our lovemaking there. But she would not let me. She moved away. She placed her chin on my shoulder and held it there, so that I could not see her, so that all I could do was guess how she looked.

"Rachel," I called, and it did feel as if I were calling her, not just saying her name, but calling her from somewhere far away to come back and be with me. I could not understand how it was possible, but I began missing her. I felt neither alone nor with her, but somehow masturbating in her presence. I needed the confirmation of her eyes.

"Rachel," I called, but the more I tried, the more she seemed to fade, pull back; not her body—her body was right there, and I was inside it—but something else that I could only call her soul. And I wanted her soul. I wanted her thoughts. I wanted her all, but all she gave me was her body. The rest was fading like a lovely song on a car radio, speeding away from me, fading.

"Rachel, Rachel . . ."

Knowing nothing of love or lovemaking, I wondered if perhaps this was how women—I thought of her as a woman now and I tried thinking of myself as a man—that this was how women behaved at such moments. Perhaps they had to pull back, to go away and then return. Perhaps if I waited patiently she would come back. But my own body refused to wait. It had a clock of its own and its time was running out.

"Rachel." I called her name as I came inside of her.

She replied, but once again I could not understand her.

"What did you say?" I whispered. "Rachel, tell me."

She held me tightly as if I were an idea she were clinging to and not I, not me, not myself.

Tension was leaving my body. Blood was returning to my head. I was getting my bearings again. I turned my head and saw the album on the floor. It had fallen open to a picture of my father. He looked at me from the album as if from a grave, that smile of his curling his upper lip slightly.

I shut my eyes. Somebody knocked loudly on the front door.

"Did you hear that?" Rachel said.

"Yes."

"You expecting somebody?"

"No."

Having waited to hear her voice, I found the words she said stupid. I found my replies stupid. Yes. No. Here we were talking about a third person, and I wanted to hear about us.

There was another series of knocks, even louder than the first.

"Who do you think it is?" Rachel sat up.

"I don't know."

I didn't look at her.

"Maybe you better go see who it is."

"Yes, I probably should."

I was getting depressed. We were saying words anybody could say and the words made us seem just like anybody else. Not special. Not the chosen two. We spoke just to speak, almost glad for the interruption.

I had thought my trousers were off. They weren't; they were around my ankles. I pulled them up, looking down at them as if I had to see in order to zip up, in order to buckle my belt. I flipped the photograph album closed and went to the door.

"Hello, Daniel." It was Mrs. Dewey. "Sorry if I . . . but I didn't know what else to do." Her left eye was blackened, swollen shut, and as she stammered excitedly, she made up for this lack of vision by tilting her good eye toward me.

"What's wrong?"

"Well, you know . . . Bimbo being Bimbo and me being me and things being the way they are . . . well . . . as you can tell . . ."

She tried to chuckle, but all she could do was smile and even that seemed to hurt.

"I didn't know what else to do, so I came here."

"You want to stay here, is that it? What, is he after you?"

"Oh, no, no. Nothing like that. Larry's after him."

I found it hard to listen to her. I felt as if I were underwater, uprooted, floating.

"You see," she went on, "when Larry saw what Bimbo did to me he got all crazy . . . He really did . . . You know how Larry gets . . . Well, he got that way . . . and he said he was going to wait for Bimbo when he comes out from work and kill him. He said kill. I don't know if he was serious, but I just couldn't sit at home and wait to find out . . . ."

"Kill him?"

"Yeah, that's what he said. It's a real mess. I can't even cry. Seems·like I need two good eyes to cry with and all I got's one. So, I don't know. I thought maybe you'd come and talk to Larry or something and get him to calm down."

"Oh, I see." I was beginning to understand at last. "Sure, I'll be right back. I'll just . . . I have to . . . I'll be right back."

"Who is it?" Rachel asked when I went back to her. She was all dressed. Two buttons were missing from her shirt. We looked at each other to show that we could do it, but it felt odd, full of effort.

"Something's come up," I said and quickly explained the situation. Although I was telling the truth, I felt as if I were lying. She paid attention to every word and her attention seemed like a lie too. We were skipping over something, and we both seemed relieved for the opportunity to cover up that something.

"Want me to come with you?" she asked.

"Yes, sure."

We left.

"Hello." Mrs. Dewey looked at Rachel and then at me.

I made the introductions. With her one good eye Mrs. Dewey took in the two missing buttons on Rachel's shirt, and then all three of us rushed to her car.

"I don't know what I would've done if you hadn't been home." Mrs. Dewey kept talking. "I think I would've just stayed there, knocking on the door. What a mess. I tell you . . . ."

Rachel got in the front seat. I was going to join her, but she shut the door behind her. I got in the back.

"I called Billy." Mrs. Dewey was very talkative as she drove. It was as if Bimbo's punch in the eye had loosened her tongue. "And his mother—she really is a bitch—she said he was at some Patty's house. Took me forever to get the number from her. So I call Patty and who should answer but Patty. I ask for Billy and she wants to know why I want him. Anyway, I finally got Billy and he said he'd go right over to the firehouse and keep an eye on Larry. I just couldn't leave it with Billy. He's a nice guy and all . . . but . . . I'm sorry if I spoiled anything by coming like I did."

"You didn't," Rachel said.

"Of course not," I added from the back seat, leaning over.

"That eye looks bad." Rachel tilted her head to take a look at it.

"It seemed all right when he hit me. Then after a while it just started swelling up." She went right through a red light on Indianapolis Boulevard, making a sharp, reckless right turn. "Bastard Bimbo used a fist. First time he used a fist on me."

"Your husband's name is Bimbo?" Rachel asked.

"No, my husband's name is asshole, but I call him Bimbo." Mrs. Dewey tried to chuckle again.

Rachel moved toward her. Their shoulders were almost touching.

"Does he beat you often?"

"He used to threaten a lot and beat a little. Now he's doing it the other way around. I guess he's changing. He's getting old and he doesn't like it."

"Is he older than you?" Rachel asked.

"I ain't old, honey. I may be a lot of things, but I sure as hell ain't old."

"No, I didn't mean it like that."

"I know you didn't. I just felt like sounding tough. I always do that after I get pummeled." This time, pain or no pain, she chuckled. Rachel smiled. I leaned forward some more. They had just met and yet they seemed to be easy with each other.

"He's in his early forties." Mrs. Dewey went through another red light. "But men around here fall apart after forty like old cardboard boxes." She chuckled again and nudged Rachel with her shoulder. Rachel did not seem like the type of person who would like being nudged like that and yet she seemed to enjoy it, seemed to respond to the gesture.

"I don't know why you stay with him if he beats you." She let her arm rest on Mrs. Dewey's shoulder.

"I don't either. I ask myself that dumb question all the time and

I can't seem to find the answer. I think maybe I stick around hoping to find out why I do it. That don't make sense, does it?"

"No, it sure doesn't."

Both of them laughed. Mrs. Dewey was getting real giddy. Maybe it was just having another woman to talk to.

"If I get hit enough times, I'm bound to find something out."

"You love him?"

"Bimbo?"

"Yeah, Bimbo." Rachel laughed.

"Do I love Bimbo?" Mrs. Dewey laughed too, repeating his name for Rachel's benefit. "That's the one question I don't ask myself. You want to know why?"

"Yeah, why?"

"Because he asks me that question so often, I'm sick of it."

She nudged Rachel with her shoulder and both of them laughed again, like it was some private joke that only they knew.

When Mrs. Dewey started talking about Misiora, I jumped in from the back seat and began jabbering away about Larry, trying to impress Rachel with my links to other people and at the same time drown out the memory of our lovemaking. I really wasn't sure any more if my impressions of that lovemaking were correct. Maybe that was the way it always was. Maybe I was expecting something that doesn't happen. What did I know of women?

"The thing about Misiora," I went on, "is that he talks and talks but sooner or later . . ."

Maybe nothing had gone wrong after all. Rachel seemed fine. There she was, smiling and laughing with Mrs. Dewey. Here we were, speeding along in a car. It was probably just me and my ignorant expectations. The more I talked, the more it began to sink in that I had made love to Rachel. That I had actually made love. I had done it. How could I possibly forget that? I had done it. The thrill of that accomplishment hit me suddenly. The fact of it obliterated the memory of the process. Rachel, I thought, had probably loved it. She was probably sitting up there thinking about it, about me. Suddenly I felt so glad that Mrs. Dewey had come along. If she hadn't, I might have said something to Rachel. I might have spoiled it all with a word or two. It was just me. I had only misinterpreted everything. It was wonderful and I just didn't know. Next time I would know. Destiny had saved me again. Destiny had sent Mrs. Dewey just in time.

"Don't worry, Lavonne, I'll take care of Larry." My voice got very loud as I talked. I was almost shouting, leaning forward, thrusting my head between them, looking at one and then looking at the other, reassuring Mrs. Dewey, letting Rachel know how happy I was after all, wondering if she had been aware of my doubts, hoping she wasn't.

"It's a good thing we were at home," I kept shouting. "We didn't know who it was when you knocked. We had no idea. We were just . . . well . . . never mind what we were doing." I laughed semihysterically and continued ranting, using "we" every chance I could and touching Rachel on the shoulder whenever I used it. We. We were we now, weren't we?

"There's Billy," Mrs. Dewey said, and I saw Freud waving with one hand, shielding his eyes from the glare of the headlights with the other. I could see the new brick firehouse about half a block behind him, but I couldn't see Misiora.

Mrs. Dewey stopped the car. Freud came over.

"Hello," he said to Rachel and took off his hat.

"This is Rachel," Mrs. Dewey said.

"Hello," Freud said again and put his hat back on.

We got out of the car. Freud brought us up to date. Misiora was waiting for Bimbo by the firehouse. Freud had tried to talk to Larry, but Larry had told him to go to hell. He had tried talking to him again and Misiora threatened to hit him. So he left. His slow delivery made it seem we were all gathering here to go to a movie.

"I better go talk to him," I said.

"Won't do no good," Freud said. "I tried. He's got a lead pipe in his hands."

"We might have to take it away from him," I said. I was shouting. I couldn't keep my voice down.

"I don't think we can get it away from him without getting hit with it," Freud said.

"We'll have to try," I shouted pompously. "We'll just have to try. This is one of those things that could ruin his life and we can't let that happen. At least I can't."

Why was I talking like this? Maybe I was trying to sound mature and manly for Rachel's benefit. I didn't like the person I was imitating, so I have no idea why I thought Rachel would. Without daring to check, I was sure she was watching my every move, my every gesture.

"C'mon, let's go," the person I was imitating said.

Freud and I walked together. Mrs. Dewey and Rachel followed.

"Who's Mrs. Dewey's friend?" Freud whispered.

"She's my friend," I said. "We're lovers."

"You're what?" Freud stopped. I had to take him by the arm to get him going.

"Bimbo's a fireman?" I heard Rachel say behind us.

"He moonlights as a volunteer. You know . . . just to be with the guys."

"What do you mean, 'lovers'?" Freud whispered again.

"You know what lovers are?"

"Sure I know. But is that what you meant? Did you mean what you said?"

"Yes. We're lovers."

He turned his head to look at Rachel, and since he was Freud, he couldn't turn his head and keep on walking. He stopped. I grabbed him by the arm again and pulled him along.

The moon was out, looking bluish through the damp haze. I couldn't see any stars. Just the moon. Our shadows stretched toward the firehouse.

"What the hell is this?" Misiora jumped out of nowhere.

Everybody stopped. Freud took off his hat and wiped his forehead. Mrs. Dewey and Rachel joined us, forming a semicircle around Misiora.

"What the hell's going on?" He looked at Mrs. Dewey. "Eh, Lavonne? What is all this? A carnival, or what? You selling tickets or something?"

"Hey, Larry," I said.

"Don't 'Larry' me in that voice. Just don't goddamn 'Larry' me."

"See what I mean," Freud whispered.

"Don't go crazy like that," Mrs. Dewey pleaded. "You don't understand, Larry."

"I understand." Misiora waved his lead pipe. "Oh, I understand, all right. Remember what you said, Lavonne. Do you?"

"Sure I remember," she said. There was a guilty sound to her voice.

"You said if he ever hit you with his fist . . ."

"I know. I know. Oh, Larry," she pleaded.

"You know how I feel. Jesus Horrendous Christ, Lavonne, you must know how I feel . . ."

"I know. I know. It's just . . ."

The side door to the firehouse opened and two beerbellies came out, followed by two more. One of the beerbellies belonged to Bimbo. He was tucking his shirt in when he saw us. He stopped tucking when he saw Mrs. Dewey.

"Whatcha doin' here, Lavonne?" He ambled toward her, stopped and spread his legs apart, putting his hands on his hips. The three other guys joined him.

"It's three against four," Freud whispered in my ear.

Misiora looked at Mrs. Dewey. He seemed to be giving her a chance to do something, say something. I looked at Rachel, but her eyes were measuring Bimbo.

"Didn't you hear me, Lavonne?" Bimbo said. "Whatcha doin' here?"

She shrugged nervously.

Bimbo looked at his three cronies and smiled as he turned toward her again.

"What happened to your eye?"

The three cronies chortled.

"I ran into an asshole, that's what happened to my eye," Mrs. Dewey said. "And now I smell of shit so I thought I'd go out and air out a bit!"

"Ha!" Freud let slip his single-syllable laugh.

"C'mon, Lavonne, let's go home." Bimbo sounded weary and threatening. He took a step toward her. He was about to take another when he found a lead pipe sticking into his gut.

"She's not going anywhere with you," Misiora said, pulling the pipe back and then sticking it into his gut again for emphasis.

"Huh!" Bimbo grunted, looking at the pipe and at Larry. "Who the hell are you?"

"Let him be," Mrs. Dewey pleaded, flapping her hands.

Bimbo's cronies advanced in a group.

"Yup," Freud whispered in my ear, "I'm sure of it now. Three against four." He took off his father's hat and his father's vest and laid them on the ground.

"You fat slob." Misiora continued to abuse the bewildered Bimbo. "You like to beat up women. You're supposed to be nice to women and you just don't know how to be nice to Lavonne."

Something clicked in Bimbo's head.

"And you do? You been nice to my wife. He been nice to you,

Lavonne? You tell me, Lavonne, you goddamn better tell me, this punk been nice to you?"

The thought that somebody might have been nice to his wife made Bimbo look meaner than ever.

"Yeah, he's been nice to me, what of it?" Mrs. Dewey just couldn't seem to make up her mind if she wanted to be the peacemaker or the instigator of a fight. Rachel tried to pull her back, but she jerked her arm free. "Somebody's got to be nice to me, Bimbo. I gotta have somebody be nice to me!"

"And he's been nice to you." He looked at Larry again. "You, you been nice to her!"

It sounded on his lips like the treachery of the century.

"You!" Bimbo couldn't get over it. "Him, this young punk's been nice to you . . . this . . . this . . . this . . ."

Maybe it was the frustration of not being able to come up with another word that made Bimbo swing with his fist. I could see the punch coming from where I stood. Misiora certainly saw it. He even had time to drop his lead pipe, deciding he didn't need it, duck the punch and hit Bimbo in the gut with a punch of his own. Larry was a wrestler, not a boxer, so he really didn't hit him hard.

"There, there's a biff for you," Misiora taunted him. Bimbo swung again and missed again. "You missed, Bimbo." Misiora kept it up. "You're a mean bastard, but you sure are slow. C'mon, Bimbo, try it again. C'mon, here I am." He danced around him, stopping for a split second to offer himself as a target and then ducking or skipping away as Bimbo threw a punch. "I think you missed again, Bimbo."

Bimbo's three cronies looked on.

"You'll pay for this, Lavonne." Bimbo threatened Mrs. Dewey and kept chasing Misiora. "When we get home, you're gonna pay."

"That's all I do is pay," Mrs. Dewey shouted. "I'm tired of paying, Bimbo."

"C'mon, Bimbo." The three cronies began cheerleading. "Kill 'im!"

"C'mon, Bimbo," Misiora taunted him. "Here I am. Kill me, Bimbo! Hit me, Bimbo."

"Kill the fucker," the cronies shouted. "Kill 'im!" They were all getting angry and agitated and eager for blood.

Rachel looked on as if she had never seen a fight. She watched Misiora dancing around, bobbing, weaving, and she seemed to be enjoying the show, her face reacting to his sudden graceful moves. She winced. She bit her lower lip. It wasn't that I was jealous. It was just that I wanted her to look at me like that.

She smiled. She covered up her face with her hands and then peeked through her parted fingers like a kid. Our eyes met. Hers were sparkling between her fingers like fireflies. I tried to read what they said.

"Kill 'im, Bimbo!" The cronies shuffled in place, shaking their fists, belching, shouting. Their clothes were too tight for them. Their skin seemed too tight for them. Uncomfortable.

Rachel looked on. The fight between Larry and Bimbo was still a silly, harmless affair, but there was trouble in the air and she seemed to love it, she seemed to be waiting for it. My heart began to beat faster. Her eyes appraised me, moving merrily from Misiora and Bimbo toward me, flashing messages, sparkling, earrings dangling.

One of Bimbo's friends made the mistake of pushing me. He was trying to follow the fight and I was in the way, so he pushed me aside.

"Who you pushing?" I snapped at him. It sounded strange to talk to an older man like that, a man old enough to be my father.

"Shut up, will yah!" he roared.

"Why don't you shut me up?" My heart was beating faster and faster. I looked at Rachel. She was bouncing up and down, up and down on her toes, chewing on her fingers, watching my every move. "You want to shut me up?" I said to the man. "C'mon and do it!"

Freud tried to intercede and play the peacemaker. "Hey, this ain't right, you know. We'll just start something. I don't like to hit older men. My father always told me . . ."

He didn't get a chance to finish. One of the cronies pushed him from the back. "Who the fuck you calling old?"

"I didn't say you were old, I just . . ."

"Who the fuck you calling old?" The man pushed him again.

"Hey, c'mon." Freud tried to wave him off. "I don't like getting pushed."

"Who the fuck cares what you like?"

Freud tried backing away just as he backed away from Coach Lukach.

"You think I give a damn about what you like, you dumbass punk?"

"We came here to stop a fight," Freud said.

"So he thinks we're old," the last crony joined in. "That's what he thinks. Is that what you think? I'm talking to you, dumbass."

"I don't like being called no dumbass." Freud stood his ground.

"Whodafuck cares what you like?" My crony left me and went after Freud.

Freud still kept trying to keep peace. "You guys should be ashamed," he muttered, "talking foul language like that. Old guys like you . . ."

"Whodafuck you calling old? You greenass punk!"

"You callin' us old? 'S that whatcha doin', eh?"

Bimbo was stumbling after Misiora across the cinders. His cronies had surrounded Freud and were poking at him with their fingers. I was left alone.

"Don't poke me." Freud slapped their hands away. "I don't like getting poked."

"Whodafuck cares what you like?"

"Hey, don't poke my friend." I pushed one of them aside.

"Whoyah pushing?" he snorted. "You pushing me?"

"You poked me." Freud kept trying. "You started it."

"Yah, you guys started it," I joined in. "You want to finish it or what? Or you want to just talk all night?"

"Shut the fuck up, you snot-nosed punk."

"Why the fuck don't you shut me up, you fat slob," I said. It felt strange to be talking like that to men of their age, but I liked it. It felt like something I had wanted to do for a long time. It was strange and fearsome, like picking a fight with a policeman.

"C'mon, fat man," I began taunting. "C'mon, grampa. Let's see what you got."

I didn't really know what was making me do it. Maybe it was because Rachel was there, watching me. Maybe it was because we had made love that night and I felt that entitled me to step into another world. I didn't know what it was, but I knew I liked it. They were old enough to be my father, and I liked that, too. The weird light from the misty blue moon made it all seem strange.

"You got any balls," I continued taunting, "or are you all beer-belly and bluff? C'mon, grampa. When this is all over, we're going to go and fuck your wife. Somebody has to."

He threw a punch at me. I stepped aside. And the fight was officially on.

Misiora had Bimbo. I had one of his cronies. Freud had the other two. Walking or sitting, Freud looked like a shaggy, lethargic bear, but when he really began to move, he became quick and graceful.

"All right," Misiora shouted when he saw us fighting, "here we go."

It was a strange fight. They kept swinging clumsily and missing. Neither Freud nor I could bring ourselves to hit them, really hit them. Even Misiora seemed to be holding back. We called them names, anything we could think of with the words "fat" and "old" in them, and they called us "punks," "fucking punks" and "mother-fucking punks." They ambled after us and we skipped around them, crouching low in our wrestling positions, moving our arms in front of us more for show than anything else. I kept wanting to hit. To hit an older man. A man old enough to be my father. To see what it felt like. It was like a word I was told I couldn't say and I wanted to say it. The only contact we made with them was to slap away their fists. They were cursing and snorting and belching and chasing after us. My fingers curled up into a fist of my own.

Mrs. Dewey and Rachel stood together. They began by standing to the side, but as the strange fight continued, they wound up in the middle, surrounded by the rest of us.

"Isn't this something?" Mrs. Dewey shouted at us. "You guys are really something."

I couldn't tell if she was talking to us or to Bimbo's friends. Rachel looked on. Even when I didn't see her eyes, I felt them. I danced around her, catching brief glimpses of her profile, a quick flash of her turquoise earring, white teeth, parted lips.

My fist hardened. I saw a face in front of me that was old enough to be my father's and I let go. I hit the face, and the face fell back. For a split second I expected the clouds to part and God to appear and strike me dead with a lightning bolt, but nothing happened. I grew bolder. Cinders slipped under my feet as I ran toward the man I'd hit and I hit him again. Nothing happened again. No God. No lightning bolts. I hit him again. It was my father I was hitting now, and I hit him again. I had lost the championship just to please him and I didn't want to please him anymore. I had tried to shrink myself down to his size and I didn't want to do it anymore. No more.

I heard women screaming and it sounded good to me. It made my erection harden. I wanted to take it out, show it off, show it to them, show it to my father—there, look at it! I'm not hiding it anymore.

They screamed and called my name and I loved it. The more I pummeled the face in front of me, the more it seemed that I had done it all wrong with Rachel. All wrong. This is how I should have done it. This is how she wanted it. Hit her hard. Ram her hard. Knock the wind out of her. And when I wanted to see her face, pull her back by the hair, not plead. And when I wanted to hear the words she was saying, pull her hair back, not plead. Pull it back and hit her hard. That's how women liked it. That's how they wanted it.

"Daniel! Daniel! What're you doing?"

Rachel was pulling me by the back of my shirt. Mrs. Dewey was crying. Freud and Misiora were standing up. Bimbo and his cronies were sprawled on the cinders. Patty was there too. I hadn't seen her come, but there she was, trying to lead Freud away.

"Are you crazy? What is the matter with you?" Rachel screamed at me. I stood up and spun around. She backed off.

"C'mon, Billy." Patty tried to lead Freud away. She pulled on his elbow, trying to get him to move. "C'mon, let's get out of here."

Mrs. Dewey was still crying. Bimbo lay on the ground and she crouched by his side. "You'll be okay, honey," she sobbed, "really, you will. You'll be fine." He tried to get up, but his knees gave out. His feet slipped on the loose gravel. Mrs. Dewey caught him just as he seemed ready to fall. Her arms slipped under his armpits and she struggled as she wept, trying to keep him from falling. His face looked terrible. It was torn and bleeding. Small cinders were stuck in the blood. Larger ones fell off as he dropped his head on Lavonne's shoulder. "Sure you will. You'll be just fine, honey," she sobbed. He leaned against her and her hands slipped down his exposed, fat waist and pulled up his trousers. He looked pathetic: too old, too fat, humiliated.

His friends didn't look any better. The two near Freud were trying to help each other up. Their clothes were torn, their flesh exposed, cinders caught in the rolls of fat, blood everywhere. Freud looked at them. Then he looked at me and seemed to be wondering if I could explain why he had done this to them.

"Please, Billy." Patty kept trying to move him, but he seemed rooted to the spot. "C'mon. Let's go home. It wasn't your fault."

The man I fought with looked the worst. Maybe it was because

I felt responsible for him. He was still on the ground. Both his eyes were swollen shut and his lower lip hung down as if torn at the corners of his mouth. He looked like some strange creature that had dropped down from the sky onto the wrong planet.

"That's right, honey." Mrs. Dewey led Bimbo to the car. "You see, I told you you'd be fine."

"C'mon, Billy. Let's get a ride back with them." Patty kept tugging at Freud. He kept looking at me. He didn't want to leave until somebody explained how all this had happened.

"I don't know," he moaned as if he had been the one that was hurt. "It was . . . they kept calling me names . . . and . . . I don't know."

"It wasn't your fault, Billy." Patty was desperate to leave.

He finally seemed to hear her. It wasn't his fault. He wanted to hear more. Maybe Patty had the answer. He ambled away with her.

One by one, Bimbo's friends got to their feet. I didn't look at them. I heard their feet crunching through the cinders as they walked away.

"You're crazy, Lavonne," Misiora shouted after her. "You don't know what the hell you want. You hear me, Lavonne. Lavonne!" He picked up the lead pipe and seemed ready to run after her and Bimbo and kill both of them. *"What the hell do you want from me?"*

Mrs. Dewey turned around. I couldn't see the expression on her face, but I saw the head turn.

"You remember what you told me, do you, Lavonne?" Misiora took a step forward. Mrs. Dewey said nothing. She looked at him for another full second and then, supporting her husband, one shoulder high in the air, the other sinking under his weight, she walked with him toward her car.

Misiora looked around, trying to find a direction in which to go. He seemed to be talking to himself. He ran out on Indianapolis Boulevard and stopped again. Then he began walking slowly, swinging his lead pipe, methodically demolishing the windshields of the parked cars.

Rachel stood about ten yards from me. I suddenly felt like Freud. I wanted her to come to me, to tell me how it wasn't my fault and to lead me away. I waited. But she just looked at me, her hair moving in the breeze. Down the boulevard, at regular intervals, we could hear Misiora smashing the windshields of parked cars.

I took a step toward her, but she gestured for me to stop. I did.

She seemed terrified of me. Why, then, didn't she leave? Why didn't she run away? What did she want?

"Rachel." I whispered her name, but she put her finger to her mouth. She didn't want me to speak. I obeyed.

But didn't I obey earlier as well? Didn't I see a look in her eyes that told me to do what I had done, and while I was doing it didn't she seem to like it? "You liked it, didn't you, Rachel?" I whispered again.

I took a step toward her and she took a step back. If she was afraid of me, why didn't she leave? The light from the moon made her face indecipherable, mercurial, now one thing, now another. Why was she chewing on a strand of her hair like that, nibbling on it with her lips? She seemed terrified of me and at the same time, unless it was the weird light of the moon, she seemed to be wondering again what it would be like to be loved by this person she saw. She seemed to be weighing the possibilities.

"Tell me," I asked her.

She kept nibbling on a strand of her hair. Far down the boulevard, I could still hear Misiora smashing away at the windshields. A part of me wanted to take that lead pipe and smash Rachel's head open and rummage through it for an answer. But I obeyed. I stood where she wanted me to stand and did not advance. I did not speak. And when she sensed that I was myself again and that she had nothing to be afraid of, she left. I wondered how she looked, what she was thinking about as she walked away.

I began to shiver. My shirt was wet with sweat and the breeze chilled me, caused me to shrink and shiver, and the physical act of shivering, of trembling, made me feel that I had done something terribly wrong.

Loose change was scattered across the gravel. A wallet belonging to one of the men had fallen there. It was ripped and some snapshots and cards lay among the silver coins. I thought about picking them up, but I just stood still. I couldn't move. I kept waiting, hoping this time, for God to appear and that lightning to strike and burn the sickening, sinful feeling from my stomach. I wanted to vomit, but I couldn't. I couldn't move and I couldn't stop shivering.

I looked up. The dark spots on the moon's surface made it look like a face mask, through which my father looked down at me.

"I'm still alive, Daniel."

Chapter 16

I t was a little before midnight when I got home. My mother was still at work.

Everything looked the same. Nothing in my house seemed affected by the events. No traces of disturbance. The kitchen table and the chairs looked normal, almost cozy, and even the couch in the living room where Rachel and I had made love seemed untouched and unloved on, eventless.

I had a glass of milk. After the strange events in the night, the milk looked astonishingly white. I kept looking at it between sips.

The fridge kicked on. The faucet dripped. The worn linoleum floor creaked as I walked to the sink. It was back to zero: home.

I went to the bathroom. In the medicine-chest mirror I saw my face. Gravel dust had clung to the sweat and the sweat had evaporated, leaving a black coating. I looked gaunt. I swung open the medicine chest and watched myself take a shower. I had bruises on my elbows and the water made them sting. Caked blood and dirt dissolved and went down the drain.

It was me. I could see myself in the mirror. Same eyes. Same face. Same body. There I was, coming into focus.

I kept soaping myself and washing off the suds and then soaping myself again. I shampooed my hair. I alternated hot and cold water. The sudden changes in temperature made me feel athletic and clean. My body tingled with simple sensations, easily understood. Hot and cold.

It was me. I brushed my teeth and then went to the kitchen and had another glass of milk.

The telephone rang.

Rachel. It had to be Rachel. Her voice would complete my transformation and restore me totally.

I picked up the phone. "Hello?"

"Daniel." It was my father. "Hello, Daniel."

I covered myself with a wet towel. It was as if he had materialized in front of me. All it took was hearing my name, hearing him say my name, to see the way his lips pulled back on the "D" in Daniel.

"Hi, Dad. How are you?"

"Still alive."

It was a strange connection. It had an echo to it. His voice seemed to be coming out of his bedroom at home.

"Glad? Are you glad?"

"About what, Dad?"

"That I'm still alive."

"Yes, of course I'm glad."

"I did a terrible thing, Daniel," he whispered. I saw the tip of his tongue as if he were going to lick me with it.

"What's that, Dad?"

"Your mother. I made your mother cry. She came to visit me and I made her cry."

I waited for him to explain. He said nothing.

"I'm sure you didn't mean to," I said.

I waited for a reply. He still said nothing.

"I'm sure . . ." I began talking. I couldn't bear the silence. "It's probably, you know, being in the hospital and all and . . . well . . . I'm sure she understands that you didn't mean to. It's just . . ."

I paused, but he didn't speak.

"Dad?"

"Yes? What is it?"

"Well, you didn't say anything and I . . ."

"Did you think I died?"

"No, of course not. It's just . . ."

"He died."

"Who died, Dad?"

"The man. The other man. The other patient in my room. He died. He is lying dead in his bed. I can see him. Nobody knows he died except for me. He died cursing Loretta. Do you know her?"

"No."

"He died cursing her. Your girl?" He whispered.

"My girl?"

"Yes. Her name? What is her name?"

I didn't want to say her name, not to him. I didn't want him to say her name.

"I don't have a girl, Dad."

"Oh, yes. A girl with a name. Your love, is that what she is?"

"No, I don't . . ." I stammered.

"In the crossword puzzle. Yes. She is ten down. Or is she five across? Rebecca. Is that her name?"

"Yes, Dad. It's Rebecca. That's her name."

I could hear him breathing into the phone. Was he laughing?

"Not nice. That's not very nice, Daniel. Lying. I know her name. Six letters . . . ten down, Rachel."

He grinned when he said it. I was sure of it.

"Both of you. Six letters. Daniel. Rachel. Six letters. I've been counting. Keeping score. There. Is she there now?"

"No."

"You're alone?"

"Yes."

"Lonely?"

"Oh, I'm . . ."

"Yearning. Is that what you're doing? Yearning for me to come home?"

"Yes, Dad," I said.

"Didn't mean to, eh?"

"What's that, Dad?"

"You're sure. Your mother. You're sure I didn't mean to make her cry?"

"I . . ."

He hung up. I put the receiver down. Maybe he would die soon. I was afraid of his disease reaching out from the hospital, infecting me, infecting Rachel, infecting us. It was as if he had known that this was my first lovemaking, known and enjoyed the way it had turned out.

I picked up the phone. I needed Rachel. I needed her love to help me fight the disease. I couldn't fight it by myself. Her father answered. I hung up. I didn't want to speak to anyone's father. I didn't trust any of them.

I went to bed imagining Rachel and myself making love again. It would be different next time. We had to do it again. Soon.

Sometime later, the light came on in the kitchen. My mother was home. She came and stood in my doorway. I could hear her crying. She stayed there, hoping to wake me with her crying, but I pretended to be asleep. I just couldn't get involved in her problems. I didn't want to hear about what had happened in the hospital. She stayed there crying. My eyes were half shut. Over her shoulder, through the window of the living room, I could see the moon.

Chapter 17

I t was too late. I got up early the next morning just so I could get out of the house without seeing my mother, but she was up, waiting for me.

She sat at the kitchen table, drinking coffee, smoking, still in her flannel nightgown. She looked tired, eyes puffy, yet when she saw me she smiled. I wanted to keep going, but she motioned to a chair. "Sit down, Daniel."

I sat down. For all my rebellious feelings, I was struck by how quickly I obeyed everyone: my mother, my father, Rachel. Do. I did.

She poured me some coffee into a demitasse cup the color of Rachel's earrings.

"You sleep good?"

"Yeah," I said. "And you?"

"No. Not so good." She sighed.

I looked down. I didn't want to know why and she wanted to tell me. We sipped our coffee.

Now that I was sitting down and drinking coffee, a part of me wanted to tell her, to brag, that I had made love to Rachel right there on that couch. I wanted to ask her—she was a woman, surely she knew—I wanted to ask her about women and how they liked their men to be, what it meant when they pulled away, when they looked tempted and terrified at the same time.

"Your father," she said softly. I looked up. Our eyes met. "Tsk! Tsk! Tsk!" She shook her head.

No, her mind was not on me.

"He talks to me." She paused. "He says . . . strange things, Daniel."

I looked down again. I didn't ask. I didn't want to know. When he was at home his presence dominated the house, and now he was far away and still he ruled.

"Poor man," she said. "He is very sick."

"Yes, I know."

"And now his hair, it is falling out. He is so proud of his hair and it is falling out. From treatments they give him. It makes it happen."

"Yes. I've heard of that."

"He thinks it is the hospital that is making him be sick. He wants to come home, Daniel."

I put the cup down and looked up at her. No, I wanted to tell her. Don't let him come home.

"But he should stay in the hospital, Mom. They have doctors and nurses there and . . . it's a very good hospital. I've read about it. They specialize in . . . cancer."

"I talk to the doctors, Daniel. Three doctors. And they tell me there is no hope. He will die, they say. But they also tell me that his head is not right. The cancer is all over his head, and they say to me, these doctors, he can be dangerous man and do dangerous things."

"He should stay in the hospital. They have people there who can look after him. They have nurses and medicine . . ."

"He wants to come home, Daniel. To die at home."

"But if he stays in the hospital, he might get better, Mom. People recover. Even from cancer. I've read about it. It happens."

"The doctors tell me there is no hope."

"I know what they've told you, but sometimes . . ."

"And something else, too. The insurance money. It is soon run out. One more week and then no more. Look, Daniel . . ." She reached down for her purse. "I will show you." She placed the purse on the table and took out of it a little green bankbook. "It is all the money we have," she said, looking at the little book. She opened the covers and then began flipping the pages slowly, looking at the dates and entries from years ago.

"I remember this. Your father got big check and we put it in bank. I remember that day." She pointed with her finger at an entry and then flipped to another page, looking it over, remembering, perhaps, other dates, other entries. This was her diary.

"You see." She turned the little book in my direction. "This is how much we have."

The last total showed: $9,200.

"We have almost ten thousand dollars." She whispered when she said the amount. The Devil might hear, otherwise. "I have worked very hard, I have saved money. Maybe buy a house without landlord. Maybe for you for college. Almost ten thousand dollars," she whispered again. She was very close to me. She smelled of coffee, cigarettes and bedclothes. I could see the white line of her scalp where her hair was parted.

"But hospital is so expensive. These treatments that kill your father's hair . . . so expensive. We have only one week and then no more insurance, Daniel. If these doctors say there is hope, then I give money from the bank to make your father live. I give gladly. You know that?"

"Yes, Mom. Of course."

"But they say there is no hope. Do we give them our money for no hope? No hope is very expensive in America. What do we do, Daniel?"

"I don't know, Mom."

"I don't know, too, Daniel. He wants to die at home. But doctors say he has 'violence' in him." She had learned a new word at the hospital. "They say it comes and goes. One hour he is normal person. Next hour there is violence. I am afraid. I don't know what he will do." She looked at the bankbook again. "So many years it takes to get almost ten thousand."

"Yes, I know."

"And so quickly it will go for treatments of no hope."

"I know." My voice was getting an edge to it. I just wanted to get out of the house. What could I tell her? Spend the money, Mom, and keep him away from me.

"You are smart boy, Daniel. What do you think we should do?"

"I don't know, Mom. I don't feel very smart. I don't know about these things. I can't think about it now. I just can't. I have things of my own." I got up.

"Where do you go?"

"I have to . . . some friends . . . I have to see them. I told them we'd meet. I gotta go, Mom."

She looked disappointed. She slipped the little green book into a plastic envelope and held it in her hand. "He is torturing me, Daniel," she said, wanting to tell me more.

I ran out of the house.

It should have been raining, but instead the sky was as blue as it gets in East Chicago and the sun was shining. The woman across the street was washing her windows and singing along with the radio.

Violence. The word stayed with me. "He has violence in him." I blamed my father for the violence that had erupted in me the night before. It was his fault. It was a trait I inherited from him. Like father, like son. I wondered what other traits of his were developing inside of me.

I spent the day circling around Aberdeen Lane, hoping to run into Rachel, but destiny took a day off. I didn't dare walk past her house, but from various corners I could see the sprinkler I had fixed —we had fixed—spraying water into the air. I took that as a favorable sign. Maybe it was her way of telling me not to worry. Maybe she was sitting up in her room, looking at it, thinking of me.

It was almost five o'clock. My mother had left for work and I was heading home. I turned right off Homerlee Avenue and saw Freud. He was ambling down the block toward me, kicking a tin can. When he saw me, he stopped. I stopped too. We stood there, pretending we hadn't seen each other. We were far enough away to pretend. I didn't want to talk to him. I didn't want to be reminded of what we had done by the firehouse and neither did he, probably. He bent down, picked up the tin can and looked at it as if reading the label. Then, just as I was deciding to be generous and walk toward him, he turned around, dropped the tin can on the sidewalk and began kicking it down the block in the opposite direction. I took the long way home, to make sure I didn't run into him again.

I watched TV. On the news they had a story about a "windshield vandal" who had smashed the windshields of more than fifty cars. They had no idea who it was. They suspected an out-of-town gang, and cited statistics about teenage violence on the rise.

The telephone rang. Instantly I thought of Rachel. It was Mr. Misiora. He sounded worried. Larry hadn't come home last night and he still wasn't home and they had no idea where he was. He wondered if I knew. I didn't. He thought he might be with me. I told him he wasn't. I promised to call him if I found out anything. He thanked me and hung up.

Chapter 18

I stayed in bed the next morning. When I heard my mother walking toward my room, I coughed several times. She came in.

"What is wrong, Daniel?"

"Oh, nothing." I coughed. "I just feel a little sick. I'll be fine. I just need to stay in bed and rest."

She looked worried. Her husband was dying. Her son was sick. "Does your chest hurt?"

"No, it's just . . . a touch of flu." I acted a little too brave and this made her suspect that I was hiding something. She came over and felt my forehead. Her hand was gentle and cool.

"I'll be fine, Mom, really." I tried to reassure her, but it seemed to have the opposite effect. "I just need to sleep some more."

"Yes, okay, I let you sleep."

I shut my eyes. She left. I felt guilty for pretending to be sick, but I could think of no other way. I wanted to stay home. For some reason I was sure that Rachel would call, and I wanted to be there when she did. But I didn't want to talk to my mother. I didn't want to hear about her visit to the hospital. About my father. I wanted to be left alone.

She tiptoed around the house. I lay in bed and waited for Rachel to call. I lay in my bed and I pictured my father lying in his. Maybe he was dying. Maybe on the very day that the insurance money ran out he would die. That seemed like one of those ironic possibilities, one of those coincidences that my mother would talk about for years to come. Yes, she would say, it is true. On same day that insurance stopped, he died. It is like he knew. She would cross herself and add, "May God rest his soul."

I pictured his funeral. My mother was on one side, Rachel on the other. Rachel had her arm under mine. My father's death had brought us closer together, closer than ever. I lay in bed and loved him for dying.

Something rattled in the kitchen. A short time later I heard grease sizzling and then caught the scent of crepes frying in a pan. My mother was making my favorite dish. How do I eat the crepes, I wondered, and still carry on as if I were sick?

She appeared in the doorway with a plateful of jam-filled crepes in one hand and a steaming cup of tea in the other. She watched me as I ate. I coughed and ate. I drank tea and coughed. She took the dishes away, and while she washed them in the sink, I waited for Rachel to call.

My mother left for work. Yes, I told her, I was feeling much better.

As soon as she was gone, I jumped out of bed. I checked the phone. It worked.

I got dressed. I was getting angry. I was sure Rachel knew I was waiting for her to call. I went in and out of the house several times thinking that as soon as I stepped out, the phone would ring. It didn't.

I began to feel stupid. I slammed the door shut and left, but my ears were still straining to hear the sound of the phone ringing as I walked away.

Our mailbox was on the front of the house, and sticking out of the mailbox lengthwise was a letter. Rachel, I thought.

I pulled the letter out. It had no stamp on it, but in the upper lefthand corner I saw a name: William Freund. William, yet! I couldn't believe it. Freud had written me a letter.

I walked up 149th Street toward Indianapolis Boulevard, staring at the envelope. I half suspected what he'd have to say and I just didn't feel like opening it. I threw it away in a trash can and then I went back and fished it out. I looked at the envelope some more. I imagined him sneaking up to the house, sticking the letter into the mailbox and then sneaking away. As if somebody his size could ever sneak.

I wondered if my telephone was ringing, if Rachel was calling, and I hated myself for wondering, hated her for not having called earlier. I had made my mother worry for nothing.

I stopped on the corner of 149th and Indianapolis Boulevard and the sound of the trucks and cars going by drowned out the noise in my head. I sat down on the bus-stop bench and opened the letter. The first thing I saw was a graduation picture of Freud. It fell out of the folded sheet of notebook paper. I started to read.

Dear Daniel,

I know this is stupid, but I am writing to you. I guess you know that by now. You know what's real stupid? All these years I knew where you lived, but I didn't know your address. So I had to walk to your house and drop it off in person. I was going to come and see you but I couldn't. And then I was going to call you on the phone, but I couldn't do that either. That's why I'm writing. I wasn't sure whether I could write you either, but I guess I can. I'll tell you why I'm writing. This is why, Daniel. It's because of what happened yesterday. You know, when we saw each other on that stupid street and then we stopped and then I walked away. You know what I was thinking when I walked away? I was thinking this: What the hell's wrong with you, William, you're walking away from your best buddy. That's what I was thinking. My best buddy and I walk away from him. I felt terrible right away and worse and worse afterwards. You're my best buddy and I do that. Walk away like that. Was I and am I ever sorry!

Here's why I did it. You know, after that night by the firehouse and all, what we did and all, seeing your girl and all, boy, is she pretty. Anyway, I don't know why I did it. I sort of know before I start writing, but as soon as I start, it gets lost. I just don't know. What can I tell you when I don't know. I just couldn't keep walking toward you. I was afraid we'd say something to each other that would make both of us hurt. I was afraid you were going to walk away first, so I thought I'd do it first before you did it. Maybe that's why I did it.

Anyway, here's the thing. It feels lonely not having you for a buddy. I'm still not sure what happened exactly by the firehouse, but it seems to me if we're real good buddies, we can forget about it, the hell with it, you know, let's forget about it and be like we were before. Can we do that, Daniel? That's really why I'm writing to you. To ask you if we can do that. Just forget about it and be like before. I can't be like I was before by myself. I tried. It makes me feel weird and lonely and makes me hurt all over being like this. So, how about it? Yes or no?

The reason I'm doing all this like this, you know, writing instead of coming to see you or calling you on the phone, the reason is this. If you say no, I won't have to hear it from you. So, if you read this letter and you still want to say no, please don't call me on the phone or come to my house to tell me. Please don't. Write me a letter. I guess if you do write me a letter,

I'll know you're saying no without even opening it, but I will open it and read it. I promise.

Anyway, that's why I'm writing.

Your old buddy,
Billy

P.S. I'm sending you my graduation picture. We never did exchange pictures, you know. I thought we did, but now I don't think so. If we did, I lost yours.

I folded the letter and looked at his picture again. It was a nice shot. He looked rugged and handsome, one of those faces you see on *Look* magazine's all-American team: square jaw, strong neck, long but neatly combed hair, white teeth, a crooked smile, a look bordering on shyness. You would never think that a person who looked like that would be called Freud or be writing a letter like this. On the back of the picture, he had signed his full name and written the date: William Francisco Freund, Summer 1961.

I put the picture inside the letter and the letter back inside the envelope.

A bus pulled over and stopped. I waved it off. Freud's letter weighed like a brick in my hand. What the hell was I supposed to do?

Indianapolis Boulevard was the business detour for U.S. 41, and trucks rolled and tumbled past me in both directions. I wished I were on one of them. I didn't want to be anybody's son anymore, anybody's friend, lover. I didn't want to have an address or a telephone number, or a home. Nothing. I was tired of it all. A bum, that's what I wanted to be. One of those derelicts who sleep on benches, pee in public and poke through trash cans. I felt as if I had lived long enough, seen enough, heard enough. I could live without Rachel and my mother's crepes.

A Sunrise Oil Company truck roared past me through the light. The cartoon mascot on the back smiled his huge smile. The sun always shines. Where was Misiora, I wondered. His father had sounded so worried.

I lay down on the bench. Yeah, just like a bum. I pulled my shirt out. The hell with it. A bus pulled in and let off some passengers. They walked around me. Those staying on looked at me through the windows. Maybe some of them knew me or knew my parents.

I wondered what they were thinking. Isn't that Mrs. Price's boy, Daniel? Look at him! What a shame. A bum. And I hear he got an A in English Lit. His poor parents.

The bus pulled away, the driver aiming the exhaust right in my face. Sometime later, a woman carrying a baby almost sat down on my head. She screamed. Then she nearly apologized. Then she walked up the boulevard to wait for the bus at another stop. I could see the baby's face peeking over her shoulder.

I thought of writing letters to everyone I knew, telling them of my decision. Dear Mother: Please don't look for me. I'm happy and healthy and a bum. You can rent my room and make some extra money.

I recognized the car's color first, sky-blue, as the Packard came to a stop at the intersection. It just rolled into my field of vision. I recognized the scratch on the passenger side, and looking up, her elbow on the rolled-down window, her chin resting in her hand, was Rachel. Her father was driving, but I only saw his hands on the wheel, fingers tapping, waiting for the light to change. Their radio was playing.

Rachel looked directly at me. The right side of her face was pushed up by her hand, wrinkled, squinty-eyed, like she was aiming at me lazily, reading my mind, shooting down my thoughts with thoughts of her own. Her lips, puffy from the pressure of her hand, seemed ready to move, to speak.

I lay there, determined not to move or be moved. I had retired from the service. I was a bum. She tilted her head, her right earring dangled into view, and then, just as the light changed, she smiled, a sly crack of a smile as if telling me that she and I had a secret and a past. Her father slipped the car into first and drove her away.

I wanted to continue lying there, at least the bum in me did, but the other bum, the panhandler for love, hope and destiny, made me sit up. I started thinking, analyzing, reappraising the situation, decoding Rachel's smile. It was just a crack, but a crack in a door that gave me a glimpse of hope.

"Rachel." I spoke her name out loud and the tuning fork inside me vibrated to the sound of her name.

It was no accident. It was all preordained. I looked at Freud's letter as further proof of Fate at work. If he hadn't written me a letter, I would never have sat down on this particular bench to read it. The chances of my being here just as Rachel drove by seemed remote. And yet it had happened. It could not have happened for nothing. It was destiny.

I saw a crossword puzzle where Daniel and destiny met at the letter D. Daniel down. Destiny across. And the "l" in Daniel becoming the "l" in Rachel. The fact that both of our names ended in the same letter struck me as a revelation. It all meant something and it was all there in her smile.

I stood up.

Chapter 19

My mother was still asleep when I left to take my position, my observation post. Men in summer suits were appearing in the doorways of Aberdeen Lane at regular intervals, getting into their cars and driving off to their jobs. One of them came out carrying a cup of coffee. He sat in the car drinking it. He lit a cigarette. He turned on the car radio. He looked at himself in the rear-view mirror. He opened the car door as if he were going to go back in the house and then changed his mind, slammed the door shut and drove away.

I sat down on the grass. Through the spaces left by departed cars, I could see Rachel's house. I leaned on a tree trunk and waited.

An hour or so later, she appeared in the upstairs window. Her father must have said something to her. She turned her head. I heard the music of her voice and then she looked out again, looked up at the sky and put on her earrings, paying no attention to what she was doing, first the right one and then the left. The pajama top she wore was unbuttoned, but I couldn't see how far down. It was too big for her. She reached inside and rubbed the back of her shoulder, making her chin, her lips, her nose disappear inside the crook of her elbow. Only her eyes showed.

A door must have opened somewhere in the house and the cross-wind made the curtains in her window fly out. White, veillike curtains fluttering, filling with air, rising, falling, dancing across her face.

Then she left. I readjusted my position and settled in once again. A woman came out of the house behind me. It was her tree I was leaning on, her grass I was sitting on. She smiled quickly at me, a little disturbed by my presence on her property, but somehow accepting it as the way things were these days. She put what looked like a shopping list into her purse and walked in the direction of Kroger's Supermarket.

I didn't see a sign of Rachel for the next two hours. I began to feel hungry, but the hunger felt fine. It seemed to intensify my concentration and made me pick out the shapes of individual leaves on individual trees. Hunger also turned my snooping into a job. Yes, I was hungry, but I would not leave my post. I had a job to do.

A little after noon, she appeared in the doorway. She came out wearing a pleated tartan skirt and a blue T-shirt much too big for her. It hung at the armpits. She carried her shoes and socks in her hand.

I was going to get up and cross the street toward her, but the thrill of observing her undetected had by now grown too strong. It was as if I expected to see something I hadn't seen before, for her to reveal a part of herself she kept hidden from me, something that would complete her, explain her once and for all. I had no idea what I was looking for, but I did feel a hungry purpose and an exhilarating sense of danger hiding there, waiting for clues.

She sat down on the front steps and pulled on her knee socks. She slipped a couple of rubber bands high above her calves and then rolled the tops of the socks over to hide them. She got up and jammed her feet into her shoes, starting to walk before she was quite inside of them.

Her father came out. "Rachel. Where're you going?"

"I'll be back."

"Don't forget, I have to—"

"I don't forget." She cut him off and kept walking.

He stood in the doorway, wearing the Japanese bathrobe, and even from the front I could see the bulging outline of his huge calves. I lay low until he went inside and then I ran after Rachel, ducking behind cars when I suspected she might turn around.

From a bum to a sleuth in less than a day.

Usually when she walked her hips moved hardly at all, like a hurdler's. Now she swung them left and right on purpose, looking down to watch her kilt sway.

I followed her to the library. I found another hiding place and waited for her to come out.

Misiora, "William" and I used to go to the library to do our homework and whisper. I remembered making plans to read the entire encyclopedia before I graduated from high school. I began with Aardvark and stopped at Abyssinia. The first had a hairy body and powerful digging claws. The second was now known as Ethiopia.

An old Jiminy Cricket song popped into my head and I hummed it to myself, waiting for Rachel.

"Curiosity, people say, killed the kitty cat
One fine day
Well this may be true but hear me,
Here is what you do
For curiosity:
Get the encyclopedia
E-N-C-Y-C-L-O-P-E-D-I-A"

Freud, Misiora and I used to sing this song sometimes on our way to the library. We sang it like a hymn, marching in step, swinging our arms. The last line was our favorite part. Our voices got deep, our faces stern as we marched up the library steps spelling out: E-N-C-Y-C-L-O-P-E-D-I-A.

Misiora was still missing. I had called his parents the night before. The phone hardly had a chance to ring before his mother answered it. She was hoping I knew something and was greatly disappointed to find that I didn't. We talked for about five minutes, each of us reassuring the other that Larry was fine. I bet, I kept saying, I bet he's fine. I bet he just went somewhere for a drive. I bet he'll be back soon.

The library door opened and Rachel came out carrying three huge books.

She walked home slowly, looking through them, stopping now and then to stick a finger inside her knee socks and rub the place where the rubber band pressed against the flesh. When she bent over, the hem of her skirt rose and a large tendon on the back of her thigh tightened.

I suddenly remembered, as if it were something I could have forgotten, that I had actually made love to her. The fact of having done it thrilled me all over again. I wanted to make love to her once more. The desire was different this time. It wasn't so much a physical craving as a need to prove to myself that there had been no mistake. That she was mine.

Her father was sitting on the steps waiting for her. They looked through the big books together, pointing at pages, laughing. He put his arm around her. She put her head on his lap. They looked so easy and relaxed that I couldn't quite pinpoint which I missed more: that my father and I had never had a moment like this or that Rachel and I hadn't.

Her father looked at his watch. He tried to lift her head off his lap, but she relaxed, playing dead, so that it took some doing to extricate himself. He left her sprawled across the steps and went inside. She put the books under her head. He came out carrying a camera. Once again they played. He had to step over her and when he did, she grabbed the cuff of his trousers. He stumbled and laughed. He wanted her to come with him. She sat up by raising her legs and then dropping them, letting their momentum raise her body. He urged her to come with him. She shook her head. He got into his car and drove off.

A newspaperboy rode down her side of the block, throwing papers on the lawns. She suddenly jumped to her feet and ran out, stopping at the sprinkler. She jumped around, attracting his attention, bashing her fist into her palm, like an outfielder. The kid got the message. He flung the paper high in the air toward her. She waved off the other imaginary ballplayers and snared the paper with one hand. The kid laughed. She waved the paper high over her head. Then she just stood there, watching the kid riding his bike down the block. She seemed to want to run after him. And then some weariness came over her. She let the paper drop on the grass and just stared at it as if she had made a mistake letting it fall, but didn't have the energy to bend down and pick it up.

I watched her, mystified, wondering what was going through her mind.

Slowly, dragging her feet across the grass, she walked to the side of the house and turned the water on and off, making it shoot out of the sprinkler and then die in midair, only to shoot up again. She did this for ten or fifteen minutes, her face leaning on the siding, her free arm swinging. Then, slowly, dragging her feet across the wet grass, she went inside, taking the books with her.

The woman whose lawn I was using as my hiding place returned from the supermarket, not very pleased to see me still there. She carried her shopping bags high, up to her nose, and she looked at me across two loaves of Wonder bread. She pulled her curtains shut when she went inside.

I wondered what Rachel was doing. Maybe she was calling me. Maybe she had a diary and was writing in it. When she had turned the sprinkler on and off, I was sure she was thinking of me.

I leaned on my tree and shut my eyes. I began daydreaming about what it would be like the next time Rachel and I made love. The first time was consummation. The second time was the final surrender. She would talk to me afterward and tell me everything. For some reason I saw her crying in my daydream, and for some reason I loved wiping away her tears.

Two quick slam-bangs made me open my eyes. By the time I looked, Rachel was out on the lawn again, the doors slammed shut behind her. She was wearing my jacket over her T-shirt and she seemed like another person, full of energy, her hair bouncing as she walked. She kicked the newspaper back toward the house and took off down the block. Hiding behind trees and cars, staying low and out of sight, I took off after her. I felt like a hunter, stalking his prey. She was wearing my jacket!

She walked fast, skipping at times, determined, it seemed to me, not to give in to weariness again. She might have been humming a tune. I followed her for several blocks in one direction and then for several blocks in another. She seemed to be just walking, instead of heading anywhere. She stopped at a clearing near an overpass. It was a little field of bleached grass that wasn't yet an official park. They were still trying to come up with a name for it. She stopped and looked. I crouched low and moved up to see what she was looking at.

There on the field, I saw four cheerleaders from my high school. They were dressed in purple and white cheerleading outfits and were practicing. Staying in shape for next year. They had a next year. Juniors.

They waved their arms in unison, they jumped, they smiled, their purple and white standing out in sharp contrast to the gray of the neighborhood and the bleached green of the grass.

"We are the riders
Mighty, mighty riders

Everywhere we go-o
People want to know-o
Who-o-o we a-are
So-o-o we tell them
We are the riders
Mighty, mighty riders
Everywhere we go-o . . ."

They kicked together, beaming and sweating, their short purple skirts flying off their rears. And then Rachel joined them. She stayed where she was, but she moved as they moved, tentatively at first, picking up the steps and the gestures and then, getting the hang of it, imitating them in perfect synch. Arms left, arms right, high over the head and then kick, dip down and do it again. She moved like one of them.

"Victory, victory
That's our cry
V-I-C-T-O-R-Y!
Yeah!"

The practice lasted another half an hour. Then the girls collapsed on the grass in a little group, talking and laughing. Rachel stood and watched them. I watched her.

She wanted to join them. I could tell that. Anybody could tell that, just by seeing her. Usually confident and supremely self-possessed, even manipulative, she now stood there like an outcast, hoping for an invitation.

Then, suddenly, she started crying. I couldn't see the tears, I couldn't hear the sobs, but I saw her lips distort, saw her head bend down, saw her wiping her eyes with the sleeve of my jacket, her body shaking in spasms.

To go up to her now, I knew, would be a mistake and yet I wanted to, as terrible as it sounded, to make the best of an opportune moment. I didn't know why she was crying. I loved her so much that my heart ached for her, but at the same time I sensed that if there ever was a chance for me to move back into her life, this was it.

Crouching low, almost running on all fours like a dog, I scurried back in the direction from which we had come. I stopped a couple of blocks later and crossed to her side of the street. I could see her from there: skirt, knee socks, my jacket.

I waited.

A few minutes later, I saw her turn and head in my direction. I started toward her, looking down at the ground, pretending I didn't see her, absorbed in my own thoughts. I tried not to overdo it. I was halfway down my block, she was halfway up hers, when I heard her call my name.

"Daniel!"

I looked up and pretended to be shocked. She ran toward me, wiping her eyes. Something told me to pay attention, watch her closely and remember the sight of her running toward me, arms open, calling my name.

"Daniel!" She flung her arms around my neck. "I was just thinking about you. And here you are! You're getting a kiss. No, two. And two more!"

She kissed me on my cheeks, making loud sounds, kissed me on one ear and made it ring. I hadn't expected this. I was hoping to reconnect our severed ties gradually, perhaps get another smile out of her at best. Her welcome overwhelmed me.

"What're you doing here? Tell me, why did you come this way?"

"Oh"—even my "oh" was a lie—"I don't know. I sort of had a feeling I might run into you."

"Did you really? Really and truly?"

"Yes."

"I love it when that happens." Her eyes shone.

She grabbed one of my arms with her two and dragged me home. It became impossible to scrutinize her when she was that close to me. I became a part of her landscape, an extension of her mood, and I loved it.

She talked nonstop. She had checked out some books from the library. One of them was a picture book of Greece. A woman in the book had on the same earrings she had. Exactly the same. She talked about Aberdeen Lane. It must be nice in the fall when the leaves turn. When they just begin to turn. We'll have to make sure to see the first, the very first leaf that falls.

I didn't really understand why she was so loving toward me, what had caused it to happen, nor could I think about it at that moment. I would figure it all out later and make it fit. For the present, I listened to the music of her words, I felt her body, and more than anything else I loved hearing about the two of us. The fall. We were together in the fall. That was months away. I told her about a hill outside town where in winter we could go sledding, and about Cedar Lake, where kids went ice-skating. She loved ice-skating. My immediate future was being insured, as if she were signing a contract to be with me through autumn.

We sat down on her porch steps. She put her head on my lap and as I reached across to play with her earring, I suddenly remembered hiding across the street, looking at her lying down, just like this, with her head on her father's lap. I was sitting exactly where he had been sitting. I could see the very tree from behind which I had observed them. For a split second I was in both places at the same time, and I had the unsettling feeling that the "I" behind the tree was detecting something that the "I" on the porch steps couldn't see.

"Do you think a person can ruin his life?" Rachel asked, casually, lazily, as if asking what movies were playing in Hammond.

I looked away from the tree.

"What person?"

"A person. Any person. You know, you hear people say: He ruined his life. She ruined her life. You think it's possible?"

"Sure."

"You do?" She sat up. "Really?"

Having expected a rambling exchange, I wasn't prepared to defend my position.

"Yeah, don't you?"

"How?" she asked.

"How what?"

"How can you ruin it?"

She seemed to be staring at my mouth, from where the answer would come. It made my lips go dry.

"How? You know how . . . you know . . . making mistakes." I thought of my father as I stammered.

She shook her head.

"No," she said, "I don't think it's possible. You want to know what I think? All that stuff that people call 'ruining your life,' all it means is having a different kind of life than the one they thought you should have. Or even you thought you should have. Plans." She nodded. "Plans can be ruined, friendships, affairs and omelettes, but not life. I'm positive of it."

But she wasn't. When she was positive of something, she didn't bother to check to see if I was convinced of it. She did now. The hem of her skirt reached just above the knees and her knees were brown and bumpy. She reached over and pushed down her knee socks. There were two red ridges left by the rubber bands, and I ran my finger over them. Her legs were warm from the sun.

The telephone rang inside her house. She didn't budge. Not a move.

"Aren't you going to answer it?"

She shook her head across my lap. "No."

It rang and rang. It made me tense to hear it ringing. I couldn't understand how she could just lie there. I found it fascinating and threatening. Would she do that when I called, too?

It finally stopped.

"I wonder who that was?" she said.

"Well, why didn't you answer it?"

"Because then I'd know for sure. Now I can wonder and wonder the rest of the day."

That's just what I did all the way home. If I expected to get to the bottom of her, there was still a long way to go.

It was getting dark. I walked slowly. I had put in a hard day's work following Rachel around and now I was slightly tired, slightly frustrated, and more in love than ever with a girl I didn't really know.

The telephone was ringing when I stepped inside my house. I rushed to pick it up and then I stopped a few feet away from it. I let it ring. I forced myself to stand still and not answer it. If she could do it, so could I. I wrestled with her as the phone continued to ring. It rang and rang.

Chapter 20

Do you have to go?"

"Sure. I must."

It was Sunday and my mother was going to visit my dad at the hospital. She was even skipping church to do it. God, she told me, He will understand. She was certain of His understanding. She was certain of everything. She was wearing a black skirt and blouse that she had knitted herself. The lightweight wool clung to her body, making her look, at least to me, very unmotherly.

"It is wrong," she told me. "Other women, they come and visit their men in hospital and they look so miserable. They wear ugly clothes. They don't comb hair. They look more sick than people they visit. It is wrong. When you go to hospital you must make sick people remember how beautiful life is outside. So I go and look beautiful."

She wasn't bragging, just stating her policy. She took a couple of pencils and sharpened them with a kitchen knife in the sink. She sharpened them the same way she peeled potatoes. My dad probably needed them for his crossword puzzles. She put the pencils in her purse and looked at me.

I thought she was going to ask me to come with her. For once I was ready to go.

"It is very nice outside," she said. "You should go for a walk."

"Yes, I will."

"Okay. I see you this evening."

She left, her purse bulging. She carried her black high-heeled shoes in there. They weren't good for walking, but she would put them on when she got to the hospital.

It was hot in the apartment. The windows were open but there was no breeze. Sunshine was pouring in, making picture frames on the walls.

I picked up the telephone and called Rachel. The phone rang and rang. She wasn't at home or she wasn't answering. She would never make a definite date the day before. I had to call or take a chance and go there.

I was sorry my mother had gone. I felt like being her son, being something more certain than Rachel's lover. I felt very lonely, maybe because it was Sunday and because I missed my former life. One by one those ties had been severed. I hadn't seen Freud since that awkward moment in the street. I hadn't seen Mrs. Dewey since the night by the firehouse. Misiora had vanished. It was as if my past was vanishing as well. My present was something I was trying to get through. All I had was a future, and my future was in the hands of a girl I loved but a girl I hardly knew. I no longer carried my life and my identity with me wherever I went. I had to be with Rachel to feel it. I had to go and see Rachel to feel myself coming into focus. River Rachel was carrying me away, making me seem like a stranger in a town where I had spent my entire life. It wasn't that I objected to being swept away. It was the uncertainty, the intermittence, the whimsical nature of the sweep. Having to wait for it.

I called her again and once again the phone rang and rang and nobody answered. I slammed down the receiver and left the apartment. It was cooler outside. As I walked past the mailbox I remembered Freud's letter.

I had nowhere to go except to hang around Aberdeen Lane and wait for Rachel to show up.

Freud would be glad to see me, I thought. Surely he was still my friend. I would apologize to him for having remained silent so long. He would understand. Put it there, Billy. We would shake hands and from a clumsy handshake we would stumble into a clumsy but warm embrace. I saw it all.

Part of my past waited in Freud's garage, and I hurried toward it.

Sunday afternoon traffic was light. People were either dressed for church or the beach.

I took the alleyway when I got to his street. There were always puddles in Freud's alley, cinder lakes everywhere. Even when it didn't rain for weeks, there were always puddles there. I could hear a radio blaring from Freud's garage. Perry Como was singing "Yellow Bird." Over the song I could hear hammering. Still fixing it up. His own place.

I was a few yards away when a telephone rang. The hammering stopped. The music stopped. The phone rang once again and then I heard Freud's voice.

"Hello. Oh, hi, Patty."

I stopped and leaned on a steel drum that he used as a trash can. The steel was warm, almost hot.

"I'm doing nothing," Freud said, and although he was speaking softly, his foghorn voice spilled out of the garage. "Just messing around in the garage, fixing it up. Yeah, I'm in the garage. How? I had a phone put in, that's how! I told you I was going to have a phone put in the garage. Well, it's in. I'm talking on it. Yeah! It's just an extension but it's still my personal phone and not my mother's."

There was a short pause.

"It's a wall phone."

Another pause.

"Because I like a wall phone, that's why. I mean, with a wall phone you always know where it is. Well . . ." Although I didn't see him I could imagine him shrugging. "I didn't know you didn't like wall phones, Patty. You never said nothing. I guess the subject never came up, eh? Ha!" His sudden laughter exploded and died. "Black. It's black. You like black?"

I waited. I didn't want to interrupt anything. I had imagined Freud sitting in the garage lonely and silent when I arrived. That was how I wanted him: shocked and thrilled by my appearance. Patty was ruining it all.

"No, I don't need a rug, Patty. You see, what I like is taking a hose and hosing down the floor. If I had a rug . . ."

"William!" His mother's voice rang out, not as deep but just as loud as Freud's. I peeked around the corner and saw her standing inside the back door of the house.

"William!"

"Hold on, Patty," Freud said. "It's my mother." Then his voice boomed out. *"What the hell you want, Mom?"*

"I want you to get off the phone, that's what I want!" she shouted back.

"Hey, Mom?" Freud stayed in the garage. He didn't have to come out. If she had been two blocks away she could have heard him. *"I'm talking to Patty. You mind?"*

"I don't care who you're talking to. I have to use the phone."

"Hey, Mom?"

"Yes?"

"You can have the phone in a little bit. Okay?"

"No, it's not 'okay.' I want you to get off the phone now."

"Hey, Mom?"

"Yes?"

"Why don't you come here and get me off, then!"

She went back inside. He went back to talking to Patty.

"It's just my mom. It's nothing. She's just a bitch, that's all."

Suddenly his voice changed.

"Hey, Mom. Get off the phone, will you? It's my extension and I'm talking to Patty. Say something, Patty. No! Don't hang up. I want to talk to you. No, I don't want to talk to you later. I want to talk to you now."

Then his voice changed again.

"Mom, goddammit, you made her hang up. I mean, what kind of a bitch are you, Mom? That's right. That's the word I used, all right. Bitch! Sure I'll say it again. Bitch! You want me to spell it out for you, too?"

My entrance, I figured, was ruined. Patty and Mrs. Freund had taken care of that. It seemed like a bad day to try to reconnect with Freud. I walked away, through the puddles, the way I had come.

"B-I-T-C-H," his voice thundered behind me.

When I got out of the alley I crossed the street and took another alleyway, and then another. Down the alleys I went, poking along past backyards and Sunday barbecues. It was as if I had run away from Rachel and after many years returned to visit the town where I was born.

A stranger.

Long before I got to Misiora's house I saw the orange and blue flame of the Sunrise Oil Company burning high in the air. Since there was no wind the flame burned straight, like a huge cigarette lighter. A sense of duty and necessity drove me to his house.

I knocked. His parents opened the door. They stood close together in the doorway. Both of them smiled, glad to see me.

"Come in. Come in."

I went inside. It felt pleasant to see people who still remembered me.

Mrs. Misiora's inevitable cookies arrived on a tray. Pumpkin cookies, of all things, truly terrible but in a nostalgic, familiar way, and I kept eating them, much to the delight of both of them.

Larry's high school diploma was on the wall above the TV set in a dark wood frame, their most treasured possession.

His mother asked about my mother, his father about my father. I told them what I could. How was I doing? Fine, I told them.

Then, we all knew, it was time to talk about Larry. It was my turn to ask. They didn't know anything. He had left in his car and they hadn't heard from him since. I tried to theorize about his motives for disappearing the way he had. They both listened to me attentively, so attentively it hurt. They thought I knew something they didn't. Something bordering on reverence for those with an education was in their eyes.

"I kind of knew," I claimed, "that he would do something like this. He hinted to me that he needed some time to himself. He'll be back soon, I bet. I just bet he will. You know Larry . . ."

It was clear they didn't. The more I talked, the more I realized that I didn't really know him either. First the poem and now this. His unpredictability angered me. He was my friend. I had known him for years. I was supposed to know him. More than anything else it angered me that he had done something I wanted to do and couldn't: run away.

"I know Larry. He'll be back. You'll see."

His parents listened to every word I said. They sat close together, like a couple of bookends, but as close as they were, they could not hide the painful emptiness between them. Nor could I fill it. I was a voice and they listened to it. But they wanted their son back.

I had some more pumpkin cookies and then I got up. Both of them saw me to the door. Both of them thanked me for coming. I thanked them for the cookies.

The sun was setting. I had stayed longer than I thought. Across the street the cartoon Sunrise characters smiled and waved from the huge steel tanks of the oil company.

There was really only one more place I could visit. So I headed toward Mrs. Dewey's house, no longer expecting anything, but merely determined to finish off the list. I had tried to reconnect with my past and I felt lonelier than ever. I couldn't imagine where Larry was, but the thought of him being free filled me with envy and resentment. Why couldn't I run away?

Night had fallen by the time I shuffled to Mrs. Dewey's house. Bimbo's car was gone but hers was parked outside. The curtains were parted and I saw her in the living-room window. She was playing a violin. I stood there listening for at least twenty minutes, trying to discern the melodic line, but I think the piece that she was playing was unfamiliar to both of us.

It felt strange being there without Misiora and Freud. The three of us. It had always been the three of us. Even when she stopped playing, I couldn't get myself to go to her door. Not alone.

Chapter 21

I continued seeing Rachel every day, and every night I'd lie in bed trying to incorporate some newly discovered details of her personality into the existing portrait. She seemed young, almost childish, one day, and the next she would be, or seem to be, a woman much older than I. She would hold on to me as we kissed goodnight, not wanting to let me go, and then when she saw me the next day she would be distant and cool as if the night before had never happened. I couldn't tell if she was doing this just to frustrate me, or if it had nothing to do with me. I couldn't tell why she smiled when she smiled; why she suddenly felt a need to pick on me; why she cried when she cried. When I pressed her about her tears she just waved me off.

"I don't know. Just something sad I remembered."

"What? What was it?"

"Oh, just something. Nothing to do with you."

What bothered me the most was the lack of continuity, a sense of progress in our relationship. My life stopped when we parted at night and when I saw her the next day I wanted it to pick up where we had left off, but hers seemed to have continued without me and I was always trying to catch up, trying to figure out where we were, without having the slightest clue how we got there.

I tried to remind her of the plans we had made for the seasons ahead. If I couldn't have continuity in the present, I figured I would try for the future. I talked about ice-skating in winter on Cedar Lake.

"Are there cedars there?" she asked.

That was hardly the point. I couldn't really remember having been there but once.

"Yes, there are. Countless cedars." I thought maybe she liked cedars. "It's real nice," I went on. "Ice-skating with all those cedars there."

She didn't seem interested in either.

"I used to go up to Lake Oscawana when I was small." She changed lakes like she changed topics, out of the blue. "Lake Oskar Werner, we called it." She smiled. She could tell by my face that I didn't know who this Oskar Werner was. "You don't know who Oskar Werner is?" She frowned. "Don't you go to movies?"

"Sure. I love movies. Want to go tomorrow?"

"And you don't know who Oskar Werner is?"

"I told you . . ."

"He's only the loveliest, saddest actor I've ever seen. Like a sad bird. I guess his movies wouldn't come to East Chicago. He doesn't play the boondocks." Her eyes flashed and she leaned back for one of those scrutinizing looks. "Daniel Boondocks Price." She started to laugh. "It's funny."

"No, it's not."

"How wrong you are, Boonie-boy. It's real funny."

She wanted to hurt me, and as long as I feigned indifference she kept going after me. Finally I couldn't pretend anymore. I walked away. She ran after me, past me, and walking backwards, so she could look at me, she peered into my downcast face.

"You know what?" She seemed genuinely apologetic. "It's not funny. I made a mistake."

I hated being manipulated. I wanted to resist, but I couldn't. She looked so beautiful, sashaying backward like that. And then she spread out her arms and began sliding her feet across the sidewalk as if she were ice-skating with me, going backward across Cedar Lake. I took her actions as a reaffirmation of our plans, and I was hooked again.

It rained the next day and we spent the afternoon sitting on her porch. Raindrops clung to the screens like cobwebs. The newspaperboy rode by on his bicycle in a yellow raincoat. He threw the paper onto the porch steps. She made no move to get it. She just sat, rocking in a rocking chair, and when she lit a cigarette she reminded me of my mother, but I didn't know why. I stood up and got the paper. I made a big show of being wet when I came back inside, but she didn't look. I sat down and slipped the rubber band off the paper. I thought of her knee socks, but she wasn't wearing them. I wondered if she remembered, as I did, my finger moving across her warm flesh. Her father appeared in the window behind us and smiled at me. I smiled back at him. Rachel just rocked.

I opened the Hammond *Times*. There was a picture of John and Jackie Kennedy on the front page. I hated baseball, but I checked the scores. Ernie Banks had hit two home runs. They had an article on his wrists. It was all in the wrists. I checked the movies, looking for something with Oskar Werner. *Ben-Hur* was playing at the Parthenon. "Want to go see *Ben-Hur?*"

She shook her head.

I flipped through the paper and then stopped when I saw a picture of Larry Misiora. "Still missing," it read under his picture. It was a short article, quoting his parents as saying they had no idea where he was, no idea why he disappeared, but they hoped to God he was all right. I didn't know where they got that picture of him for the paper. It didn't look like the mean Misiora I knew. His hair was combed, his eyes soft, and in place of the sarcastic grin there was a boyish smile. When did he feel like this, I wondered, and who was there to snap the shutter?

Still missing. The phrase stung me. It covered all the people I had abandoned for Rachel's sake. I looked at her, wanting something right then and there in return.

She rocked, staring straight ahead, through the enclosure of the screens, through the rain, across the lawn. There, reflected in the car window, I saw her father, looking at us through the parted curtain of the window behind us. I froze. I didn't want him to know that I saw him. I pretended to be looking at the newspaper, but I couldn't take my eyes off his reflection.

This went on for several minutes. Her father withdrew. Her face changed. It began to rain harder.

"Maybe you were right," she said.

Out of nowhere. I hadn't the slightest clue to what she was talking about.

"Right about what?" I asked. It wasn't often that I was right around her, and even though there was a "maybe" attached to it, I wanted to know what it was.

"What you said."

I racked my brain, but I couldn't think of anything I had said. "What I said when?"

She frowned. "You mean you forgot already?"

"I'm sure I didn't forget, it's just that I don't know . . ."

She got up. The rocker continued rocking. She seemed disgusted with me.

"Rachel, how am I supposed . . ."

She covered up her ears, not wanting to listen. Then she walked out in the rain, across the lawn, down the block. Gone.

Her father came out with a drink in his hand. I didn't want to stay, but I didn't want to jump up and leave, either. The empty rocker continued to rock, and for some absurd reason I decided to leave when the rocker stopped, as if that were the accepted, sociable thing to do.

David toasted me with his glass and took a sip. He glanced at the downpour.

"What a chaser, huh?" He smiled.

I smiled.

The rocker stopped. I made a great show of folding the newspaper. I got up. "I guess I better . . ."

"Still guessing?" He cut me off. It was a courteous cutoff. Friendly. Intimate, almost. I didn't like it. He looked at me as if he knew me well. I left.

My mother no longer came to my room at night after work. She bore whatever she was bearing alone. Either she sensed that I didn't want to know anything about my father, or she chose to be heroic and keep it all to herself. On different days, I came to different conclusions. New wrinkles were forming in her face, old ones deepening. I could always tell when she had spent the night crying, but I never asked why.

My father was becoming a memory of my father. He didn't really exist anymore. He had evaporated, vanished. If nobody mentioned his name, he would never come back.

Every now and then in the newspaper or on television there would be a story about some famous person who had died of cancer, and if they happened to mention "the agony of cancer" or "medication to relieve the suffering," only then would I be forced to think of my father as a real human being, lying in a real bed, crying out with pain. When I could not keep that image out of my mind, I rushed to Rachel for relief. She was the living proof that I was capable of love, of inspiring love in others, and not the monstrous person who could ignore the agony of his father's dying.

The first normal, comprehensible thing that Rachel did was to catch a cold. It was a delight to watch her sniffle, see her sneeze, her nose runny and red. She seemed like a regular human being after all. I had never seen her as accessible as when she had a Kleenex in her hand.

The sun, according to her, was the best cure for a cold, so she took a blanket and we went to the little clearing where the cheerleaders had practiced, to lie in the sun.

Behind us, the Indiana Tollroad stretched east and west. A construction crew was building an entrance ramp. This was one of the many jobs Misiora, Freud and I were going to get. We would stay fit, get tanned, and make a lot of money.

Rachel blew her nose. It was relaxing and wonderfully pleasant to be near her when she was sick. What our love affair needed more than anything else was for Rachel to get a two-year cold.

I lay on the blanket and watched the bulldozers and road-graders. I remembered that trip we were going to take. Misiora, Freud and I and Mrs. Dewey. Wisconsin Dells. I still didn't know what a Dell was. "You ever been to Wisconsin Dells?"

"No." Rachel spoke through her nose. "What's that?"

"It's this tourist thing they have in Wisconsin."

"I can hardly wait."

A couple of young kids rode their bikes across the clearing. They had raccoon tails hanging from the handlebars and Popsicle sticks rattling against the spokes. Rachel followed them with her eyes.

"I sure liked being a kid," she said. "A lot of girlfriends, short skirts. Long, long days."

She sneezed. A butterfly balanced on a dandelion unfolded its wings and flew off.

"We used to chase after them." Rachel smiled. "Me and my little band. All girls. Skirts and blouses and ribbons on pigtails." She was remembering it all as she spoke. You could see it in her eyes: treasures from the past. I wondered how long it would take for her to look back on our time together in the same way. Maybe this was one of the days she would remember.

The uncut grass was slowing down the kids on bikes. They were standing up now, pressing down on the pedals, inching along. I was in a good mood, full of generosity. I rooted for them. I was a nice guy.

Rachel plucked a dandelion and blew away the seeds. The wind carried them off like tiny paratroopers.

"I thought I'd be a kid forever," she said. "Didn't you?"

"Sure."

"I mean, I thought grown-ups were people who weren't good at being kids. And since I was damned good at it, I thought . . ." She paused and tossed away the stem of the dandelion. She took off her earrings and dangled them, one in each hand, looking intently at them. She did this for a long time before she spoke again.

"And then on my sixteenth birthday it happened. We had a party at my house. A cake with candles. Decorations. All that stuff. My little band of girlfriends was there in party dresses. Sam Cooke was singing 'Only Sixteen' on the hi-fi. My girlfriends were giggling and making faces at me. Somebody turned out the lights so that only the candles on the cake lit the room. It was time for me to blow them out. And then this older man, a friend of my father's, I had seen him around for a couple of years without saying a word to him . . . he just came over to me and put his hand around my waist." She put the two earrings into her palm and shut her fingers around them. She made a face, as if searching for words. "That's all it was. A hand around my waist, but . . ." She shook her head, puzzled herself by what happened. "But, you see, up to that point, whenever men touched me it was always on the shoulder or to rub the back of my head, you know, always kind of rough and playful. So when he slipped his hand around my waist, I almost fainted. This strange feeling suddenly awoke. I didn't know what it was. I didn't know I had a place on my waist that could do that to me. His hand guided me to the dining room, toward the cake and candles. I could hardly walk. I looked at my girlfriends as I walked past them and I wanted them to help me, to save me, to rescue me from that hand and that strange feeling. I blew out the candles. Everyone applauded. I started crying. I couldn't stop. Everyone thought I was upset because I didn't blow them all out at once. I wasn't a kid anymore. And it hurt. And that's why I was crying. For hours and hours . . . God." She wiped her nose and smiled. "Silly. Sil-ly stuff."

She seemed open as never before, and I saw a chance for that final breakthrough. There was a crack in the door and I would step through it and into Rachel's soul. That man with the hand, was he the one who had stood between us and was it his hand that had pulled her away from me that night we made love? I wanted to know. I wanted to hear that her heart was all mine now. She seemed open and unguarded and ready to surrender. I decided to make my move.

"When I was thirteen," I said, after a couple of minutes of silence, "I used to keep a diary." I laughed. It was a lie. The laugh, the diary, the pause before I spoke. All of them a lie.

"Really?" She suspected nothing. "Me too. I still do," she said, squinting at the sun.

"I'm kind of sorry I stopped." I spoke slowly, casually, holding back. "It'd be nice to go back and read all that stuff. You make entries every day?"

"No, just when something happens."

"I don't suppose I made it in your diary yet."

"You did."

"Really?"

"Yup."

"Oh, I know. I bet you made an entry on the day we met."

"That's right. Destiny Day." She smiled and, waving two Kleenexes like pompoms, she did a little cheer:

"Destiny, destiny
That's our cry
D-E-S-T-I-N-Y!
Yeah!"

I remembered following her. I laughed at the cheer and pressed on.

"Did you . . . let me see . . ." I paused as if I had no idea what to ask next. Strictly random. Casual. "Did you, mmm, make an entry that night we made love?"

My voice betrayed me. She noticed something. Her eyes narrowed.

"Yes," she said, "I did."

"What . . . what did you write?"

"How I felt. How it felt."

"And how was that?"

"You were there, weren't you? Couldn't you tell?"

"Sure, it's just, well, I wonder what you had to say . . ."

"It's private."

"Why?"

"Because it is."

I could tell that the door was closing, but I still pressed on. "What, it's a big secret or something?"

"No," she said simply, "secrets are something you hide because you're ashamed. I'm not ashamed."

"Then why can't you tell me?"

"I can. I just don't want to. I like having it all to myself."

"I tell you everything," I began whining.

"If you do, *if* you do, it's because you want to. If I don't, it's because I *don't* want to."

"When people love each other, they tell each other everything."

"I'll tell you something, Boondocks, people do all kinds of strange things when they love each other. But the one thing they don't do is tell each other everything."

"If they really love each other, they do," I went on, badgering her, telling her how she could tell me anything. How I would just love her all the more for it. How she could trust me. Finally she put her hand on my mouth and shut me up.

"Go away, Daniel. There's still some sun left and I want to stay in the sun, but I don't want you to stay with me anymore." She wasn't angry. Her tone was parental, motherly. "We were having a lovely afternoon, you and I, weren't we?"

"Yes."

"I don't want to get mad at you. You'll feel bad enough as it is because you ruined our day. So, go away now and feel bad by yourself."

She shut her eyes. She didn't open them when I got up to go. She just sat there peacefully, self-contained, her eyes shut to the world. I stood and watched her, but although she had to know I was still there she was oblivious of my presence. Not an eyelid fluttered, not a line changed on her face. What thoughts, I wondered, were going through her head?

I left, frustrated by the realization that I loved somebody I could not threaten or control.

That night, since I could not sleep, I stayed up and tried to understand her, tried to find a crack in her personality through which I could insert my conclusions.

"People do all kinds of strange things when they love each other. But the one thing they don't do is tell each other everything."

I analyzed the meaning of those sentences. Maybe, I reasoned, she did not understand my need to be told everything. Maybe she did not understand doubt, did not feel it herself and could not understand how anybody else could. Maybe—I continued my theories—she loved me so much, she expected me to know it without being told.

I loved that last theory. The more I thought about it, the sounder it seemed. Rachel in retrospect was everything I wanted her to be in person.

I walked around my room feeling terribly wise and profound. Then I sat down at my table and took a sheet of paper and a ballpoint pen. I clicked the point in and out several times and finally, unable to resist, I began writing. I smiled. I laughed to myself. It was just a joke.

I, Rachel Temerson, do hereby swear that I love Daniel Price with all my heart and soul and will love him with all my heart and soul forever and ever and even when I don't look like it, or act like it, I'm really loving him and am always thinking of him and coming up with more and more reasons why I love him and him alone, to the exclusion of all others in the world. So help me, God.

And then I signed it:
Rachel Temerson.

Chapter 22

I was asleep, dreaming that words I wrote left the sheet of paper and entered the hearts of people I knew. The word "adore" flew off the page and went straight into Rachel's heart, where it began to glow.

The telephone rang. I heard it ringing but I did not want to leave my dream. R-r-r-r-ing! R-r-r-r-ing! The Rs passed through my dream like a caravan. And then each letter turned into Rachel and each Rachel was slightly different.

I woke up. The telephone was still ringing. I stumbled out of bed and turned on the light. It was a little after midnight. I rushed to the living room and picked up the telephone.

"Hello?"

"Hello, D-aniel." It was my father, dropping that hard D into my ear.

"Father, is that you?" I said, trying to get my bearings.

"Yes. It's me. I'm still here, Daniel. Still alive. Holding on. The little man is holding on." He paused and then asked, "Did I wake you?"

"No," I said. It was automatic to lie to him. "No, I was up, Father."

"Couldn't sleep?"

"No, I couldn't."

"Couldn't sleep from worrying about me, is that it?"

"Yes, Father."

The word "Father" just didn't sound right the way I was pronouncing it. I kept thinking that I had to say it right. I reached over and turned on the lamp. When I heard his voice in the darkness I felt that he could pop out of anywhere.

"How are you, Father?" I tried to say the word right and failed. He ignored my question. I could hear him breathing into the telephone while I waited for him to speak.

"Daniel."

"Yes, Father."

"There's going to be hell to pay, Daniel," he said.

"I don't understand . . ."

"Your last name is Price, isn't it?"

"Yes, of course, Father." I kept trying to, but my lips and tongue just could not make the word come out correctly. I was so conscious of it that it was becoming hopeless.

"There's going to be hell to pay when I come home," he said. "Did she tell you?"

"Who's that?"

"Your mother. Did she tell you?"

"Tell me what?"

"Ask her. Ask her now."

"She's not home yet, Father. She won't be home for a while."

"Then you can ask her when she comes home. She will tell you. Goodnight, Daniel. Soon. I'll see you soon."

It sounded like a threat, and with that he hung up. I put down the phone slowly. It almost seemed that the phone conversation had been an extension of my dream and that only now was I beginning to wake up. I went to the kitchen and ate a piece of bread. There was some cold Turkish coffee left over in the pan and I took a couple of sips until I got down to the grounds. The coffee finished the job. I felt fully awake. In the present. The telephone conversation receded to the past. I turned on the tap and washed the pan slowly under hot water and then I went back to my room. Just as I stepped through the door, a voice called my name.

"Daniel."

My knees buckled. I spun around ready to defend myself, and there in my open bedroom window I saw a familiar face. Misiora!

"Larry!" I screamed.

"Sonovabitch!" He smiled. "How's that for luck. I thought I'd ride past your place thinking you'd be asleep and what do I see? The lights are on!"

He put his elbows on my window sill and scratched the back of his neck. As happy as I was to see him, to see that he was all right, I think I was even happier just to know that he was back where I was and not out there somewhere alone and free. His return proved the folly of trying to be alone and free. It was wonderful to see that he had failed. I was elated.

"Damn, Larry. You sure had us guessing. But I knew you'd be back."

He seemed amused when I shook his hand, as if we were performing some exotic ritual. His nails were long, his hands rough.

"I need some advice, Danny," he said. "I was thinking of letting my beard grow. What do you think?" He grinned.

I could hardly keep from gloating. He was back. I wanted to hear how it was terrible out there where he had been. I wanted to hear him say what a mistake he had made even to try it.

"You sure seem glad to see me," he said.

"Of course I'm glad to see you," I gushed.

"Yeah, but the way you're beaming you'd think your prick just grew a couple of inches." He grinned, but his blue eyes weren't smiling. He was scrutinizing me. My true motives seemed to be showing. I looked away and covered up as best as I could.

"Where the hell were you all this time?" I asked with a new voice and a new face. "We've all been worried about you. I know your parents—"

"They were born worried," he broke in.

"Well, anyway, you're back and that's all that matters." I spoke too loudly. My voice sounded false. Its sound reminded me of the way I had spoken in Mrs. Dewey's car while she and I and Rachel were driving to the firehouse that night.

"Yeah"—he nodded—"I tried to stay away but I couldn't. I got as far as Pennsylvania in my car but the mills there reminded me of the mills here and I had to come back."

"Of course you had to come back." I tried shading my voice, disguising any traces of satisfaction. "This is your home, after all."

"That's right. It is. And I have a room in my home. My parents call it 'Larry's room.' Clever of them, huh? And if I play my cards right I'll have a job and they'll call it 'Larry's job.' And 'Larry's foreman.' Because if Larry has a job Larry will have to have a foreman. And then there'll be 'Larry's vacation.' And 'Larry's paycheck' will be the talk of the block."

"That's how it is," I said. "Sooner or later . . ."

I stopped. I couldn't finish. His eyes made me too ashamed to continue. He looked so sad and disappointed.

"Yeah, that's what I was thinking while I was driving around. Sooner or later. That's what I was thinking, Danny. Everything has to happen sooner or later." He wouldn't take his eyes off me. It was as if he had missed me, thought about me, while he was out there alone and free. "So this is what I decided." He forced himself to grin. "I'm going to turn over a new leaf, Danny. I've been mean and nasty long enough. I'm tired of it but I guess that was bound to happen sooner or later, right?"

"Sure, Larry," I said. I knew he was leading me somewhere but I didn't know how to stop him.

"So that's why I came back, you see. To tell you the big news. I wanted you to be the first to know. No more mean Larry. You know what I've decided to be?"

He waited for me to ask. He enjoyed waiting, but that sad, disappointed look stayed in his eyes.

"I really don't know, Larry."

"Then I'll tell you. I'm going to be a hero." He winked at me. I took it as a joke and laughed.

"I'm not kidding around," he said. "I'm very serious about this whole thing. I think I'd like being a hero."

"Oh, c'mon, Larry, what're you talking about?"

"I'm talking about heroes." He winked at me again. "Good guys. I'm talking about white hats and silver bullets. Robin Hood and Zorro. Gene Autry and Roy Rogers. I'm talking about all those guys, Range Rider, the Lone Ranger, Lash La Rue, Wild Bill Hickok. Heroes. That's what I'm talking about." He seemed to be putting me on a bit, but at the same time he seemed very upset, on the verge of tears. "The thing is I'm new at this," he rambled on. "The hero business. I'm just starting out. So I need your help, Danny. A few tips, you know. Leads. Yes, I think I need a few leads. So I was wondering if you know of any decent hardworking homesteaders who're being terrorized by power-hungry cattle barons. I thought you and I could offer our services to them. Just to get us started. What do you think, Danny?"

He was talking faster and faster, getting more and more upset. Everything he was saying sounded childish and silly, but there was genuine sorrow in his eyes.

"Huh, what do you think, Danny? What do you say we help the homesteaders?" He seemed impatient for my reply.

"Why don't you come inside, Larry." I offered my hand, ready to pull him through the window. "It's late. It's the middle of the night and . . ."

He wouldn't take my hand. He started singing softly, looking at me as if he were serenading me.

"Out of the night when the full moon is bright," he sang, "comes the horseman known as Zorro. This bold renegade carves a Z with his blade, a Z that stands for Zorro."

He really did seem ready to cry. As soon as he stopped singing he started talking again in that rambling, painful way of his.

"I see your point. Yeah, I do." He nodded as if agreeing with me, and although I hadn't said anything he launched into his reply. "You're quite right. I can't just jump in and be a hero just like that." He snapped his fingers. "No experience, right? I'll tell you what. I'm willing to take on a job as an apprentice hero. You know what I mean. A hero's sidekick. That's what we'll do, you and I. We'll become a hero's sidekicks. I'm talking about Tonto now, Pat Buttram, Jingles, Dick West—you know Dick West, the guy who rides with Range Rider. I'll take it. What the hell. I'll be a hero's sidekick. I even know of a good job we can do. There's this damsel in distress. Swear to God, Danny, she's in distress. Her name's Lavonne Dewey and she needs to be rescued, and since I'm only a hero's sidekick I gotta find out real fast who and where the hero is so I can hook up with him. So I thought I'd come and see if you knew."

"Larry—" I tried to keep him from talking but he wouldn't let me.

"Oh, I see your point," he said. "There's no heroes, right, Danny? No openings. Too bad. What a world. Right, Danny? What a world. Even hero's sidekicks are out of work. I don't know about you, but do you know how it makes me feel when I'm ready to turn over a new leaf and stop being mean and nasty and go into the hero business only to find out that it doesn't exist anymore? Do you know how it makes me feel? It makes me feel meaner and nastier than ever before."

I tried putting my hand on his but he pulled it away.

"You remember those western movies we used to go to? You and I and Freud. Do you, Danny?"

"Sure, I do."

"And there would always be that scene in a town. The town's full of townsfolk and the heroes ride in from one side and the villains from the other and the townsfolk are crossing the street. Maybe they're all right. Maybe, you know, it's not as bad as I think being one of them, but I just can't be a townsfolk. All they're good for is to run and hide in a house or get shot down in the crossfire without ever getting one shot off themselves. I can't do that. I can't be one of them. And it looks like I'm not going to be a hero. What a world, huh?" He started laughing. "Jesus Horrendous Christ, what a world."

He put his head down on the window sill. He seemed tired, ready to fall asleep right then and there. I remembered his poem and I wanted to tell him how good I thought it was but I just didn't know how to begin. He lifted his head and smiled.

"You doing anything?" he asked.

"No." I shrugged.

"Let's take off. My car's over there." He pointed across the street where his car was parked. "I've still got some money left over from all those jobs I had. Maybe if you came with me, you know, maybe if we left together, the two of us, we'd never have to come back. What do you say?"

"What're you talking about, Larry?" I tried to reason with him. "You just got back and you're talking about leaving. Why don't you come inside? C'mon. Here." I offered him my hand again but he just looked at it.

"Come with me," he said.

"Oh, c'mon, Larry." I pretended to laugh. "Get off it. I can't come with you."

"You can't, huh?"

"Of course I can't."

"Then I guess I'll have to leave alone, buddy boy." He pushed himself away from my window. I reached out and grabbed his wrist. I was determined not to let him escape. He winced, puzzled by my action. The disappointment in his eyes undermined my resolve. My grip weakened and he pulled his wrist loose. And then slowly, facing me, he began backing away.

"Larry!" I clutched the window sill, sticking my head out into the night. "Larry, dammit. You can't leave. You just can't go on like this!"

"Like what, buddy boy?"

I blew up.

"Like what! Like a bum, that's like what. You want to be a bum, is that what you want?"

"No." He spread out his arms. "I want to be a hero."

"Larry." I was desperate. I remembered lying on the bus-stop bench daydreaming about leaving town and becoming a bum, and since I was unable to do it, I couldn't bear the thought that he was living out my daydream. "A bum, that's what you'll wind up. A no-good bum. You'll see. What the hell are you going to do when your savings run out? Tell me that. What will you do then?"

"I don't know," he said. "You got any ideas?"

"Larry, dammit, listen to me!"

"I'm listening, buddy boy." He stopped in the middle of the street and began shifting his weight from one foot to the other. The light from the streetlamp made a little island around him. He looked so self-contained and defiant that I felt my heart shriveling up with envy.

I lost all control. There was only one other person I knew who could stand alone like that without looking lonely and afraid, and since I could not bring myself to attack Rachel, I went after Misiora. I went after both of them. I started babbling, telling him how he was going to ruin his life, telling him how selfish he was, turning his back on his parents and friends, accusing him of being whimsical and immature, warning him about dangers I was afraid to confront myself, insisting that I knew what was best for him, babbling in that mean-spirited hysterical voice that I just could not control.

"You'll come back," I taunted him. "You'll see. When the money runs out you'll come back. Brad Davidson came back and you'll come back, too."

I finally stopped when I recognized my father speaking through me.

"I thank you for those words of wisdom, buddy boy." Misiora touched the brim of an imaginary hat. "You're probably right. I'll be back. Sooner or later, as they say."

He turned and walked to his car. He got in, started the engine and, hitting the horn a couple of times, floored the accelerator and sped away.

I felt like an old man. My neck felt wrinkled and scrawny as I craned it to keep the car in sight. Then I pulled my head inside. The edge of the window sill was pressing on my biceps, cutting off the circulation in my arm. It was falling asleep. I let it, pressing down even harder, enjoying the numbness. I wanted it to spread throughout my body. There I stayed for fifteen or twenty minutes when the front door opened and my mother entered the house.

It was too late to turn out the lights and pretend to be asleep. I heard her footsteps coming toward me, across the kitchen linoleum, across the living-room rug. I turned. She stood in the doorway.

"Daniel," she said.

I dreaded hearing my name said like that, soft and agonizingly tender. It was always an introduction to pain.

"Yes, Mom."

She walked into my room, Daniel's room, and stopped a few feet away from me. I could see the pain in her eyes. I could almost smell it on her body.

"Your father . . ." she began, but I interrupted her.

"I know. He called. I know, Mom."

"What, Daniel? What is it you know?"

"You saw him today and he said terrible things. You cried. I know."

"Daniel," she said softly.

I felt like screaming. I wanted to be out in the night with Misiora.

"Yes, Mom?"

"Your father is coming home. It has to be. There is no other way."

"When?"

"Friday."

"Tomorrow!"

"Yes." She nodded slowly, as if just realizing that Friday was indeed tomorrow. "We will have to prepare ourselves."

"I can't, Mom. I really can't prepare. Let's just see what happens, and . . . but I just can't prepare."

"All right, Daniel."

She reached out with her hand as if to soothe me, but when I pulled back, her hand mothered the air, soothing the atmosphere between us. Then she left. Across the living-room rug, across the kitchen linoleum and into her room.

I turned off the lights and lay down on my bed, Daniel's bed. I turned over and lay on my stomach, the weight of my chest cutting off the circulation in my arm. I fell asleep clutching that numbness to my heart.

A police siren woke me later in the night. I opened my eyes. I heard the sound coming closer and closer. I saw the glare of the flashing red light speed past my window. I fell asleep again and fell right into a nightmare. I saw my father's face—his whole head, actually, severed from his body, but alive—crammed inside the siren light, revolving as the flashing red light revolved. His head spun around and around. His mouth was open. He was screaming. Calling my name.

Chapter 23

My mother cleaned house all morning. I had seen her do the cleaning before, but never like this. It wasn't the thoroughness that was new so much as the manner in which she went about it. Slowly, she moved slowly and steadily, keeping time to a whole new rhythm, and when she spoke to me, it was slow and steady. The cadence of her words had almost liturgical overtones.

"No, Daniel. It is fine. I do not need help. Thank you, son."

I tried to stay out of the way. I sat down and watched her work. She went down on her knees to scrub the kitchen floor. It all seemed like some old Byzantine ritual of preparing the house for a death in the family. I ate and watched. She seemed to forget that I was there.

Later, I helped her take down the old curtains in the living room and hang new ones. They were heavier than the old ones, and darker. Dark blue. We stood together, side by side, and looked at them when we were finished. She pulled the cord to close them and then she pulled another cord to open them; she pulled slowly, to a rhythm, a ritual, like lowering the flag.

I stood and watched.

She took a bath and went into her room. When she came out again, she was wearing her Sunday clothes. The tight blouse made her large breasts show. She had put on lipstick and was wearing earrings. I thought I detected the scent of perfume, but I wasn't sure. She carried herself like someone who knew that this was how she was supposed to look at a time like this, this was how she was supposed to act.

She left a little after noon to catch the one o'clock train to Chicago. She told me, slowly, that she would be back in an "abulance" around five o'clock with my father, and then, slowly, she walked out of the house, silently shutting the doors behind her.

The new curtains made the whole house feel different. They were longer, heavier, like judicial robes, and their dark-blue color contrasted sharply with the beige of the couch where Rachel and I had made love.

It would be his house again. My father was coming home.

I still found it hard to believe. The events had all been pointing toward a different conclusion. Father gets sick. Father gets cancer. Father dies in the hospital. His return seemed almost unnatural.

Would he remember that I didn't visit him, not once, that I didn't even bother to call, or would he be too sick to remember?

I tried to sit down on the couch, but I just couldn't. My mother had pushed in the chairs around the kitchen table and I didn't feel comfortable spoiling her work. I stood wondering what to do. I just couldn't get used to the idea that he was coming back, that he was actually coming back.

I considered running away, but how could I leave without Rachel? I couldn't just take off as Misiora had done. I began hating both of them: Rachel, because I loved her so much that she could hold me in place; Misiora, for doing what I couldn't.

Maybe, I thought, maybe something will happen. Maybe on the way home from the hospital the ambulance will have an accident. A car crash. A railroad crossing. A man, dying of cancer, dies in a car crash. Just because it was so improbable, it sounded possible. One of those twists of fate. I could hear my mother telling and retelling the story for years to come: "I had a feeling as soon as we got in the 'abulance' . . ."

I walked around the house, waiting for the phone to ring, waiting to find out that what I had imagined had come true.

It was almost three o'clock. He was sitting or lying in the ambulance with my mother, and the ambulance at this very moment was moving along U.S. 41 toward me.

I picked up the telephone and called Rachel. I needed reassurance. I needed to know that I wasn't alone, that there were two of us, that we were a couple, that she loved me. The sound of her voice alone would remind me that I was here. My momentary flirtation with running away, with freedom, made me now want all the more to belong to her.

The telephone rang. I knew where it was. I pictured it ringing. It rang and rang. Nobody answered. I put the receiver down and walked around the house. I peeked into my mother's room. It, too, was neat and clean. No clothes on the chairs. No socks on the floor. The bedspread looked as flat and wrinkle-free as a table top. Is that where he would lie again? Their wedding picture sat on the dresser. He stood proudly next to my mother, almost a foot shorter than she, his face beaming. Yes, I did look like him.

I called Rachel again. I let the phone ring a long time. Nobody answered. What if she was just sitting on the steps listening to it ringing? I wondered if she knew, somehow knew, that it was me calling.

I wanted to run over to her house and find out. But when I checked the time, I saw it was a little after five o'clock. I couldn't leave. I just couldn't. If my father came while I was gone, I would have to enter the house with him already there. It seemed easier to remain and face his entrance than to plan mine.

A few minutes later, I heard a car brake to a stop in front of our house. I ran to the window and peeked through the curtains. The engine of the red ambulance was still running. The driver, all in white, was out, checking the neighborhood as he opened the back-door. My mother got out. She reached inside as if to offer help and then pulled her hands back and stepped aside. Next I saw my father's head emerge. It startled me. I just caught a glimpse of it and pulled back from the window.

He looked like a ghost. Had I seen correctly? Did he really look like that?

A car door slammed. And then another. And then the ambulance drove away.

I didn't know where to be when he came in. In the kitchen? In my room? What should I say first? Should I look happy to see him or concerned about his appearance?

The front door opened. The door to the kitchen opened. My mother walked inside. She cast a quick glance at me. I came toward her. I heard the sound of shoes shuffling through the corridor and over that sound, another: tap, tap, tap, like the slow, distant tapping of a gavel.

He entered in bits and pieces. A black cane appeared in the doorway first, tap, and then an emaciated hand on the handle of the cane, tap, and then a shoe, a bit of shoulder, a knee, and then I saw my father's head entering my home again.

His small eyes looked large now. The flesh on his face was gone and the skin that remained was stretched tightly over his bones. He seemed to have no wrinkles. Cancer had eaten up half his body and his old clothes hung on him like robes. And his hair! I could see bare gray patches of the skin covering his skull. Strands stuck out here and there like mad thoughts planted in the brain that had now broken through the surface.

"Hello, Daniel." He spoke first for once, tapping the cane on the floor on the letter "D."

"Hello, Father."

"I am home."

"Yes, I'm glad to . . ."

He hit the floor with the tip of his cane. My mother walked past him and shut the doors.

I waited for him to say something else, but he just stared at me with his new pair of eyes. He walked by placing his right foot forward, bringing the left one even with it and then leading with the right again. He used the cane to support himself.

In this way, silently except for the feet shuffling and the cane tapping, he walked past us. My mother and I followed.

It seemed improbable that a man so fragile and faded could stand, much less walk. Each little half-step exhausted him, but he took another, and since my mother and I dutifully followed every move-ment he made, his exhaustion infected us: he walked with difficulty, we looked on with difficulty; he strained, we strained. His cane tapped on the floor. There was a tapping in my head like the first pounding beats of a migraine on the way.

He sat down on the couch. Did he know Rachel and I had made love there? He seemed to know. My mother and I stood in front of him like petitioners.

"Are you hungry?" my mother asked him.

"No."

"Thirsty? Are you thirsty?"

"No."

"Can I get you something from the store?" I asked.

He saw right through that question. He could tell I wanted to get out of the house. "No." He almost smiled. "I am content to just sit and look at my wonderful wife and my wonderful son."

When he saw our discomfort, he seemed pleased. We stood there, squirming, waiting to be dismissed. The cane lay across his lap. His wrists were not much thicker than the cane.

"Do you want to go to bed?" My mother tried again, after a couple of minutes. "Are you tired?"

"No."

"A bath? Do you want a bath?"

"No."

It felt as if it were my turn again to ask him something, offer my services. I couldn't think of anything.

"We cleaned the house," my mother said. "Daniel helped me."

"Daniel is a wonderful son. You are a loving wife. And I am a lucky man. Is that how it is?"

My head was beginning to throb. Why was I just standing there? Why couldn't I just move my feet and walk away?

"Are you comfortable?" my mother asked him.

"I am in pain," he said. "I hurt."

"You made me throw out all the pills. I don't have pills now to give you. What can I do? You said to throw them out."

"That's how it is," he said. "No pills. Just pain."

"Is it very bad?" she asked him.

"Yes. It is." He took a deep breath, as if to sigh, and without any warning, he screamed: "A-a-a-a-a-a!"

Both of us flinched. He looked at us and screamed again: "A-a-a-a-a-a-a!"

My mother rushed toward him, but he stopped her with the tip of his cane. "That's how it is," he said softly. "The pain. Just like that. All the time."

"I have prescription." My mother wrung her hands. His scream had shaken her. "Maybe I can go to store and buy more pills."

"I'll go, Mom," I offered.

"Worse pains," my father said. "There are worse pains." He looked at my mother. "Isn't that right?"

She shrugged, trying not to cry.

"Smile for me," he whispered.

"I . . . how can I smile?" she pleaded.

"You know how." And once again he whispered, "Smile for me."

"But I don't know . . ."

"You know. Sure, you know. I remember everything," he said. "The night. The smile. Summer night. Yes. I want that smile. Smile for me."

It was clear that he was torturing her, but I didn't know how or why. I just stood there, waiting my turn. There was a drum in my head and somebody was beating on it.

"I want to go to bed now," he said.

No, he refused to sleep in his old bed with my mother. He didn't want to be in a room with a door, in a bed with somebody else. He chose the couch, the couch where Rachel and I had made love, as his place. My mother brought out pillows and blankets and sheets and made the bed for him there.

"I will now go make some hot milk to drink," she announced. She kept making these little announcements the rest of the evening, as if my father's presence dictated that she declare her intentions before every move. "I will wash the dishes." And then later: "I will now take a bath." And finally: "I will now go to sleep. Goodnight."

He said nothing.

"Goodnight, Mom," I said.

"I will turn off the lights." She turned off the light in the kitchen and disappeared inside her bedroom.

My father lay on the couch, fully dressed. I sat in a chair not far from him. Why I was sitting there and how I came to be there, I don't know. Maybe I was waiting for something to happen.

He sat up and leaned back on the armrest of the couch. He put the tip of his cane on the living-room rug. He seemed ready to get up but remained in that position for the next five minutes or so. Then he asked for the telephone. I brought it to him and placed it on his lap. He dialed and handed the receiver to me. The hospital where he had been answered. I hung up.

"Easy," he said. "It is easy to call the hospital. I thought maybe it was difficult and that's why you never called. But it seems to be easy."

"Father, I . . ."

Tap! Tap! Tap!

He hit the floor with the tip of his cane, cutting me off. A few minutes later, he spoke again.

"Television. Did you watch television while I was in the hospital?"

"Oh, I . . . yes. A little."

"To get your mind off my sickness. Is that why you watched television? So you wouldn't worry yourself to death over my sickness?"

"Yes."

"Eat sandwiches, hmm? Did you eat sandwiches while I was being treated? Roast-beef sandwiches?"

"I suppose. I don't know."

"Because your mind wasn't on the food. Because you were too preoccupied. Worried. Because you were worried about me. Right?"

"Yes," I lied.

"Wonderful son." He grimaced. "I am blessed with a wonderful son."

"Father, I—"

Tap! Tap! Tap! He stopped me.

"Did she?"

"Who's that, Father?"

"She. Did she?"

"Did she what, Father?"

"Smile for you. That special smile. Did she?"

"Who's that, Father?"

"What's her name? Gretchen. Yes, Gretchen. Is that her name: Gretchen?"

"Yes, that's it."

"Was she here?"

"No."

"I think she was here."

"No, she wasn't."

Tap. Tap. Tap. He hit the floor with the tip of his cane.

"Right here! That's where she was. You." He pointed the cane at me. "You want to have what I couldn't have. Is that it? Is that what you want?"

"Father, I don't think I—"

Tap! Tap! Tap!

"My son. You are my son. Do you know what that means?"

"Yes, I—"

"In my footsteps, that's what that means. You can't have what I couldn't have. In my footsteps."

Tap! Tap! Tap!

"Your last name's Price. To pay. You have to pay when you have that name. Oh, yes. Like father, like son."

I didn't dare look at him. I kept my head bowed. It was pounding. Expanding and contracting to the beat of his words.

"Wretched son. From me. Yes. That's what you are inheriting from me. No use fighting it. You and I. We are not men who make women smile that special way. No. Doomed. Born doomed, both of us. Yes. Six letters, four across: Doomed."

He continued talking. The word "doomed" kept coming up: "Not a bad word, 'doomed.' Sounds bad at first, but then you get used to it. Why me? Yes, you say why me at first, but then you get used to it." At some point, I ceased to hear anything except the pounding in my head.

I got up.

"I am going to turn out the lights, Dad," I said and clicked the lamp off. The streetlights, shining through the curtain, made his face look blue.

I went to my room. For some reason, I couldn't bring myself to shut the door completely. I went to bed.

"*Rachel,*" he whispered. "That's her name. I know. I remember. I remember everything. Six letters, five down: Rachel."

He tapped on the rug with his cane. I shut my eyes. He continued talking to himself, his voice whisper-soft but filling the darkness like escaping gas.

Chapter 24

A routine evolved. I stayed with my father when my mother went out to shop. When she came back, I went out. We took turns being with him. That was the routine for the first weekend and for the weekends to follow. The weekday routine was similar, but revolved around my mother's job. She had to continue working. We had no other source of income. As soon as I got up in the morning, I would leave the house and not return until it was time for my mother to go to work. Then I would take over and stay with my father until she came back late at night. At that time, I would either go to bed or go outside for an hour by myself. Every now and then, all three of us would be in the house at the same time. That would happen only when Rachel didn't feel like seeing me and I was just too tired of walking the familiar streets with nowhere to go.

There were times as I shuffled back and forth between my house and Rachel's house and envisioned spending the rest of my life going back and forth between these two points that I yearned for Misiora to appear in his white Chevy and take me away. I saw Mrs. Dewey driving around in her car several times. I saw Freud and Patty sitting on the library steps. But no Misiora. I walked past his house twice hoping to see his car parked outside, but it wasn't there.

The window in my room, especially at night, became associated with him. It was Misiora's window. And lying in bed, analyzing yet another scene I had had with Rachel, listening to my father crying out in pain or taunting me from his couch in the living room, I stared at the window waiting for Misiora to reappear.

No matter how early I got up in the morning, my father was up already, waiting for me, propped up on the couch, cane tapping on the floor.

"Good morning, Daniel."

"Good morning, Father."

"Did you sleep well?"

If I said I did, he would accuse me of not giving a damn; here he was, a few feet away, dying while I slept. If I said I didn't, he would tell me that it was because my conscience, if I had any left, was bothering me. Or he would accuse me of lying.

"You slept. I heard you. You are lying. I heard you. Yes, snoring. While I die! My God, how could you!"

I couldn't understand what kept him alive. He hardly ate. He hardly seemed to breathe. Every day he seemed to get worse— thinner, more ashen, his eyes larger, glassier. He was like a man with a mission. He would not die until he did what he had to do. And only he knew what that was.

"Where are you going, Daniel?"

"Out."

"Your love. To see your love, is that where?"

"No, I'm just going out."

"Your one and only love," he went on. "What's her name? Gretchen, is that it? No, that's not it. Rachel. That's the one. Rachel. To see Rachel, is that where you're going? Go ahead, then. Go. I'll be here when you come back."

And when I returned in the afternoon, when my mother left for work, he would start up again, only not right away. He would wait and make me think that his mind was on other matters. He would ask if it was nice outside. If it was sunny. Did it look like it was going to rain? He would say he was tired. He would shut his eyes, and just when I thought he would go to sleep and I began to relax, he would tap the cane on the floor.

"By the way, Daniel, how was Rachel? Is that her name? Rachel? Yes, that's it. Love you. Did she say she loves you? Did she? Smile for you? That special way. Did she?"

Sometimes he smiled when he said this, a smile so cold and hateful that it seemed dipped in venom. At other times, the word "smile" took him somewhere else, out of the house, made him drift away to some other time and place, and while I sat there watching him, or stood by my door, he would start weeping like a little boy.

"Oh-h," he would whimper, "oh-h, why? Why me?"

It broke my heart to see him like that. Whatever defenses I had put up, went down. I couldn't bear all that grief and I would go to him.

"Father, don't. Please. What is it?"

"Why?" he sobbed. Where were his tears coming from? He looked so dry, a bleached skull, yet tears were rolling out of his eyes. "Why did she do that?"

"Who, Father?"

"She. I loved her so, and she . . ."

"Who was she, Dad? Who?"

Suddenly everything changed. His faraway look vanished, and with a birdlike flick of his head, he turned on me.

"Rachel, that's who. Isn't that who? That's who it is, Rachel. Here you are. Right here. And she? Where is she? Where do you think she is now? And with whom? Her lips. Spreading her lips into a smile. That's what she is doing. Not for you. No-o. Somebody else. She is spreading them for somebody else."

The only thing he knew about her was her name, but he loved to plant doubts in my head about her; gross, ugly images in my head about her. The more I resisted, the more I hated him for it, the more the doubts sank in, and along with them, the same old desperation and uncertainty. I would go to her in the morning, expecting her to undo all the damage my father had done, instantly reassure me of her love—not just love, eternal love.

She tried at first. The weekend when my father came home and she saw the state I was in, she assumed, and I did nothing to correct her, that I was out of my mind with worry about him. She held me in her arms. She talked to me like an adult to a child and I loved it. She would take care of everything. That's how she made it seem. We went for a drive in her father's car. A part of my body was always touching hers. Whenever she seemed ready, even for a minute, to just stare at the road ahead and think her thoughts, I would do something to focus her attention back on me. This happened several times, and although she obliged each time, there was a growing resistance to my demands.

In the days that followed, the pattern repeated itself. My father drained me. I expected Rachel to replenish me. My father could sense how things went between me and her on a given day. If things went badly, he would sympathize:

"That's how they are. Women. Yes. The more you love them, the

more they'll hurt you. Don't let her. Give her up now. Beat her to
it."

If things went well, he jeered at my stupidity:

"Doesn't take much, does it, for you to come home all starry-eyed.
What a fool you are. You sit there—how can you sit there, hoping,
when you don't even know what she's doing at this very moment.
Do you think . . . of you . . . do you think she's thinking of you?
It's nighttime now. Do you know what women do at nighttime? I
know. In my footsteps. Yes, that's where you're headed. Like father,
like son. . . ."

When he tired of attacking her, he attacked me:

"Her! How can you love her when you don't love your own
father. Animals! Even animals love the ones who gave them life. I
am your father." He started to weep. "Your one and only father. I
want you to love me."

His eyes looked at me, waiting to be filled with love, crying for
it. I could not bear the need I saw in them.

"Of course I love you, Dad."

"What 'of course'? Where is this 'of course'? Make me feel it.
Look at me and make me feel you love me. My God, make me feel
it before I die."

"But I do. I love you, Dad."

"Where?" He spread out his arms, waving his cane through the
air. "Where is it? I don't see it. I don't feel it. Nothing."

I recognized something of myself in his despair. Was I really
following in his footsteps?

"Nothing. There is nothing. You cannot love. You do not love.
And she knows it. Rachel knows it. And she'll find someone who
can. That's where she is now. She's with someone who can."

Late that night, long after my mother had returned from work
and when I was sure my father was asleep, I got up, and by the light
of my little table lamp I reread the pledge I had written in Rachel's
name. It was almost a joke when I wrote it. I remembered smiling
as I wrote it. Now it was something else. It stated clearly what I
wanted from her. There it was in black and white. That's what I
needed for my happiness:

". . . forever and ever and even when I don't look like it, or act
like it, I'm really loving him and am always thinking of him and
coming up with more and more reasons why I love him and him
alone, to the exclusion of all others in the world. So help me, God."

Maybe it was because it was so late at night and I was so tired, but it seemed like a reasonable document.

"You're kidding," Rachel said the next day when I showed it to her. She seemed ready to be amused by it and only waited for a signal from me that yes, of course, I was kidding. "You gotta be kidding."

"Of course I'm kidding." I caved in when I saw her reaction. The document looked all wrong, even to me. It had looked fine late at night, under the light of a table lamp, but there, on her lawn, with the wind blowing and the sunshine streaming through the leaves, it looked ridiculous. I blamed my father. He was making me behave like a lunatic. "A thing like this. Sure, I'm kidding," I stammered.

"You're not kidding, are you?" She made a face. She seemed truly worried about me. I lowered my head. "Daniel." She put her index finger under my chin. I resisted. "Daniel, I'm talking to you."

"It's a joke," I mumbled. "Can't you tell it's a joke? I mean, God, I signed your name, even. I thought you'd laugh."

"All right. It's a joke. Neither one of us is laughing, but I'll take your word for it. It's a joke. Can I keep it?"

"Why?"

"I can never remember jokes. So I'll keep it, okay? Can I?"

"Sure."

She folded it once and then she folded it again.

"C'mon," she said, "let's go fly a kite."

"Why don't we go for a drive instead?"

"Because"—she pointed to the street—"we don't have a car."

"Did your father go somewhere?"

"Yes. Let's go fly a kite," she said hurriedly, creasing the edges of my folded "joke" with her fingernails.

The kite was yellow. She ran through the park several times until the wind caught it and made it rise. Then she stood there and watched it go higher and higher. I walked up to her. We stood shoulder to shoulder, but her total attention was focused on the yellow speck in the sky. Her head was tilted back and her earrings fell back into her dark hair. When she moved her arms in a certain way, little valleys formed under her collarbones. I looked up and watched the kite and although I was smiling, I wanted the kite to fall.

Two days later, as I was walking down Northcote, toward her street, I saw her father. He was driving from the opposite direction.

Both of us turned down Aberdeen at about the same time. I waved to him, but he didn't see me. I turned the corner and saw him park in front of his house. I kept walking. Rachel ran out and stopped in the middle of the lawn. He got out of the car. I kept walking. Neither of them took notice of me.

He looked all different. His clothes were wrinkled. A pocket on his sport coat was turned inside out. He needed a shave, and his silver-gray hair, usually combed back, stuck out around his ears.

I stopped.

Rachel looked down at the grass and then, taking a deep breath, looked up at him. He shrugged and spread out his hands, palms upward, in the helpless gesture of a man who could not do something he wanted to do. She went to him slowly. He didn't move. She combed back his hair with her fingers. She adjusted his jacket and pulled it down by the ends. She pushed his turned-out pocket back inside his jacket. Then she moved aside and he, looking down, started to walk toward the house. When she saw me, she just shook her head, telling me that she could not see me now. They walked into the house together, in step, her body positioned to shield him from my eyes.

Chapter 25

Ⅰt was Saturday evening. My father was asleep on the couch. My mother sat in the kitchen.

"Goodnight, Mom," I said softly, not wanting to wake my father.

"Goodnight, Daniel," she whispered.

I left to see Rachel, shutting the door quietly behind me.

I walked slowly to her house, letting the dusk change to night. My head was full of plans. My stomach hurt with desire for her. Maybe we would make love in the park. Or in the car. Maybe we could drive to the beach and make love in the sand. I wished that I had some exotic disease and a letter from a doctor informing Rachel that only making love to her could keep the disease from becoming fatal.

I coughed. I remembered the way the patients in *The Magic Mountain* coughed. There was a touch of poetry in the way they did it, but then, they were on a mountaintop and I was in East Chicago. I had read that book in my junior year. I read all kinds of books that year, going out of my way to read those that were not assigned, feeling superior because of it, telling nobody, not even Misiora or Freud, about them. From novels I went to short stories, from short stories to poetry, and from poetry I went into my senior year and worries about jobs and things that waited for me as punishment for graduating.

I turned the corner on Aberdeen Lane and as always, no matter that I had been disappointed countless times, I felt a sudden surge of hope as I walked the half-block to her house. Anything could happen.

Her porch light was on, and I started up the steps but then stopped. She was sitting there waiting for me. She stood up when she saw me. The rocking chair she had been sitting on continued to rock by itself. She came toward me. I backed away to let her come through the door.

She wore a black blouse, black trousers and high-heeled black boots. Her hair was combed differently from the way she usually wore it, fuller on the sides. Turquoise dangled from her earlobes. She wore makeup: lipstick, mascara. She looked as beautiful as any human being I had ever seen.

I coughed and took another step back.

"Hello, Daniel," she said as she came out, slamming the porch door shut behind her on purpose. It was as if this was her way of letting her father know she was leaving. She stopped in front of me and smiled. "I look good in black, don't I?"

"Yes." I nodded. "You do."

My stomach began to ache even more. She looked too beautiful. Anything I wanted to do to her would spoil the way she looked. She took me by the arm and, twirling her car keys, led me to the car. As we drove away I saw her father looking out of the living-room window.

She turned on the radio. We drove past the public library, down Magoun Avenue, past my old high school, and down Indianapolis Boulevard toward Whiting. Songs changed as we drove but I wasn't paying attention to them.

"They're playing a lot of nice dancing music tonight," she said, moving to the beat of the music. I found it difficult to watch her. Her beauty was depressing me. My stomach was killing me.

"Yes," I said, "it's perfect dancing music. Nice and slow."

She hummed along with the Drifters, moving her shoulders, tapping her fingers on the steering wheel.

"It's very Greek, you know," she said, running her hand down her outfit. "Black. Whenever I feel I'm being pulled in several different directions at the same time, I put on my black outfit. It makes everything seem simpler for a while."

"Like what?" I asked.

"Everything." She smiled, and although she was still moving to the beat of the music and although she was smiling, she did not seem happy.

"I mean, what kind of things are pulling at you?" I asked.

"You," she said. "Aren't you pulling at me?"

She suddenly took a left turn off Indianapolis Boulevard. I recognized the road. We were going to Whiting Beach. She turned up the volume of the radio as we bounced across the railroad tracks. She kept looking at me, smiling, but there was something purposeful in the way she did it. It reminded me of the way she had slammed the porch door shut behind her as we left so that her father would know. I wondered what she wanted me to know.

There were about half a dozen cars in the parking lot. Rachel drove past them and parked in front of the concession stand. It was closed. The lifeguard's chair was empty, the beach deserted. She shut off the engine and the radio and got out. I followed.

The moonlight shining through a thin cover of clouds made them seem fluorescent. We walked toward the water, her high-heeled boots tapping across the cement and then suddenly becoming silent as they hit the sand. A breeze was blowing from across the lake, warm and humid. Her blouse fluttered. Her hair blew back. I could see the lights of Inland Steel in the distance. The water smelled of industry and jobs. To our right, a hundred yards or so away, a bonfire was burning, a transistor radio was playing music and the kids from the cars in the parking lot were shouting and jumping around. For some reason they all sounded like juniors to me.

"A beach party." Rachel smiled, looking at them. Her lips moved as if she were getting ready to say something else. Her body seemed poised to move toward the fire.

"It's just a bunch of kids," I said. "They're going to drink beer till they throw up."

The kids around the fire started laughing loudly and Rachel smiled, as if she were among them.

"I wonder what they're saying," she said.

"How stupid their teachers are. What fools their parents are. Things like that."

She wasn't listening to me. She was listening to them. I felt a little annoyed. I had hoped we would be alone on the beach. Make love in the sand. I took her hand and tried to lead her away. "Why don't we walk down a little?"

"No." She gripped my hand but would not move. "This is fine." She sat down in the sand and pulled me down with her. I positioned myself in such a way as to block the fire and the kids from her view.

"It's all wrong," she said.

"What's that?"

"My whole outfit." She shrugged. "My Greek black."

"You look beautiful."

"I know, but it's all wrong for a beach party. These boots. These earrings. All this makeup. I bet if I walked over there they'd think I was some older woman or something."

"They're just silly kids, Rachel." I, a genuine high-school graduate, felt no hesitation in condemning a bunch of juniors.

"Nothing wrong with that," she said. "Being a kid."

A girl screamed. A boy laughed. Rachel, hearing them, smiled and looked away. I could feel her drifting away from me. I could feel the breeze blowing between us. What was she thinking about? She lay back on the sand. I lay back too, to keep her from seeing the fire and the kids. Just me. I wanted her to see just me.

"Why so sad, Boone?" she asked.

"I thought you liked me sad."

"Not that kind of sad." She ran her hand over my face as if trying to rearrange my features. "What I like is real sorrow. You know . . . tragedy." She smiled. "Not that."

Her hand felt wonderful on my face. Her eyes, looking at me, loved something they saw in me, but I didn't know what.

"A boy," she said, letting her hand glide up and down my cheek. "A boyfriend." She said the word slowly. "I have a boyfriend."

She seemed ready to cry out, but since I could see no reason for it, I thought it was my imagination.

"My mother would really like you." She nodded. "And if she were here, not here on the beach, but here in East Chicago waiting for me at home, I would tell her all about you. If you love somebody you want to tell your mother all about them. You told your mother all about me, didn't you?"

"Yes, I did."

"You see. And I want to tell mine, too. She would be so happy that there is this boy who loves me." She left her hand on my cheek. "This boy with a smooth face." She bit her lips and pulled her hand away. She scooped up a handful of sand and flung it into the air.

"My outfit isn't working." She tried to sound casual about the whole thing. "Maybe I need a new outfit, Boone. Things are still pulling at me. This way, that way . . ." She dug her heels into the sand, trying to anchor herself to one spot. She seemed ready to laugh or cry or jump up and run away.

"I don't understand what these things are, Rachel. These 'things' that are pulling at you." I spoke softly, carefully, sensing that our whole night could be ruined with one wrong word.

"I told you, didn't I? You're pulling at me."

"And who else?"

"David's pulling at me," she said, looking right at me.

"He's just worried about you," I rambled, trying to sound wise and experienced. "Fathers are like that."

"You know nothing about it, Daniel."

"About what?"

"Fathers," she said. And then her eyes changed. She squinted, and after a slight pause during which her lips moved, she asked me: "You've seen him. Does he act like my father?"

Her voice sounded strange and direct. I didn't know she had a voice like that in her.

"Well," I stammered, startled by the sound of her voice more than anything else, "my father doesn't act like a father either. I'm sure he loves me, but . . ."

I had to stop. I wasn't prepared for the pain those words caused me to feel. I'm sure he loves me . . . Suddenly I wasn't sure of anything except that I, too, wanted to be a junior again or somebody else entirely, someone far older and much wiser who no longer worried about love at all.

"Don't," she said, pulling me gently by my shirt. "Don't get sad again. I can't bear it, Daniel. You see"—she smiled, still pulling on my shirt—"now I'm pulling at you. How's it feel?"

"It feels real nice."

"It does, does it?" She smiled, pleased to have such an immediate effect on me. "We'll show those kids down by the fire. We're going to have more fun than they are, that's what we're going to do."

She winked at me and put her finger on my lips.

"C'mon, Daniel. Take my lipstick off."

She moved toward me. I saw the fluorescent clouds above her head and then I shut my eyes as she kissed me. In the distance I could hear the transistor radio blaring music, the kids screaming and laughing, and either it was my impression or I was absorbing Rachel's, but it felt as if we were in their midst. I kept my eyes shut. I was afraid if I opened them I would see something in her eyes that might lead me to ask more questions to which I would get more answers which, as always, answered nothing. She ran her tongue over my lips, she put her hands under my shirt. I shuddered, and even though she was kissing me I could feel her smiling, enjoying the tremors she was causing, the game we were playing. I knew we couldn't make love, not with those kids so close, but I found it difficult to control myself. I felt no resistance in her at all, no hesitation, no boundaries that could not be crossed. I rolled on top of her. She inhaled to let me pull her blouse out of the belt and exhaled as my hands moved inside her blouse and up to her breasts. Her arms were wrapped around my bare waist. I could feel the warm breeze blowing across my neck.

"Rachel," I whispered. I wanted us to go someplace where we could be alone, move further down the beach, go to the car, drive to some motel. "Let's go somewhere else."

She shook her head and kept kissing me, holding me tighter around the waist.

"Rachel." I tried again after a few minutes. I felt her embrace loosen suddenly, and thought that perhaps she was now willing to go. I opened my eyes.

Her head was resting on the sand but her eyes were looking away toward the fire. The music from the transistor radio and the noise of the kids seemed to be coming closer to us. I looked up the beach and saw them. They were all leaving, heading back to their cars and making a wide detour around us.

I was glad to see them go. They whistled and yelled some encouragements to us and then they all laughed. The boy with the transistor radio swung it back and forth as he walked. A girl started running. The boy with the transistor ran after her and the rest followed, laughing and screaming.

I couldn't wait for them to leave us alone. They disappeared around the concession stand and only then did I look at Rachel. She seemed lonely. I was lying on top of her—my hands were still on her breasts; if I moved a couple of inches forward our lips would be touching—and yet she seemed lonely. It was clear that she missed the kids. I could not understand that at all. She didn't know them. I didn't know them. They were just some strange, loud kids who had finally left us alone. What was there to miss?

We heard the cars start up, and then we heard them drive away one after another.

Rachel sat up. I had to scramble to get off her. She checked to see that her earrings were still in place.

"It was nice with the music and noise and all," she said, looking at the now deserted fire. She seemed truly sad.

"You want to go down and sit by the fire?" I offered.

"Just the two of us?" she asked simply, not really trying to hurt me, and then she shook her head slowly, answering her own question.

She got up and brushed the sand from her blouse.

"Let's go home. The party's over." She tried to smile and began crying.

I didn't understand a thing.

"Rachel, what's the matter?"

"I'm crying."

"But why?"

"Because I'm sad. That's what I do when I get sad and my outfit isn't working. I cry. Don't worry." She took me by the arm. "I'll stop."

She tried to run through the sand, but after a couple of steps she gave up. We walked slowly to the car, she leading, I following. She tucked her blouse back inside her belt as she walked.

Had she not cried and looked so sad, I would have been angry with her. Denied my anger, all I felt was frustration and confusion. My stomach still ached. She looked more beautiful than any human being I had ever seen. I stared at her as she drove, thinking that if I stared long enough and hard enough I would be able to understand her.

"I'm a real mess, aren't I?" she said as we came out of the side street into Indianapolis Boulevard.

"I just don't know why you do all these things, Rachel. That's all." Although I was trying very hard to be grown-up and mature, I felt my lower lip swelling up into a childish pout.

"Don't do that," she said softly. "Don't look as if I've short-changed you. I get enough of that."

"It's hard keeping up with your whims." I felt the anger I was trying to hold down beginning to surface. I did feel shortchanged. "I don't know what you want from me. Sometimes you want me to be old and sad and then you want me to be young and happy. You want tragedy. Then you want a boyfriend. You look like you want to make love and then you don't. Back and forth. Back and forth."

"Now you know how I feel," she said.

"No." I was getting real angry now. "I have no idea how you feel. It never lasts long enough for me to find out."

"Then you're lucky, Daniel. You see, I know how you feel. I know how David feels. My mother is a couple of thousand miles away and I know exactly how she feels. I know how I would like to feel. I know everything and all these things I know are pulling at me."

She turned on the radio. The loud music absorbed our anger. She turned it off when we crossed the steel drawbridge over the Calumet River Canal.

"He tried to run away," she said.

"Who?"

"David."

"Your father?"

She blew up.

"Every time I say his name, you say 'your father.' I know who he is. Don't you think I know? His name is David. Can we call him David?"

She turned on the music again and left it on until we drove past my high school. The rhythm of the radio going on and off reminded me of my ride from the state finals with Coach French.

"Remember that day last week?" she said after a while, trying to remain calm. "You were coming down the street and David drove past you and got out of the car. Remember the way he looked?"

I remembered him clearly. Clothes wrinkled, pocket turned out, standing on the lawn looking down at the grass.

"Do you?" She repeated the question.

"Yes."

"Well, he left. He tried to run away but he came back. You saw the way he looked."

"Why did he want to run away?"

"Because he thought it would be better for me. One less thing pulling at me. But he couldn't stay away."

She turned down Aberdeen Lane. All the lights were off in her house. He must have turned off the porch light after we left. She parked the car in the same spot and looked at the dark house.

"I'm all he has," she said, and then as if days had suddenly passed, not seconds, she changed before my eyes. She smiled, her eyes shone. "God, it was nice, wasn't it, with the music and the kids and all?"

She looked so happy, it seemed so important to her, that I couldn't possibly disagree. "Yes, it was," I said.

"A beach party!" Her whole face beamed. I could almost see the bonfire in her eyes. "With my very own boyfriend." She kissed me suddenly, holding me tightly as if it were cold outside and she wanted to absorb all the warmth she could. Then she removed the car keys and jumped out. I watched her run across the lawn and into the house.

I got out of the car and shook some sand off my trousers. A light came on in a room upstairs. I imagined her father standing up there in front of her the way he had stood that day on the lawn: arms hanging helplessly, his head bowed, eyes looking at the ground. I imagined her going up to him the way she had that day. I began imagining other things, bizarre things I had never thought about in my whole life. My own brain frightened me. I ran home to keep from thinking. I blamed my father, his sickness, his madness, for my thoughts.

Chapter 26

My father could no longer walk, not even with the help of the cane, so my mother bought him a wheelchair. It was now a part of my job to push him around town in his chair. He enjoyed going outside, and although I hated doing it, hated being coupled to him in such a direct fashion, I preferred it to just sitting in the house listening to him attacking me, attacking my mother, attacking Rachel, or suddenly bursting into tears pleading for me to love him. It was simpler this way. Both of us faced in the same direction and so we didn't have to look at each other. The noise of the streets covered up his words. The rattling, swaying motion of the wheelchair seemed to pacify him, and he would fall silent for minutes at a time. Sometimes he fell asleep, and then I felt as if I were pushing his corpse to a funeral home. The days got longer, hotter, but he was always cold, always shivering despite the blankets that covered him. My shift began, as before, when my mother went to work. We stayed out from around four o'clock until the sunset, and during that time it was my duty always to steer the wheelchair toward the sunny side of the streets. If we stayed in the shade for too long he complained bitterly that I was trying to kill him. He insisted on carrying his cane in his lap, and whenever we saw an attractive girl in the street, he pointed with his cane.

"Is that her? Is that your love? Is that Rachel?"

I used to say "No," and then, just to spite him, I began saying "Yes."

"Yes, that's her."

He'd point to another one.

"That's right, Dad. There she is again."

"There is no Rachel." He laughed. "Making her up. That's what you're doing. You're just making her up."

"That's right, Dad. You know everything."

He hated it when I disagreed with him, but he hated it even more when I agreed with everything he said. He tried to twist around in the chair so he could look at me, but he was too weak to manage it. I watched him struggle as I pushed the chair, and quite often I went out of my way to steer the chair over a bump or a pothole just for the pleasure of getting him upset. Whenever one of his tirades got too long and unendurable, a good bump would make him drop the subject so he could scream at me and tell me to keep my eyes open and look where I was going. I hated it when he said Rachel's name, and whenever he did I managed to find a bump to pay him back for using it. Sometimes I shut my eyes as I pushed the chair, imagining myself being somewhere else. At other times it seemed as if I were handcuffed to it and would go through the rest of my life pushing him up and down the streets of East Chicago, waiting for him to die, getting older waiting, dying myself in the end while he kept getting smaller, even more cadaverous, but continued to live.

The wobbly front wheels of the wheelchair, when my eyes were shut, sounded at times like a distant train rattling along the tracks, and invariably I would push my father past the public library to the railroad crossing. A couple of times I was lucky and got there just as the train was going by. I stood there imagining being on the train with Rachel, leaving East Chicago forever. When the train rattled away and I heard the sound of the gates at the railroad crossing going up I returned to reality, but a reality of my own creation. I wheeled my father home past the library, steering clear of Aberdeen Lane, and saw Rachel and myself as a couple of doomed lovers held in tragic destinies by our fathers. The tragedy seemed so real, the music of the tragedy so audible that I could almost hear the words of a poem that would go with the music. The rhythm of the music was always the sound of the railroad wheels rattling away: Ra-chel, Ra-chel, Ra-chel.

She didn't wear black again, nor did she put on makeup or lipstick. She left her hair uncombed and seemed in general to be going out of her way to look unattractive, at least when I saw her. It bothered me that she usually wore something of her father's, his polo shirts or his long-sleeved plaid shirt with the sleeves rolled up above her elbows. It bothered me even more when I caught a glimpse of him wearing one of these shirts himself a few days later. He stayed out of sight whenever I came to the house. He never answered the door; he never even replied when Rachel called to him from the doorway to tell him she was going out.

"He's all involved with his work," Rachel said when I asked her about him. When I tried to get her to talk about him some more, she refused.

"It's not right," she said, "for the two of us to be chatting about him." She made a face when she said "chatting," as if it were something distasteful.

I was sure that he had taken a dislike to me. I felt him coming between Rachel and me just as my own father had come between us. He had returned and occupied the couch, the only place where we had ever made love. No other place seemed to work. Now Rachel's father was occupying her thoughts. It was like a conspiracy of fathers. I imagined the two of them calling each other on the telephone when Rachel and I were together and devising new strategies to drive us apart.

"Your father doesn't like me, does he?" I asked Rachel.

"Please, Daniel." She spoke slowly, shutting her eyes. "Don't start that again. He likes you. It's not you . . ."

She left the sentence unfinished, but she looked so tense I was afraid to say anything.

My only way of coping with my life was to imagine explanations to unanswered questions, imagine scenes between Rachel and myself that I was dying to have in real life, imagine killing my father, going to jail, writing love poems to Rachel from my cell. The things I imagined frightened me sometimes. It seemed, in my mind at least, very easy to push my father in front of the train. When I felt guilty about these thoughts I imagined him making love to Rachel and the murder seemed justified. It took hours to get over the shock and disgust that some of these self-inflicted images produced. To get over them I had to create other images. It was becoming habitforming, compulsive. Rachel's father had a darkroom in the basement. I carried mine with me.

"Is that her?" My father continued to point at girls in the street. "Is that Rachel? Is that my darling son's Rachel?"

"Yes, that's her."

"No, it's not." He was getting wise to my game. "I wonder where she is."

I ran his wheelchair into a lamppost on purpose, but he was getting used to that. It didn't seem to bother him anymore. His body was dead. He felt nothing with it. Only his head, sticking out of the blankets, worked. His eyes. His ears. His mouth.

"I know where she is." He laughed. "With someone else, I bet. Smiling for somebody else. Yes. Spreading her lips into a smile for him. I bet she likes it better with him."

"There's nobody else, Dad."

"You know that?"

"Yes."

"Oh, you're a genius, then. If you know that, you're a genius. My son is a genius!" he shouted. I pushed the chair faster and faster. I began running, hoping the speed would distract him.

Did she love him? he kept asking my mother. How much did she love him? When she tried to answer he cut her off. It wasn't enough. It wasn't the kind of love he wanted. More. He wanted more. Not the kind of love she offered but some other incontestable love.

It struck me more and more that what he wanted from my mother, the kind of love he wanted from her, I wanted from Rachel. His style was different, his words were different, but the objective was the same. The less I wanted to be like him, the more like him I was becoming.

I knew cancer wasn't contagious, but there were nights when I lay in bed and felt it creeping toward me across the living-room floor, under my door, up my sheets, up my legs.

In his footsteps. Like father, like son.

His words stayed with me. His gestures. The doubts he planted and continued to plant about Rachel stayed with me. At times my eyes looking at her felt like his eyes looking at my mother. "Smile for me," I almost said to her several times.

"Do you love me?" I kept asking her.

"Of course I love you," she answered, both the question and the reply making her impatient, tired.

"How much?"

"Enough. Isn't that good enough for you?"

If my questions angered her sufficiently she told me to go home and leave her alone. Sometimes, however, she seemed to take pity on me, and with eyes full of concern she would try to make me feel better.

"What's the matter with you, Daniel? You're only eighteen. You're my boyfriend. Be happy."

"I don't want to be your boyfriend," I said. "I want to be your lover."

"I need a boyfriend, Daniel. I really do."

She refused to make love to me. On weekends, the only evenings and nights we had, we would get in her car and she would drive around town playing music on the radio. Sometimes two or three cars full of kids would go past us and she would follow them, clearly pretending that we were part of some group. We followed one such car to Hammond, to a strange house on a strange street. There was a party in the house. Music was playing. Through the windows we could see the kids dancing inside. Six kids jumped out of the car we were following and ran to the door. Rachel wanted to follow them inside.

"We can't do that," I said. "We don't know anybody here."

"C'mon," she pleaded, "they won't kick us out. We'll go inside and make friends."

I wouldn't go. We stayed in the car and watched. She refused to leave. A half an hour later the music stopped, the lights dimmed and we heard a large happy chorus singing "Happy Birthday." Rachel sang along softly with them, looking past me through the car window at the party inside.

The lights came back on. The music returned. They began dancing again. She held the steering wheel with both hands, moving her shoulders to the music, mouthing the words of a Sam Cooke song. We stayed there until kids began leaving, and when she drove home I had the distinct impression that she was pretending we had spent the evening inside the house, with the others.

We parked in front of her house, her father's house. She began kissing me. This was the ritualistic conclusion to our weekend nights. Nowhere else, not on the beach, not in the park, not even on the couch in the living room where we once made love did her desire for me seem nearly as intense. I could feel the surface temperature of her skin rising wherever my hand touched her. Her heart beat faster. Her breathing became audible. My hands could go wherever I wanted them to go, but a moment would always come when I wanted to make love, when I felt her wanting it herself, and at that very moment she would pull back, button her father's shirt, pull the keys out of the ignition and run inside the house.

I stayed in the car feeling used, but I could not tell how or why.

Had she just teased me I would have understood it, but that was not the case. Her own desire seemed so genuine, so intense, and yet her need to rush across the lawn with that desire intact baffled me. If I didn't know for certain that only her father waited inside I would have suspected her of having a secret lover waiting for her there.

I turned my desire for her into dreams, into anger, into attempts at poetry. What did she do with her desire for me?

In my imagination I followed her inside the house and on different nights I imagined different things. I saw her writing in her diary and I imagined I saw what she was writing.

My father, she always began. I saw her writing. I saw the diary. I saw the words on the page. My father does not believe that Daniel really loves me.

On other nights I imagined him coming into her room and turning on the lights and just standing there, head bowed, looking at the floor like a human question mark.

I was sure that he was responsible for her strange behavior. He kept her from giving herself completely to me.

Maybe, I reasoned, he was very strict. Maybe Rachel had been hurt by someone before and he wanted to keep it from happening again. I was sure he did not understand the nature of my love for her, and I was determined to find a way to convince him of it.

As I walked home I imagined having a scene with him. Sir, I told him, perhaps you are used to meeting young men my age whose intentions leave a lot to be desired. Let me assure you from the start that I am not one of those. My intentions are honorable. I love your daughter dearly and wish to marry her. I saw him smile with relief. He apologized for any suspicions he might have had about me and then the two of us went out on the porch to tell Rachel the happy news. You can do no better than him, he told her, putting his arm around my shoulder.

"Ra-chel, Ra-chel, Ra-chel." The train rattled past the library, heading east. My hands rested on the handles of my father's wheelchair. The wind created by the train moved the tassels on the blankets that covered him. His head was slumped over. He was asleep. It was only Tuesday. I had to wait three more nights before I could have another night with Rachel.

When I think, Rachel, of the nights we've already missed . . . I shut my eyes and tried to write my poem.

Maybe it was this particular railroad crossing, the proximity to the library, that made me suddenly remember Misiora and Freud. The three of us had walked to school down this same street, across those same railroad tracks, stood countless times as I was standing now to watch the train go by. The three of us. Buddy Plans. "For golden friends I had . . ." A line of someone else's poetry rattled through my head.

When I think, Rachel, of the friends I lost for you . . .

It surprised me that I missed them. It shocked me that I hadn't thought of them for weeks. We had been inseparable.

I missed the life I had. I missed Freud leaning on me and Misiora's mean blue eyes losing their meanness on Mrs. Dewey's porch. The walks to and from school, the wrestling practice, the junior year with a year to go, the feeling that next year would be my year, I missed it all. I knew what it was like to make love to a girl but I missed the wonder of it and the airy open-window feeling in my head, where now a darkroom stood developing images and scenes I never envisioned in that, my earlier life.

How was it possible? Had I become somebody else? Standing there I felt as old as my father, and the memory of my days with Misiora and Freud was like a memory of someone else, another friend called Daniel that I had once had and lost.

I waited for the long freight train to go by. Maybe when it did I would see the two of them on the other side with a space between them reserved for me. I would cross the tracks and resume the life I had abandoned. The three of us.

But when the caboose went past me I saw only a line of backed-up cars. Night was falling and their headlights were on. The sound of the departing train filled my head with the sound of her name. "Ra-chel. Ra-chel. Ra-chel." Each rattle of the wheels produced a syllable, each syllable a different image. The syllables came together to form a name, but the images of Rachel never came together into one person.

"Ra-chel. Ra-chel. Ra-chel." My heart beat to the rhythm of the train. The front wheels of my father's chair as I pushed him home chattered her name.

The three of us, I thought. First it was my mother, my father and me. Then Misiora, Freud and me. And now Rachel, David and me. The symmetry of these images made me think that my life was following some plan, that I was moving in some natural, evolutionary fashion toward my destiny. But in the darkroom of my brain other images appeared, and these were not natural or rational or something I wanted to see.

When I think, Rachel, of the nights we've already missed . . . I forced myself to concentrate on poetry again as a way of keeping the demons away.

Chapter 27

It was her father's blue plaid shirt that made me lose control. I came to take her for a walk. She was waiting for me on the porch. I didn't even hear her slamming the door shut behind her. I saw that blue shirt coming toward me and I felt like ripping it off her body.

"Hello, Daniel." She smiled her weary smile, her afternoon smile.

"Yes, hello," I said, beginning to tremble.

I hadn't slept much that night. I had spent hours trying to write my poem to her without getting anywhere. When I turned off the light and went to bed, I saw disgusting images of her and my father. When I turned the light back on and tried to write, nothing came. I got up in the middle of the night and tried to take a hot shower but there was no hot water. I masturbated in order to fall asleep, and the proximity of my father dying on the living-room couch where Rachel and I had made love made the act of masturbation feel loathsome. My own sperm had the odor of hospitals and medicine and my father's dying body.

I fell asleep near dawn and slept late into the day. My mother woke me up to tell me that lunch was on the table. When I came out of the room my father began screaming at me. How could I sleep? Didn't I care that he was in agony? What kind of monster was I?

My mother brought him soup. She offered to feed him herself but he knocked the plate over with his cane. She took it back and put it in the sink. She washed it for at least ten minutes with her back turned to us. When she and I sat down at the table to eat, he began screaming again. Was that all we thought about? Food? Our stomachs? Was that the kind of monsters we were? He seemed tiny lying there on the couch, covered up with blankets so that only his head showed, an infant, but his voice carried. His voice had teeth and fingernails that bit and clawed.

In the middle of our eating soup, Mr. Kula, our landlord, came in without knocking. He stayed there framed by the kitchen doorway but refused to come into the kitchen itself. He complained about my father. All that screaming! People were stopping in front of the house, he said. If the man was that sick he should be in a hospital. He had been in the hospital, my mother told him. We had no money left. We couldn't afford to keep him there anymore. Mr. Kula said he couldn't afford to have the reputation of his house ruined. My mother began defending my father. He was sick. He had cancer. He had a right to his agony. God would punish him, she warned Mr. Kula, if he did not have sympathy for my father. She seemed ready to cry.

"Who's there?" my father kept screaming from the couch. "I'm not dead yet. My replacement, is that who it is?"

When Mr. Kula left I waited a few seconds and then got up and ran out of the house. Once in the street, I realized I was still carrying my soup spoon. I didn't know what to do with it. My whole life came to a stop while I stood there wondering what to do with the soup spoon. Take it back? Put it in my pocket? Stick it under the door? I wanted to throw it away, but although I had thrown many things into the street, I had never thrown away a soup spoon. I kept looking at it, getting more and more paralyzed by my options. I could stick it in the mailbox and on my way home take it back inside. Finally I flung it away and called Rachel from the pay phone. I have to see you, I told her.

I hurried to her house, making sure not to forget a single problem I had. I wanted her to take care of them one by one. And then I caught a glimpse of that shirt on the porch. Instantly I came to the conclusion that she had worn it on purpose just to spite me.

It was one o'clock. At four I would have to be home again to replace my mother. Three hours. We walked to our little grassy field where I had seen the cheerleaders practice. It was deserted. In the distance the highway crew was working on the interstate.

We sat down on the hot, dry grass. Rachel pulled out a blade of grass and began chewing on it. She rocked gently, thinking. Her shirt was open—*his* shirt was open. I could see her breasts. As she rocked, the loose fabric kept touching the tips of her nipples and I saw, or imagined I saw, the nipples harden.

"Aren't you hot in that shirt?" I said.

She was deep in her thoughts. Hearing my voice, she focused on me slowly, as if waking up. There, I thought. There's something I have never seen. Rachel waking up.

"What did you say?" She smiled.

"Your shirt. It's flannel, isn't it? Aren't you hot?"

"It's all right. It's loose. Feels good on a day like this."

"It's too big for you."

"That's why it's loose," she said slowly, and seeing that it was unbuttoned too far down, she lazily slipped two buttons through the buttonholes.

"I was daydreaming when you called. I guess I still am." She looked past me into the distance at the highway crew. I was going to ask her what it was she was daydreaming about or give her a lecture about how wonderful it was that she could daydream while inches away I was going through hell. But then she saw something and smiled again, a different smile this time.

I turned and looked. All I saw was the highway crew. Dust. Bulldozers. Sun bouncing off the hard hats of the crew.

"What are you smiling at?" I asked her.

"Just something." She chewed on the blade of grass.

"I know it's something. But what is it?" I couldn't bear her privacy anymore. I didn't have the energy or the patience to keep on wondering. I simply wanted a straightforward answer for once.

She hardly noticed my hostile tone. She pointed into the distance.

"It looks like they're making ruins," she said.

I looked again. She was pointing at a half-finished overpass. The concrete posts and the structure they supported did in fact look like the ruins of some temple.

It annoyed me that she was right. It annoyed me that she could notice, think to notice, take time out to notice something that inconsequential when I was sitting there in torment and when she was the one responsible for it.

"We can't go on like this, Rachel," I said.

"I know." She nodded, still looking at the overpass, thinking her thoughts.

"Can't you at least look at me when I'm talking to you?"

"Sure," she said and looked at me. But she was still thinking about something else.

"It's been very hard on me, Rachel. These last few weeks."

"I know. It's been hard on all of us."

"Can't we just talk about you and me?" I screamed. She didn't so much as flinch. She seemed underwater.

"We can try," she said. She looked at me as if she were remembering me. As if she were far away and I were a memory.

"Rachel. I don't know what's going on anymore. I love you. You say you love me."

"I do," she said.

"Then why does it feel like it's all falling apart?" I wanted to put her on the defensive, to get her to deny it and reassure me that it was not true. She did nothing of the sort. She chewed on her blade of grass. Then she spoke.

"The only way you can tell that something is really yours is if you feel free enough to ruin it. If you have to worry about things, look after them, make sure they're doing well, then they're not really yours. By ruining things you make them your own."

"I'm not talking about things, Rachel. I'm talking about us." I was the one who was now going on the defensive. "If you love somebody you don't want to ruin it. It doesn't make sense, and when things don't make sense—"

"People still do them," she cut in. "They really do, Daniel. I do."

Her "I do" sounded simple, declarative and final. I could see the period at the end of it.

She got up. Her father's shirt fell down her hips. She stood there looking into the distance. "Maybe that's why I love Greece so much," she said. "The ruins!" She spread out her arms as if they stood in front of her. As if she saw them. Then she turned slowly and started to walk. She looked back to see if I was coming. She wasn't inviting me to come, nor was she telling me not to come. She just seemed curious.

I watched her go. The soup-spoon syndrome was taking hold of me again. Every impulse I had for action was paralyzed by a counterimpulse. Follow her? Stay? Call her back? Remain silent? Rachel was pulling me up. The earth wouldn't let go. The hot sun was weighing me down. My eyes were shutting. I could feel myself falling asleep. There, I thought. There's something I can do.

I dreamed about extension cords. All the people in the dream had extension cords sticking out of them. I was plugged into Rachel, and although she wasn't there I knew which cord led to her. I was plugged into my father. My mother. There was a cord that led to Freud's garage and another one that just trailed off into the distance, attached to Misiora. A door-to-door extension-cord salesman appeared and wanted to sell me more. I have all I can use, I told him, but he wouldn't listen. I needed one for a church. Another one to plug into a factory where I worked. You're not a kid anymore, he kept telling me. You need more. He kept plugging them into me. My temperature began to rise. I felt overloaded. I was sure I would go up in flames.

I woke up. The first thing I saw was my wristwatch. It was a quarter to three. When I got to my feet I felt dizzy. The back of my head was very hot. I stumbled across the field toward Aberdeen Lane.

Half the street was in the sun, the other half in shadows cast by the tall trees. I walked in the shadows, still dizzy but feeling better with each step. Sprinklers were on in the lawns. The air felt cool and friendly. It reminded me of the day I made my leaf collection.

Amazing, I thought, what a little sleep can do. That was all I needed. Feel like a different person. Too bad Rachel's not here to see me like this.

Even when I saw her father outside her house I didn't react in my normal way. There he was sitting on the steps drinking something. He seemed like any other man. I walked toward him. It seemed like a perfect time to have my chat with him about Rachel. What seemed absurd was that it had taken me so long to get around to it. He had a right to know how I felt about his daughter.

"Hello," I said.

He turned. The ice cubes knocked against the glass in his hand. He hadn't seen me approaching.

"Hello, young man."

He was wearing a polo shirt and shorts. His legs were white, and even when relaxed his calf muscles looked powerful. There was a round red mark on the top of his thigh as if he had been holding the glass there for a long time.

"It's very hot," he said, looking up at the sun through the treetops. The wrinkles in his neck disappeared when he looked up and then returned when he lowered his neck.

"Sure is," I replied.

"Can I offer you something?" The fingers on his free hand fanned out.

"No, thank you."

"I can't offer you anything?" He wanted to smile when he said this, but he didn't. He wanted to look at me, but he didn't. A little vein in his temple was pulsating. He put the glass against it.

"Well, there is something," I said. I considered calling him David but changed my mind. "It's about your daughter, sir." I liked the formal tone of this sentence. It sounded mature and yet preserved the difference in our ages.

He took the glass away from his temple.

"Rachel?" He raised an eyebrow. Then he laughed without moving his lips, as if the laugh were coming from his chest. "You want me to offer you Rachel?"

I laughed too. He was making a joke and it behooved me to laugh. The word "behooved" seemed terribly appropriate. Formal. Mature. Just right for the occasion.

"No, sir. Not offer. I would just like you to understand how I feel about her."

He put the glass carefully on his thigh, determined, it seemed, to cover the imprint left there.

"Don't you think I know how you feel about her?" he said, pressing down on the glass and grinding it slightly into his flesh.

"I hope you do, sir. But just in case you may have lingering doubts about the nature of my intentions, I would like to set your mind at rest."

He laughed again without moving his lips.

"If you can do that, young man, you'll be doing me a great favor. The nature of Rachel's intentions"—he used my words with a slight bow of his head as if seeking permission—"certainly isn't setting my mind to rest."

"Your daughter loves you very much, sir."

The glass sank deeper into his thigh. The vein in his temple began to throb a little faster.

I continued. "And I'm sure you love her equally as much, sir."

"If not more, right?" he said.

"Yes, sir. If not more," I agreed readily.

"So, then." He almost looked at me. "Let me see if I have this whole thing right. Rachel loves me very much and I love her as much if not more."

While he spoke, since there was no eye contact, I looked at the vein on his temple. He spoke slowly but the vein throbbed faster and faster. Ra-chel. Ra-chel. Ra-chel.

"And if all that is true"—he stared inside his glass—"it just leaves one question unanswered." He paused and turned the glass some more. "How do you fit into all this, young man?"

Finally, I thought, we get around to me.

"I love your daughter very much."

Ra-chel. Ra-chel. Ra-chel. I couldn't take my eyes off his temple.

"But unlike most young men my age," I continued, "my intentions in regard to her are honorable in the extreme." I didn't know why I added "in the extreme." It just came out. The scene wasn't going quite the way I thought it would. The glass turning and the vein throbbing were beginning to upset me. My own heart began beating to the rhythm of the vein on his temple. I was aware of its speed. It became a contest. I wanted my heart to beat faster.

"I love her more than anyone else in the world, sir." Although I spoke slowly, measuring my words, my heart was racing along. He hardly moved, and his was, too. Ra-chel. Ra-chel. Ra-chel. I was gaining on him.

"I know you do," he said. "I do too."

"I know you do." I repeated his words and felt my heart passing his. Boom. Boom. Boom. Like a train passing another train. "It was just important to me to have you understand exactly how I felt so there wouldn't be any unnecessary misapprehensions." I used the word for the first time in my life. A phrase popped into my head: "Intercede on my behalf." I wondered how I could find a way to use it. It seemed perfect for the occasion.

He lifted the glass off his thigh. A red mark much more prominent than before stayed there. He leaned back a little as if hearing somebody inside calling him. I heard no one. He did it again, only this time he turned his head and I saw his eyes and in them some desperate need to be called away. But the house was empty. Whom was he waiting for?

"Naturally," I said, "since I'm so new at all this, love and all, there will be times when even Rachel misunderstands the true nature of my feelings and at such times I would deeply appreciate it, Mr. Temerson, if you could intercede on my behalf."

He suddenly rose to his feet. Both of us had been still for so long that his abrupt rise was startling. He looked right at me. His lips moved, but whatever those words were, he chose not to say them. He tried to smile and looked at his glass.

"The ice has melted," he said and emptied the water into the grass. "And since there's nothing I can offer you . . ." He shrugged, turned around, opened the screen door and walked inside.

I was going to leave myself. I was just getting ready to thank him for his time when he stopped. His back was to me and when I saw his head begin to turn I thought it was in order to say goodbye to me. Instead it stopped in profile. He seemed to be looking down at somebody on the porch.

I imagined, just before I left, Rachel lying on the cool cement looking up at him.

Chapter 28

I stayed in bed Thursday until almost two o'clock.

"I'm not hungry," I told my mother when she came to tell me that lunch was ready. Her eyes looked worried, maternal, but she left me alone. I couldn't hear my father. Maybe he was sleeping.

A strange, sweet paralysis held me fast. I lay in bed, shut my eyes, and imagined. Soup-spoon syndrome. Darkroom dreams.

My bed was a raft and I was floating down the Mississippi with Huck and Tom. I coughed and I was instantly one of those doomed poetic souls atop the magic mountain. It was easy and pleasant to be somebody else.

When I decided to be myself again, I thought of Rachel. I imagined her lying on the cool cement of the porch listening to my conversation with her father. Then I imagined her writing in her diary.

Daniel and David had a long talk. David seemed very taken with Daniel's maturity and the sincerity of his love for me. I finally feel that everything is going to work out perfectly.

Having made sure that my own life was working out well, I turned over in my bed and went back to being somebody else.

It began to rain when my mother left for work. My father looked out of the window.

"I guess we won't be going out today," he said.

"Not unless it stops."

We sat in the living room. I didn't know what he was thinking, but I was not in the living room at all. I was with Rachel. We were driving to Cedar Lake. It was winter. Our ice skates were in the back seat. I was driving.

"Daniel." My father called me. His voice was weak. There was no anger in it.

"Yes, Dad."

He had nothing to say. He just wanted my attention. He called me back several times from my trips.

It got dark. Rain continued to fall.

"Daniel."

"Yes, Dad."

His eyes shone in the darkness like buttons on a doll's face.

"When you were a baby and your mother wasn't around, I used to tell you things."

"What kind of things, Dad?"

"All kinds. How I felt. How I loved you. But you don't remember, do you?"

"I was just a baby. You said yourself . . ."

"Do you remember when I dressed up as Santa Claus?"

"No, I don't."

"I did," he said. He seemed to be smiling. "I picked you up in my arms and my beard scared you and you started crying." He laughed. "It was so funny. It's just me, I kept telling you, it's just your daddy. But you didn't recognize me and you screamed and screamed. Poor little thing. So scared."

I suspected him of treachery. Why else was he telling me this? Why else was his voice so soft and loving? He sensed that I was drifting away and he wanted me back.

"And do you know what happened then?" His little hand waved in the air. "I looked out of the window and saw your mother. She was carrying groceries. I remember it all." He seemed delighted. "And do you know what I did? I ran out of the house with you in my arms screaming away. I knew what I was doing. Well, when your mother saw us! She recognized the sound of your voice right away. Those peasant women are like that. She stopped in her tracks. Her baby. Who is that strange man in a red suit and a beard who's running off with her baby?" He cackled merrily. "You see, I started running. I knew what I was doing. And then she starts running after us. She is chasing us and screaming, telling me to stop. And you're crying. I was laughing so hard I had to stop. Yes. She pulls me by the shoulder and my beard falls off. And you! You were just a baby, but when the beard fell off you recognized me. It was Daddy! And you smiled and reached up to touch my face with your little hands."

He started crying.

"The three of us walked home together," he said, wiping his nose. "Through the snow. I kept putting on my beard and taking it off and you just screamed with delight every time. Yes. That's how it was. And because I was making you happy, your mother looked at me and smiled in a very special way. Such a loving way. And through the snow we went. The three of us. My favorite Christmas ever."

I was in bed when my mother came home from work that night. My father went after her right away. He called her a slut, a whore. He wanted to know where she had been.

"*Husband!*" she cried out. Her voice shook the house. I jumped out of bed and stood in the darkness with my ear to the door. Neither she nor my father said another word.

I went back to bed. I had never heard my mother's voice sound so defiant, so strong and yet exhausted. I imagined her holding a kitchen knife in her hand as she cried out.

I'm not the only one, I thought. She too can be somebody else.

Chapter 29

It continued to rain on Friday. No lightning, no thunder, no wind. Just rain.

I got up late again. My father was looking out of the window.

"I guess we won't be going out today," he said.

"Not unless it stops," I said.

"It won't stop." He shook his head.

After lunch my mother told me that she was taking a day off from work. She said she was tired and needed to rest, but I think she was doing it for me.

"You go," she said. "Spend evening with your friends. Enjoy yourself."

She seemed concerned about me, her dark eyes full of love and worry. I would have given anything to see that look in Rachel's eyes. I stayed in the kitchen with her and even when she turned her back to do the dishes I felt cradled by her eyes. I was in her thoughts.

This is how it will be with Rachel someday, I thought. I'll be sitting here, she'll be doing the dishes and without her saying a word I'll know she loves me and is thinking of me.

"It is raining," she said as I started to go outside. "Take your jacket."

I took it but didn't put it on. I called Rachel from the pay phone on the corner. Before I could tell her the good news that we had tonight to ourselves, she told me that she and David were leaving for the weekend. They were just packing. I put the phone down and rushed to her house. It was only a little after four, but the overcast sky made it seem much later. I was soaking wet when I got there. I carried my jacket over my shoulder and I was positive the first thing Rachel would tell me when she saw me would be to put it on.

She didn't. She was coming out of the house carrying a suitcase. I insisted on taking it from her.

"David wants to shoot some pictures of university campuses in Indiana," she told me, although I didn't ask her where they were going. "So we're going to go look at Indiana University, Purdue, and something called Ball State."

I put the suitcase in the back.

"Thank you," she said. It seemed like such a strange, polite thing to say and she said it in such a strange, polite way.

"You're very welcome." I tried giving my voice just the right touch of irony, hoping to make her smile. She didn't. She seemed very preoccupied about the trip.

"Where will you sleep?" I asked her, slinging my jacket over my other shoulder. She didn't notice.

"Oh, there's motels everywhere, I imagine."

"Were you going to call me to tell me you were leaving?" I asked.

She didn't answer. Her father came out of the house and she went to him. He had a raincoat draped over his shoulders to protect the cameras he was carrying. She said something to him as they walked to the car. He just shook his head in reply.

I slung my jacket over the other shoulder. I felt I was waving it like a flag.

"Hello, young man," her father said as he walked past me.

"Hello, sir."

He shook the rain off his raincoat and got into the car. He took the passenger seat. Rachel came toward me twirling the car keys.

"Listen," she said, not looking at me, "we'll be back."

Again, I thought it was a strange thing to say.

"I certainly hope so." I tried for irony one more time. I smiled. She didn't. She got into the car and drove off without turning on the windshield wipers.

It was all so quick and strange that it took me more than fifteen minutes just standing there in the rain before I could do anything.

The porch door was unlocked so I went inside and sat on the porch. The more I thought about it, the more sense it made. The two of them had probably discussed in detail my talk with David and had jointly decided that she could do no better than to marry someone like myself. She was very happy and he was happy for her. But after the initial joy the realization came that I would be the man in her life from then on and not her father. So they were going off for one last time, father and daughter, on a farewell trip of sorts.

My conclusions sounded so comforting that I felt a need to see them in writing. Somewhere inside the house, unless she had taken it with her, was Rachel's diary. It would all be in there. Not just this last entry but all the other entries as well. Her whole past. I imagined finding it, reading it, and understanding finally who she was and how she felt about me. The proximity of the prize made me try the door. It was locked. I tried the window on the porch. Locked. I went outside and, making sure nobody saw me, tried all the windows and the back door. All locked. For a moment I considered breaking one of the windows and forcing my way into the house, but some fear kept me from it.

She probably had taken the diary with her, I decided. I didn't know where to go. I couldn't go home. My mother had taken a day off from work just so I could have an extra evening to myself. Enjoy myself. I couldn't disappoint her.

I walked in the rain with the word "motel" rattling around in my head. She was going to sleep in a motel. Misiora, Freud, Mrs. Dewey and I were all going to drive to Wisconsin Dells and sleep in a motel ourselves. Where the hell was Misiora now? A Dell! I still didn't know what the hell a Dell was.

That familiar paralysis was creeping into my body. Is this what it would feel like, I thought, if Rachel ever left? Left for good?

I wound up standing in front of the public library. I just stood there getting wetter and wetter, trying to think of something to do. Dells. I finally had a flash of inspiration. I could go inside and look up Dell in a dictionary. My mother wouldn't have to know how I spent my evening.

The library was empty. When the door shut after me, a head appeared behind the desk, only a head. It was the same old librarian who had been there as far back as I could remember. She smiled.

"I bent down to pick up a card and my back locked up on me," she said. "Arthritis, you know." She took a deep breath. "Here goes." She grimaced and grunted and wiggled around and straightened herself. She exhaled with relief.

"Happens whenever it rains for a while. It's the dampness. I don't know why it's the dampness, but it seems to be. You'd think damp things would be loose and flexible, but no."

She had curly gray hair, glasses dangling around her neck, and she wore a lot of rouge. She had looked this way for years and years. I stood in the doorway, dripping wet, hesitant to mess up the clean floor.

"Come in," she said. "Come in. It's all right. Everybody has his job. There's a night man whose job it is to clean the floors. Our job is to mess them up."

Her telephone rang.

"Hello, library. Yes, we certainly are open. You're welcome." She put the phone down. "What do they think? Just because it's raining, I'm not going to open the library? Honestly!"

A touch of palsy made her head shake. She looked at me as if trying to remember me, and then she put on her glasses and looked at me some more.

"I thought I . . ." she said. "Ah, never mind. I just thought I . . . well . . ."

She took her glasses off and began going through some cards. I walked toward the bookshelves in the back.

"*Now I remember you.*" She banged on the desk.

I stopped and turned around. She pointed at me.

"You used to come in here with two of your friends to do your homework, didn't you?"

I did. I nodded.

"One was this real big boy." She spread out her arms. "He had this terribly loud laugh, and the other one was blond and bothered the girls all the time. Right?"

"Yes."

"Well, I thought I . . . So, the three of you are all done with school?"

"Yes. All done."

"I'm certainly glad you didn't forget about us." She spread out her arms, motioning to the books. "Most kids, you know, once they graduate, never come back. I miss them. Well, we all have our jobs, I guess. Can I help you with anything?"

"No, I was just going to . . ."

"Browse? You go right ahead."

I turned to go and she banged on the desk again.

"*James Donovan.* That's your name, isn't it?"

She seemed so happy that she had remembered it and so sure that she was right that I didn't have the heart to tell her she was wrong.

"Yes, it is."

"Jimmy Donovan?"

"That's right."

"I never forget a name. Well, you go right ahead, Jimmy. Browse away."

A little puddle had formed on the floor where I was standing. I walked toward the back, disappearing inside the free-standing bookshelves that divided the rear part of the library into narrow corridors. The old smell of old books!

She banged on her desk again. I couldn't see her, but I could sure hear her.

"Ha!" she laughed. *"Isn't that how that friend of yours used to laugh? Ha! Like that?"* She did a pretty good imitation of Freud's laugh, for an old lady.

"Yes," I shouted, *"that's how he did it!"*

"He used to startle the daylights out of me," she shouted back. *"I'd be sitting here going through the overdues, and all of a sudden, there'd be that 'Ha!' and I'd practically fall out of my chair. Honestly!"*

She started typing. I continued browsing. It was like visiting an old neighborhood. Here and there, a newcomer had moved in. The Faulkner shelf used to end on the bottom of a row. Now it ended at the top of another row. *Moby Dick* was still torn. *A Tale of Two Cities* was in exactly the same place. I took out *The Catcher in the Rye.* It was the very copy Misiora had scribbled in. I even remembered the page numbers and flipped to them. On page 37 he had written in the margin: LOOK ON PAGE 64. And then on page 97, he had written: DID YOU LOOK ON PAGE 64?

I put it back and continued browsing. The library smelled of autumn and falling leaves.

The librarian typed away. Tap. Tap. Tap. I walked slowly, running my hand along the books, as if along a picket fence. Every now and then, when I saw a title I had never heard of, or a book I had never read, I pulled it out and took it with me. In this way I gathered five or six books. I sat down at a large wooden table and went through them one by one, reading the last page. That was how I used to select books to read when I used to read. The ends of things fascinated me: how it all turned out. I never read *Tender Is the Night* because I read the last sentence first and I didn't like it.

The last sentences of the first three books didn't do much for me, either. And then I read the fourth: "And out into the world I went."

I read it again.

"And out into the world I went."

It sounded so simple and wonderful. I wondered what kind of person it took to do something like that. Go out into the world. And out into the world I went. Just like that.

"*Here it comes, Jimmy!*" the old librarian shouted.

"*Excuse me?*"

"*The train! Here comes the train, right on time.*"

I heard the locomotive whistle and then the clatter and the rumble of the train along the tracks outside the library. I reread the last sentence again. And out into the world I went. I shut my eyes and hopped onto the train. I was somebody named James "Jimmy" Donovan and I was sitting inside the train, heading out into the world. I rocked and swayed, imagining looking out of the window at East Chicago, at the region, for the last time, and only when the train was gone and I heard the ding-ding-ding of the railroad-crossing gate going up did I open my eyes.

Tap. Tap. Tap. The old librarian was at the typewriter again. I was myself again. But I wanted to be James "Jimmy" Donovan. A man without a father. Without a mother. No girl in his life. Just a man with a name, going out into the world.

"I forgot my library card," I told the old librarian when I took the books to her desk. I took all of them, even the ones whose endings I didn't like. I suspected it made her happy to have somebody checking out a lot of books.

"That's all right." She took off her glasses. "Seeing as how I know you, I'll just issue you a new one."

She put a card in the typewriter and typed in "James Donovan." I gave her my real address. She typed that in and handed me the card. "Here you go, Jimmy."

Then she rummaged behind her desk and brought out a plastic bag. "Can't have the books getting wet, can we?" She looked on as I put the books in the bag. You would've thought she was placing orphans, she looked so pleased.

"I certainly didn't expect any visitors on a day like this. I'm so glad you came. And tell your friends to stop by sometime." She recited the hours during which the library was open and the holidays when it was closed.

"Bye."

"Goodbye, Jimmy."

As soon as I stepped outside, I remembered that I had wanted to look up "Dells" and hadn't. It was still raining.

And out into the rain I went.

Chapter 30

It was like a trick. When I pretended to be James "Jimmy" Donovan, everything changed, and although everything remained basically the same, everything still changed.

The rain finally stopped. I lay in my bed. Jimmy Donovan lay in his. I was in my room. He was in a motel room somewhere, and although it was the same room as mine, I preferred his. Both of us had the same memories, but we looked at them differently. I was inside mine. He was outside his, and although they were the same memories, I preferred his to mine. To him, everything that happened, happened a long time ago, he remembered it all, but he remembered it the way I remembered movies on a week-end afternoon. He saw his past. I saw through it, partially blind-ed by it.

It really was like a trick of some kind.

Both of us got out of bed. Even though my door was shut, I could hear the man next door breathing with difficulty. He was my father. To Jimmy, he was just a man in a room next to his. He had no father. He had no mother. His parents had died a long time ago. He remembered both of them, but he remembered them the way I remembered the books I had read. My father's breathing irritated me as if the air he was breathing were my air. Not Jimmy. He heard it, but he did not listen to it. He knew that a time would come when he too would be sick and old and near death. His heart went out to the old man in the next room. He reminded him of his father, who had died years ago.

I sat down at my table, turned on the lamp and read the last sentence again: "And out into the world I went." Then I began at the beginning. It was Maxim Gorky's *Childhood*. It began with his father's death. Destiny, I thought. It was destiny that made me choose this very book.

Not Jimmy. He didn't believe in destiny. He read, looking over my shoulder, but he didn't really feel like reading. He ran his fingers through his hair and he remembered Rachel. Rachel Temerson. He remembered the pain she had caused him without feeling it, the love he felt for her without yearning for it. She was his first love, and although there had been many since then, she occupied a special place in his heart. The sound of her name alone could set a tuning fork vibrating in his soul and make him see once again turquoise earrings dangling in the lamplight of Aberdeen Lane. He wasn't a poet for nothing. He wondered whatever became of her. How her life turned out. Where she was now. He wished her well.

I stuck a pencil in my mouth. Jimmy placed a cigarette between his lips. Both of us shut the book I was reading. Jimmy took a drag on the cigarette and placed an empty page in front of him. I wondered what he would write. He knew. He looked around the room. It looked familiar to him, but then, after a while, all motel rooms looked familiar.

TO RACHEL, he wrote at the top of the page. He knew she might never see it—he had no idea where she was, if she was alive, even —but he had been thinking of this poem for years and only now did he feel free enough to write it. The wind was blowing through the open window. Jimmy's mind wandered for a second. He thought of Misiora. An open window always made him think of Misiora, just as every unanswered letter made him think of Freud. Buddy plans. He smiled.

Then he said her name out loud: "Rachel."

The tuning fork began to vibrate. He heard music. Words followed.

TO RACHEL

> The list of things
> that I've already missed
> is long. On it
> are centuries of faces

cities and landscapes
that are gone.
The Rome that was.
The Greece that was.
There was a time
they tell me
when Lebanon
was covered with trees.
Then the Phoenicians came
cut the cedars down
and sailed away. So
I'll never know
the cedars that were
and the Lebanon that was.

"The Last Supper" is
being restored
but I'll never know,
never, never see
the colors on the wall
that were there on the day
when Leonardo
put the paintbrushes away.

They say Comanches
looked awkward on the ground
and glorious on horseback
but I'll never know.

I'll never know my father.
His photographs show a man
smiling at the camera,
easy to love and be loved by
but I'll never know that man,
never, never, find a way
to know what it was like
to be his son for a day.

The list, as they say,
goes on and on.

And having already missed
so much, why then, Rachel,
should I mourn
that I'll never see
you waking up in the morning
in my bed, next to me?

Chapter 31

Rachel returned on Sunday night. I called her from the pay phone across the street from my house.

"Hello," she answered.

I hung up. I just wanted to see if she was home.

I took out my poem and reread it for maybe the twentieth time. I had reread it in my room, in the bathroom; I couldn't get enough of it. Now I read it once again in the phone booth, turning the pages to catch the light from the streetlamp on the corner. It seemed like the best poem anyone had ever written. It had Rome and Greece and Da Vinci in it. It rhymed in places. I just loved it. I almost knew it by heart, but it was much more thrilling to read it off the pages, to see the words: "the cedars that were and the Lebanon that was."

Nobody, I thought, since time began, had ever written those words. I was the very first person in the history of mankind to put those words in that order.

I read it out loud, making my voice deeper than normal. It sounded wonderful. It didn't sound like me, but it sounded wonderful. Better than anything Misiora could write.

"... why then, Rachel,
should I mourn
that I'll never see
you waking up in the morning
in my bed, next to me?"

If that wasn't wonderful, I didn't know what was. I folded the poem and put it in my pocket. From where I stood, I could see the light in the window of my living room. My parents were inside. My father had been trying to make my mother cry all evening. Maybe she was crying now.

The next morning, I got up early and made three copies of my poem. One was for me. One was for Rachel. I had to have the third just in case the other two got lost. I put Rachel's in an envelope and addressed it to her. I put the other in my pocket. I put the spare inside my leaf collection.

"Where are you going?" my father wanted to know.

"Out."

"Me too. Take me."

"I'll be back right away," I lied.

"Take me."

"Mother will be up soon. Maybe she'll take you out."

"My last summer. To see. I want to see it." It hurt him to speak. His lips were cracked. His tongue was black. "Where is it?" he asked.

"Where's what, Dad?"

"I don't feel it. You know why I'm dying?"

"Because you have cancer, Dad."

"No. I am dying so I'll feel it. You and your mother. Especially her. Love. A dying man—" He got angry. "A dying man is supposed to feel it. It's your last chance. If not now, when? Tell your mother to get up. Wake her. Tell her to do it. A dying man is supposed to feel loved. It's the law."

"I'll be back soon, Dad. I gotta go."

He called after me, but he was too weak, it hurt too much to scream.

I mailed my poem to Rachel. I checked the collection schedule on the box and hung around for the next hour and a half until the mailman came and took it away. I figured it would take three days for her to get it. Wednesday. So I decided not to see her, not to call her, until then. It seemed like perfect strategy. She was bound to wonder what happened to me. She was probably expecting me to show up today. By Tuesday she would start worrying and then on Wednesday, just when she was getting frantic, doubting if I'd ever come again, bang, the poem would arrive and shortly after the poem, the poet would arrive in person. I had to smile.

I walked toward Kosciusko Park, seeing not only the reception on Wednesday, but the events that were bound to follow.

. . . why then, Rachel,
should I mourn
that I'll never see
you waking up in the morning
in my bed, next to me?

That would get her. She would read those lines and realize how much I loved her, what a wonderful person I was, and the least she could do in return was to grant me the very thing I had generously accepted I would never get: a whole night with her and the sight of her waking up in the morning, in my bed, next to me.

We would go to a motel.

We would make love in a motel. On neutral territory. Not in her father's car. Not, even if we could, on my father's couch. In a motel. Everything would be different this time. She would be mine. She would get pregnant—no, I would get her pregnant—and then she would be mine forever, and while the baby grew inside her womb she would reveal herself to me, tell me everything. I would get to the bottom of everything.

Good thing it rained, I thought. Had it not rained, I never would have gone to the library, never been called Jimmy Donovan, never written the poem. It was destiny.

"Destiny, destiny
That's our cry
D-E-S-T-I-N-Y!"

I hummed the cheer as I entered the park.

It was noon and the swimming pool was open. Kids were rushing in, screaming and jumping into the water. Last summer I was one of them. Misiora, Freud and I. The scent of chlorine in the air brought it all back.

I sat down on a bench and took out my poem. Reading it in a new place was almost like reading it for the first time. I had never read it in the park.

The only thing that bothered me about the poem was that, properly speaking, I hadn't written it. James "Jimmy" Donovan had written it, and when he did, he had no plans for it. He had no intentions of using it to get Rachel into a motel room. It bothered me a little. Made me feel like a thief. Maybe that's why I kept rereading it so often: trying to make it mine.

Cedars that were. I wondered if that phrase would make Rachel remember Cedar Lake and ice-skating by moonlight.

I looked up. Not far away from me was the tree where I had first told her that I loved her.

"*Ha!*" I heard Freud's laugh without seeing him. It was too distinctive to be anyone else's. I looked around. There he was, lumbering through the trees in his size extra-large city uniform, his face tanned and sweaty, dragging a rake across the grass. He was with some other guy in the same uniform. When he saw me, he stopped. He blinked a couple of times and then he smiled.

"Hey, Daniel!"

"Hi, Billy." I waved and put my poem away.

I had forgotten that he worked in the park. He walked toward me as if I had come there just to run into him.

"So, goddamn, here you are." He seemed awfully glad to see me. I moved over on the bench, making room for him, but he remained standing, leaning on his rake, one foot on the bench.

"Here I am, all right," I said.

"So, how've you been an' all?"

"All right, I guess. And you?"

"I dunno." He shrugged slowly, in sections. "Maybe I've been all right too. Who can tell? *Ha!*"

"Hey, Billy!" the guy in the uniform called. "You coming or what?"

"Nah, you go ahead. I'm not hungry. I'm gonna talk to my old buddy here. Victor, this is Daniel. That's Victor." He pointed to the guy.

Victor and I waved hello and goodbye in one wave. Victor left. Freud took out a cigarette and lit it.

"What's this?" I asked him. "You smoking now?"

"Oh yeah." He took the cigarette out of his mouth and showed it to me. "I started smoking. Yeah. It'll be three weeks next Sunday. My mother hates it when I smoke around the house, so I guess as long as the bitch is alive, I'll be puffing away. Ha!" He laughed and took a puff. He looked older—maybe it was the tan—and definitely heavier.

The kids in the pool must have started playing tag. They screamed in chorus. Both of us looked toward the pool.

"Hey, you remember . . ." Freud pointed to the pool.

"Yeah, I sure do."

"Amazing, huh?"

"What's that?"

"Summer's almost over and we never swam. Not once."

We listened to the kids screaming. We sniffed the chlorine in the air. Freud smoked his cigarette, taking it out of his mouth every couple of puffs and looking at it as if he still couldn't believe that he was really smoking.

"I got your letter, Billy," I finally said. "I read it and . . ."

"Oh yeah, that." He looked down, embarrassed. He shrugged. "I don't know why I did that. I mean, I did it. But I don't know. I guess I just did it, huh?" He smiled nervously.

"I'm sorry I never called you, but you see, my dad's been very sick and I . . ."

"Hey, c'mon. Forget it, huh. How's that old saying go?"

"What old saying, Billy?"

He winced, trying to remember.

"Shit, I can't think of it now. It's one of those old sayings. Ah, the hell with it." Suddenly his eyes widened. He raised a finger in the air. "Water under the bridge! That's the one. It's water under the bridge, you know what I mean."

I smiled. He smiled. He seemed to be straining. It was as if for the last month or so he had been somebody else and now, for my benefit, he was trying to be the old Freud again. The faces he made, the shrugs, even the laughter, were like something he was reciting. I wanted to tell him that he didn't have to do that, but I didn't know how. I felt like I was in the park remembering Freud, instead of being with him.

"How're you and Patty doing?" I asked.

"I dunno how we're doing. She tells me we're in love and maybe we are. I mean, who am I to say we're not?"

"Don't you know?"

"No. How can you tell? I've never been in love before. I got no, shit, what's the word, you know, like in Supreme Court?"

"Precedent?"

"Yeah, that's it. That's what I don't have. I got no precedent. I was never that good in school. Hell, I had to rupture myself to get C's. Patty, you know, she was a real good student. Smart. So if she tells me we're in love, who am I to say she's wrong?"

He lit another cigarette, took a puff and took it from his lips and looked at it at almost arm's length. Then he took another puff.

A whistle blew in the pool. Everybody had to get out so the water could be tested. Shivering bodies pressed against the cyclone fence. Freud and I looked at them.

"I saw Mrs. Dewey," he said.

"Oh yeah, how is she?"

"Okay. She says she's okay. She says she and Bimbo, they're okay, she says. She asked me about Misiora, but I didn't know any more than she did. You seen him at all?"

"No," I said.

"Me neither. Amazing, huh?"

"What's that?"

"I don't know. Everything."

"Hey, Billy!" Victor called him.

"Be right there, Vic." He took his foot off the bench. "Gotta go back to work."

I stood up. He seemed to be relieved that he had an excuse to go.

"I don't get it," he said. "I skip lunch, I smoke, and I put on weight. Amazing, huh?"

"Sure is."

We shook hands. It felt awkward, but we did it.

"Nice to see you, Billy."

"Yeah, it really was. You too. You know. The thing is I gotta go . . ."

"You go ahead. You got a job to do."

"Yeah, don't I know it. See you, huh."

"Yeah, see you, Billy."

We waved the way we did in the old days, as if we would see each other that night or the next day at the latest. He walked away, dragging his rake behind him. Victor joined him, and a few steps later Victor turned and looked at me. Freud was probably telling him all about me, the two of us, the three of us.

I sat down on the bench. Ten minutes later, the whistle blew in the pool and screaming kids jumped into the water. I tried reading my poem, but I couldn't.

Chapter 32

Tuesday afternoon, I was out in the streets, pushing my dad through town. I went down Northcote Avenue and stopped as we came to Aberdeen Lane. I looked down the block. Rachel's father's car was parked in its usual place, but there was no sign of either of them outside. According to my calculations, my poem had been sorted out by a clerk in the post office and placed in a little box of mail destined for Rachel's place. Tomorrow the mailman would deliver it. I saw her opening my envelope, standing in the doorway of her porch, reading my poem. I saw her looking puzzled, wondering where the poem was heading, and then I saw her smiling as she read the last five lines. I saw it all.

"Why aren't we moving?" my poor dad complained.

"I was just resting."

"Who knows what you're doing back there?" His voice was weak, the anger in it lacking authority.

My poor dad. I found it possible to think of him in those terms as long as I thought of myself as Jimmy Donovan. I used that trick as often as possible to remove myself and from a distance feel for him. Poor man.

I pushed the wheelchair past the corner. In the chair was my father. In Jimmy Donovan's chair were only memories. His father had died a long time ago, but he remembered him, poor man. He remembered Freud and Misiora and Rachel, of course. He remembered it all. He looked around East Chicago as we walked. He was glad he came back to visit the place where he grew up and from where he went out into the world.

That night as I lay in bed trying to decide if I should fall asleep as myself or Jimmy Donovan, I began to worry if the ease with which I could go from one to the other was not perhaps a symptom of madness. Jekyll and Hyde came to mind. So did Mr. Geddes. Perhaps at this very moment he was in some institution thinking he was fine, thinking he was somebody else.

To counter this worry I came up with more acceptable examples. Men who joined the foreign legion took on different names. Maxim Gorky was not born Maxim Gorky: he chose the name himself. And all those movie stars. Same thing. Everybody who was anybody was really somebody else.

I fell asleep as Jimmy Donovan and dreamed dreams I had never dreamed before. His dreams. The old librarian was his godmother.

The next morning I was on Aberdeen Lane, alone, hiding in my old hiding place across from Rachel's house, waiting for the mailman to show up and deliver my poem. I was early and I had to wait until eleven o'clock for him to come. He went up the side of the street I was hiding on first. He seemed to be taking his time. He went past me, sneezing. His face was not what I expected from a messenger of destiny.

He went down Rachel's side of the street, dawdling, almost loitering. I felt like screaming at him to pick it up, get going. He stopped at her house and stuck some letters into the black mailbox attached to the outside of the porch. Then, as far as I was concerned, he vanished from the earth. All I could see was the mailbox and the letters sticking out of it. Was my poem in there?

Her father's car was in its usual spot. I could see nobody moving inside the house. The curtains were drawn. Maybe they were still asleep.

I just wanted to know if my poem had been delivered. I crossed the street. If she came out, I would tell her I had come to see her. I pulled the letters out of the box. I began going through them. *Yes! There it was!* I pulled it out and stuck it in front, so it would be the first thing she saw. Then I ran away.

I wanted time to move fast. I ran past the library, halfway down to school. The factory sirens blew at noon and I was still running. It was half-past when I got back to Aberdeen Lane, and halfway down the block I saw the mailbox. It was empty. She had read it, or was reading it now.

I stopped and waited. I gave her another half an hour to reread it several times. With each reading, my position improved. I stood there, feeling smug, like a bank account gathering interest. "I had no idea you could write something like this," I heard her say to me. "I had no idea you felt like this."

"Now you know," I said out loud.

I cut across her lawn and tapped the mailbox for good luck as I went inside the porch. I knocked on the door.

I knocked again.

Her father appeared. He wore a T-shirt I had seen Rachel wear. His eyes were bloodshot, he needed a shave and he was not happy to see me.

"I thought it was you," he said.

"Is Rachel home?"

"Yes, she is," he answered. He just stood there. He didn't invite me inside. He gave no indication that he was going to call her. He just stood there.

"Can I see her?" I finally said.

"Why ask me?" He made me feel as if I were insulting him. I didn't know what to say. "It's up to her, isn't it?" he said.

"Yes, I suppose . . ."

"*Rachel,*" he called, turning his head. "Your young man is here. He wants to know if he can see you!"

His voice was hostile. He looked me right in the eye for once and then moved away as he heard her coming.

"My young man?" She came out. "And so it is. It's my young man, all right."

He slammed the door shut behind her as soon as she cleared the threshold. She didn't so much as blink. She wore her "Greek black" and a big smile and she walked right past me and kept walking. She didn't stop until she was in the middle of her lawn. I followed her out. Her smile told me she had read the poem. And liked it.

"I almost gave up on you," she said. "You didn't call. You didn't come over. What's all this, I thought."

Yes, she missed me. She missed me. She had read the poem. And loved it.

"I had things to do around the house and I . . ."

She didn't seem to hear me.

"What are we going to do now?" She looked up and down the block. "There's really only two choices. We can walk or we can drive around in the car. That's it, isn't it?"

I just wanted to hear about my poem. It didn't matter to me where we were.

"I don't care," I said. "Whatever you want."

"That's just it." She winked at me. "It's a tough choice."

"We could flip a coin—" I reached inside my pocket.

"And let destiny decide?" She spread out her arms, smiling.

"Yes, why not?"

"It all comes down to a flip of a coin. I like that, Boone. Let's do it. Here." She stuck out her hand. "Let me."

I put a quarter in her hand.

"You ready, Boone?"

"Sure am," I said.

"Me too." She just kept on smiling. It was beginning to bother me. I smiled myself. "Here goes, then." She shut her eyes and moved her lips. She was saying something to herself. When she opened her eyes, she wasn't smiling anymore. She flipped the coin into the air. It veered to her left and landed on the sidewalk. We ran over to it.

"There it is." She looked down at the quarter without picking it up. It was heads. That was all I saw. She embraced me suddenly. "You know what that means, don't you?"

"No, you never said."

"It means . . ." She kissed me on the cheek. "It means we walk." She pushed me away abruptly. "That's what it means. So let's go."

She hurried off. It annoyed me just a little to have to run after her. As a private citizen I didn't mind, but as a poet I was annoyed. I wanted the focus to be on me for once.

When I caught up with her, I expected the conversation to turn to my poem. It didn't. She talked compulsively about her weekend trip and the strange towns with strange names they had driven through: Kokomo, Terre Haute, French Lick, Beanblossom. Through it all, I expected her to stop suddenly and tell me about my poem. I even justified her rambling as an introduction to the theme. She loved to change topics abruptly. It would come out of the blue, when I least expected it. I walked alongside of her, pretending to be listening, but I was merely waiting for the unexpected. Valparaiso, Elkhart, Wabash, Troy. Nothing about Cedar Lake or cedars of Lebanon, not even when she mentioned Lebanon, Indiana.

"Can you imagine: Lebanon, Indiana?" She rambled on. "It's like this place we saw on the map: Athens, Georgia. That's not the Athens I want to see."

Even when we turned around, when she turned around to go
back and I followed, even then I didn't think it was too late. I
actually visualized how it would happen. She would bring up the
poem just before she ran inside. "Daniel," she would say, "the poem
is beautiful. It is."

"Peru," she said.

"What?"

"Peru, Indiana. This state's full of towns with names like that.
You ever been there, to Peru?"

"No," I said.

"You know what I did?" She went right on talking, telling me
how she lost their house keys and how they had to break into their
own house. "Look." She pointed to a broken basement window. "I
had to crawl through there. David kicked it in with his foot. It means
something, what do you suppose it means?"

"What?"

"Losing keys. I know finding keys is supposed to be good luck,
so I suppose losing them is bad luck." She stopped suddenly. "It's
still there." She pointed to my quarter on the sidewalk. I bent down
to pick it up. "No, don't," she said. "Leave it there. Somebody will
come along and find it and it'll make them happy. We'll never know
who it was, but that's all right."

She started going inside. I couldn't believe it. Not a word about
the poem.

"Rachel," I called.

"What, Daniel? What is it?"

I looked her right in the eye and waited. The left side of her face
was twitching. She tried to smile but it just kept on twitching.

"I have to go," she said and then shook her head. "No, that's a
lie. I don't have to go in, but I think I better."

She turned and went. I could have shot her in the back. What
kind of a goddamn girl was she, not to say anything? I walked to
the corner of Northcote and Aberdeen Lane and attacked the steel
post that held the street signs. I shook it. I tried to bend it. I tried
to pull it out of the ground.

I had no pity for my dad that afternoon. I pushed his wheelchair
over every bump I could find. His body bounced around like a bag
of bones. He cursed me. I cursed him back.

"Like a book. I know you like a book, son. Bad day with Rachel.
Is that what it was?"

"Just shut up, Dad."

"Yes, that's what it was, all right. Bad day with Rachel. Just like me. You're just like me."

I pushed the wheelchair hard and let go. It rattled down the street, heading for a parked car. I lost my nerve and sprinted, catching it just in time.

I reread my poem that night, looking for flaws. Maybe she didn't like it. Maybe she didn't want to hurt my feelings. I couldn't find any flaws. It was wonderful. Better than ever.

"Daniel," my father called from the living room.

"Go to sleep, Dad."

"Tell me. Your bad day. Tell me about your bad day."

"I didn't have a bad day."

"Tell me. And I'll tell you about mine."

"I had a wonderful day, Dad. A peach of a day."

And then later on:

"Daniel. I'm afraid of dying, Daniel."

"No, you're not, Dad."

"I'm so afraid."

"Everybody dies."

"Come here," he pleaded. "Look at me while I'm alive."

"I'll look at you tomorrow."

It took all the discipline I had the next day not to ask Rachel, point-blank, if she had read my poem and what she thought of it. But it wasn't for me to ask. I had written it. It was up to her to say something.

She was standing outside, waiting for me.

"Look," she said, "nobody found it. It's still here."

I picked up the quarter off the sidewalk and threw it away. It landed in the street and rolled down the pavement till it hit the curb.

Her father watched us from the living-room window.

"Let's go for a drive," I said.

"I don't have the car keys."

"Can't you go in and get them?"

"Yes, I can. But I don't want to."

She seemed tired. She tried shaking it off while we walked, but couldn't.

"I was going to water the lawn today," she said, "but that thing you fixed broke again, and I couldn't get it back on."

It was either my imagination or she was ready to cry.

"I'll fix it again," I told her.

"I tried and tried, but I couldn't get it to stay on." She was breathing funny, running out of air and then taking in huge amounts at one time.

"You all right?" I asked her.

"Didn't sleep much. David was . . . never mind."

"David was what?"

"Never mind."

"Fine," I said, "have it your way. You always do."

We walked silently as if it were our job to walk together.

"Did any of your old friends write you?" I couldn't resist asking. She shook her head.

"No, none of my old friends wrote."

Here it comes, I thought. But it didn't. We went a whole block without saying a word.

"A boy sent me a Christmas present once," she said as we stepped up on the curb. "I couldn't imagine what was inside. Or rather, I imagined all kinds of things. Different things on different days. I decided not to open it. To have an unopened present. It was the loveliest gift anyone had ever given me."

"So what was it?"

"I don't know. I never opened it."

"What do you mean, you never opened it?"

"Never. You know what 'never' means?"

"Sure I know what 'never' means. I've never heard of anything like that. That's what 'never' means."

She said nothing. We walked some more.

"Didn't he ask you about it?" I said. "That boy. Didn't he want to know what you thought of his present?"

"Yes. He asked me if I liked it." She smiled at the memory.

"Yes, and what did you tell him?"

"I told him I loved it."

"You lied, then."

"No, I didn't. I told him the truth. I did love it."

Had there been a pin on her body that I could have pulled to make her explode, I would have done it.

"How could you say that if you never opened it?"

"I opened all those others," she said slowly, calmly. "All those years of all those opened presents and the one I remember and love the best is the one I never opened at all."

I threw up my hands. She hardly noticed. We turned around, or rather she turned around, and I followed, half a step back. It was such a wonderful plan. From a poem to a motel. I couldn't believe the way it was falling apart. I didn't know if she was telling the truth about that boy and his goddamn present, or if she was making it up as a way of telling me something about my poem. Motel! How the hell was I going to get her to a motel if I couldn't even get her to respond to a poem I had written.

"You see." She took me to the side of the house and showed me the fitting on the hose. The brass ring was cracked. "It's broken," she said. "It all began with this and now it's broken."

Why did she look so sad?

"It's all right," I said. "It's no big deal. I'll fix it."

In less than a minute, she took the poet in me and turned him into a plumber. Then she went inside, leaving me there with a hose in my hand. I flung it to the ground.

My dad really went after me that afternoon.

"Two days. Two bad days in a row with Rachel."

"Keep it up, just keep it up, Dad."

"That's how it begins. One day, then two days, then two months, then two years. That's how it is for the likes of us."

I pushed his wheelchair, trying not to listen.

"Love," he went on. "That's all we want, you and I. But they won't give it to us."

My unhappiness was a comfort to him.

"I'm not alone in this," he said several times. "It's not just me."

He asked me, but I wouldn't answer: "I'm not alone in this, am I? It's not just me, is it?"

He wanted to feel that whatever had filled his life with despair was not his fault. That it was a general condition. He was not the exception. And for his theory to work, he needed to hear of others like him.

"There's many like us. I warned you, didn't I, not to hope. There's millions like us who loved and hoped and lost. Yes, my poor boy. That's how it is."

The sun was setting, and in the reddish-orange afterglow, I felt myself slowly surrendering to my father's despair. I was only eighteen. I thought of all those years that lay ahead, all that life that had to be lived day by day, wondering each day if tomorrow would be the day when everything would fall into place, and when it didn't, going on, looking for love, waiting for Rachel to drop the veils and reveal herself, year after year. It seemed too much for me. It seemed better to give up now. Then, years from now, I could at least say: It just wasn't worth it. I didn't even try.

A car horn startled me as if out of a dream. We had strayed into the middle of the street. I pushed the chair to the side. The car went past us slowly, the driver looking out. He looked like Coach French. It wasn't him, but it looked like him. The memory of my wrestling match came back. The memory of giving up. The long ride home.

I began to shiver. I had come so close to giving up again. My dad started speaking, but I wouldn't let him.

"It was all a lie, Dad. I had a wonderful day with Rachel. Do you know what she told me? She told me she loved me and me alone." It didn't matter to me what I said. I just wanted to drown him out. "She told me she stayed up late at night, thinking up more and more reasons why she loves me. I wrote her a poem and she said it was the most beautiful thing she'd ever read. We're going to a motel this weekend. She and I. We're going to make love in a motel."

When he tried to raise his voice, I started singing and drowned him out: "Destiny, destiny, that's our cry. D-E-S-T-I-N-Y!" I shouted at the top of my lungs. "There's a word for you, Dad. Seven letters, six across. *Destiny.*" And then I started singing again.

"I'm not the only one: I can't be the only one!" he shrieked, but I just kept on singing.

Chapter 33

I stood in front of a hardware store the next morning, waiting for it to open. Through the window, I could see a man inside the store, putting money into a cash register. Behind him was a large wall calendar with a picture of a girl in a bikini, driving a tractor. I looked at the calendar and saw that today was Friday the thirteenth. It didn't bother me. I had it all figured out. Rachel was going to marry me.

The man inside the store checked his watch, fussed around with the displays and opened the door, flipping the Sorry, We're Closed sign to Yes, We're Open.

I went in and bought a hose and walked out. I carried it, slung over my shoulder, down Chicago Avenue. I hadn't slept much the night before, but some time near dawn it all came to me. Rachel had read the poem. She had loved it. She had interpreted "waking up in the morning in my bed, next to me" not as an invitation to a motel, but as a marriage proposal. She showed the poem to her father. He got upset. Losing a daughter and all. He got her upset. Then she got me upset. And then, like a fool, not realizing what was at stake, I failed to propose to her. Naturally, she thought I had changed my mind. She couldn't say anything about the poem without sounding foolish. And then, when the fixture on the hose cracked, she took it as an omen that it was all over between us.

Sometimes you can rack your brains for weeks and not get anywhere; at other times it just comes to you. It all made perfect sense to me.

Will you marry me? I had never said those words before. Rachel, will you marry me?

Rachel Price. Yes, it sounded much better that way.

Price had five letters. Rachel had six letters. Destiny had seven letters. Marriage had eight letters. The progression revealed itself to me.

I sneaked through the alley, over the wooden fence in the back, and fastened one end of the hose to the water outlet at the side of Rachel's house. I attached the other end to the sprinkler. I moved the sprinkler to the middle of the lawn.

The old, worn-out hose lay at my feet. It had done its job well, but now it was time for a new one. I turned on the water all the way. No leaks, no drips; the water shot high into the morning sunshine and then fell back like a lace veil on a wedding gown.

I didn't hear the door open, but when I came around to the front, ready to go inside and knock on the door, I saw her father standing on the porch, wearing only his bathrobe. He shook his head as if he didn't quite believe he was seeing me. I stopped. Drops of water fell on the back of my neck.

"*Rachel!*" her father called, keeping his eyes on me.

As soon as she came out she saw the sprinkler behind me, and her body slumped over as if she were too moved to speak.

"Didn't you tell him?" her father said as she walked past him. "I thought you told him."

She walked out on the lawn. She was wearing a sleeveless summer dress, white, as white as any wedding gown. Her feet were bare and her brown legs shone.

"I knew you'd do this. I just knew it," she said. "Oh, Daniel."

She walked toward me, the outline of her thighs draped in white muslin.

"Rachel," her father called.

"I'll be back soon," she said. She walked around the car to avoid getting wet. I followed her.

"Told me what?" I asked her. "Your dad wanted to know if you told me something. What is it?"

"I used to walk barefoot all the time," she said. "I think my feet have gotten soft. The sidewalk's warm already." She turned and looked at the sprinkler. "I really did know you'd do that."

"You see"—I took her arm—"everything's fine. Destiny goes on with a little help from a hardware store."

She sighed, shutting her eyes.

"Told me what?" I asked again.

"Tell me, Boondocks, are you really that blind?"

"Blind to what? I'm not blind. Blind to what?"

"I love ruins," she said.

"I know that. You told me and I remembered. I remember everything you say. What's that got to do with being blind?"

"And I love you. Do you know that?" She asked as if she really wanted to know. "Do you?"

"I guess I do."

"Don't guess anymore. It's time you knew, Daniel."

"All right. No more guessing," I said. The thin strap on her dress slipped down her shoulder. I stopped and, as tenderly as I knew how, pulled it back up. She was so close, her shoulder was so warm, that I knew I would ask her right then and there.

"Rachel, will you marry me?"

She looked at me the way her father had looked at me: Was I really there? Did she really hear those words? Maybe, I thought, she had given up hoping I'd ask her and now she couldn't believe it.

"Nobody," she said, "has ever asked me that."

"You knew I would, didn't you?"

"Yes." She covered her mouth with her hand. "I suppose I did."

"The poem I wrote you said it all." Having assumed the answer to my marriage proposal was yes, I began fishing around for literary acclaim. "You probably won't believe this, but I've never written a poem before. It was only because of you. It all just came out. As soon as I began, I knew . . ."

"Daniel." She cut me off. "I didn't read it. I never opened it."

There was no room in my plans for this information. No provision for it. So I rejected it. I had to, for my world to make sense.

"Sure, you read it. It came in the mail. You opened the envelope and you read it."

"I never opened it. I saw that it was from you. I almost did open it."

"Almost?"

"But at night, do you know what I do? I lift up the envelope to the lamp and I can make out certain words. Comanches, that's in there, isn't it?"

"Yes, 'Comanches . . . on horseback,' " I said. All I could do was repeat the words she said. My mind refused to accept the basic information.

"And Greece. Did you put that in for me?"

"Yes, 'The Greece that was,' " I said, and picked up where that line left off: " 'There was a time, they tell me, when Lebanon was covered with trees . . .' "

"No, no," she interrupted. "I don't want to hear how it goes. I just want to keep it in the envelope. Pick out words here and there and imagine for a while. Save it for when I need it. There's bound to be a day . . ."

I wanted to interrupt her, but I just didn't know what to say. I couldn't get my bearings.

"One of those days, you know. One of those interminable Sunday afternoons when it's looked like rain for days and it still refuses to fall and you need something."

"I need something!" I shouted. "You haven't read it! I've been wondering for days what you thought of it and you haven't read it! It's not that long, dammit. You open the envelope and you read it. What's the point of having post offices and mailmen if you don't open the envelope? That's what envelopes are for. To be opened. That's what poems are for. To be read. That's why I wrote it!"

"I was hoping you'd understand," she said.

I lost all control.

"Understand! What do you think I've been doing since I met you but trying to understand? You say weird things, you do weird things, you change subjects out of the blue, you smile and I don't know why, you frown and I don't know why, you kiss me and I don't know why and all I've been doing is trying to understand what kind of a weird person does things like that and why and what it means and I just can't keep it up anymore. Me! When the hell are you going to understand me? I wrote the poem, I had it all figured out what you thought of it, and you, you tell me you haven't read it."

She seemed rather unshaken by my outburst.

"I've been thinking about Comanches ever since I saw the word through the envelope."

"It's not about Comanches, Rachel. It has nothing to do with Comanches."

"But it made me happy to think about them."

"I don't care if it made you happy. You're supposed to open the envelope, read the poem, and then you're supposed to be happy. My poem is supposed to make you happy. I'm supposed to make you happy. That's how it's supposed to work. Instead, you just go around and make yourself happy. What about me?"

"You're free to do what you want, Daniel."

"No, I'm not. I'm not free to do anything. How can I be free if I spend all my waking hours trying to figure out what the hell you're talking about? Ruins and Greece and all that kissing in the car and then running off and then telling me you love me."

"I do love you."

"Then why don't I feel it? Make me feel it. Do something normal for once. I had it all figured out, Rachel, and you, all you had to do was see it. It all made sense. It was all beautiful and it all made sense."

"To you," she said.

"All I want is to make you happy. To know I make you happy. I imagine you happy. I think of things to do to make you happy . . ."

"Make me happy sounds like it's against my will. Force me to be happy."

"There you go again. There's the weird talk again. I can't take this anymore."

"Maybe you won't have to," she said.

"There's no 'maybe,' Rachel. I don't have to. Nobody should have to."

She was standing still, and without realizing it, I had been backing away and shouting. The next thing I knew, I was about ten yards away from her. I knew she wouldn't come to me. There was nothing else to do but go to her or leave.

"If you want to get married," I shouted, "give me a call. Otherwise you'll never see me again."

I rushed away. Until I turned the corner, all I could think of was making sure not to trip or stumble. I wanted to look good rushing away.

Calm and in control; that was how I tried to be with my dad as I pushed him around town that afternoon. I could have gotten out of doing it, but I didn't really want to. I didn't want to accept that what had happened had really happened. Rachel made no sense at all. It would make even less sense to be affected by it, to be upset by it. Calm and in control. Disciplined. My dad talked, but I said nothing. He baited me, but I said nothing. Discipline. Nothing happened, I kept thinking. If something had happened, I'd be feeling terrible now. I'm not feeling terrible; therefore nothing had happened. I'm pushing my dad around town. It's just another day.

"Where are we going?" he asked. "You alive back there?"

"Yes," I said. Calmly. "I'm alive, Dad."

"I'm cold."

"You're always cold, Dad."

"Not like this."

The sun had set and we were halfway to Whiting, a long way from home. I will be so tired, I thought, that as soon as I get home, I'll fall asleep. That was going to be the ultimate proof. A person who is upset stays up all night. Not me. I would fall asleep.

It was late when we turned around. Dark. No moon, no stars. Occasional headlights. My father was shivering. I began to feel cold myself. I'm only wearing a T-shirt, I thought; that's why I'm cold. Also, it's late at night. Two good reasons why I'm cold.

A half-hour later, still far from home, I began to shiver too. I didn't eat anything, I thought; I'm only wearing a T-shirt and it's late at night.

"It's cold," my father said.

"Same as every other night, Dad. No difference." My voice was not only calm, but almost gentle. Goose bumps were popping up all over my body.

We crossed the steel drawbridge over the Calumet Canal. I couldn't see the water, but I could smell it. If I were upset, I thought, I would push my dad into the canal and jump in after him. Instead, we're just crossing. The evidence was piling up that I was calm and cool. To top it off, when I got home, I would go right to sleep.

"There it is!" My dad pointed at a house on the corner of Indianapolis Boulevard and Perry. The house with a green door. "There it is! That's where she did it!"

I pushed on. He tried to turn in the chair so he could keep looking at it. I remembered following him, going out at night to look for him, finding him and then following him to this very house.

"Stop!" he shouted. "Go back!"

The difference between my dad and me, I thought, is that he gets all upset and I don't. The only similarity between us is that we're both shivering.

He started cursing my mother, calling her a slut, and then he started in on Rachel.

He's just trying to get me upset, I thought, and I won't let him because there's nothing to be upset about.

"Rachel, is that her name?"

"Yes, Dad. Rachel Temerson."

I gripped the handles on the wheelchair harder. I tightened my body. I clenched my teeth. I wanted to stop shivering. It was a summer night. It was cool, but it couldn't be that cold. Not cold enough to shiver. If I stopped shivering, I would have nothing left in common with my father. I tried to remember my poem. I couldn't. There, if it had meant that much to me . . .

"And is she tall and dark? Is she? With black hair like your mother's?"

"Yes, Dad. She's quite tall and quite dark. And yes, she has black hair. She also has turquoise earrings. The last time I saw her, she wore a white sleeveless dress . . ."

"The last time! No more Rachel, is that it? The last time!"

We had gotten off the boulevard and were going up Magoun Avenue. We were approaching the railroad tracks by the library.

"No, you misunderstand, Dad. I didn't mean it was the last time I would see her. I meant it was the last time I saw her."

The library was dark. The houses around the library were dark. A mist was blowing past the streetlamps.

"The last time!" He shivered the words out of his lips. "Not just me. I'm not alone! Now you know what it's like. My poor boy. Now you know."

I just wanted to stop shivering. It seemed to me if he stopped, I would stop. I was picking it up from him. Like father, like son.

In the distance, through the mist, I heard a locomotive whistle.

If I didn't stop, I would start picking up other things from him. Other symptoms. Other traits. Other destinies.

"The last time," he went on. "That's what I should've done. But I didn't. Good for you, my poor boy. Never see her again."

Lines from the poem started coming back. Never see. Never see. I'll never see you waking up in the morning, in my bed, next to me. Why then, Rachel, should I mourn . . .

"Dad, please, don't say any more . . ."

I couldn't stop shivering. I couldn't keep the poem from coming back. He wouldn't stop talking. Was it possible? Was it really possible that I would never see her again? He was beginning to make me believe it. He had to stop.

I lodged the wheels of his chair between the ties of the railroad track and started running.

"Daniel!" he called.

I turned around. He was trying to dislodge himself, but his arms were weak, his efforts futile. A cold mist was swirling around—how could it be so cold?—and through the mist I heard a locomotive whistle again, closer this time, and through the mist I saw a light. I will be so sad when he dies, I thought, so very sad that Rachel will lie in my bed, next to me, to comfort me. I will be so very, very sad, I kept thinking.

Where the puppy came from, I don't know. It just appeared through the mist, ran past me, tail wagging, rear shaking, ears flopping around.

"Daniel," my father kept calling. "Daniel."

And the puppy went right to him. It just went right to him. And jumped into his lap.

My father let out a cry and his weak arms were strong enough to embrace the silly little thing. "Daniel," he kept calling, hugging the puppy, crying. The puppy was licking his face, head wobbling, ears flapping. "Look, Daniel," my father cried, "look, he loves me. Oh, look."

He didn't seem to hear the train coming closer.

My impulse, I think, was to save the puppy. I couldn't bear to watch the silly thing die. I ran, thinking I had to pull it from my father's arms. But when I got close, I saw something I hadn't seen for years. My father looked happy. His cadaverous face was beaming, his eyes were filled with tears, his thin arms were wrapped around the little bundle of fur.

I felt my heart break. He looked so happy. I pulled the chair off the tracks. The locomotive rumbled past us, and then the passenger cars, the steam from the locomotive mixing with the mist in the air. I shivered. The earth seemed to be trembling. And then it was just my father and me and the puppy in his arms.

Ding-ding-ding, the railroad crossing gates went up. The puppy began squirming. The tighter my dad tried to hold it, the more it squirmed. It broke free and jumped to the ground.

"Puppy," my dad called, "little puppy, come here."

It ran around, darting about, changing directions. My dad laughed. The puppy yelped, tail wagging, ears flopping, and then it stopped. It crouched low on its front paws, nose to the ground, rear in the air. It yelped a couple of times and took off.

"Puppy," my dad laughed, thinking it was coming back. But it kept going.

"Daniel." He pointed. "Don't let him get away."

The pup stopped, eager to be chased.

"There, he's waiting for me. Daniel, please. He loved me."

We set off after the pup.

"There he is!" my dad shouted. "I see him."

I ran, pushing the chair.

"Puppy," my dad called.

"Puppy," I called.

It loved to be chased, but didn't want to be caught. It appeared suddenly behind cars, in front of us, behind us; it waited until we got close and then took off. We went after it.

Then it just disappeared. We waited, looking around.

"Pup-py!" my dad called. And then again: "Pup-py!"

He seemed to realize that it wasn't coming back. He began to cry. I began to cry.

"You saw, didn't you, Daniel, you saw how he loved me."

"Yes, Father," I sobbed, "I saw. I did."

I didn't really know why I was crying, but I couldn't stop. It was like something I had been meaning to do for a long time. Maybe it was the relief of knowing for certain that, however insufficiently, I did love my father. But it wasn't just that. It was seeing him happy. How little it took. It was the thought of Rachel slipping through my fingers. The memory of Freud in the park, with the scent of chlorine in the air.

We went home slowly, and although we knew it was gone, we still looked around for the pup. Just in case. It got colder and colder.

My mother was waiting for us in the street. When she saw us, she clutched her head. She seemed relieved. "You make me so worried. Where have you been?" She pointed to her wristwatch. "It is so late."

All three of us were shivering. My father screamed and cried as we carried him into the house in his chair. He didn't want us to shut the door. The puppy might come. My mother understood none of it and kicked the door shut with the back of her foot. She looked puzzled and tired. But yes, tall and dark like Rachel.

When he saw that he was really inside the house, that the doors were really shut and that the little dog was not in his lap, he went to pieces. My mother looked at me for an explanation. I had too many, so I gave none.

"You"—my dad pointed at her—"do you know how much I loved you?"

"Husband, please." She sounded so tired.

"Husband." My dad clenched his pathetic little fist and beat on his chest with it. "Yes, husband. That's all I wanted. Husband and father. So why did I have to see . . . why did I have to live to see? Why?"

She said nothing.

"See what, Father?" I asked.

"It is nothing," my mother said. "Go to bed, Daniel."

"To see . . ." My dad covered his mouth, trying not to speak.

"Go to bed, Daniel."

"See what, Father?" I asked.

"My wife," he said, "the woman I loved. See her coming out of his door. I saw her. Didn't I? Didn't I see you?" He seemed to be willing to be told that it was all a misunderstanding. He wanted to be told. But my mother was tired.

"Yes." She nodded slowly. "You saw me."

Her admission, the calmness of it, enraged him.

"I followed her. To his house. I followed her there. Inside. She went inside and stayed there. She stayed there for hours, while I"—he beat with his little fists on the chair—"while I waited in the street like a dog. Like a dog!" He got distracted. He looked around the kitchen. Maybe he was looking for the puppy. Another betrayal. It wasn't there. I wanted to go to him, but he didn't want me. My mother stood still, leaning on the wall.

"A dog! Like a dog I waited. For hours. And then the door opened. The two of them—she and that man with the moustache—the two of them came out and they stood there in the doorway and he kissed her on the lips. Didn't they have enough inside? No. On the lips he kissed her. The woman I loved. On the lips. And her hand, her fingers went into his hair. The slut. The whore. And even then, while they were still kissing, even then I was willing to forgive her. I loved her, so I was willing. But then she turned around and I saw a smile on her face. Never! I had never seen such a smile on her face before. Such joy! Such pleasure! Such womanly satisfaction!" Each word was treachery to him. He made them sound ugly. "Never such a smile. And he. The man in the doorway. He put it there on her lips. Not I!"

My mother just looked at him. His anger and accusations didn't seem to touch her. Only his pain, the retelling of the agony he felt, softened her face into pity. Not love, not the love he wanted, but pity. He shook his head, as if rejecting it.

"No, not I. Not I who loved her. Not I who adored her. He! The moustache! He put that smile on her lips. He put it in my brain, he planted it there." His little fists pounded on his nearly bald head. "I see it. It's still there. That smile. I tried. I said nothing. Even then, I was willing to forgive. Even then! For weeks, I tried to put that smile on her face myself. To cause it to happen myself. For months. To know I put it there. I tried. To love her even more. To love her in such a way that she would smile for me, just once, like she had smiled that summer night in the doorway of a stranger's house. For years I tried. It never came. Never happened. And I realized it never would. Not if I lived two hundred years. I would never make her as happy as he. Never, never, never."

His voice had grown weaker. The "nevers" sounded slurred, like a single word, like never itself. My mother looked at him. There was love there in her eyes, not just pity, but I knew it wasn't the kind of love he wanted. I knew the kind of love he wanted.

The fridge kicked on.

"Oh, husband," my mother sighed.

"It won't go away," he said. He had no anger left. "The memory. Of the smile. Still there in the brain. I thought cancer would eat it up. No. It's nibbling all around. Destroying everything. Except the smile. Even cancer has let me down."

I had never imagined the possibility of such a sentence being spoken. I had nothing left with which to respond to it. I imagined Jimmy Donovan, but I could not imagine how he could respond to it either. Maybe, I thought, tomorrow I'll know what to do. Or the day after.

I distanced myself and saw the three of us in the kitchen, my whole family, like a snapshot. Jimmy Donovan looked at the snapshot, and as he went out into the world he swore to himself that he would try to live his life in such a way that he would never be capable of uttering those words: Even cancer has let me down.

Chapter 34

I shivered all night. I was sure I was coming down with some sickness and I looked forward to it. I needed a rest. I would stay in bed. There was nothing I could do if I was sick. I had forgotten to shut my window, and a cold wind was blowing through it, but I was too cold to get up and shut it. Besides, I kept thinking, the wind can't be that cold. It's summer. I must be sick.

I fell asleep, I awoke, I fell asleep again. The previous day had too many things in it to seem real. The hose, the marriage proposal, the railroad tracks, the puppy, my father sitting in his wheelchair in the kitchen: Even cancer has let me down. I would awaken and find that I had been sick and that the whole day had been a nightmare.

Sometime in the night I awoke again to find my mother covering me with a quilt. It's summer, I thought, and she's throwing a quilt over me. I must be very sick.

"Daniel." She put her hand on my cheek. "Are you awake?"

"Yes."

"You must know, Daniel. I did what I did. It is true. But I loved your father as much as I could."

Then she left. But maybe it was all a dream.

The quilt was on top of me in the morning. I wrapped myself in it and got out of bed to shut the window. I saw people in the street. They were all bundled up in winter clothes, jackets, mufflers, gloves. I could see the breath coming out of their mouths, steam coming out of car exhausts. I had the strange sensation of having slept through a whole season. The last thing I remembered was that it was summer and I was wearing a T-shirt. Now this. I closed the window. The glass felt cold.

The previous evening, if it had not been a dream, seemed a long time ago. The last time I saw Rachel seemed even more distant. It was summer. She wore a white sleeveless dress and walked barefoot on green grass and warm cement. And now this.

I shivered inside my quilt, looking out of the window. A kid walked by, with the earflaps on his cap pulled down. There was no snow, but it seemed like winter. I had never seen Rachel in winter clothes. I pictured her wearing woolen mittens, a loose-fitting parka and a shawl wrapped around her face like a Turkish veil, revealing only her green eyes. Cedar Lake was probably frozen over. We would go ice-skating. Silver skates across a silver lake, turquoise earrings dangling loose. And we would wait for the first snowflake to fall. It was like a vision: Rachel in snow.

Dishes rattled in the kitchen.

My father was asleep on the couch, covered with blankets. My mother was wearing her winter bathrobe and fur slippers. She was making coffee. She turned when she heard me.

"Everybody sleep late today," she said.

I thought it was still morning. The clock in the kitchen read three-fifteen.

"So cold," she said and held her hands over the flame of the gas range. She touched my cheeks with her warm hands. She smiled a little, a maternal smile, happy that I didn't pull away.

"These kind things," she said, going back to making coffee, "they happen all the time in old country. Here not so much. But in Montenegro, once three foots of snow fall in July."

She was talking about the weather. I didn't know at first.

"It will not snow. But it is very cold for summer."

It was still summer. Yesterday really was yesterday. That's what she was saying. We sipped our coffee. She smoked and looked at me. She seemed to be looking for signs in my face. What did I think? Did I hate her? Did I still love her? Did I understand? I tried to imagine that smile on her face, but I couldn't. Only my dad knew what it looked like.

We had no oil for the stove. The house was cold. My mother turned on all the burners on the gas range and lit the oven, leaving the door open. My father slept. I dressed and went out.

"Cold enough for you?" a man laughed, walking past me. There were more people in the street than usual and they all seemed thrilled and talkative. One man remembered a freak cold front like this passing through back in the thirties.

I just couldn't get used to it. The clothes people wore, the cold, the dark damp fog that shrouded houses half a block away. Even the clouds were obscured by the fog. Several people were gathered around a man in a car. The car was parked but running, and the radio was on. The announcer was carrying on about the weather. An all-time record low for this day!

When I got back home, the clock in the kitchen read six-thirty. My mother had changed clothes and was standing in the archway that separated the kitchen from the living room. She said nothing. I sat down. She just stood there.

"Listen," she said.

"What is it?"

"Listen." She gestured me toward her. When I came, she took me by the arm.

I didn't know what I was supposed to be listening for. The gas burners on the stove fluttered like moths. I heard that. Was that it? I looked at her but she just squeezed my arm, directing to me to listen. And then I heard it: a strange sputtering sound, like bubbles bursting. I could see the quilt and the blankets on top of my father moving in rhythm to the sound. He was hiccupping. That was all. He was just hiccupping. The quilt and the blankets jumped in spasms.

"What is it, Mother?" I asked. I couldn't understand why she looked so concerned, why she was holding on to me like that.

"You hear?"

"Yes, he's just hiccupping."

"It's a sign," she said. "It is now only matter of days. He will die soon. I know."

"He's just hiccupping," I said again.

"My own father," she whispered, "he did same thing before he died."

"Mother, c'mon, you don't really believe . . ."

"God is coming for his soul, Daniel." She looked at me as if she knew. I could disagree with her if I wanted to, but I could not change her mind. She let go of my arm. "You stay here. I have to buy candles."

"What're you talking about?"

"We have no candles. We need candles to burn. Without candles, when it is darkness, Devil can come and steal away his soul. We need candles to burn so God can see. You stay here."

"I'll go get the candles," I offered.

"You don't know these things, Daniel. We need special candles. From church."

She put on her coat. She seemed very calm, as if she were going out to buy a carton of milk.

"Don't be afraid," she told me. "It is bad for a person who is dying to see afraid. Calm and brave, that is how you must be."

She left.

I sat down slowly at the kitchen table. I thought I had prepared myself for his death. Now I realized that the death I had imagined was different from the one that was coming. My father wasn't going to get smaller and smaller and finally vanish from the earth. No, it was going to be different.

"Ha-ka!" he hiccupped. The blankets moved. I blinked. The burners on the stove continued to flutter, as if trying to escape.

Death was on its way. God was coming to take his soul. What if it happened now? Right now!

I held my breath.

"Ha-ka." The blankets moved. I blinked.

God was coming. And God knew everything. He knew how I felt, what I was thinking. He knew what kind of son I had been. That I had wished my father dead. That I had hoped he would never come back from the hospital. That I had never called him and that in his absence, I had taken over the house and behaved as if it were mine. I had made love on the couch where he was lying and denied any resemblance to him and even now—would God know this?— even now, while those flames fluttered and small, spasmodic explosions shook the life that was left in my father, shook it loose, pried it loose from his body, even now was I not thinking of Rachel, was I not remembering her on the couch, was I not waiting for the phone to ring so that I could hear her voice, and if it came would I not run out to be with her and let even the Devil come and take my father's eternal soul? Would I not? Yes.

Would God know this?

"Ha-ka!" The blankets moved. I blinked.

Why was I suddenly thinking of God, when I had never thought of God before? Was it because He was coming for me? My mother would come with the candles. I would look at her and then I would hear something and I would turn my head and see my father rising from the couch, recovered, walking toward me with blankets in his hands, ready to cover me. Don't be afraid, my mother had told me before she left. Did she know? Be brave and calm. She must have known. She was getting the candles for me.

"Ha-ka!" I clutched the table. It was me. It was me hiccupping!

"Ha-ka!" I did it again.

My throat felt constricted. Something was stuck.

"Ha-ka!"

My father would start to rise any second. He would come, carrying the blankets. The flames on the stove were rising too, their wings growing, sucking up the air. I couldn't get any air into my lungs.

"Ha-ka! Ha-ka!"

I wanted to get up, but my left leg would not move. A cold hand landed on the back of my neck. I screamed.

"Daniel!"

No, I didn't want to die.

"Daniel!"

It was my mother. She was slapping me on my back, trying to get my hiccups to stop.

"Daniel, what is wrong?"

She brought me a glass of water.

"Here, drink."

She fed me the water like a baby. I drank. Then I took the glass from her hand and finished it. Between drinks, I gulped in air. My chest was heaving.

"What is wrong?" she wanted to know.

"Nothing. I . . . I just . . ." I looked around. I looked at her. I looked at the blue flames burning on the stove.

"Ha-ka!" The blankets on top of my father shuddered.

"Daniel, do not make me worry. Are you sick?"

"No, I'm fine. I don't know . . . I'm fine."

She didn't quite believe me, but she didn't press me. It was good to breathe again, but I was waiting for my hiccups to return. Then slowly the tightness eased. I sighed.

"I bought the candles in Catholic church. I was going to buy the candles in my church, but it was too far away," she said. "I also had a thought. Your father, he is Catholic." She shrugged, holding the candles like a bunch of flower stalks. "So for him, I buy Catholic candles." She looked at them. "They are not as very nice as candles in my church. Candles in my church are thicker, but . . ." She shrugged. "But we will light them."

She went into her room and brought out two candlesticks. She wiped them with a dish towel and placed them on the table in front of me.

"You are now head of family. It is for you to light the candles. One is for the dying and one is for the living."

She spoke slowly, softly, as if repeating instructions she had been given. She gave me a book of matches, and then, without saying a word, she made it clear that I should stand when I lit them. I stood up. She crossed herself.

I struck the match and lit one candle.

"That is for the dying," she said. "For the soul of your father."

She blew out the match. Then she nodded that I should light the other candle. I struck another match.

"And this is for the living," she said. "May God watch over us and forgive our sins." She smiled and spread out her arms, her hands cradling the flame. "Look, Daniel. Look, you see. The flame on candle for the living is brighter. That is good sign."

I couldn't really tell if it was brighter or not. Having gone through the motions of performing a ritual I knew nothing about, I went through the motions of agreeing with her. She seemed to know everything. Unlike me, she had no doubts about the signs she saw. The candle for the living looked brighter to her. That made her happy. She knew my father would die soon. There were no doubts about this. There were no doubts that the other candle would keep the Devil from stealing his soul. She looked peaceful. She had, and she knew she had, loved my father as much as she could. She had, and she knew she had, caused his heart to break with a smile. But it couldn't be helped and if it couldn't be helped, it was not a sin and if it was not a sin, her soul was still clean, and so with a clean soul she went about the business of making my father's last days on earth as serene and proper as possible. She lowered the shades in the kitchen and she lowered the shades in the living room. Everything she did seemed like a ritual; even the way she walked across the floor seemed to be different, in keeping with the spirit of traditions I knew nothing about. She whispered something into my father's ear and then she put her own ear next to his lips. I couldn't hear what she said or what, if anything, he replied, but she continued to have, or to pretend to have, a conversation with him in this manner. All I could do was look and wait to be told what came next.

She made coffee. I think she just couldn't bear to see the gas being wasted. She took out a cigarette and then put it back. Perhaps one was not supposed to smoke at a time like this. We sipped our coffee. My cup rose when hers did. It came down when hers came down. When she looked to her left, at my father in the living room, I looked to my right and did the same thing. The candles for the living and for the dead flickered between us. Her gold tooth shone as she began talking, and the rhythm of her voice, like the rhythm of her gait when she walked, was once again stately and in keeping with a tradition she knew.

She talked about the dead: about her father and how peacefully he had died, about her brothers who were killed fighting the Germans; she remembered all the dates and she crossed herself at the mention of every name and asked God, her God, to be gentle with their souls. Then she talked about the more distant relatives and how they had died and the kind of day it was when they were buried and the kind of tombstones their sons and daughters had put up for them. Some, in her opinion, were second-rate tombstones and she asked God to forgive the cheap sons and daughters who had put them up.

"No good will come to them from the money they save in that way. That's right, Daniel."

She used my name every few sentences. She used it like a bridge between thoughts: a chant, almost. Yes, Daniel. That's right, Daniel.

She told me that when I was lighting the candle for the living, she had been afraid, because if the flame had gone out, that would have meant there would be another death in the family. Yes, Daniel. She, herself, had been in a house where such a thing had happened. Signs, she told me, were God's way of speaking to us on earth. There were too many languages that human beings had invented and God had too many things to do, He was too busy to learn all of them, so He speaks to us in signs. The Devil tries to trick us. He sends false signs to try and tempt us.

"Yes, Daniel. And sometimes we make mistakes. What can we do? We are human beings and we are not very perfect. We must then ask God to forgive. The Devil, he hates it very much when we ask God to forgive us. It's true."

She crossed herself, sitting erect, as if both God and the Devil were watching and she wanted to impress God with her faith and the Devil with her defiance.

Yes, she told me, she had sinned. The flesh of her body had driven her to the door of another man. It was like a fire that could only be quenched by another fire and into that fire she had leapt, yes.

"Your father . . ." She crossed herself. "He loved me so very much. I loved him, too, Daniel, but not so very much as he loved me. It is not a good thing to be loved so very much. I am now telling you things about what it is like to be a woman, and every woman, she wants man to love her. I am no different. But when man loves too much, when man loves nothing else except woman, not even God, not even himself, not even his soul, when man only loves woman, he puts up bricks, every day, he puts up bricks with his love, every day he brings another brick and every day the woman sees that the man is making a wall around her, a prison, to protect and keep her. It is like making her dead, to love so much. That's right, Daniel. Just like that. And so woman, she breaks out of prison. She is not dead. She is alive. So she runs to another man, to a house where she can be woman again. Yes, Daniel. I am mother. I am wife. But always I am woman. It is something God gave me and it is something that man can love, but never take away."

The coffee had become cold. She almost turned her cup over to read her fortune, but she stopped. Perhaps that too was not done at a time like this. My father continued to hiccup in a soft, unbroken rhythm, and at times the sound became so familiar that it appeared to have stopped. The fridge kicking on, or a car horn in the street, would make me aware of it again. Make me aware of him again. Make me wonder how I could have forgotten, and then I would forget again. My mother, on the other hand, gave the impression of always being aware of him, of never losing the thread of the occasion. She was at peace. Maybe it was because she honestly felt that she had loved him as much as she could, and still did. I did not understand her peace. I marveled at it.

The ritual continued. I couldn't tell if she was making it up as she went along, or if she was following procedures handed down to her from her old-world ancestors. I had no idea what would come next. I was in a house where I had lived all my life and yet suddenly I was a stranger. The shades were pulled down. Candles for the living and the dead were burning. My father was dying. My mother was drifting farther and farther back to that Old World she had left, and outside, in the supposedly real world, a cold wind was blowing in July, forcing its way through the cracks in the window, moving the shades, making the candle flames flicker and sway, so that neither the outside world nor the inside world felt like mine anymore.

"When your father is dying, Daniel—" My mother crossed herself. So did I. "When he is taking his last breath of air in this world, and when the moment comes and his soul leaves his body, you must not cry, you must not be afraid, you must let his soul go to God. You understand, Daniel?"

I nodded. I didn't understand.

"It is very important that his soul rise free. The Devil will be there watching. Yes, he will. And he will whisper words to your father's soul. He will say: Look, look at your poor son who is crying. Look at your woman. Look how they weep, how they love you. Can you bear to leave them? Stay. Stay with them. That is how he will whisper. It is Devil's trick. And I have been in houses where the soul of dead did not leave. Where it stayed with the living. Where the ghost of the dead and the soul of the dead was not allowed to go to God and it caused terrible things to happen. Such things that make me afraid to think of them. We must not listen to Devil. He will whisper to us, too. He will tell us: Look, it is not too late. Do not let him go. Keep him with you. Tell him how you love him. You will regret if you do not keep him. And we must say no. We must let him go. We must not try to do in his death what we did not do in his life. That's right, Daniel. It is very important."

The telephone rang. Rachel. It's Rachel, I thought. It was my world calling.

I rushed to the telephone.

"Hello?"

A strange voice came on, asking for my mother.

I handed her the phone.

She tossed back her hair and put the receiver to her ear.

" 'Allo?" she said, keeping her voice down, and then began talking in her own language. I had no idea whom she was talking to or what she was saying, but the strange words and sounds intensified even further the impression of being in somebody else's world, where not just the rituals but even the language was not my own. She looked at my father as she spoke; a couple of times she even gestured with her free hand toward him, as if the person on the other line could see. She put the phone down.

"It is foreman from my work. He told me I was late for work and I told him I was not late. I am never late. I am not coming because my husband is dying."

My dad said something, but I could not hear it. She went up to him and put her ear to his lips. He spoke again.

"Am I dying?" Is that what he said? I couldn't be sure.

"Yes," my mother said gently. "You are, my dear man. It is true."

He said something else.

"No," she replied, "summer is not over. But it is very cold outside."

I walked toward them.

"Cold," my father said.

"Yes, so-o very cold," my mother replied.

"And the ground . . ." He spoke with difficulty. "They will bury me . . . ha-ka . . . cold ground!"

"Do not worry, my dear, it is just your overcoat we will bury in cold ground. Your soul will not be cold when you embrace God. He will put his arms around you and He will rock you on His bosom like mother a babe she loves, like father a son who comes home from the war. Like that He will do to you and you will not be cold, you will never be cold again."

"Is . . . is it . . . ha-ka . . . is it really true?"

"Yes, it is true."

I took another couple of steps toward them and stopped. His head stuck out of the blankets. He seemed to be trying to crawl out, to rise.

"Now . . . I am . . . ha-ka . . . I am to die now." He tried to get up, as if it were an appointment he had to keep. "Is it now?"

"No, no, you wait . . . He will call you when it is time . . ."

"Cold . . . I am cold . . . ha-ka . . . s-s-o cold."

"I will make you hot bath. That will make you warm."

"W-warm . . ." He reached out with his hand. She took it in hers and pressed it to her breast.

"Yes, so nice and so warm. That is how you will be."

She put his hand back under the covers and got up to leave. He let out a cry.

"I am just going to make hot bath," she said. She waited to see if he understood, and, satisfied that he did, she left and in that stately processional way walked across the living room, across the kitchen and into the bathroom. I heard the water running.

I waited for my father to say something to me, but he looked past me, toward the sound of water falling into the tub. He looked thirsty for the warmth it offered.

"Father," I whispered. Perhaps I had whispered too softly. All he seemed to hear was the water falling. His eyes waited for my mother to return.

"Ha-ka."

"Daniel." She came back. Her sleeves were rolled up. "Bring your father."

His eyes stayed on her as I carried him to the bathroom. The mirror was steamed up. Steam rose out of the tub and out of the spigot where a trickle of hot water was left running. We undressed him. I took him in my arms and lowered him into the tub. His paralyzed left arm hung from his body, touching and sinking into the water first.

My mother knelt on the floor by the tub. She kept him afloat with a single hand on the back of his neck. He seemed insubstantial enough to float on his own. He tried to smile. The hot water made him happy.

I went back to the kitchen, shutting the door behind me. I peeked behind the lowered shades. It was dark outside. The few people walking in the street were dressed for January. The cold wind was still blowing in through the cracks. In a single day, a season seemed to have slipped past me. It had been months since I had seen Rachel. She alone was my world now.

I waited. I didn't know what I was waiting for. For the ritual to continue, perhaps. For Death to come into my mother's house. It was her house now. She was in charge.

I listened. She was singing something in the bathroom, strange words, and the wind whistling through the cracks sang along with her, and the candle flames, flickering in the wind, danced along with her song. It was her world and she was in tune with it.

I tiptoed toward the telephone. I dialed. All I wanted was to hear Rachel's voice. I needed to hear it to know who I was. The telephone rang. I pictured it ringing. I imagined her hand lifting the receiver. It rang and rang.

The bathroom door clicked open. I put the phone down. The floor creaked. My mother appeared in the kitchen, carrying my father in her arms. He was still naked. His pale body had turned red from the hot water, and he was steaming. His head rested on her shoulder, his lips and nose touching her neck. She carried him effortlessly. I gestured my willingness to take him, to carry him myself, but she shook her head slowly.

"He wants to lie in bed with me," she said. "He wants his old bed again."

Two drops of water dripped off his heel and fell upon the linoleum. He was beginning to get cold again. "Ha-ka." His head moved back when he hiccupped and then fell forward again, pressing against her neck. She looked down at him, and then she swung him gently around and carried him across the threshold of her bedroom, feet first.

This, too, looked like a ritual. Everything did. She came out to take the blankets and the quilt off the sofa and carry them into the bedroom. She pushed the door behind her, so that it almost shut. It seemed purposeful that a narrow opening remained. The floor creaked in her room. I heard drawers open and close. The bed creaked. Was this also a ritual, that they go in there and that I stay out here, waiting for further word, further instructions, keeping an eye on the candles? Was that what I was? A keeper of the candles?

The bed creaked again.

Maybe I had done everything I was supposed to do. Maybe my part was over.

I waited.

I tried not to imagine anything.

The candles flickered. The gas burners on top of the stove roared.

I waited.

For what?

They had forgotten about me. Maybe they expected me to know, to realize, that I was supposed to leave. Maybe the last part of the ritual called for the son to leave.

I checked the candles. It seemed safe to leave them. They were thick and they burned slowly and still had a long way to go.

I dug out my warm high-school jacket with black leather sleeves and a large purple letter I got in wrestling sewn on the right side, a large purple R for Roosevelt High School. I slipped it on and tiptoed out of the house.

Chapter 35

The cold wind blew as if it were trying to blow out the street-lights. The stop signs moved, buffeted by the wind. Wisps of fog blew past me. I put my hands in my pockets, and there in the pocket of my jacket I felt the outline of a ballpoint pen I thought I had lost. The pen, the jacket, the way I walked when I wore my jacket, and the icy wind all intensified the impression that the summer was not only over, but had been over for a long time and sometime, a long, long time ago, I had seen and known Rachel, I had loved her, and without losing her and without ceasing to love her, I had not seen her since. A few more patches of fog blew past me, like ghosts rushing to a reunion. The letter R on my jacket—ah, yes, it was destiny after all, wasn't it, that made me choose that very jacket— the letter R was my passport through the cold night to her. I wondered if she would be amused by it. Would she run her fingers across my chest, tracing the outline of the letter? Would she smile at the coincidence and welcome me back to the world we had, where I still had a part to play?

Everything that was loose and light gave way or flew with the wind. The treetops all bent one way; even the few cars that went by all went with the wind. I alone seemed to be going against it. Did not Ulysses have to battle the Fates, too, to get back to his home, his world and the one he loved? I loved the comparison. Time had gone by. Seasons had gone by. And just like the first time we had seen each other, it was night again and destiny was in the air.

The treetops swayed on Aberdeen Lane. Some of the leaves from some of the trees fell off and were caught in invisible gusts, as if in nets, and whisked off through the air. From the corner I could see that Rachel's father's car was not there. Her house was dark. A small light shone in the basement, but that was all. Something seemed to be swaying in the wind, a sign or something on the lawn in front of her house, but since I saw it from the side, I couldn't tell what it was, and my eyes kept straying up to the second-story window where I had first seen her.

The steel sign on her lawn scraped against the steel posts holding it up.

R. I saw the letter R first. My eyes went to it as if I had been trained to spot Rs wherever they might be. FOR SALE read the sign. The sign moved. The letters moved. I stood still, and for several seconds, at least, I was convinced that it was no longer an impression created by weather and the events but that months had in fact gone by, slipped by, gone, and Rachel with them.

FOR SALE.

My hands were in my pockets. I was clicking the ballpoint pen in and out and I could not decide if I had stayed away from Rachel too long, or if I had never met her but imagined the whole thing. Maybe I had just got out of Coach French's car after my defeat in the state finals. There was a For Sale sign then. There it was again. It was the same sign. I kept clicking the ballpoint pen in and out.

I shut my eyes and opened them again. The sign was still there. The light in the basement was still on.

I walked up to the door. I banged on it. I called her name. I wanted to peek through the window to see if anything of hers, of theirs, was still there, but the house was dark. I tried to open the windows, but they were locked. I banged on the door and called her name again.

"*Rachel! Rachel!*"

I ran back out on the lawn to see if her light came on upstairs. It didn't. There was only one light, the one in the basement, and it drew me forward. The wind had partially dislodged the cardboard in the broken window. I finished the job with my foot and lowered myself through the opening.

A single bare light bulb on a black, dangling cord illuminated the basement. Cardboard boxes were scattered about. A blue flame sputtered at the base of the water heater. A white laundry rope hung loose between two posts. Shadows stretched out in all directions, like black stains across the walls and the floor.

The basement seemed divided into various areas. I saw at least three different doors. Two were open, one was shut. I just wanted to find my way upstairs to see if anything of Rachel's remained.

A sudden explosion startled me. The burner under the water heater came on. I walked through one door; it led nowhere but into a closet that smelled of coal dust. I tried another one, feeling my way forward with my hand. I touched a string in midair. I grabbed it and pulled it. A red light came on. This turned out to be David's dark-room. It wasn't very large, but it was crammed with all kinds of gadgets and things I had never seen before, things that looked like huge microscopes, things that looked like clocks. There was a large sink, with a dripping faucet. On the shelves above a countertop were bottles of various sizes. The whole place reeked of alcohol and mildew.

Then I saw the pictures. They were held up by clothespins nailed to the wall. There were three of them, and all three were black and white pictures of factories in East Chicago: smokestacks, railroad cars, men with lunchbags walking through the gates. The large countertop, I now saw, had stacks and stacks of pictures on it. Each stack had a weight on top of it. A couple of stacks had old-fashioned irons holding them flat. I removed the weights and looked at the pictures. More studies of East Chicago. I recognized the streets, the factories, the refineries, the Calumet Canal. The drawbridge on Indianapolis Boulevard was lifted. Cars were waiting on both sides and a tanker was moving through the canal.

The last stack I looked at (there were others, but I never got to them) were not pictures of East Chicago. They were all of Rachel.

I sat down on a swivel chair and began going through them. The first picture was an extreme close-up of her face in profile, her eye looking askance at the camera, her shoulder bare, her hair held up by her hand, revealing the line of her neck and the fingertips peeking through the hair.

The second picture showed her either taking off or putting on her earrings. Both hands were pressed around her right earlobe, and through the cage of her fingers you could see the dangling turquoise earring, like an exotic bird in a cage. Her left earlobe was bare. Her shoulders were bare. Her neck was bent, her dark hair hung to one side and on her lips was a smile I had never seen before. It was like a smile of someone very tired, pleasantly tired, surrendering to sleep, yielding to the occasion, already dreaming.

My hands began to shake. I tried not to imagine why she looked the way she did. It was just a chance expression on a chance occasion. Just a picture.

The next one showed her brushing her teeth. Her back was to the camera, her face reflected in the mirror. She had a toothbrush in her mouth. For some reason, I could tell it was taken at night. The lateness of the hour seemed reflected in her eyes; memories of what had preceded the click of the shutter were right there in Rachel's eyes. The curve of her bare back, the curve of her smile, the curve of her neck as she smiled, all the lines of all the curves on her face and body leaned toward the camera I couldn't see, toward the man behind the camera I couldn't see; leaned toward him, yielded to him, spoke to him about the day spent, the hours spent, and carried promises of the hours still to come. It was all there. I didn't have to imagine a thing. Not a thing. Nothing except what followed the click of the shutter.

There were more pictures. I tried looking through them, but I kept going back to the third one—back to the mirror, the toothbrush. It was the ordinary, everyday nature of the moment that enthralled me. Rachel brushing her teeth. It reminded me of hundreds of similar moments I had never seen. Rachel waking up in the morning. Rachel coming through the door with the day's mail in her hand. Rachel on the phone. Everyday moments that didn't have to be earned, but were simply scattered throughout the day and shared with someone. I had shared other moments with her, but none like these, and without them our moments together remained scattered, pearls without a string. I could no longer console myself that she was incapable of those moments. They were all there in my hand, revealed to someone else. Her father!

I flipped through the other pictures, but could not bring myself to examine them the way I had examined the first three. I saw quick red-lit glimpses of Rachel naked. Her body half obscured by shadows, her flesh the color of buttered toast, and—the most revealing and the most exposed—the naked smile on her lips, the disrobed look in her eyes. Her eyes looked right at me, but I knew and could not forget that when the pictures were taken, she was looking at someone else and he had made her look and smile that way. Not I.

The front door slammed shut upstairs. I heard footsteps above my head. I flinched, like a rodent caught nibbling at food. I heard

Rachel's voice. Her father laughed. And then something or someone fell to the floor.

I waited, holding Rachel's pictures in my hand. My eyes felt small, my heart tiny, my motives damp and dirty as the floor of the basement, as the smell of the sump pump. I felt degraded. To sneak out through the window the way I had come in seemed even more degrading. Something had been started. Something would be finished if I went upstairs.

Another door led out of the darkroom. I went through it and saw the outline of a stairway going upstairs. I went up one slow step at a time, clutching her pictures to my chest. The stairway creaked.

I heard their voices again. I stopped.

"I can't anymore, Rachel. I just can't," her father groaned.

"C'mon, get up, at least," she pleaded.

"And stand on my own two feet." He started laughing. A sound covered up his laughter, a sound like a heavy piece of furniture being pushed across the floor. I stared at the space between the threshold and the door at the top of the stairs. Light and sound from the other side escaped through it, spilling down the dark, silent stairway toward me.

I waited, like a rat, like a witness with evidence in his hands, waiting to be called, waiting for the right moment to make my appearance. In my position it was easy to hate, to think murderous thoughts, to feel trapped, afraid and full of spite at the same time. I wanted to hurt Rachel.

"What're you doing?" Her father sounded drunk.

"It's cold," she said.

"Old! Did you say 'old'?" He laughed.

Metal pokers rattled. Something like a rusty metal gate creaked open. Something fell.

"Old." Her father laughed. "It's so old in here. It's the oldest day of the year."

"David," she said, "for God's sake . . . must you?"

He said nothing. I listened. It was like a radio play. I imagined him trying to speak.

"We've never been in a house with a fireplace," she said. Her voice was soothing, conciliatory, like a peace offering. I could imagine her face as she spoke. She had made those offers to me. "And now we're going to leave soon. Might as well try it once before we go. It's a good day for it. Would you like a fire?"

What a soothing voice. Like the voice of a loving nurse, asking: Would you like me to tell you a story?

I heard paper rustling. Maybe I heard a kitchen match being struck.

"Why don't you come here?" she said.

I almost thought she was talking to me, inviting me.

"Why don't you?" she repeated. "C'mon. Come here. Don't be like that."

My mind, my personal darkroom, developed instant images of her face as she spoke. I could see her smile, her eyes; I could see her lips and the way she pressed them close together while waiting for a reply, causing tiny wrinkles to appear around the corners of her mouth. No matter what she said, she had a way of making it seem that she was saving the best, the most wonderful, for later. She had a way of doing that simply by tilting her head to one side and making her eyes glow with words yet to come. I saw that, too.

Smelling the smoke and hearing the crackle of the fire, I went up the few remaining steps and stopped at the door. I put my hand on the knob and waited for something to happen to keep me from opening it. And then, maybe just to get away from the darkness, where images of her kept developing and appearing, I opened the door and stepped across the threshold to the other side.

They didn't see me. They didn't hear me. Rachel sat by the fireplace, her chin resting on her knees, her hands holding on to her ankles. She was rocking gently. The fire crackled. It was still in the early stages. Her father lay on the floor, not far from her, face down, legs close together, arms stretched out. An end table lay not far from him, and an overturned lamp that had been on top of the end table lay next to his head. The lampshade was turned up. He seemed to be staring at the bare bulb. Rachel stared at the fire. The fire crackled, engulfing more wood.

I stood in the middle of the dining room, next to the door that led down to the basement.

"You'll feel better once we leave," Rachel said, without moving her head. "You will. You'll see."

"Leave what?" Her father tried to get up and gave up the struggle. "What are we leaving? We're not leaving anything, Rachel. It's all going with us. I'm tired of it."

"You say that now . . ."

"Yes, and if I were a man—"

"Don't." She cut him off.

"When is it going to end, Rachel?" He sounded drunk, his struggles to get up those of a drunken man. "I just want to know when, that's all. When, Rachel?"

"David, please, why do you . . ." She turned her head. She stopped in midsentence. She saw me. The shock in her eyes lasted for a second or two and then, when she was sure that I was in fact there, that she was not imagining my presence, her face hardened with anger, her beautiful eyes filled with hate. She began trembling and waved me away, waved me away like a fly. Go away. Go! She did not want David to see me and she did not want me to see him lying on the floor. Go! Go away! Go down to the basement, go through the basement, go, go out the way you came. Go! I would not. I stood there, clutching the pictures of her to my chest, a witness for the prosecution.

"When, Rachel?" Her father struggled with his body, with his words, running his hand through his long gray hair. "If I were a man . . ."

"Stop it," she snapped at him. She didn't want him to continue with me there. She still seemed to be hoping that I would leave without his having seen me.

"If I were a man, I would've stopped it a long time ago. . . ."

"David! That's enough!"

"I need a drink. I want to throw up and I haven't drunk enough." He brought his hands to the side of his chest and tried to push himself up, and when he couldn't, he rolled over and sat up. That's when he, too, saw me. He looked at me and then he looked at Rachel and then he started laughing, scratching the back of his head.

"By God, Rachel, you've got them coming out of the woodwork. One sitting down and one standing up. Here, young man." He pointed to the spot on the floor where he was sitting. "Here, you sit down for a while and I'll stand. We'll take turns." He tried to stand up. He put his hand on another end table for support, and on his way up, the table fell over with him on top of it. The legs of the table broke.

"Forgive the mess." He laughed. He rolled off the debris, winding up with a table leg in his hand. For all his drunken stupor, there was something about the handsome, granite features of his face that remained intact. The body was that of a drunken man. The words and the laughter were, too. And yet his face held and even his lips moved crisply and cleanly when he spoke.

Rachel ignored me and directed her attention to him.

"C'mon, David." She spoke as if I weren't there. "C'mon, get up."

"Here's how I see it, young man," he said to me. "If I get up, I will just have to drop down again sooner or later. So I might as well stay where I am." He turned to her. "Your young man is standing. Look at him. Young and strong. With an athletic jacket, yet." He flung the table leg away, aiming at, and missing, the fireplace.

"*Why are you here?*" Rachel screamed at me. Frustrated by David's behavior, angry that I was witnessing it, angry that she had been unable to do anything about it, she took it out on me. "What do you want? What is it you want from me?"

No words would come to me, so as a reflex, as a defensive move, I showed her the pictures.

"Like this," I finally said. "Smile for me like this, Rachel."

I stepped toward her. Her large, beautiful eyes narrowed; her lips whitened from the pressure. She looked hateful.

"Get out of here. Get out!" she hissed through her teeth.

"Oh, c'mon. Smile for him, Rachel," her father muttered, sitting up.

"Get out!" She slapped my face. She tried to take the pictures from me, but I wouldn't let her have them. I clutched them close to my chest again. "Get out! Get out!" She hit me again and again. She tried to pull me out of the house, but I held my ground, dodging as many blows as I could, trying to remember the accusations I was going to hurl at her. It seemed a little late in the game to accuse her of not loving me.

"She's a stubborn woman," David muttered. "When she doesn't want to smile, she won't."

I wouldn't go. I could think of nothing to say, but I wouldn't leave.

"What is the matter with you?" Rachel, tired of hitting me, but not tired of screaming, seemed almost to be pleading with me. "Can't you understand? Leave! Get out of here, damn you!"

"I have got to get a hold on myself." David tried to get up again. "Stand on my own two feet. Like a man." He tried to use the TV set to pull himself up. He made it up to his feet, and then the TV set, sitting on top of a stand with wheels, began rolling away from him. He held on to it, stumbling after it, but it slipped out of his hands. He fell to the floor again. The TV set rolled forward, knocking over the iron pokers by the fireplace.

"See what I mean?" David crawled across the floor. "I try to walk like a man and look what happens."

"David, damn you!" Rachel pushed me aside and ran to him. "Damn you, David!" She tried to pull him up. She damned both of us. Me, standing, cold sober, and David, crawling on the floor, dead drunk.

"Do you think she's nice now?" David asked me, as she tried to pull him to his feet. "You once said she was a nice girl." He turned to Rachel. "I didn't tell you this, Rachel, but that's what he told me. He called you 'nice.' And I said . . . I can't remember what I said . . . What did I say, young man? Do you remember?"

Rachel was furious. She couldn't get him on his feet and she couldn't get me out of the house. The fire roared. All the stacked-up logs were now ablaze and shadows of furniture, shadows of the three of us, danced around the living room.

She pulled at him and he let himself be pulled, but he refused to rise, to stand.

"Love," he said. "Didn't I once say that love is both a sickness and a cure . . . I said that, didn't I?" She let him go. He sat on the floor, his legs sprawled apart, his head hanging down. "I can't tell anymore, Rachel, which is which . . ."

"David, I beg you . . ."

He lifted his head and stared into the fire. "I really can't," he said. His wrinkles deepened. He shook his head and then he turned and looked at me. "You're still here, huh? Waiting. That's the spirit. Wait it out. Because if you wait long enough—not all that long, actually—she'll be yours. Won't you, Rachel?" He turned the other way, looking for her. "Won't you, Rachel?"

She sighed, lowering her head.

"Sooner or later, you're going to leave me," David said. I couldn't see his face. His neck was twisted, the flesh on the back of the neck creased with wrinkles. "So why not do it now?"

Rachel shook her head as a reply.

"Why not, Rachel? Let me go. Either do that or swear that you'll never leave. Will you swear to that?"

She shook her head again.

"You will leave me then, won't you?"

She nodded.

"You see"—he turned to me—"it's not very pleasant living like this . . . knowing this . . . it eats at me. She's so young, you're so young . . ."

"Youth's not everything," Rachel whispered.

"When, Rachel?" he moaned, looking at the fire again.

"When it's over," she said, "and it's not over yet."

"I can't . . . I just can't anymore . . ."

He lowered his head and raised his shoulders. He was trying to hide that he was crying.

"David, please . . ." She went up to him. She put her hand on his shoulder, forced it in between his shoulder and his chin, so that her palm came to rest on his wrinkled face. As much as he wanted to, he could not resist her touch.

"Don't." She leaned over and whispered in his ear, "Don't." She kissed him on the cheek.

I had left my home where my father was dying, only to stumble into another house where another ritual was unfolding. Candles flickered in my home. A fire roared in this one. Shadows danced in both.

"Don't you understand?" David kissed her hand. "The knowing for certain . . . and yet not knowing when . . . it's so hard, Rachel . . ."

"Yes, I know," she whispered, kissing his cheek. "I do." She kissed his eyes. "I really do." She rocked him gently left and right, left and right, their bodies moving like a pendulum in front of the fire.

"I wish you'd find someone else, Rachel."

"Yes, I know you do. I thought I had. But it's still you. Yes, it's still you I love." She kissed the corners of his lips. "Still you, old man."

"Rachel . . ."

"Yes, you are an old man. A wrinkled old man. But I love you, and you love me and it can't stop until it's over."

"And when I get to be too old . . ."

"Then I'll leave you. You know I will." She kissed his lips. "But it can't stop till it's over."

They talked as if I weren't there. They talked as if they'd had this conversation many times before. I sat down on a wooden chair next to the overturned lamp. I sat down, thinking that I had to leave, but it was all I could do to sit down. The fire, their voices, their bodies, swaying back and forth, had a hypnotic effect on me, a paralyzing effect on my will.

"Did you talk about me . . . when you were with your young man, did you talk about me . . . did you tell him things . . ."

"Some," she whispered. "I told him some things. Just some."

"And do you love him?"

They were talking about me! About me! As if I weren't there.

"Yes, but not like you." She kissed him over and over again. She had kissed me just like that, light butterfly kisses on my eyes, on his eyes, on my lips, on his lips.

"He loves you."

"I know he does."

"And there'll be others?"

"Yes, there will. There'll be others."

"Swear to me you'll never leave. Please."

"No, I can't do that."

"Please."

"No."

"Rachel . . ." he pleaded and tried half-heartedly to pull away, anticipating and then surrendering to her response. Her arms pulled him back. Her fingers went into his gray hair and pulled his head back. She kissed him on the lips. My hand reached down and found the lamp switch. I flicked it off. Maybe I was trying to draw attention to myself, to remind them that I was there. Maybe I was hoping that the scene I was watching could be so easily switched off. All it did was to put me further in darkness and focus the light from the fireplace on the two of them.

She began to undress. For some reason it seemed quite natural. She was close to the fire. It was hot. She removed her blouse, with a brief, ever so brief glance at me, and flung it to one side. I just sat there. I could not move. Could not blink. Could not think or form an opinion of what I saw. And as I looked, she undressed and he, stumbling, moaning, crying, gave in to her like a little boy being undressed by his mother, not wanting to obey, but obeying; wanting to resist, but not resisting.

The fire roared. Licks of flame shot out of the logs, reaching up toward the damper. His hand, fingers outspread, landed gently on her stomach. She twisted, as if in pain, to the touch. They embraced and I saw the smile on her face, the smile I had seen only in pictures —I saw it right there in front of me. They made love in front of me and I looked on. Never having seen how true love was made, I looked on. The initial gentleness slowly turned into a struggle, with power shifting from one to the other. Rachel smiled; even when she seemed to be losing, she smiled, sensing that the power was all in her, loving it, and only when she knew that she was totally in control did she deign to surrender. I saw everything in detail.

Her knees were propped up and I watched a drop of sweat trickling down her leg, down the loose, relaxed calf, down along the Achilles tendon and then finally disappearing under her heel. David's enormous calves were taut, swelling as if the motion of his hips were pumping blood into them. Rachel looked at me every now and then, telling me that this was what love was like, that this was the man she loved, rejecting me, and yet there was something in her eyes that wanted to hold me, to keep me at a distance but hold me, something in her eyes that held out a promise, and with that promise she wanted to hold me, not in an embrace, not yet, but in an orbit until my time came. She was making love to David and making an offer to me. A place in her galaxy.

She shut her eyes. David's calf muscles rose and tightened as if in a cramp and then they relaxed. He sighed, his head slumped over on her breast. Her arms encircled him. He was all hers. He seemed dead.

I stood up. The chair creaked. I put her pictures on the seat of the chair and left.

The wind was still blowing, still in the same direction, only this time I went with it, carrying in my mind, as my father had carried in his for years, memories of smiles on a summer night. I clung to my pain, and by clinging to it, I clung to Rachel. I sensed that if I let go of the pain, I would be free, but on that cold, windy night, freedom did not seem enticing. I considered, despite everything, Rachel's silent offer. I could see a new destiny taking shape. I would mourn forever the proximity and the possibility and the eventual loss of my first love. I could imagine devoting the rest of my life to it. It was like a secure emotional occupation, a fixed orbit. Freedom was nothing. Freedom was a leaf blown down the street, and I wanted to be connected to something, to someone. Better pain than nothing. A lifetime of freedom was a terror I was not ready to face. I even saw a ray of hope in Rachel's offer. It gave me a goal, it gave me a "maybe someday." Freedom meant free from pain, free from hope, unanchored, cast adrift. What did a free man do? What did he dream of? What did he hope for? Nothing. Nothing. I could not imagine being free. All I could see was a void. And I needed to see a "maybe someday." I needed a role and a destiny. Even as I walked home, I imagined myself in the next few years becoming a "character" in my town: Daniel the broken-hearted. Everybody would know about me and the girl I had loved and lost and how I was still hoping and waiting for her return. His father died. His girl left him. Everybody would understand why I was the way I was.

The candles were still burning on the kitchen table when I came inside. My absence was probably as unnoticed as my return.

I lay down on the couch in the living room. There were no blankets left. Shivering and watching the candles burn, one for the living and one for the dead, I fell asleep.

My father died the next day.

Chapter 36

I did what my mother told me. I put on a clean white shirt. She finished ironing my trousers and brought them to me. I put them on. They were still warm. I polished my shoes, as instructed. I combed my hair. From my room, I could hear her talking on the telephone in her own language. Making preparations. She made several calls. The word "Libertyville" came up in all of them. Then she came to get me.

"Daniel." She opened the door to my room. She, too, was dressed up: black skirt, black blouse, lipstick, earrings. She looked beautiful. Behind her, in the living room, I saw my father's wheelchair, empty now.

"He will die soon," she said. "Remember, he must die in peace. You must not cry too much. It will make him upset. Think nice things about his life. That's what you should do."

I tried to remember everything she said. I wanted to lose myself in procedures, have nothing in my head except directions to follow.

We set off together.

The shades in the bedroom were pulled down. Two candles were burning, one on each side of the bed, one for the living and one for the dead, but I no longer knew which was which. My mother knew. I would do what she said.

My father lay in bed, his head propped up on pillows. The white pillowcases reflected the light from the candles. I could see his face, every feature on it, as if a spotlight were aimed at him. He blinked, looking at us.

We took our positions at the foot of the bed. He looked at my mother for a long time. Then he moved his eyes and looked at me.

I tried to think about something nice from his life. I remembered him laughing with the puppy in his arms.

"Do you see," my mother asked him, "what a handsome son you have?"

"Yes," he whispered, "my son."

"The bloodline will continue through him," she said. "You have done your job. Your name will live on in his children. You have worked hard. And now, soon, you will rest."

He listened to her, as if she knew everything.

"Husband," my mother said after a short pause, "do you know that you are dying?"

"Yes." He nodded.

"There are things I must do. Preparations. It is important that you understand and give approval. I will do what you want."

He looked at her as if he couldn't get enough of her. How was it possible, I wondered, that he could still love her the way he did? As she talked, his eyes moved and took me in. I could tell he loved me. But he loved her more. How was it possible?

"I can bury you in Catholic cemetery." My mother was giving him his last options. "And I can make promises that I will visit your grave all the time, but God forgive me"—she crossed herself—"I know I would not. I would like very much to bury you in Serbian Orthodox cemetery. There I will go every Sunday and plant flowers to grow on your grave. And I will take care of flowers. And when other women come and they start to talk about their dear departed ones, I will talk about my years with you. So, this is what I ask you: Does that meet with your approval?"

"Yes." He nodded.

"I am so glad," she said.

And what about me, I wondered. What would I be doing on those Sundays? Why wasn't I included? I wanted to hear, I wanted to know what was expected of me.

"And I will put expensive monument on your grave," my mother went on. He couldn't get enough of her. "And on monument, I will put picture of you when you were young and handsome with hair so lovely. And I will tell them to put words in stone. These words will last forever: Beloved husband. Beloved father."

"Beloved," he whispered, his eyes filling with tears. "Really? Is it really true? Beloved."

"Yes," she said, "it is true."

"Beloved." He repeated the word, looking at her.

I could not understand the deathbed love scene that was taking place. Maybe it was because I felt left out, but I wanted him to say something cruel to her that he could never take back. Something that would hurt her for the rest of her life. Tell her to put these words on the tombstone: She cheated me of a smile. I saw myself lying in his place, saying those words to Rachel, and I wanted him to say them to my mother.

All he said, for the fourth time, was that single word: "Beloved."

"We have made peace, husband." My mother crossed herself. "May peace be with you."

When, I wanted to know, when did they make this peace? While I was out crawling through Rachel's basement? Did I, too, have to lie dying to feel at peace?

My father's face changed. My mother noticed instantly.

"Daniel," she said, "it is here. He sees death. Go to him."

I took a step toward him, but she pulled me back.

"No," she said, "you are the man of family now. Go to his right side. I will go to left."

I did as I was told. She knelt down and took his left hand. I did what she did and took his right. I saw all three of us in the mirror above the dresser.

Death was in the room. My father's eyes saw it. His hand squeezed mine. His eyes widened. He saw it. A sound like a yelp escaped his lips.

"Do not be afraid," my mother whispered to him.

He began to choke.

"Easy. Do not stop breathing. Make it easy. Let out the air. Like a sigh."

He obeyed.

"Yes, like that. Do not rush. Death will wait. Now you breathe in. Now out. Like a sigh."

He relaxed and did what she said. He inhaled, he exhaled.

"Yes," she said, "you are doing fine. Like a hero you are dying. At peace. Look at death. Only you can see it. Show you are not afraid. That's right. Like a hero."

He inhaled, he exhaled. He seemed calm. I would never know what his thoughts were at this moment. There was so much about him that I would never know.

He inhaled. He exhaled. I could not help wondering if he was dying with a memory of my mother's smile, the smile his whole life had denied him. Pity gripped my heart. For him. For me. Pity for the living and the dead, for all those who were denied the one thing they craved.

"Daniel," he whispered.

"Yes, Father."

"Forgive . . ." His lips hardly moved.

"Who, Father?" I didn't know. "Who should I forgive?"

His lips moved. He said something. A word. A name. I couldn't hear. He inhaled. He seemed ready to speak again. He exhaled. And with that, he died.

My mother said a prayer in her own language. She shut his eyes with her fingertips.

"Daniel," she said, "blow out your father's candle."

I didn't know which one was his. She told me. I blew it out. The other one continued to burn the rest of the day.

The next few days were filled with new people and constant activity in preparation for the funeral. In the end, however, I remembered those days as a series of impressions which, in time, became disassociated from the funeral.

"Thirty-two long," the salesman said, measuring me with his weary eyes. Then he looked at me from the waist down. "Thirty-two, I'd say, unless you like it high. If you like it high, thirty-one."

I needed a black suit for the funeral. I had taken a bus to Hammond and got off at Robert Hall Clothes. The store was nearly empty. Three salesmen stood together at the far end of the store and silently decided whose turn it was to wait on me. The tall man in the middle stepped forward. He was about fifty, and as weary as any man I have ever seen. I told him what I needed, and with his tired eyes he took my measurements. He wasn't doing it to show off; he wasn't especially proud of being able to guess correctly my waist size, my inseam, the length of my sleeves. He just did it. He was like a man who had lived before and died and come back and died and was reincarnated once again as the same person, doing the same job in the same store. I only saw one day in his eyes. This day. Neither his past nor his future seemed to exist.

My father's body lay in an open coffin in the funeral home. The casket was surrounded by flowers sent by my mother's Jugoslavian friends. There were two wreaths from the factory: one from the management and one from the union. There was also a wreath from Billy Freund and Patty Campbell, signed William and Patricia. I sat up front. Sunlight shining through the door of the funeral home followed the hallway leading to the casket, creating a corridor of light, and when people came to pay their respects, they first appeared as long shadows. I sat up front and watched the shadows, heard the shadows whisper, heard the footsteps of the shadows, and when the actual people walked past me, I shut my eyes and kept them shut until I heard them leave. Then I opened them again to watch more shadows coming through the door.

The cemetery was in Libertyville, Illinois. To my mother, that was the place where the Serbian Orthodox monastery and the Serbian Orthodox cemetery were located. To others, it was the place where Adlai Stevenson lived. It was about a three-hour ride from East Chicago. My mother and I rode in the back of a black Cadillac supplied by the funeral home. Behind us, a convoy of cars followed, with their lights on. I kept looking at my mother, wondering why she seemed so different. And then, just before we pulled off the four-lane highway to a county road, I realized why. She was a widow. She had a new identity, a new word to wear. There was no word for a son who had lost his father.

The pallbearers carried the coffin from the parking lot along the narrow path lined with tombstones to the gravesite. I saw Billy Freund and Patty walking arm in arm behind me, and directly behind them I saw Mrs. Dewey and her husband. Mrs. Dewey was weeping openly and loudly. My mother kept turning her head to look at her. Others, too, seemed curious to know who this woman was and why she was crying, grieving more than anyone else in the funeral procession. I thought I knew. She wasn't crying for my father. She was crying for herself, and for once she was in an atmosphere where she could cry openly and freely in front of her husband, and he couldn't stop her. She had come to do just that. She cried and cried.

In the crowd of mourners around the gravesite, I noticed an unusually tall man. He had dark hair, a dark complexion and prominent cheekbones. He also had a moustache, black, sprinkled with gray.

He kept looking at my mother during the eulogy. I waited for her to return his stare. When she did, the man's face changed ever so slightly. Was this the man, I wondered, was this the one who had made her smile on that summer night long ago?

The coffin was lowered slowly into the ground. Down at the far end of the cemetery, another group of mourners was arriving, following another coffin. The mourners and the relatives of the deceased from that group looked at us and we looked at them. We looked at each other across the tombstones. The monastery bell began to toll, and neither side seemed quite certain for which funeral the bell was tolling.

Across from the old monastery, there was a brand-new building of brick and glass. There, inside a large hall, we held a funeral feast for my father. Food and drink were laid out on a series of large folding tables. Mrs. Dewey drank and cried, ate and cried. Bimbo just drank. Freud, dressed in his father's suit, came over to me and said something about how the two of us were so much alike; neither of us had a father. Patty shook my hand and gave me her condolences. The man from my father's union did also. He told me to call him if I wanted a job in the plant. The priest talked to me in broken English. The Jugoslavian women talked to me in fluent Jugoslavian. The tall, dark man with the moustache remained aloof. He got drunk first. Then Mrs. Dewey got drunk. Then Freud got drunk. Then I got drunk. I don't know who got drunk after that.

Chapter 37

The cold front came and went. Warm weather returned. Then it was hot again. I tried to ignore the change. My heart was still in the cold front, and my thoughts were autumnal. Despite the heat, I continued to wear my black funeral suit every day. I even found an old black shirt and I wore that, too. I walked the streets, looking at people watering their lawns, washing their cars; I stopped to look at kids playing baseball, or couples talking to each other, holding hands, and wherever I went, I tried to cast my black shadow of doubt over them. Couldn't they see, couldn't they smell the rot of impermanence in the air? Their hopes and plans, weren't they like a sunny afternoon that at any moment could be, would be, swept away by change, by another cold front coming through? I pitied them. I was so full of black, fatalistic wisdom, a prophet of doom, that I even understood why they chose to ignore me when I stared at them. They didn't want to know the truth. Only I knew the truth. We would all die. Love would die. Hopes would die. Even the thick-trunked trees on Aberdeen Lane would someday die. That's what "someday" had in store for us: death. The earth, the planets, the sun, the moon and the stars, all of them had a someday waiting for them and that someday was death.

I saw my future clearly. The black suit would become my trade-mark. I would walk the streets of East Chicago and, in time, those who knew me would die and the next generation would whisper half-substantiated rumors about me as I walked by. Maybe they would know about the girl who had broken my heart. Maybe they wouldn't. But everyone would know of me, my black suit, my withering glance: Old Man Daniel, the man in bitter black.

I couldn't stay at home. Everything my mother did annoyed me. Cooking, cleaning house, buying groceries—they seemed so unrooted in any philosophical outlook on life, except to keep life going. Why did she comb her hair? What was the point? She took the funeral register home and wrote letters to everyone who came to the funeral. I just shook my head. The eventually-to-be-dead writing to the would-be-dead to thank them for coming to the funeral of the one who actually died.

"We need milk," she said.

It struck me as preposterous that she could think of something like that.

"What for?"

"To drink. That is what for. To drink."

I just shook my head.

"You shake your head too much, Daniel. All the time now. I say something and you shake your head."

I shrugged and got up.

"Daniel," she called as I went through the door. "Get milk."

Had she only known how she diminished herself with that word, she never would have uttered it. Milk. My father was not in his grave even a full week and she could think of milk. No, there was no way she could have loved him. Had she loved him, her mind would not be on groceries. Something about her—maybe it was the sudden intrusion of a totally inappropriate topic—reminded me of Rachel. My father and I had both been betrayed. We were both martyrs of love at the hands of savage women.

A curse on them both!

A curse on their fickle hearts and on the men who made them smile!

I went to Kroger's for milk. The supermarket was packed. Women shopping. Women with carts loaded with food. Damn women everywhere. I withered them all with my glance.

The checkout line was long. I stood there with my carton of milk, aloof and proud that I only had one item. I was surrounded by steaks and pot roasts and boxes of cereal. The line moved slowly. I looked down and thought my dark thoughts.

When I looked up again and saw the woman at the cash register, I wanted to switch lines. But it was too late. She saw me. It was Mrs. Dewey. She was wearing the pale green smock of a Kroger's employee with a name tag over her right breast: LAVONNE. She bagged the groceries for the woman in front of me and then it was my turn.

"Hello, Daniel." She smiled, pushing back a strand of hair.

"Yes, hi." I put my milk on the counter.

"This all you got?"

"Yes, that's it."

She rang it up and put it in a bag. I paid her. She gave me back my change. I made sure to take it without touching her hand.

"Evelyn," she called as I walked past her. "Evie, take over for me for a sec, will you, hon?"

She followed me out of the store. I didn't want to talk to her, but when she came up to me in the parking lot and stopped, I stopped too. The smock made her look shorter and older.

"I needed a break," she said. "I've been at it five hours straight."

I said nothing. I had nothing left to say to women.

"Three weeks now I've been working here," she went on. "It's not that bad. Gets me out of the house and . . . well . . . you know."

Yes. I nodded. I know.

She chuckled like she used to do and shook her head.

"Endives," she said. "Do you know what endives are?"

"No." I suddenly remembered that I still didn't know what Dells were.

"Well, I tell you." She looked away. "I saw this thing the other day. It's like a catalogue from which the store manager orders food from the suppliers. I don't know why I was looking at it, but I was. Flipping pages in this ring binder. And there it was on page 127: Endives!" She looked at me and chuckled again. There was something sad in her eyes. "Well, I tell you. I just looked at that word and looked at it. Endives. Before I knew it I got all depressed. I mean, here I am almost thirty and I don't know what the hell endives are. I could tell it was a vegetable because it was on the vegetable list, but so what, right? When I asked around the store one of the girls told me, oh yeah, endives are wonderful. She had them all the time back East somewhere. Naturally I just got more and more depressed. You know, I started thinking." She looked away again. "Maybe there's all kinds of things, you know. Maybe all the songs I like, all my all-time favorites, maybe there's other songs I'd love even more if I heard them. But where do you go to find out? You see, that's what got me. Not knowing where to go." She seemed ready to cry, but instead she chuckled and shook her head. "It all started with endives." She threw up her hands. "I tell you . . ."

When she saw that I wanted to leave, she put her hand on my shoulder. Not like she used to do, easy and playful. It was a different hand. A different gesture.

"Have you seen Larry at all?" she said.

"No. Not for a while."

"Me neither. He used to drive past my house at night and then he stopped."

"Yes, I know," I said. "He did the same thing with me."

"I'm too old for him." She started playing with her name tag, pulling on it. "I'm almost thirty, and he . . . well . . . he's got his whole life ahead of him." She sighed and then her eyes widened as if she had just remembered something. "How long do you think that lasts?" she said slowly, softly.

"What's that?"

"You know. How old can you be and still have your whole life ahead of you? Where's the line? I remember when I was in high school people used to tell me all the time how my whole life was ahead of me. And then they stopped telling me. So, I guess . . ." She shrugged. She looked at her watch. Then she pointed at my milk. "Your milk's getting warm. You better . . . and I should too . . . I'll see you, all right?"

"Yes."

She spun around on her heels and walked back inside the store.

I walked home carrying a half-gallon carton of milk, thinking of all the women, all the girls, I had known and the harm they'd done. The useless dreams inspired by Diane Sinclair. Misiora's despair over Mrs. Dewey; the fight she caused. The years of despair my father spent, waiting for a smile that never came. And Rachel!

I stopped on the corner of Northcote and Aberdeen Lane and cast my withering glance down her block. The For Sale sign was still in front of her house. David's car was parked in its familiar spot. It was like a personal insult directed at me that his car would be where it had always been. As if nothing had happened! As if nothing had changed! Life went on as usual and only those sensitive enough were doomed to suffer. I saw no contradiction in the fact that I was sensitive enough to suffer and at the same time vengeful enough to envision Rachel in agony, tormented by guilt, begging and pleading for me to forgive her. No! Never!

"Here," I told my mother, handing her the milk as if I were

handing her a signed confession of her own insensitivity. "Here is your milk."

"Put it in fridgerator," she said.

I just shook my head.

"You will stop doing that, Daniel. I don't like your head shaking at me."

I shrugged.

"Also, you will not shrug at me. Shrug and shake, that is all you do. No more. Also, you stink. I am washing clothes today. Give me your black shirt so I can wash it."

"I like it the way it is."

"It smells like a horse, Daniel. This is house, not a barn. Take shirt off."

"I don't want to."

"This is free country, Daniel. You can don't want to whatever you don't want to. This is also my house and you will do what I say until you pay rent."

"Would you like me to leave?"

"I would like your black shirt to wash."

"If you want me to leave, I'll leave."

"Put milk in fridgerator, Daniel." She spoke calmly. "That is what I want."

I threw the milk in and slammed the door shut.

"Now take off shirt."

"No."

"Goodbye, Daniel. Come back when you are ready to obey."

"All right, I'll leave. That's what you want, I know. You've just been waiting for me to leave, so you can resume your affair with that guy with the moustache. I know."

"Daniel, come here."

I came toward her and stopped. She pointed to a spot in front of her.

"Come closer."

I did. She slapped me across the face with the back of her hand and then once again with her palm.

"Now, go outside. You are angry. I am angry. It is no good to be together."

I stayed out all night, wandering through town, contemplating committing suicide and leaving a note behind that would make my mother and Rachel feel responsible. I hung around the railroad tracks by the library, waiting for the train to come along. I would throw myself under the wheels and let the New York Central crush the life out of me. But I had no paper and no pen or pencil on me. I couldn't write my note. I didn't want to die unless I knew for certain that my mother and Rachel would spend the rest of their lives tormented by guilt.

I moved on, contemplating another possibility. I would run away. But how would I know the impact my departure would have on Rachel and my mother? Nothing short of daily reports of their agonized guilt would make me happy. Who would send me the reports? And what if they didn't feel guilty? What if they really wanted me to leave, to run away, so they wouldn't have to see me and be reminded of their treachery? No, it seemed better to stay in town and find a way to torment them in person.

I got thirsty thinking about it.

The lights were off in Rachel's house. Asleep, probably. Both of them. Both in the same bed. I turned on the water spigot on the side of the house and drank greedily. I drank the water, I drank the memories associated with the sprinkler, I cursed Rachel and I longed for her. I loved her still and I hated her more than ever and I drank and drank.

I left the water running and walked away.

Everywhere I went was somewhere I had been before, and I could remember something with which each street or part of a street was identified. Here I had seen the cheerleaders cheering. There I had walked with Rachel. I walked through the park and recognized the tree where I had told her that I loved her. Not far from the park were the streets where my dad and I had gone on our late afternoon jaunts, me pushing his wheelchair, and without even seeing them I could visualize the streets Freud, Misiora and I had taken together when we were inseparable. Every part of the town was filled with memories. There were no vacant spots. My whole past was here, scattered around, and I walked through the night making the rounds of my life.

I sneaked into the house carefully so as not to wake my mother. If she was still awake, I wanted to sneak into my bed quietly so she wouldn't even know I had returned, so that she would continue to worry and wonder where I was. I really could have used a glass of milk, but I didn't touch it. Not a drop.

When I awoke the next morning, I found my black shirt washed and neatly folded on my dresser. She must have got up in the middle of the night to do it. It looked so damned motherly lying there, the way it smelled, the way it was folded. It angered me that I was touched by it, that my bitterness could so easily be assuaged by an act of motherly love.

I put it on.

"Mother," I called.

I looked in her room. The bed was made. She was gone.

Chapter 38

She went back to work the next week. I had nothing to go back to. I spent my days at home and my evenings and nights walking around town. I watched TV a lot. I'd pull out my father's wheel-chair to the center of the living room, turn on the TV and then just sit in the wheelchair for hours, watching daytime heroes on the screen. I liked sitting in the wheelchair. When I got hungry, I'd wheel myself over to the fridge, take something out to eat and wheel myself back in front of the set. I let myself imagine whatever I felt like. I was a veteran, wounded in the war, and I came home to find that the girl I loved had fallen in love with somebody else. I enjoyed being wounded, enjoyed pretending that my manhood had been snuffed out by an enemy's grenade. I understood why Rachel could not love me anymore. I had long scenes with her in my head, where I told her it was no good this way. I'm just half a man. You need somebody whole. Go and be happy with somebody else.

It all made sense as long as I stayed in the wheelchair and played paralyzed. When I got out of the chair and began walking the streets at night, my hatred and anger returned. Why didn't she love me the way I loved her? All I wanted was an explanation. I wanted to be convinced that David was better for her, made her happier. I just wanted to know why. Why, Rachel? For all I knew—and this is what I found intolerable—she misperceived me and rejected me without really knowing who I was, what a wonderful person I was. I wanted to know exactly what she saw in me, in minutest detail, so that I could defend myself point by point, detail by detail, and only then, if she still wanted to reject me, could I accept it. My mind cranked out scenes and I walked the streets playing them. I sued Rachel for not loving me and took her to court. A team of lawyers represented her. I represented myself. I spoke passionately to the jury. I cross-examined Rachel mercilessly.

"Tell me, Miss Temerson, what, exactly, don't you love about me?"

"I don't know. It's hard to be exact in cases like this."

"Let me rephrase the question. What, exactly, do you love about David?"

"I just do."

"You're also on record as loving me, are you not?"

"Yes, I am."

At this point, I introduced a series of snapshots as evidence. They were all pictures of Rachel and me, pictures I didn't have, but pictures that my mind carried as memories, and I offered my memories to the jury as exhibits A to Z.

"Do you recognize these pictures?"

"Yes, I do."

"Would you say that in these pictures, your face is showing love for the plaintiff?"

"Yes, I remember those pictures. I loved him in those pictures. I did."

"All right. Think back. From the time these pictures were taken to the time that you 'changed your mind,' did the plaintiff do *anything* wrong, did he perform some treachery, did he let you down, did he betray you—did he, in short, by word or deed, do anything at all to cause you to cease loving him?"

"No, I can't say he did."

"I bet you can't."

I turned to the jury and began ranting about innocent lovers who, through no fault of their own, are abandoned without cause. Was there sufficient provocation, I asked them, or was this a case of whimsical, willful abandonment? Furthermore, did the defendant show any proof as to why she is better off with this older gentleman? Did she show any proof that precluded the possibility that I could make her smile—no, not just like he did, but even better? I went on and concluded by saying that if we allowed this woman to stop loving me, we would be sending a signal to the women of the country that they, too, could use whimsy instead of reason in their dealings with their husbands and lovers. We're setting a precedent here, I went on. We're placing a value on the human heart and if somebody breaks it, the person either has to put it back together again or pay. If somebody hits your car and ruins it, he is liable. Surely, then, if somebody ruins your life, that person too is liable and should make restitution. I rest my case.

It didn't take long for the jury to reach its verdict. It found Rachel guilty on all counts. The judge, admitting that it was an unusual case, passed sentence. If Rachel did not want to love me, she could not love anyone else, and if she was caught loving anyone else, she would be imprisoned and fined. I was totally exonerated. Landmark decision, the newspaper headlines read.

Sometimes, when my mother was not at home, I rummaged through her room, through the dresser drawers and the closets and the shoebox filing system she kept. Just as I had looked for my father's diary, I now looked for hers. It didn't matter that even if she kept one it would be written in her own language. I wanted to find it. I would take it to somebody who could translate it for me, and then and only then would I find out why she had gone to that other man on that summer night and what it was that he had that my father didn't. I wanted to know where the difference lay. I found nothing except old photographs of her as a young girl: old photographs of her and my father, and as hard as I tried to read their faces, I could not read their minds. I found no pictures of that other man. The desire to know, to get to the bottom of people I knew, became as intense as the frustration I felt, caused by that fruitless search.

Everybody, I decided, should be required to keep diaries where they record their motives, their impressions of people close to them, and those diaries should be made available for inspection. How else were we to know for sure the nature of people we loved? How else could we understand them? How else could we correct their misperceptions about ourselves? I could not be sure that there was a single person who knew me, nor a single person whom I really knew. And unless somebody did something, it would go on like that for the rest of my life.

I imagined myself becoming a scientist, developing a process that could unroll the human brain on a screen so that there, in precise images, we would be able to see what people really saw in us. If they really loved us, and why. If they didn't, and why. We would know who they were and who they thought we were and we would at last get to the bottom of the human soul.

Halfway through her work week, my mother had a talk with me.
"Summer will soon be over," she said.

"Good." I couldn't wait for fall, for winter. A long winter.

"What are you going to do, Daniel?"

I knew what she meant, but I avoided the question.

"I don't know what you mean. What am I supposed to do?"

"You have finished high school. Now what will you do?"

"I don't know."

"If you want to go to college, I will work and I will give you money for college."

"No, I don't want to go to college." I looked at the floor. "It's too late, anyway, for this year. You have to apply and all and be accepted."

"Then you must find job. You must do something. It is wrong to stay home and do nothing."

"I don't mind."

"I don't like it. It is wrong. You don't look good, Daniel."

As she was preparing to leave for work that day, she looked around the house. Her eyes stopped on my father's wheelchair in the corner. I kept it there when she was around.

"You will take wheelchair back to store. Maybe you can ask the man at store to give you back some money for it."

"It's not hurting anyone where it is."

"It is hurting me." She crossed herself. "It has been here long enough. Take it back to store."

"All right."

"I will see you tonight."

"Bye, Mom."

I wheeled the chair out after she left and sat down in it. I hated parting with it. Its presence in the house seemed to confer a special status on me and made me feel exempt from jobs and future plans and the general odious notion that life must go on. It fit my body and my mood, and sitting there, I would have given anything to be suddenly struck with paralysis and in that condition be allowed to continue my speculations about the things that really mattered.

I pushed the chair out of the house, wondering if there was a place where I could hide it and use it whenever I felt like it. Freud's garage seemed like a good spot, but I couldn't do my research, my thinking, with him around. There was a letter in the mailbox. I took it out. It was addressed to a Mr. James Donovan. I almost put it back in

the mailbox when I remembered that I was James Donovan. The
letter was from the public library. I opened it. DEAR MR. DONOVAN:
YOU ARE NOW OVERDUE. It was a form letter, and in the space below
the greeting were the names of the books, including Maxim Gorky's
Childhood, that I was supposed to bring back or be fined ten cents
a day from that day on.

I reread the letter several times. James Donovan YOU ARE NOW
OVERDUE.

I put the letter inside my suit jacket and pushed the chair up 149th
Street toward Indianapolis Boulevard. The empty chair rattled and
seemed harder to steer than when my dad sat in it. I had known him
all my life and yet I didn't really know him at all. Did my mother
see him in the same way that I did? Did he carry an image of himself
inside his head that had nothing to do with our view of him? The
peace I saw on his face as he was dying . . . did he really feel it?

I took a left on Indianapolis Boulevard, and after a couple of
blocks, I stopped in front of a store whose only name was Hospital
Supplies. In the window display were all kinds of hospital-room
accessories: bed pans, stethoscopes, syringes, steel tables with wheels
on them. Off to the right was a display of canes and walkers and
wheelchairs, stacked one against the other like folding picnic chairs.

I pushed the chair inside. A little bell rang above my head, tripped
by the door, and then rang again as the door closed.

The proprietor was standing behind the counter. Behind him was
a sign: ASK ABOUT OUR GUIDE DOGS. He was talking to a customer
who was blind. The blind man had a white cane and wore dark
glasses and seemed to be grinning when he talked and when he
listened. His buck teeth were stained yellow.

"Be right with you," the proprietor said to me. The blind man
turned toward me. His grin got broader by way of a greeting. They
resumed their conversation.

"It's highly unusual," the proprietor said.

"Yes, I know." The blind man grinned. "Everyone I talk to tells
me they never heard of such a thing."

"Oh, I've heard of it happening before. Yes, I've heard of it. But
it's still highly unusual. Most unusual, as a matter of fact. He just
took off, eh?"

"It appears he did. I was sitting on a park bench . . ."

"McArthur Park?"

"No, Kosciusko Park."

"Ah, yes."

"I was sitting there," the blind man went on. "I had my hand on the handle. Then I let go of the handle and, you know . . . I started talking to him. I liked talking to him. I talked to him a lot. You know, you forget it's a dog at times and you just talk to him. I used to tell him everything. So, anyway, there I was chatting away and then I reach down for him and there's no dog there. I feel around the bench. Nothing. I feel around some more. I got all worried. I thought maybe the dog had a stroke or something. But, no. He wasn't there . . . He just, eh . . ."

"Took off, eh?"

"It appears he did. I called him and called him, but nothing. Some kids came along and I asked them if they'd seen a dog with a harness around his shoulders and a leather handle sticking out. I described him real good, so there'd be no mistake. And they said yes, they did see such a dog. And he was, according to them, running like a bat out of hell. Their words."

"What was his name?" the proprietor asked.

The blind man really grinned this time. The proprietor grinned too.

"I called him . . . Puccini!" The blind man seemed both embarrassed and proud of the name.

"Puccini, eh?" The proprietor looked at me and shook his head.

"It comes from . . ." the blind man began, but the proprietor cut him off.

"Yeah, I know. It's Italian."

"No, no." The blind man began laughing.

"What do you mean, 'No, no.' Of course it is. It's Italian."

"Yes, I know it's Italian, but . . . No, I can't tell you. It's embarrassing."

"Oh, c'mon. He's gone anyway, so what the hell, eh?"

"Well, all right." The blind man paused and bit his lower lip with those huge teeth of his. "It comes from Pooch. You know, Pooch, like a dog."

"Pooch?" The proprietor seemed puzzled.

"Yeah. Pooch. You know: Poochini."

"Poochini?"

"Yeah, Poochini!"

"*Poochini!*" The proprietor started laughing. The blind man joined him. Their hands touched across the counter. "No wonder he left," the proprietor roared. The blind man's body moved jerkily in rhythm to his laughter. "Maybe he ran off to New York to join the Met. Poochini, eh?"

They laughed and laughed. Then, after a couple of sighs, it was back to business.

"I'll put another order in. I'll give you a call when the dog comes and the two of you can meet and see what you think of each other. Might take a couple of weeks. Okay?"

"You have my number?"

"Yeah, I got it."

"Well, bye-bye, then."

"Bye."

The blind man tapped his way to the door. The bell rang twice and he was gone.

"Quite a character." The proprietor winked at me. "So, what can I do for you?" He looked at the wheelchair. "Need a tune-up?"

"I'm bringing the chair back."

"I can see that. Something the matter with it?"

"No, my father died and we don't need it anymore."

"Sorry to hear that, young feller. I suppose you'd like to sell it back to me."

"Well, my mother said . . ."

"Yeah, I imagine she did. All right," he sighed, "what's the name?"

"Donovan," I said. "James Donovan."

"Let's see." He started looking through some files. "A, B, C, D. Here it is. Donohue . . . Dobosh . . . Dreiling . . . no Donovan. That's my chair, all right, but I don't have no Donovan in the books."

"That's because . . . eh . . . my mother probably . . . you see . . . I was really adopted when I was thirteen. They let me keep my name: Donovan. Their name is Price. It's probably under Price."

"It's not under Donovan, that's for sure. Let's see . . ." He flipped through the cards again. "Ah, here we are. Price!"

He looked at the chair again. He ran his fingers over the rubber on the wheels.

"Kind of worn, eh? Well, tell you what I'll do. Last thing I want is to have a nice young orphan kid like you get in trouble with his mother. I'll give you thirty bucks for it."

"Okay."

"You drive a hard bargain, kid. Here you go . . . ten, twenty, thirty." He put the three ten-dollar bills in my hand. "If you see Poochini and bring him back, I'll give you another ten."

He laughed. He liked saying the dog's name. He waved. The bell tinkled above my head.

James Donovan.

I walked down Indianapolis Boulevard, trying a new gait to go with the new name. James "Jimmy" Donovan. I put my hands in my pockets. Thirty dollars. I had a suit and three ten-dollar bills. I had just got out of jail, where I had spent ten years for . . . I couldn't decide what crime I had committed. I considered murder. I considered having killed Rachel. Temporary insanity. It didn't sit right with me, so I lowered my sentence to five years and left my crime vague. Then I decided that I hadn't committed any crime at all. I was innocent but framed. A set-up job. Rachel set me up.

James Donovan. Home after five years in the pen. Innocent going in. Not so innocent coming out. You grow up and grow up fast in the pen.

I stopped on the corner of Chicago Avenue and Indianapolis Boulevard. For five years I had waited for this moment, to be free again, to find Rachel again and plunge my dagger into her treacherous heart. You framed me, Rachel. I was innocent and you framed me.

"Just remember, son," the prison chaplain told me as I was leaving. "Revenge is mine, saith the Lord."

James Donovan at the crossroads.

I crossed the street slowly. A short girl with blond hair walked out of the bank on the corner, bouncing up and down on her toes as she walked. Our eyes met for a brief second.

The worst thing about the pen was the absence of women. I followed her. A cute kid—it'd be a shame for her to get mixed up with somebody like me. Still, I contemplated my introduction. "Hi, I'm new here. Jimmy Donovan's the name, but everyone calls me J.D."

She went into Woolworth's, bounced right in, and I went in after her.

New stock had arrived and the stockboys were unpacking boxes of school supplies and putting them on shelves and display cases. Big Chief tablets, crayons, bottles of glue, pencils, protractors, rulers, loose-leaf binders and reams of loose-leaf paper. The girl bounced through the aisles, waving merrily to the stockboys, her white smock shimmering past the perfume display. She paused to look at some makeup and lipstick. She combed her hair, checking herself out in one of the mirrors on the shelf, and then she skipped and bounced behind the lunch counter. A waitress. I would start a new life with her. Someday I would tell her all about my past.

Right at the place where the stationery department ended and the perfume department began was a large bin full of hard-covered books with "1961" stamped on their covers. I stopped and picked one up. It was a diary. They were all diaries. The whole bin was full of diaries. All empty.

"They're on sale," a saleswoman told me. "Fifty percent off. I guess they figured the year's more than half over, so . . ."

They were all the same color. Red.

"You have any in black?" I asked.

"No, red's it. Never seen them in black."

I leafed through the empty pages full of dates. I must have stood there flipping pages longer than I thought, because when I looked up, the saleswoman in the glasses was gone. I saw her ringing up a sale at the makeup department and got her attention. She came over.

"So, have you decided to buy one?"

"Yes . . . eh . . . Give me . . . eh . . . I'll take six."

"Six?" She pushed up her glasses with a finger.

"Yes."

"Well, they *are* on sale. Would there be anything else today?"

"Yeah, a ballpoint pen."

"We just got some piggy-back ones in stock."

"No, I don't want anything on its back. Just a regular ballpoint pen. You got black ink?"

"Blue, I'm afraid. All blue. Oh, we do have red."

"I'll take blue."

I had twenty-one dollars and change left after paying. I took my diaries and my pen and went over to the lunch counter where the bouncy blond girl was cheerfully wiping the countertop clean with a wet rag. Our eyes met again.

"Something to eat?"

"No, just coffee. Black."

She smiled and took in my suit and my shirt. "Yeah, I can see that."

She brought me the coffee. She had a little yellow pencil tucked under her ear. She wore it like an ornament, writing out my check with another pencil. On her white smock, she had a name tag: BECKY.

"Here you are." She gave me the check.

"Thanks, Becky," I said.

She bounced away.

I took a sip of coffee and opened my first diary.

January 1.

I clicked my ballpoint pen.

I took another sip of coffee. In the mirror in front of me, I saw the store reflected, and the customers and the stockboys and the salesgirls and me among them sipping coffee. From the corner of my eye, I could see Becky wiping the countertop, humming some song. I put the cup down and picked up the pen. I knew I was going to write something, but until the tip of the pen touched the surface of the paper, I had no idea what. It was only then, when the contact was made, that the thought was born.

January 1. Dear Diary: Today I met my new master. He seems like a nice man, but he sure's got a set of teeth on him. I'm back in the harness.

And with that entry, I began the diary of Poochini, the guide dog who ran away.

Chapter 39

The door opened. My mother stood in the doorway to my room. Through the darkness, I could feel her stare directed at me. I could hear her breathing. She stood there for several minutes while I lay in bed, pretending to be asleep. Then she left. I heard noises in the kitchen. She opened and shut the fridge. She moved a chair. She turned the tap on and off and then I heard the door to her room shut.

I waited for another half an hour to make sure she was asleep and then I got up. I turned on the light, pulled out the diaries from under my bed, pulled up a chair and began writing.

For two nights I had been making entries in Poochini's diary, and in those two nights I had covered a period of a little over seven months. I skipped a lot of days entirely, or merely recorded that it was raining on a certain day and then put "More rain" in the next day's entry.

April 5: It's still raining. It's nice to have a home, a master, a worthwhile occupation and a roof over my head. But, I keep thinking, it's also nice to be loping along in the rain, pausing under trees and shaking myself off and then moving on.

April 10: It's really a wonderful thing I'm doing. I'm performing a valuable service. It's not just a job, it's a calling. I am his eyes to the world. Not a mutt, not a stray, not a useless household pet, but a trained professional.

April 21: I saw this cat today. Just your run-of-the-mill tabby. But I wondered why there aren't any Seeing Eye cats. Is it that they're not smart enough to be trained, or is it maybe that they'd just as soon not get involved? Too smart, maybe.

April 22: I had a good laugh today, thinking about Seeing Eye cats. That really would be a sight for sore eyes. Ha, ha, ha.

April 23: Officially spring came several weeks ago, but today is the first day when it felt like spring. We went outside for a walk in the park and you could see a change everywhere. It depressed me that my master could not see it. He could feel it. He could smell it. He even talked about how nice it felt. "Spring is here, Poochini," he told me, and I looked up at him. He sat down on a park bench and I lay down on the ground. The earth and the grass smelled real nice. I suddenly started getting depressed. Seasons were changing. You could feel the change, see the change, and yet I knew my life would remain the same. In the harness. "Spring is here, Poochini," my master said again.

April 24: I wish he wouldn't call me Poochini. If he could see, he'd see that I just don't look like Poochini at all. But he can't see. I have to be understanding. I have to see it from his point of view. All right, all right, Poochini it is. It's just a little odd for a German shepherd to be stuck with an Italian name.

May 1: Another beginning of another month. May. Mayday! Mayday!

May 10: Mayday! Mayday!

May 13: He talks a lot. He probably talks a lot because he can't see, but it's beginning to get on my nerves. He tells me everything. As he's getting ready to eat, he tells me that he's getting ready to eat. Just before he washes the dishes, he tells me that he is going to wash the dishes. It's as if he thinks I'm blind, too. So I shut my eyes and listen to him.

May 21: God, am I getting depressed. The only thing that cheers me up is thinking of that tabby as a Seeing Eye cat, but how long can that last?

June 1: Another beginning of another month. Mayday! Mayday!

June 3: Silly things are beginning to annoy me. Why does he have pictures of this girl and himself around the house, when he can't see? Why does he try to sing arias from *La Bohème* in the shower, when he can't sing? Why must he tell me everything? And he lies. The other day he was talking to somebody on the telephone and he said: "You know what Poochini did? I was sitting in my chair feeling kind of blue and he came over, put his head on my lap and started whining. You know. Like he knew how I felt and felt badly for me."

That whole thing was a lie. I never put my head on his lap and whined.

June 13: Friday the thirteenth. The whole day I waited for something terrible to happen, hoping for something terrible to happen. Nothing did.

June 15: He lied again. He told this guy on the phone how I started howling when he was in a shower singing "Casta Diva." I certainly wanted to howl, but I didn't. I'm a professional.

June 27: When we go outside, when we go to the store, when we go to the park, when we go for a walk, we always go the same way, day after day, week after week, month after month, always the same way. I know the way so well that I sometimes shut my eyes just to make the routine interesting, just to make it a challenge. I shut my eyes more and more.

June 28: When I sit inside our apartment and look out of the window, everything looks beautiful to me. The passing cars look nice, the tree trunks look inviting, a tin can left on the sidewalk makes me wonder how it smells. But when we go outside and I lead the way, the whole wonderful world becomes a series of obstacles to avoid, to go around. There's no stopping or pausing except for the red light. I am praised for leading the way. Day after day our eventless journeys continue.

June 29: Day after day. I am beginning to see the world totally from his point of view. Everything is an obstacle. People, cars, trees, other dogs. Must not stop. Must not bump into things. Must not chase a loose leaf blown by the wind.

June 30: I shut my eyes more and more and imagine myself free, pulling nobody along, attached to no one, just free. I forget myself and want to run. "Slow down," he says. "What's with you today, Poochini?"

July 1: Mayday! Mayday!

July 2: I am so good at my job I could do it blindfolded, but instead I just shut my eyes and lead the way. I am becoming like my master. I might as well be blind. I feel angry. At times I want to bite him on the hand.

July 3: I'm thinking the unthinkable. I have been trained to stay with my master for life. Devotion has been bred into me. Loyalty has been drilled into me. But I'm thinking the unthinkable. I will run away.

July 4: It's probably no accident that I picked this day. We were sitting in the park, the same park, the same bench, and he let go of my handle. I knew that the moment had come and if I didn't go, the moment would. So I left. Forgive me, Master, but I just had to go before I too went blind. I've seen the world through your eyes long enough and it's time I saw it through mine. You will find another guide dog, I'm sure, but this one is off to see the world for himself.

I left not entirely free. My harness was still strapped around my shoulders. My past, so to speak, would stay with me until it rotted and fell off or I learned to live with it. It didn't really bother me. Nobody was holding on to it. It was all mine. I sniffed the wind, and with fireworks shooting off behind me, I shook myself and took off. *Arrivederci!*

Chapter 40

The door opened. My mother stood in the doorway of my room.

"Daniel?"

"Yes."

"It is almost four o'clock."

"Really?"

"Yes, really. How long will you stay in bed?"

"I didn't sleep much last night."

"You will not sleep much this night also, if you sleep in bed all day."

I said nothing.

"Are you sick?"

"No, just . . . no, I'm not sick."

"If you are sick, you can stay in bed."

"I'm not sick, Mom."

"I will take your fever."

"I don't have a fever."

"When people are sick they don't know if they have fever."

"I'm not sick, Mom."

"Let me see your tongue."

"Oh, c'mon, Mom."

"I want to see."

I stuck it out.

"You have big tongue, Daniel." She smiled. She felt my forehead. "You don't have fever."

"I know."

"You are fine."

"I told you I was."

"Then you must get up."

"I'm getting up, Mom."

She stood there, waiting.

"I don't have any clothes on, Mom. If you leave, I'll . . ."

"I will make coffee."

She left. Just to make sure I didn't go to sleep again, she started banging away in the kitchen. Pots rattled. Dishes clattered. I got up.

We sipped our Turkish coffee. She checked the time and sighed.

"It is almost over."

"What's that?"

"Summer."

"Yes," I said.

"People in street . . . people at work. They are talking not so loud. Even the train . . . it does not make so much noise now. It will be here soon."

"What's that?"

"Autumn." She sighed again, thinking, remembering God knows what.

"You are nervous?" she asked.

"Me? No."

"Then why do you do that?"

"Do what?"

"With your pen. Click. Click. Click."

I was clicking my ballpoint pen in and out, in and out.

"I don't know," I said and stopped. "I didn't know I was doing it. A habit."

"You are not sick and you are not nervous?"

"That's right, Mom. Neither."

"You don't look neither."

When I finished drinking my coffee, she made me turn it over on a paper napkin so that she could tell my fortune. She picked it up and peered into it with her Oriental eyes. She lit a cigarette.

"You are clicking again," she said without looking up.

I was. I stopped.

"Where are you going?" she asked.

"When?"

"When you go."

"I don't understand, Mom."

"You are clicking."

I stopped again.

"There is in your cup . . . look." She motioned me toward her. I got up and looked over her shoulder.

"You see this?" She pointed inside the cup.

I saw a lot of things.

"Yes."

"You know what this is?"

"No."

"That is road. This, you see this?"

"Yes."

"That is center of cup. That is home. And the road . . . you see . . . it goes from home. You see?"

"Yes."

"So where are you going?"

"I'm not going anywhere, Mom."

"Okay."

She put out her cigarette and took the cups and the saucers to the sink. She washed them, wiped her hands on her skirt and looked at her watch.

"Time for work. Don't click too much while I'm gone."

"I won't."

She suddenly kissed me on the cheek and left. I went back to bed. Although she had made me aware of clicking my pen, I lay in bed and clicked away. I liked the sound the pen made, as if it were a camera. I lay in bed, clicking from image to image, person to person. I saw Rachel. I saw Misiora. I saw Freud. I saw my dead father. I heard their voices and their voices drowned out mine and it felt peaceful not to hear my voice, its complaints, its demands.

I reached under the bed and pulled out all my diaries. I spread them out on the bed and clicked, flipping the empty pages every now and then, glancing at the window, where the curtains moved gently in the wind, listening to voices, seeing faces, wiggling my toes.

YOU ARE NOW OVERDUE.

I lay in bed until it got dark and then I got up and began my next diary.

The date was arbitrary, because I couldn't remember the exact date.

March 12: I met a strange boy today. His name is Daniel Boone Price. Daniel Boone, of all things. At least it wasn't Pat Boone. He reminds me of somebody whose jeans just won't fade, no matter what he does with them, and he seems ready to jump off a cliff just to fall in love. He helped me fix my garden hose. Then something really strange happened. After he told me his name, I was going to tell him mine, but he said no, let me guess. And guess what? He guessed it. He did. He really did. Rachel, he said. Just like that. Maybe it's destiny!

With that, I started Rachel's diary and began looking at myself through her eyes.

Chapter 41

The door opened. My mother stood in the doorway to my room. Through the darkness I could feel her stare directed at me. I could hear her breathing. She stood there for several minutes while I lay in bed, pretending to be asleep. Then she left. I heard noises in the kitchen. She opened and shut the fridge. She moved a chair. She turned the tap on and off and then I heard the door to her room shut.

I waited until I was sure she was asleep and then I got up. I turned on the light, pulled out Rachel's diary from under the bed, pulled up a chair and began clicking my pen.

April 1: He thinks David is my father. I always think that the obvious is so obvious that it will be obvious to everyone. Apparently not. I hate lying, but I'm doing it. I hate leading anyone on, but I might be doing that, too. I don't know yet. Maybe it is destiny.

April 15: Tonight, in the park, he told me that he loved me. God, the way he said it. Like somebody dancing for the first time in his life. And the way he says my name: Rachel. I teased him about it. I couldn't help it. I really couldn't. He watches my every move, every gesture, and when I look at him, he's trying to read my mind. It's both flattering and annoying.

April 16: David has started drinking again. He's asking me about Daniel. Sometimes, using honesty as an excuse, I hurt people. So I told David about him. Yes, I told him, he does love me. No, I said,

I don't know if I love him. I might. I added that "I might" just out of spite, just because he started drinking again.

April 19: When Daniel looks at me, he's like a blind man who has suddenly recovered his vision and just can't get enough of seeing. And because he was blind, he looks at me and sees the whole world in me. Nothing I do escapes him. Everything I do means something —in his eyes, at least. It all means something to him and he stares and stares, trying to grasp the meaning of it all. I love it.

April 20: No, I don't. I don't love it at all. It's irritating. I can't throw anything away around him. Not a look, not a smile, not a word can be said and tossed away. He collects it all. And then he goes home, I'm sure of it, and out of the stuff I threw away, he reconstructs me and comes to conclusions about me. He comes to see me expecting me to be a certain way, and out of anger, or spite, I don't really know, I do everything I can to frustrate his expectations. I will not be defined.

April 24: I feel like an emotional Indian giver. Everything I give to Daniel one day, I want to take back the next, just so he doesn't make something out of it. And yet I have never felt loved in my life the way I feel loved by him. I try to tell myself that this is a rare thing, that I'm an unusually lucky girl to be loved like this. I do. I tell myself this.

May 1: May Day!

May 3: It's been a long time since I've been around somebody my age. A kiss. What a kiss does to him! What it means to him! It reminds me of what it felt like for me, too. The thrill of it all! There is something I love about him. I think if he loved me less, there'd be more room for me to love him back. But if he loved me less, would I want to see him? It's his excess that attracts me, it's his excess that irritates me. And yet, there is that thing: the thrill of it all.

May 13: I go from one to the other. From an old man to a young boy. David is desperate because he thinks, he knows, he will lose me. Daniel is desperate because he thinks he will never have me. Just when I think I know how I feel, I find out that I don't. It does make for an interesting life, even in a place like East Chicago.

May 24: David told me I should leave him. He thinks it will be better for me and he says it will certainly be better for him, not to be waiting around for the inevitable to happen. I cried. He cried. Just when Daniel's youth and my own youth seemed so exciting, David's tragedy intruded on it and made them seem frivolous and insubstantial by comparison. I know I will leave him someday, but how can I leave him? It's like leaving somebody to die. My youth keeps him going. Making love to me makes him young. What will happen to him if I leave? Will I think about him all the time, all the time? I couldn't bear that.

June 1: I have started doing something terrible. I find it truly terrible and yet I do it. Daniel and I will kiss ("the thrill of it all") and just when I feel my body opening up to him, I pull away and rush home and give myself to David. I have done this three times now, and each time David has been fooled into thinking that he had aroused me and each time it had been Daniel. And each time it was wonderful, and each time when David slid off my body and put his head on his pillow he seemed sure of himself like he used to when we began. Only I knew that Daniel's kisses started the fire in whose glow David was basking. Never in my life would I have thought that such a thing as this was possible. It makes me wonder: What else is possible?

Chapter 42

March 23: I cried all day today and was in tears when he came home. He got very angry. I cried some more. It's no way to live, he tells me. Crying's no way to live.

So began the diary of Lavonne Dewey, only I changed her name to Lavonne Endive. Mrs. Endive.

April 2: Yesterday was April Fools' Day. I missed it. I forgot all about it till today. The boys came and sat on my porch and we talked about school. I have a feeling this will be my last group of boys. The thought of it makes me want to cry. I should be brave. But the thought of myself being brave makes me want to cry, too.

April 21: The blossoms are blooming in the trees in my backyard. Every year those trees complete their cycles. How wonderful that must feel: to fulfill your destiny once a year and then do it again. No wonder they look so peaceful and content. They leave nothing unfinished.

May 2: Yesterday was May Day. I missed it. Forgot all about it. Next year I'll remember.

June 4: Larry tells me he loves me. He tells me all the time. He told me again today, and when he left something happened. Nothing unusual. I started crying. But then something else happened. I suddenly sensed that I knew why I cried so much. It's because I've decided. Yes, I'll stay with Bimbo for life. I will complete something in my life. The thought of myself doing that filled me with both sorrow and pride. I will complete something before I die.

June 10: My heart broke watching Bimbo fighting by the firehouse.

I put Mrs. Endive's diary away and picked up Rachel's.

June 10: My heart broke watching them fight by the firehouse. The savage youth of the boys, Daniel's youth, appealed to me, but the sight of those older men lying conquered on the cinders, and the boys standing victorious over them, filled me with pain. It was their eyes. I saw the realization in those men's eyes that they were not young anymore. It was if they had forgotten till that moment. I thought of David as I watched them trying to get back to their feet. I grieved for all of them. I should learn from them. I must. So I can prepare myself for when my turn comes to stumble and fall and leave my youth behind. I cannot face life if all it has to offer is youth.

Was this what she was thinking, I wondered, as she watched us fight? As she looked at me later under the light of the blue moon? Was this it? I remembered everything. I saw everything. I saw Freud's face and I had to know what he thought, how he felt. And so I began Freud's diary.

April 1: Today was April Fools' Day. I kept waiting for Larry or Daniel to do something, you know, try some joke on me so I could say: No, you don't. I know what today is! But they didn't.

April 10: Misiora was knocking East Chicago again. Saying things like what a terrible place it is. Yeah, I nodded my head, it sure is. He and Daniel started talking about how it would be nice to leave and go somewhere else. Yeah, I nodded my head, it sure would be. Sure would.

April 15: My garage is really coming along. The more Larry and Daniel talk about leaving, the more I agree with them and the more I fix up the garage. I'm walking around all the time now feeling guilty and ashamed.

April 27: You see, here's the thing. I know there are better places than East Chicago. I'm not that dumb. I know there are.

May 10: Yeah, I nodded. Misiora was knocking East Chicago again. He called it a rathole and "the armpit of the Midwest." Yeah, I nodded, what an armpit.

June 1: Sure there are better places than East Chicago. I've never been to Dayton, Ohio, but I'm sure it's nicer than here. I know that. There are nicer girls than Patty Campbell. I know that, too. But here's the thing. I like it here. I don't know why, but I do. I feel all guilty and ashamed about liking it so I don't tell Misiora or Daniel.

June 10: We had a fight with Bimbo and his guys. It was the three of us against four of them. Boy, was it terrible. And you know what? Here's what. The most terrible part was this: I felt like I was on the wrong side. There, I said it, finally. No, I didn't. I wrote it because there's nobody I can say it to.

June 12: All day I've been going around wondering how such a thing is possible. Misiora and Daniel are my buddies. I love them a lot. And yet I wish they would leave. I like it here and they don't and as long as they're around I have to pretend that I don't, too. I like the factories. I like the smelly air. I like the way people walk in East Chicago. You know, like they got nowhere to go but they still do it. I like saying "Hi" to them. There are, I know, places much more wonderful than this but I won't see them. Misiora and Daniel make me feel ashamed for feeling this way. I have to hold my stomach in as long as they're around. I would like to let it out. It's beerbelly for me, I know, like Bimbo and his guys. Maybe in a few years' time I'll be able to say all this to Patty. Maybe that's why I'm getting to like her.

June 14: Misiora, Daniel: I love you guys. But go away so I can miss you. Let me be.

I heard his voice while I wrote. When I tried to sleep I heard voices of other people I knew, people I wanted to know better. I spent the rest of my father's wheelchair money at the dime store and bought more diaries. One for Coach French, one for Bimbo; my father's voice demanded a diary of his own; Mr. Geddes, Presley Bivens, my mother, Misiora; I heard all their voices. I wanted to arrive at some kind of an understanding of all these people I knew but really did not know. I felt as if I had overlooked them. Short-changed them all in some fashion. And I wanted to make up for it. My mind was like a radio receiving voices I had failed to hear up to now. I didn't have to leave the house. They came through the air to my room. I slept during the day. At night I got up and wrote.

The door opened. My mother stood in the doorway to my room.

"Daniel?"

"Yes."

"Do you know what time it is?"

"No."

"It is almost two o'clock."

"I thought it was later."

"It will soon be later if you don't get up from bed."

"I'm tired."

"You do nothing and you are tired. That is why you are tired. From nothing."

"I couldn't sleep."

"You are smart boy, Daniel. You have high-school diploma but it is miserable shame how wrong you are. I come home from work and I hear you snore. I stand in doorway and I look at you and you sleep and snore. And now you say you didn't sleep. Daniel, you don't know what you are doing, or you don't know what you are saying. Neither is very good sign. You must get up." She came over and began shaking me.

"C'mon, Mom. Don't do that."

"Do what? I don't know what I am doing."

"You are shaking me. I don't like it."

"I am not shaking you." She shook me. "You didn't sleep last night. Now I am not shaking you."

"All right, all right. I slept last night."

"Oh, I am glad to hear, Daniel. And did you sleep well?"

"Yes. Yes."

"Good. That means you are all rested. Get up."

She pulled the blanket off me. I clung to the sheet.

"Mom, I don't have any clothes on."

"It is not my fault. You are not supposed to be naked when it is two o'clock in afternoon . . ."

She ripped the sheet out of my hands and threw it in the corner like dirty laundry.

"Now get up and put on clothes and go wash your face with cold water."

I did as I was told. I heard her voice in the bathroom as I washed my face.

"Almost three o'clock and you are just washing your face. Do you think you are British prince or something?"

I drank three cups of Turkish coffee. I didn't have my fortune read, but I did have my future forecast. I would get nowhere fast if I continued like this, she told me. I had to get a job. I had to get out of the house and look for one, at least. And no matter what I did, or did not do, I couldn't sleep like I'd been sleeping. It was like having an invalid at home. If I was sick, I should see a doctor. If I was not sick, I should see somebody about a job. She was going to wash the dishes before she left, but she changed her mind and told me to do them.

She left. I did the dishes and then went back to bed fully dressed. She wouldn't be back for over nine hours. I could think and do whatever I pleased.

I lay there clicking my pen in and out, wondering which diary I would pick up next, waiting for somebody's voice to make a visit. I shut my eyes and saw my father as a young man. Walking to work. His mind on his job, his heart free of love and hope. And then suddenly he sees her. A tall, beautiful woman with dark hair. My mother.

Somebody knocked on the front door. I didn't budge. I didn't feel like seeing anyone. Let them knock.

The knocking made my father and mother vanish from my head. It's probably Mr. Kula, my landlord, I thought. I started thinking about him. When he was a small boy, was that his dream, to become a landlord? Even he must have had other dreams.

Knock. Knock. Knock.

It got louder. A visitor to see you, the prison guard said to James Donovan. He seemed surprised. Jimmy Donovan never had visitors.

I rolled out of bed.

Knock! Knock! Knock!

"Just a minute," I said as I walked through the kitchen. I opened the door.

"Hello, stranger."

It was Rachel. She was dressed all in black just as I was. The sight of her momentarily paralyzed my mind and my body. I could think of nothing to do or say or think. I had made no provisions for seeing her again. In her absence I had arrived at certain conclusions. I had made peace by proxy with her. I didn't want a real person there on my doorstep. I wanted to go back to my bed, my diaries, my voices.

She stood there and, as always, seemed totally uninterested in my wishes and wants.

"Mind if I come in?" she said, disgustingly confident that I would not deny her.

I moved aside. She walked past me—real life walked past me, and I found real life both unpleasant and disruptive. Her voice in the diaries I wrote for her had a spiritual quality, and the person I imagined as I wrote them possessed a wispy, fragile, dreamlike beauty. There was none of that in the real Rachel. She stomped across the kitchen floor with her boots; she took over the kitchen instantly; she pulled up a chair and sat down, crossing her legs. It wasn't so much a visit as an invasion. She sat there breathing, looking, thinking, living, those damned turquoise earrings dangling. Although I had shut the door behind her, it felt open, and more real life was blowing inside. The fridge kicked on and began rumbling. I expected the windows to fly open by themselves and the telephone to start ringing.

"So, Daniel." She picked up one of my mother's cigarettes and lit it. A bit of burning phosphorus broke off from the matchhead and flew across the room. "How've you been?" she asked.

"Fine."

"You look pale."

"I'm fine." It seemed important that I convince her of that. "I've just been staying indoors a lot."

She smoked her cigarette and looked at me through the smoke, her bottomless green eyes squinting. I wanted to cling to the Rachel of my diaries, but her presence there left no room for that other Rachel.

"Am I interrupting something?" she asked.

"No, why?"

"Just the way you look." She smiled.

"I don't know how I look. I suppose I look a little surprised to see you."

"You don't look a little surprised. You look interrupted. What were you doing before I came? I knocked and knocked."

"It's none of your business what I was doing."

"Daniel." She shook her head. Maybe I hurt her. Maybe I just disappointed her. I couldn't tell. "Don't be like that." Then she laughed, freely and easily, as if we had been together for hours having a wonderful time. "Where"—she gestured toward me with her hand holding the cigarette—"where did you get that black shirt?"

"It's none of your business where I got it."

"Daniel"—she slumped a little—"let me tell you something. This may come as a shock to you, but you really don't look good in black. Me, I look good in black, but you don't. Do you know why I wore this outfit? Do you?"

"I don't know and I don't care." I still found it hard to believe that the scene I was in was actually taking place. It was as if I were asleep and she was forcing me to wake up against my will.

"I'll tell you why I wore it." She ignored my reply. "Because I remember you liking it, that's why. I remember the way you looked at me when I wore it the first time."

Despite myself, her words forced me to remember. I saw the outside of her house, I saw the lawn, saw her standing there dressed in black talking about Greece and ruins. The memories carried emotions I wanted to keep out of my heart, but I could not separate them. She sat there smoking her cigarette, and with little effort, with her words and eyes, she was destroying the barriers I had labored to construct.

"Oh," she sighed, "the way you looked at me then. You're not looking at me in the same way anymore."

"Things have changed," I defended myself.

I wanted to sit down, but I knew if I did I wouldn't be nearly as relaxed as she was. I hated her for seeming so at ease. It was my house. I should be the one who felt at home.

"Yes." She put out the cigarette. "I suppose you're right. Things have changed. You know, I used to think that whenever something very painful happened, you learned from it. A lesson." She smiled, spreading out her arms to encompass both of us. "And I thought that I would go through life learning lessons and becoming terribly wise by the time I was terribly old. Well"—she made a face—"I don't think so anymore. I don't think I'm going to learn a thing, Daniel.

People learn from their mistakes, and nothing, nothing that happens to me seems like a mistake. I love it all."

"I don't know why you're telling me all this," I said, leaning on a chair. I needed something to hold me in place.

"It's like this, Daniel, my old friend." She took another of my mother's cigarettes and lit it. "I get to be a certain way with you and only with you and when I leave I won't ever be able to be that way again. And . . . well . . ." She wiped her eyes. Maybe it was the smoke. "I'll miss it." She nodded slowly. "I will."

I contemplated sitting down. But should I sit facing her or away from her? Should I pull the chair way out and put my feet on the table?

She looked around the apartment, her eyes stopping on the couch in the living room. "That's where we made love," she said.

I was pulling the chair out when she said that. I winced and pushed it back hard against the table. "Why must you bring that up?"

"Because it happened," she said. "It wasn't that bad."

"I don't want to talk about all that."

"You don't have to, Daniel. I seem to be the one doing all the talking. It really wasn't all that bad. Kind of desperate and frantic, but I'm glad it happened."

"Well, good for you, Rachel."

She reacted as if I had wounded her. Although I didn't know the cause, I was glad to see the effect.

"The way you say my name now"—she really did seem hurt—"like it's just another name. It used to sing on your lips. I loved the way you used to say it. Ra-chel." She tried to bring back the sound of it for herself. She shook her head. "No, I can't do it. Nobody can. You're the only one, Daniel. Will you say it again in that way of yours . . . like I'm the one and only Rachel in the whole world?"

"Things"—I bared my teeth—"have changed."

"Things"—she bared hers, imitating me—"always change. Things are bound to change again. Things will always change. But what happened between us happened. It is in the past. And you can't go back and change the past." She threatened me with her finger. "You loved me. And I loved you. And I still do."

"Yeah, I bet you do, Rachel."

"Don't say my name like that." She hit the table with her fist. "If you're not going to say it right, don't say it at all." She threw up her arms. She seemed disgusted. "I knew you'd do this," she said.

"Do what?"

"This . . . this . . ." She waved her hand, as if trying to clear the air around her. "This thing. This cowardly thing, this changing of facts, this scribbling in the margins of our past—and just because *things* didn't work out the way you thought they would, trying to turn me into somebody I'm not and never was. I find that contemptible and cowardly, Daniel Boone. I knew you'd do it. Anybody who would be stupid enough and petty enough to sneak to my house and turn on the water out of sheer spite would do this as well. And that's why I came here. If you want to know why, here's why." Smoke was blowing out of her mouth. Her eyes were flashing. She seemed on fire. "We might never see each other again and you're going to have memories of me and I'll be damned, I'll be goddamned if I'll let you have them the way you want them. If you're going to remember me, then you're going to do it right."

"I'll do it the way I want to do it." I tried to match her anger and energy. "My goddamn memories are my own business."

She almost threw the ashtray at me. "Not if they're of me, they're not. That makes them my business as well."

"I have never heard of anything so crazy in all my life." I tried laughing.

"Then you just haven't lived all that much. It's a wonder you've heard of anything, stuck here in East Chicago."

"I like it here, you mind? There may be places more wonderful . . ." I began quoting from Freud's diary, but she cut me off.

"Who do you think you're talking to?" She moved her chair closer to me. "Don't you understand that I know you? I've stayed awake nights thinking about you, thinking so hard that there were times when I felt like I was trapped inside your brain. I know you! So don't tell me you like it here. Don't tell me I didn't love you. Don't tell me I don't love you now. And don't you dare tell me that I don't have a right to come here and demand that you do things right. I have spent hours and hours of my one and only life thinking about you and that gives me a right."

She stopped, eagerly waiting for me to say something so she could attack again.

"And what about my rights?" I wished I had a cigarette so I could blow smoke in her face. "Don't I get to have any? Don't I?"

"You can do whatever you want except lie about what happened.

I never make promises, but just this once I'll make an exception. I'll promise you this. I'll remember you exactly the way you were. I'll love you as long as it lasts. If it lasts forever, then I'll love you forever. If I have to regret that I left you, then I will regret it. And if it's forever, then I'll regret it forever. But I will not distort your memory and turn you into somebody convenient to hate or dismiss just to make it easy on myself. And that's what you're doing and you better stop!"

Suddenly she smiled.

"I have to admit," she said, placing her hand on her breast, "I rehearsed that speech on the way here. I knew you'd give me an opportunity to use it." She leaned back in her chair. There, she seemed to be saying, you see how open I am. I tell you everything. In her posture, her face, in her eyes was a friendly invitation, a peace offering. But a peace on her own terms.

The sudden switch from anger to this warm, smiling friendliness confounded me and I found myself once again trying to figure out who she was, what the source of her contradictions was. Once again I felt the desire to define her, to make her fit into a point of view. All I had were a few snapshots, a few images of the time we spent together. I wanted to get to the bottom of her.

"C'mon, Daniel," she said softly, "why have a misunderstanding when we can have a tragedy?"

She moved her head, she moved her shoulders, urging me to accept.

"We found a buyer for the house. David and I'll be leaving in a couple of days, so . . ." She moved her head again, urging me toward peace and tragedy. "How about it?"

She stood up.

I thought I had reconciled myself days ago to never seeing her again, and now that she was here I found it inconceivable that she would be leaving my life forever.

"Walk me home, will you?" For once she didn't sound totally confident that I would.

She went out. I followed her. The day was ending. Darkness seemed to be rising out of the ground. To our left the sun was slowly approaching the horizon. It would sink out of sight in half an hour. Already curtains were being shut, and through the dusk I could see the light of TV sets in the windows of the houses we passed. Rachel took me by the arm, wrapping both her hands around my elbow.

"To look at us now—" she said, "if you were some old man looking out of the window and you saw the two of us like this, you'd think, wouldn't you, what a happy couple they are." She tugged at my arm, pulling me off balance, planting a kiss on my cheek. "Wouldn't you, Daniel?"

I thought of the old man looking at us. I thought of myself several days from now walking on Aberdeen Lane knowing she was not there. Winter would come. I saw myself going to Cedar Lake. The word "never" appeared in my brain and began expanding, inflating like a balloon, displacing everything else. Was it really too late? Maybe destiny was giving me one last chance, if not to reverse the situation then at least to understand it.

"Why can't you love me?" That was really the one thing I wanted to know.

"But I do," she said.

"Not like David."

"No." She seemed sorry she had to say that. "Not like him."

"Why not?" I stopped. Maybe she would say something and it would make sense to me.

"I don't know," she answered in a way that made it seem she had asked herself that question many times. "I just don't and there's nothing I can do about it."

"Rachel," I said, and before I could say anything else she started crying.

"There . . ." She pulled on my shirt. "That's how you used to say my name. And I'll never hear it again like that." She kept pulling on my shirt, crying. "I'll miss it. The one and only Rachel in the whole world."

I could no longer doubt what I saw in her eyes. She loved me. I panicked. It suddenly seemed better to risk rejection than lose somebody who loved me, whom I loved. I needed words. Magic words. Panic and terror seized me at the thought of regretting for the rest of my life not doing something or saying something, some words I had never spoken before, that would keep her with me. I could think of nothing new. What I wanted to tell her I had told her before and so I told her again: "I love you."

"I know, I know." She nodded, crying. "And you know I love you. God, we both know so much." She wiped her eyes and stomped on the sidewalk with her boots, as if determined to stop crying. Then she tossed back her head and smiled. "I bet you didn't know I was Jewish, did you?" She used the question to change the mood. She pulled me by the shoulder. We started walking again.

"You never asked me if I was Jewish, so I thought I'd let you know. You want to know so much about me. Let me see, what else can I tell you? I used to take dance lessons. I used to be fat when I was young." She seemed desperate to keep talking. "I have two brothers and two sisters and I miss all four of them. I almost had a baby. I almost got killed in a car accident. I want to go to Greece. I don't want to leave you but I will. David wants me to leave him and go back to my parents but I can't. God, it's all so stupid." She started crying again. "But what can I do? I can't stop until it's over between him and me. I know it will end. But I can't stop until it does. I want to love you and you alone. You want me to love you. David, yes, David wants me to love you . . ."

Love. Love. Love. I kept hearing the word, but I could no longer understand it. There seemed to be no bottom to anything, not even single words.

"Daniel." She stopped and flung her arms around my neck. "Did you do everything you could to persuade me? Did you? Is there something else we can try?"

"Rachel, I . . ."

"Rachel." She repeated her name. "Rachel, Rachel . . ."

The sound of her voice saying her own name seemed like one of the loveliest, saddest things I had ever heard. She was whispering it into my ear so that I would remember her the way she wanted to be remembered.

We stood there on the corner of Northcote and Aberdeen Lane, determined, it appeared, to cling to each other and avoid the inevitable. Suddenly everything changed. It happened so fast I could not tell which I noticed first, the tremor that rattled the windows in the area, the hot wind that swept past us or the brilliant glow of light like a gigantic flashbulb exploding behind us. Almost immediately dogs started barking.

We let go of each other. In the distance, over the flat roof of Kroger's Supermarket, due east in the direction of the Sunrise Oil Company and Misiora's home, I saw in place of that one flickering flaglike flame the jagged outline of an enormous blaze. It was as if a small mountain had suddenly been dropped down on the eastern horizon and set on fire.

Rachel looked at me. "What happened?"

"I don't know," I said, imagining all kinds of things. In my state of emotional disorientation I pinned my last hope on the Russians. The Russians had finally made war. Surely Rachel could not leave me at the onset of World War III.

People appeared in doorways. Some stayed there looking. Others came out and kept going, hurrying toward the fire. Cars started up. Dogs just kept barking. Rachel and I joined the people rushing toward the fire.

The traffic lights on Indianapolis Boulevard were not working. Drivers heading in one direction were trying to make U-turns and go where everybody else seemed to be going. "What happened?" people rushing out of their houses asked. "What happened?" people in cars shouted at us. I heard sirens wailing as we crossed the boulevard. They seemed to be coming from different directions.

I held Rachel's hand through it all. Although my mind was on the fire, even though I noticed everything around me, a part of my attention was still on her. I wanted to hold on to her. Our group swelled. There were over a hundred people jamming the sidewalk, spilling out into the street. Everyone walked as fast as possible without actually running.

"Look!" Rachel said and pulled her hand loose to point. The sun was setting and the western horizon seemed to be on fire too. She smiled. It was probably her cheekbones that reminded me of my mother and through her of some beautiful savage enjoying the spectacle. Her eyes sparkled as she kept looking from the sunset to the fire. She was totally in the moment. No thoughts of me or David. It was the wrong time to try to remind her that no more than fifteen minutes ago she had been crying, and for once I didn't even feel like doing it. It seemed preposterous to expect consistency from her; criminal, almost, to insist on it. When she began drifting away from me, pushed along by a small, eager group of people, I didn't try to stop her.

The closer we came to the refinery, the quieter everybody became. Even before we turned the corner I could hear the deafening roar of the blaze. It sounded like a waterfall. Like tons and tons of water crashing on rocks and exploding into flames.

We turned the corner and spread out in the street, taking our places behind those already there. At the end of the block where Railroad Avenue and 142nd Street intersected, the fire burned. Two huge oil tanks had exploded and in their place were flames two or three times taller than the tanks had been. Firemen were spraying water on the surrounding tanks to keep their temperature down so they wouldn't explode. The fire trucks, the men battling the blaze, even the remaining oil tanks: all seemed inconsequential and toylike in comparison to the enormity of the flames.

A police barricade was set up at the intersection and policemen, shouting through megaphones, were urging the crowd to stay back. It was difficult to hear them. Difficult to pay any attention to them.

"*Back!*" They gestured. "*Stay back!*"

Nobody obeyed.

I pushed my way forward through the crowd looking for Rachel. My eyes burned from the heat and the smoke. In front of me, through the flames, I could see the Sunrise Oil Company cartoon character smiling its ten-foot smile through the two-hundred-foot-high flames.

I slowly made my way forward. The initial shock of seeing the fire was gradually wearing off. I was released from its hypnotic effect to notice the people through whom I was moving. Here and there I saw faces I recognized from my high school. I saw and recognized some old people from the neighborhood. I was stunned to discover how long it had taken me to notice that several houses across the street from the refinery were also on fire. One of them was Misiora's. His parents seemed oblivious to the enormous flames dancing behind them. All their attention was focused on the little fire in front of them. They stood together watching their house burn, taking turns at comforting each other. First he would pat her on the shoulder. Then she patted him.

More fire trucks arrived, sirens wailing, red lights flashing. I saw Bimbo jump off the back of one. He had the end of the fire hose tucked under his arm and he ran with it toward a hydrant. He ordered people out of his way. They moved aside. He connected the hose rapidly and turned on the water with a huge wrench. He did it quickly and efficiently. It was like seeing an entirely different person from the one I had fought with; the lumbering, bulky, overweight wreck kneeling defeated on the cinders did not seem like the same man at all. As he ran toward the fire with his men I saw Lavonne separate herself from the crowd to wave to him. "Be careful, hon," she seemed to be shouting. He waved back, pleased by her concern but too rushed to stop. She stayed in one spot, going up and down on her toes, watching him, shielding her eyes with her hand.

Moments later, as I continued toward the barricade across Rail-

road Avenue, I saw Freud and Patty. Something about the way they
stood next to each other reminded me of Mr. and Mrs. Misiora.
Freud wore his father's hat—it stuck out above the crowd—and it
wasn't so much that he was fatter as that he looked older, his stomach relaxed, sticking out a little. He had his hands on his hips, Patty's
arm around his, their faces expressing what could only be described
as community-minded concern about the fire. He stood there rooted
in place, but to me he seemed to be sailing away toward that world
of grown-ups and adults he had feared so much not that long
ago.

Debris swirled above our heads: shredded newspapers, torn shopping bags, leaves blasted off the trees by the explosion, all seemed
to be sucked toward the refinery blaze. I could feel the wind. It
pulled the hair on my head toward it.

I couldn't see Rachel anywhere. There were too many people. I
had to stop when I reached the barricade. There was nowhere else
to go. A line of policemen blocked my way, the collars on their
jackets turned up to keep the heat off their necks. They looked
directly at the crowd. The crowd, myself included, looked past
them at the fire.

On the other side of the barricade, between the policemen and the
fire trucks, I saw a man running from spot to spot as if looking for
somebody. It was David. He had several cameras dangling from his
shoulders and he was taking pictures of anything that moved or
burned, running, stopping, shooting, looking around and then
shooting some more. He seemed possessed or inspired but he did not
seem like the David I thought I knew, just as Bimbo didn't seem like
himself. He seemed youthful. He knelt down and then jumped up
to run like a young man to another spot. His gray hair, by the light
of the blaze, seemed red, his face tanned, his aim sure. The last time
I had seen him was by the light of the fire in his fireplace. This was
another night. Another fire. Another man.

The firemen concentrated all of their efforts on keeping the fire
from spreading. They seemed to have abandoned all hope of putting
it out. They sprayed the surrounding tanks with water, and as soon
as the water hit the hot steel surface of the tanks it turned to steam.
David ran from one spot to another, loading his cameras, shooting,
throwing away the yellow film wrappers. If he seemed concerned
about anything it was to avoid getting wet, not burned. I tried
keeping up with him. Every time he stopped and took a picture I

tried imagining what he saw, but since my point of view was different from his, it was a useless exercise.

Then I saw Rachel. She, like David, had managed either to sneak her way past the policemen or talk her way past them. She was on the other side of the barricade and she didn't seem concerned about anything, not the water nor the fire. The wind from the flames pulled her long black hair, her silky black blouse rippled and her whole being seemed to vibrate ecstatically at the danger. The fire behind her roared. She moved to the rhythm of the flames. She seemed to change with each step, discarding facets of herself as if she had an endless supply, enough to throw away, more than enough to burn. I saw her from one side and then from another. I saw her look directly at the crowd on the other side of the barricade without seeing me. More—I remembered my father's words—there is more to tell. There would always be more to Rachel. The accountant in me would never arrive at her total picture by adding up the pictures I saw. The wrestler in me would never pin her to the floor and define her once and for all. No matter how many words I wrote in no matter how many diaries, the writer in me could never hope to explain away the pain she caused me nor find a way to scribble myself into her heart to the exclusion of all others. There just was no bottom to her, and my desire to crawl inside her soul and search there for clues the way I had through my father's things gave way to something else: relief, perhaps, that my efforts had been unsuccessful. Had it been left up to me there would have been less to her, and watching her move to the rhythm of the flames I was overcome with gratitude that I had failed.

I moved along the barricade, keeping her in sight. There was no longer any hope or scheme of holding her. What I wanted now was to hold on to the way I saw things, and since I saw them in such a new way I was afraid I could lose my perspective as suddenly as I had found it.

I ducked under the barricade when a policeman wasn't looking and ran to the other side. She was about thirty yards away from me when she saw me. She stopped. Her lips moved. Then she shook her fist at me and smiled, as if warning me not to forget some promise she expected me to keep.

Facing her, I began backing away.

No words came to my mind that I wanted to tell her, but with each step backward I felt something breaking inside of me, collapsing to make room for life as it was; room for her and all those others I had tried to fit into my small heart. It hurt.

A few seconds later I saw her and David. He was running. She was running after him. Both of them disappeared behind the fire trucks. Soon I was too far away from my neighborhood to recognize anybody. I turned away and headed home.

My face felt flushed, my eyes burned. My clothes smelled of oil and smoke and I had a feeling that a match lit near me could set me ablaze. I tingled with sensations.

I turned off Railroad Avenue and went down 142nd Street. The electric power had either been turned off or knocked out by the explosion and the streets were dark and deserted. Everybody was at the fire. Here and there in one of the dark houses I saw a candle burning. I was sure that for a long time to come, whenever I saw a candle burning I would wonder if it had been lit for the living or the dead.

When I turned onto Northcote a dog barked behind me. I looked back. Moving slowly down the dark street, its headlights turned off, was a car. It was too dark to tell who the driver was, what kind of a car it was, yet the shape seemed familiar. It stopped in the middle of the street, but when I resumed walking I could hear it following me.

No, I lied to myself, I have no idea whose car it is. I could hear its tires crunching rocks in the road, keeping its distance, but staying right behind me. I considered running.

When I got to the corner of Northcote and Aberdeen Lane I stopped. It was impossible just to walk past that corner. I had stopped there so often that it was automatic. I turned around.

The car slowed but continued rolling forward. It came to a stop about ten yards away from me. The headlights came on. The engine continued to run. Then the door opened and I saw Misiora coming toward me.

"Larry!" I called out. The smoke from the fire hurt my throat. I could feel his name as I said it.

"Hello, buddy." The headlights caught his grin. A two- or three-week-old reddish beard covered his face. "I thought it was you."

He stopped in the street in front of me. I was on the sidewalk. He put his foot up on the curb and offered me his hand. We shook. He seemed very nervous. Even as we shook hands, he kept looking around. "I bet you didn't expect to see me again, did you?" he said.

"I didn't know what to expect, Larry. It's been a strange time for both of us."

It wasn't just the beard that made him look so different. He was wearing clothes I had never seen him wear before. He seemed thinner, his hair longer, and his blue eyes had a wolfish glow to them.

"Yeah, I suppose so," he said. "Strange times, all right."

Although we were far from the fire, you could still see the reddish glow in the sky. He glanced at it nervously.

"Some night, huh?" He thumbed over his shoulder.

I wondered if he knew about his parents' house.

"Were you over there to see it?" I asked.

He couldn't quite believe I was asking him that question.

"Oh, c'mon, Daniel," he whispered, "you know I was over there. I was there at the beginning, you might say. That's right." He nodded his head slowly, determined to make me understand. "How do you think the fire got started?"

He grinned at my attempts to evade the obvious.

"I did it," he said. "I went and did it, Daniel."

He really seemed to enjoy watching me react.

It all felt unnatural: the headlights shining in my eyes, the fire burning in the distance, the way Misiora looked, even the way we were standing. I felt artificial perched above him on the curb, but I didn't want to go down to where he was. His foot was on the curb, his body crouched, his head thrust back so that his Adam's apple showed. He seemed both relaxed and compressed, ready to jump.

I kept looking into the distance, at the fire, while Misiora scrutinized me. Did he really do it? While I was standing there in the crowd, it had never occurred to me that anyone had set it. It had seemed like a natural disaster. I resisted connecting it with Larry.

"You don't believe me, do you?" he said.

"Why would you want—"

"Damn you, Daniel. You know why. We've known each other all these years, so don't tell me you don't know. Don't tell me that." He spat to the side.

"It's just that I didn't think you'd ever go through with it, Larry. That's all."

He softened a little.

"I didn't either. I kept trying to go away and stay away. The money I spent on gas"—he shook his head—"the gas I burned trying to get far, far away from East Chicago. This last time I went west. Got as far as Iowa and just couldn't keep going. I kept seeing that Sunrise character, that smiling cartoon. And I knew, you see, I just knew that when things got bad for me I'd go back. It would always be there, waiting for me to return. My place. My job. Walk home for lunch with my dad. All that stuff. You know, there were times when all that stuff seemed real nice and cozy and tempting. Sooner or later I knew it would get to me. And the thought of walking through those gates for the rest of my life, I tell you, it just made me crazy. So I did it. You might say I went and removed the temptation."

Had he boasted about what he had done, I might have found it possible not to believe him. But his voice was calm and declarative and left no doubts.

"They sure looked pathetic," he said as an afterthought.

"Who's that?"

"The people watching the fire. The townsfolk." He pronounced the word with distaste.

"No, they didn't." I defended myself as much as them. "I was there. I saw them."

"I saw them too. I hid behind one of the houses and watched the whole show. All those people, running to see what's going on, standing there like they were in church." He stopped and measured me with his eyes. "You too."

"What do you mean, Larry?"

"Oh"—he grinned—"nothing. You're wonderful citizens, all of you. You didn't see it 'cause you were one of them, Daniel. Everyone looked so goddam concerned and yet everyone there was having a wonderful time."

I wondered what he would say if I told him about the vision I saw while I stood there watching those people, watching Rachel moving past the flames. It had seemed like such a profound breakthrough for me, that vision of life and my place in it. Misiora, I sensed, would tear it to shreds if I let him. I wanted to hold on to it.

"You know what, buddy boy?" He grabbed me by the belt buckle and pulled. "It's too bad. All those years in school and you and I never wrestled each other in practice. Now I'd kind of like to know who was better. Wouldn't you?"

"I think both of us have more important things to worry about."

"I'm not worried about it. Just wondering. I'm not worried about anything anymore." He gave one last tug on my belt buckle and let me go. "We were good friends, you and I?"

"We sure were, Larry."

"But you know what?" He pointed a finger at me. "We could have been better friends."

"It's not too late," I lied.

"Yes it is. That's what I like about it. It's too late. Makes me feel just fine to know that."

He put his foot down on the street and spread out his arms.

"This is it, then. I've got seventy-five dollars left and I can't imagine where that'll take me. But I won't be back. Goodbye."

He walked toward the car.

"Bye, Larry."

"Listen." He stopped. "If you and I were blood brothers, if we were the closest friends that ever lived, do you know what we would say to each other right now?"

"No, I don't."

"I don't either." He shrugged. "So that settles it."

He got into his car and drove away. Once again and for the last time he fooled me. He didn't step on the accelerator the way I thought he would. He rode away slowly, stopping at the stop sign at the next intersection and then proceeding slowly again, as if determined to make a lasting impression.

I never saw him again.

Chapter 43

It took me several days before I could bring myself to walk down Aberdeen Lane, and when I did, the house was sold and she and David were gone. A different car was parked in front of their house. The hose I had bought and attached was still there, and the sprinkler was on. The new people, thinking I lived on the block and eager to make friends, smiled at me. They were from Pennsylvania and they had a small baby and a large dog. We talked a little. They told me about Scranton. I told them about East Chicago.

The fire destroyed nearly half of the Sunrise Oil Company. Newspapers wrote about it. There were stories on television, reporters in suits and ties and with microphones in their hands walking through the charred remains. Everyone talked about the fire for weeks, and soon it became official. It was the largest fire East Chicago had ever had. The cause of the "accident" was, and continued to be, "under investigation." Only I knew who had done it. I loved walking around town with my secret.

Two weeks after the blaze, East Chicago became national news. A picture of the fire made the cover of *Life* magazine. The caption read: SUNRISE BURNING AT SUNSET. Inside were six full pages of pictures of the refinery in flames, houses burning, firemen spraying, people whose faces I recognized looking on. They were all taken by David. His last name, I found out in the credits, was Zoakos. It sounded Greek to me. The issue was like a high-school yearbook at graduation. Everybody in East Chicago bought one, more than one in some cases, and people carried them around for days. I bought one too. On page 27 of the magazine was a picture only David could have taken. In front of a curtain of flames was a girl dressed in black. The flames were out of focus, a blurred reddish backdrop. The girl stood out in sharp detail. Her arms were in the air. She had tears in her eyes, but she didn't look sad. She seemed intoxicated by the flames. It was Rachel among the ruins.

I kept getting letters from the library, addressed to Mr. James Donovan, urging me, in increasingly strong language, to return the books I had checked out. I kept meaning to take them back and then I'd forget, and soon another letter would arrive. The last one, unlike the others, was a personal letter from the librarian.

Dear Jimmy,

I remember you well. If you haven't finished reading the books, I'll be happy to renew them for you. You looked like such a nice boy, so please bring the books back. I worry about them. See you soon.

Yours truly,
Miss Day

I meant to take the books back that very afternoon. And then I got to thinking about her. All those years I had known her, she had just been the old librarian. Now she was Miss Day. I wondered what her first name was. I wondered why she never got married. Maybe books were easier to understand and love than people.

One day I took a long walk. I went all the way to 95th Street in South Chicago, and on the way back I stopped on the corner of Indianapolis Boulevard and Perry. I looked at the house with the green door. I just stood there, looking at it the way my dad had done. I consciously assumed his posture. I waited for over two hours. The door finally opened and an elderly couple came out. The man felt in his pockets and went back inside. He returned with a pipe stuck between his teeth. The woman locked the door and put the keys in her purse. Then they got into their car and drove away. No sign of the man with the moustache. The two houses that had left their marks on both my father and myself were now inhabited by other people.

I tried to think of some lesson I could learn from that. Actually, ever since my father's death and Rachel's departure, I had been trying to sum up everything that had happened and extract a lesson from it. Not just a lesson, but a valuable lesson that would stay with me for the rest of my life. In the years to come, I wanted to be able to say "I learned a lot that summer." Some persistent accountant inside me was still trying to balance the books and cover my losses with "profit from experience." He would stay with me forever, that accountant, always in the background, always trying.

My mother, sensing that I was contemplating a move of my own, left me alone. We drank Turkish coffee together. We talked about visiting Montenegro at some future date so that she could show me the town where she was born. The most beautiful people in the world, she claimed, were born in that town. Men, women, children, everybody. So beautiful. She smiled, flashing her gold tooth at me. "Yes," she said. "I had to leave town and go to America because I was not so beautiful." She didn't mean a word of it. She talked about my dad, their early years together. I listened, but I was keenly aware that she was keeping a lot to herself, that she would never share everything with me. I still wanted to know, but I no longer asked. I imagined. The less I knew about something or somebody, the easier it was to imagine.

We went shopping for a tombstone for my father. She knew about a street in South Chicago where more than half a dozen monument-makers were bunched together in one block. We went from one to the other, my mother bargaining with them. The marble cost so much per foot. The inscription cost so much per letter. She haggled over feet and letters.

"My husband could not rest in peace," she told one of them, "if I let you cheat me like that."

She wanted a wonderful stone, with nice big letters, but she would not be overcharged.

"Lady," one of them said, "it's not right to quibble over a few dollars for something like this."

"Mister," she told him, "you are very right. You lower price and we don't quibble."

I found out something I had never known about my mother. One of the shops was run by an Italian family, and I was startled to hear that she could speak Italian. I was even more startled at the impact this obvious ploy had. She got the stone she wanted with the letters she wanted at the price she wanted to pay. We had a glass of wine. They spoke to me in Italian. I nodded.

"Montenegro," my mother told me on the way home, "it is very close to Adriatic Coast and that is very close to Italy. Such nice songs they sing. I learn Italian from songs. Very nice people, Italians. Catholic, but nice."

For several days I thought about the tombstones in the shops. Some were all finished; some were half-finished; some were just begun, works in progress. I remembered the names I read on them: WALTER CARNAHAN, LOUISE FARRAR, UMBERTO ADORNI.

I tried writing my diaries—Misiora's, Rachel's, Poochini's—extending their lives into the future, but I couldn't get anywhere. I was still stuck in the past and they were stuck there with me. There's a lesson to be learned from all this, I thought, but when I tried to write it down, nothing came. I reread the diaries I had written. I sniffed the old leaves in my leaf collection. I spent hours hanging out of my window at night, remembering.

Diane Sinclair got married. The most beautiful girl ever to come out of Roosevelt High was leaving. There was an announcement in the paper and so I went. Except for the fire, it was the largest turnout I had ever seen in East Chicago.

It was a crisp sunny day with a touch of autumn in the air. The churchbells rang. The churchyard was filled with people, kids from the school, waiting for the door to open and for Diane to come out. I saw former schoolmates everywhere. Freud and Patty were talking to Mrs. Dewey. Mrs. Dewey seemed to be waiting to cry. The cheerleaders were there, together as always. I made no effort to hide from Freud, but he didn't see me. Patty did, although she did her best not to show it. A large, noisy crowd separated us.

The guys in my part of the churchyard were behaving like bad actors in a school play. Their parts called for them to seem upset about the wedding, like they'd all had a chance and let the most beautiful girl in town slip through their fingers. They overacted like crazy, shaking their heads, snapping their fingers, damn, Diane was gone, out of commission. There was something touching about all of them. It didn't take much to see through their unconvincing display. They were thrilled that she was getting married. They wouldn't have to dream about her anymore. With her gone, the other girls in town would suddenly look better and everybody's life could proceed. Her beauty upset the curve. Soon everybody's grades would improve.

"Here she comes!"

The door opened and Diane emerged, as if on wheels, in her wedding gown. The churchbells rang. The crowd groaned and pressed closer together. Her husband was tall and blond, a basketball player. He seemed quite at ease to have Diane holding his arm. Maybe he had known other girls who were just as beautiful as she was. Maybe he didn't know that he was marrying the girl of so many guys' dreams.

The guys around me started whistling and cheering. Hooray, there goes our dream. Hooray, no more dreams. Yeah!

"How about a kiss, Diane!" one of them shouted. The others laughed and then picked up the cry. "A kiss! A kiss! I want to kiss the bride!"

They pushed each other, clowning around. Diane and her groom paused. She smiled. She seemed willing to oblige. Nobody made a move toward her. A lot of pushing and shoving and snickering, but nobody stepped forth. They seemed afraid to find out, now that it was too late, what it was like to kiss her. She waved and continued toward the waiting car, the Pontiac, covered with ribbons. It had a hand-painted sign on the side: JUST MARRIED. Others hurried to their cars and soon, amid horns blowing, streamers streaming and tin cans on strings trailing after them, the guy from Notre Dame drove off with Diane.

The crowd slowly dispersed. Freud saw me and wandered over alone. Patty and Mrs. Dewey joined some other people and walked off in a large group.

"There's going to be a barbecue," Freud told me. It sounded like an invitation. He told me the names of the people who were having it. I had never heard of them. He said they were "nice people." We walked a bit, but it was clear he didn't want to go anywhere. He was expected at the barbecue. So we shuffled around the church. He did most of the talking.

"Hey, you'll never guess the job I got. Really, you'll never guess." I didn't. So he told me.

"I'm going to work in the toll booth on the Skyway. It's good pay. Union job. Patty's father got it for me. All those cars going by. You know what I keep thinking? I'll be working there, you know, and sooner or later, I'll spot my dad's car. You know, the one my mother sold. And I'll get the guy to sell it back to me."

He told me he and Patty were going to get married. I would be invited if I wanted to come. Sure, I wanted to come. Both of us must have been thinking about Misiora, but neither of us said anything. And then, just before he left, he asked me.

"You don't think I could've been no all-state in football, do you? I mean, I know I don't think I could've. Do you?"

He wanted to hear a "no." I came as close as I could to giving him what he wanted.

"No, probably not."

It was the last time I saw Freud. I didn't plan it. It just turned out like that.

Summer ended. The swimming pool closed in Kosciusko Park. School began. I saw the young couple on Aberdeen Lane raking leaves. For some reason their big dog didn't seem so big the second time around. I took my leaf collection one evening and scattered it, leaf by leaf, on their block.

My mother and I went to Libertyville for the blessing of the tombstone. It was on a Sunday and we got a ride from a Serbian woman my mother knew who was going to visit her son's grave. A priest in a white beard and gold-embroidered Byzantine robes sprinkled the marble with holy water, read a service and left. We knelt on the ground. The inscription on the tombstone was just what she had promised: BELOVED HUSBAND. BELOVED FATHER. And then in smaller letters, the names of the survivors. It produced a mild jolt to see my name on a tombstone: Daniel B. Price.

My mother wept softly. I had no doubts, looking at her, that she had loved and still loved my father. But the simplicity of that word, the time when I believed that you either loved someone or you didn't, was gone forever. It didn't work that way. Everything was a matter of degrees; love, freedom, everything. I still wasn't used to it.

"Next spring," my mother said as we got up, "I will plant nice flowers on your father's grave." She thought a bit. "It is strange thing. You live with man so many years and never find out what kind flowers he likes."

We strolled through the cemetery. I looked at the tombstones. My mother visited with other women at gravesites. It was a fairly large place, larger than I remembered it, running flat and then turning hilly and steep. The bright afternoon sun made the hilltop tombstones gleam like windows.

A small group of women joined my mother. All of us strolled through the cemetery. She mentioned my name and they turned and looked at me. Sometime later, my mother stopped to look at a grave. It was overgrown with weeds. Most of them were turning brown but some were still alive, thick and tall like little trees.

"It is a big shame," she said to me. "Nobody looks after grave. Such a thing is not right."

And with that, she planted her foot on the ground and began pulling out the weeds. One of the women helped her. I watched with the rest, and then the others began looking around and found another grave in need of clearing. Soon I was pulling out weeds myself, tossing them over my shoulder the way my mother did. Something about the work became infectious, and when yet another woman called out that she had found yet another grave covered with weeds, we rushed over and began pulling. We cleared at least fifteen graves and we kept going. My mother began to sing. The women joined in. It was a song I had heard her sing around the house, a song from the old country. Not only could she speak like an Italian, she sang like one.

Two days later, it happened. I was at home alone. The phone rang. I picked it up.

"Hello there, Boondocks." It was Rachel.

My first assumption was that she was back, but naturally, this assumption, like all the others I had made about Rachel, was wrong. She wouldn't tell me where she was.

"Far away," she said. "Too far from Greece and too close to Los Angeles, that's where I am."

"How are you?" I asked. It was a simple question, but true to form, she didn't answer it.

"Listen," she said. "I did it. I opened the envelope finally, and read your poem. It's not bad at all. It's not as nice as the poem I imagined, but it's really not bad."

I told her about the people who had moved into her house. She asked me if I had seen David's pictures in *Life* magazine. We stayed away from certain questions. I tried once again to find out where she was, but she wouldn't tell me. Then it was time for her to get off.

"So," she said, "this is the way people leave each other's lives. First they say goodbye in person. Then comes a phone call. You only hear a voice . . . and then maybe . . . years from now . . . a letter arrives . . . or a Christmas card . . . and then it just stops. Right?"

I didn't know what to say.

She said goodbye. I said goodbye. She hung up. I hung up. As soon as I did, I knew. It was time to leave. It would be all too possible to stay around and wait for Rachel to call again. If she had called once, she might call again. She might come back. I saw it all, and I knew that the time had come.

My mother and I took the South Shore train to Chicago. She was on her way to work. I was on my way to the LaSalle Station to board the New York Central. She didn't ask me where I was going. She said nothing about my suitcase. When the time came for each of us to go our own way, she hugged me.

"It is no big deal," she said. "When I was your age, I left old country for America. You are my son and now you leave. Don't come back except to visit."

She kissed me twice on each cheek and left an envelope in my hand with five hundred dollars in it.

I had spent my whole life in East Chicago, and the New York Central rattled through it in less than five minutes. The library flashed past my window like a snapshot. I never returned the books. They were in my suitcase along with all my diaries. I had no idea why I stole those books.

The train stopped in Gary. Nobody got off. A bunch of people got on. A woman with two daughters sat down across from me. They looked like twins. We started talking. I introduced myself as James Donovan. I fell asleep going through Pennsylvania, and when I woke up, they were gone. I took a diary out of my suitcase.

September 29: I left home today, convinced that there is no such thing as destiny. As far as I can tell, there is only life and I look forward to living it.

With that entry, I began the diary of James Donovan.
And so I went out into the world.

STEVE TESICH was born in Yugoslavia in
1942. He came to America with his mother
and sister when he was fourteen years old
to rejoin his father in East Chicago,
Indiana. He graduated from East Chicago
Roosevelt High School in 1961. He received
his B.A. in Russian literature from Indiana
University in 1965—graduating with honors
and being elected to Phi Beta Kappa—and
his M.A. in Russian literature from
Columbia University in 1967.

Mr. Tesich is the author of seven plays,
six of which were produced at the
American Place Theater in New York. He
made his Broadway debut with his seventh,
Division Street. He has also written
screenplays for four films. He lives in
Colorado.